"YOUR FATHE
HE IN̄TERRUPTED.
"YOU'RE IN DANGER."

D0173619

"My father?" she scoffed. "Not very likely."

Luke glanced around as if expecting danger to close in on them at any moment. "There was an incident earlier today. Your father was injured, and your sister—"

"Look," Sarah interrupted, finally pulling her hand from his grasp. "I don't know who you are, but this isn't funny. And, by the way—it's a *lousy* pickup line. Now, if you'll excuse me, I have a job to do."

Luke downed the cider and grabbed his wallet from his back pocket, fishing out a couple of hundred-dollar bills and handing them to her. "For the cider."

She cautiously reached for the money. "It only costs a dollar."

"I'm guessing it'll cover what you would've sold for the rest of the hour," he said. "Now, I need you to come with me so I can get you and Eli to safety. I'd rather not have to throw you over my shoulder and drag you outta here kicking and screaming to do it, but I will. I'll do whatever I have to do to keep you safe."

The Transplanted Tales series by Kate SeRine

DECEIVED

KATE
SERINE

ZEBRA BOOKS
KENSINGTON PUBLISHING CORP.
http://www.kensingtonbooks.com

ZEBRA BOOKS are published by

Kensington Publishing Corp.
119 West 40th Street
New York, NY 10018

All Kensington titles, imprints, and distributed lines are available at special quantity discounts for bulk purchases for sales promotion, premiums, fund-raising, educational, or institutional use.

Special book excerpts or customized printings can also be created to fit specific needs. For details, write or phone the office of the Kensington Sales Manager: Attn.: Sales Department. Kensington Publishing Corp., 119 West 40th Street, New York, NY 10018. Phone: 1-800-221-2647.

Zebra and the Z logo Reg. U.S. Pat. & TM Off.

First Printing: July 2016
ISBN-13: 978-1-4201-3777-4
ISBN-10: 1-4201-3777-8

eISBN-13: 978-1-4201-3778-1
eISBN-10: 1-4201-3778-6

10 9 8 7 6 5 4 3 2 1

Printed in the United States of America

For M.E.G.H. and J.N.G.S.
The best sisters anyone could ask for.

Chapter One

This son of a bitch is going down.

Luke Rogan casually rose to his feet and tucked under his arm the newspaper he'd been using to disguise his interest in the deplaning passengers. The guy he'd been watching for had taken his sweet fucking time making his way down the narrow tunnel that opened into the bustling terminal, but the wait would be worth it if it meant getting the chance to thin the herd of one more useless waste of space.

God, it felt good to be out of a three-piece Fioravanti and back in the field. He'd spent the last three months sitting in board meetings, shepherding a merger between two of the world's leading technology companies to make sure everything went off without a hitch, but since the deal finally closed just two days earlier, he was itching for action.

He felt an immense sense of pride when it came to his track record as a consultant for Temple Knight & Associates. The status he'd gained as a titan of hardcore corporate negotiations was five years in the making, and he'd earned every damned ounce of that reputation. But it was *this* aspect of his job, the clandestine consulting arm of the operation, that he loved the most.

And the man about to be the recipient of Luke's more dubious talents couldn't have been a more worthy beneficiary.

Jonas Richter.

The name had taken root in Luke's memory like a putrid fungus. There was no place in society for sick pervs who committed rape on the women who worked for them and called it "job security" and "career advancement." But the reason he'd come onto Luke's radar had nothing to do with those transgressions—although they certainly added fuel to the fire—and everything to do with the guy's habit of selling off top-secret technology to the wrong people, the kind of people who wouldn't think twice about using said technology to take out half the United States just for shits and giggles.

When all the legal channels to take down Richter had proved to be paved with hush money, Luke had received the go-ahead to move in and put a permanent end to the unscrupulous bastard's operations.

As Richter made his way toward baggage claim, Luke followed at a comfortable distance, his small duffel bag slung casually over his shoulder, his sharp gaze trained on the guy's back. Luke kept his pace unhurried, making sure not to draw too much attention. As a six-foot-four wall of muscle with a complexion just a shade lighter than that of his Cheyenne mother, he had a hard enough time blending in.

Apparently, Richter had no such concerns. That cocky asshole swaggered through the airport like his shit didn't stink, clutching his too-expensive briefcase loosely with one manicured hand while the other was tucked in the pocket of his power suit. The only thing missing was a fake New England accent and some Botox. The son of a bitch had some serious bankroll goin' on, that was for damned sure. Apparently, being a coward and a traitor was a lucrative gig.

Luke grunted in disgust and murmured, "I'd be happy to take out this dude just for being a tool."

A quiet chuckle came through the earpiece Luke wore, letting him know his wingman, Jack Grayson, had heard him. "I'm with you there, brother," Jack replied, his smooth British accent belying his deadliness. "Let's get this over with and get the hell outta here."

Luke couldn't help the smirk that curved his mouth. "Copy that."

As soon as he did what needed doing, Luke would board a private jet back to Chicago, leaving no trace that he'd ever even set foot in the Pacific Northwest—and that was just the way he liked it.

God knew there wasn't anyone back home to miss him or wonder where he'd gone. The only ones left who *might* think of him now and then knew they were better off without him around bringing trouble down on them. At least, they should. He'd told them that often enough.

No, the only people who needed to give a flying fuck about where he was at any given time were his fellow Templars, his by-the-book commander in particular. But he knew that any concern they might've had for his whereabouts was out of necessity, not some sentimental attachment that was just bound to disappoint them anyway.

There was a reason the New Order of Templars that had formed after the Order's dissolution in the Middle Ages called themselves the Dark Alliance. They were a seriously badass group of men who'd pledged their loyalty to the Alliance. Because of the inherent dangers of what they did and the potential danger to the people they cared about, the Templars essentially chose to "go dark," cutting themselves off from nearly anyone and everyone they'd ever cared about in order to serve a greater purpose. Oh, there were a handful of exceptions, but Luke didn't see the point. Who needed the distractions? Having a singular focus suited him just fucking fine.

"You on him, Luke?" Jack asked over the com.

"Affirmative. Headed your way." Luke adjusted his black baseball cap a little farther down over his forehead and grabbed his shades from the inside pocket of his black leather jacket as he followed the mark through the pneumatic glass doors and into the surprisingly bright October sunlight.

Richter was only a few feet ahead of him as Luke's long strides closed the distance between them. Richter hailed the sleek black limousine that was slowly pulling toward the curb and raised his arms to his sides in a gesture of impatience when the driver didn't immediately hop out to open the door for him.

Prick.

"Here, let me get that for you," Luke said, his deep bass nearly causing Richter to jump out of his skin.

Richter's brows drew together in a frown as he gave Luke the once-over—well, his brows drew together as much as they could.

Botox. Check.

Richter looked like he was about to say something shitty to Luke, but he must've thought better of it after sizing him up. "Uh . . . thanks. Good drivers are hard to find, I guess."

"So I hear." Luke pulled open the door and jerked his chin toward the back seat.

Richter gave him a nervous smile and slid inside, more than a little startled when Luke slid in after him. Luke dropped his duffel bag on the floor and pulled his SIG Sauer from the holster under his jacket in one swift movement, training it on the center of Richter's chest.

"Oh my God!" Richter screeched, not so cocky now. "Please don't kill me! Listen, I'll give you whatever you want!" He fumbled at the clasp of his Rolex. "Here, take my watch. It's worth at least thirty grand."

Luke held up his left wrist. "Got one." When Richter's face went slack, the color draining from his skin, Luke growled into his com, "Move out." The car slowly pulled away from the curb, merging into the other traffic.

Richter glanced toward the divider window, his eyes going wide. "Where's my driver?" he demanded, fear allowing him to suddenly grow a pair. "Who sent you? Was it Moretti? That fucking bastard! I didn't steal his designs. He can't prove a goddamned thing!"

Luke removed his shades and stowed them in his jacket pocket, his SIG still trained on Richter. "I don't know anybody named Moretti, but it sounds like I'm doing him a favor."

"Then what the hell *is* this?" Richter demanded, his pallor replaced by the blood rising up from his neck, making him look like an overfed tick about ready to pop. Richter swallowed hard and his voice was raspy when he said, "This is about the bullshit rape allegations, isn't it?"

Luke didn't answer right away, letting Richter stew in his fear. Finally he said, "This is justice, Richter. I'll let you figure out which of your fuck-ups is gonna be rectified today."

Luke saw understanding dawn on the guy's face, and wasn't surprised when Richter began to tremble. "Where are you taking me?"

Luke shrugged. "I'm not driving."

They rode in silence for several minutes, Richter's gaze darting from Luke's face to the gun and back again, before Richter finally hissed, "If you're going to kill me, why don't you just get it over with?"

"Hard to talk when you're dead," Luke drawled.

Richter eyed him warily. "So . . . you *aren't* planning to kill me?"

Luke leveled his gaze at him. "Didn't say that."

When the limo finally came to a stop, Luke grabbed Richter by the scruff of the neck, dragging him out of the car. Jack Grayson slid out from behind the wheel and nodded toward the dilapidated boathouse on the eerily deserted wharf. The roof was half caved in, and the stench of rotting fish and mildew was enough to make Luke gag. And if that wasn't bad enough, the squawking of seagulls was like the wailing of disgruntled spirits who'd risen from their graves to seek revenge upon the living. He suddenly found himself thinking about the stories of the little people—*Vo'estanehesono*—that his mother had told him when he was a child and wondering if maybe there'd been something to them. . . .

It was creepy as shit, even to Luke. Richter had to be pissing himself.

When they entered the boathouse, Luke ducked under the door frame, which had come apart and was hanging at an awkward angle. The remnants of old fishing boats crowded the perimeter of the boathouse, the crafts having been taken apart long ago and used for scrap, making it look like the building had been the site of some jacked-up nautical autopsy. Thick spider webs clung to the rafters, and Luke fought back a shudder when he heard the scrabble of rats scurrying into the shadows to avoid the intruders.

Waiting inside was a man whose hair had once been dark but was now peppered with white. Although Luke knew the man to be in his mid-sixties, the guy still had the bearing of a soldier and the physique of a much younger man.

Senator Hal Blake had traded his combat fatigues for a suit and tie long ago, but he was still a man to be reckoned with. And if he'd taken the risk to show up for the op in person, not bothering to put some distance between himself and the meeting with Richter, there was no way in hell Richter was walking out of there alive.

Luke cursed under his breath and glanced at Jack, wondering just what the hell they'd signed up for. This was more than an attempt to wrangle a confession out of Richter and turn it over to the feds. This was personal.

Beside Blake was a petite woman in jeans and a white button-down, her thick dark hair pulled back in a no-nonsense ponytail. If Luke had to hazard a guess, he would've placed her in her mid-thirties, but a smattering of freckles across the bridge of her nose made her look younger. Her piercing green eyes pegged Richter with hatred so intense, Luke had the impression she wouldn't have hesitated to take out the asshole herself if given the chance.

"Senator Blake," Jack said with a nod of greeting to the man.

The senator's calm, practiced gaze met Richter's. "So this is the man who sold out his country and didn't even have the balls to own up to it." Blake then turned to the woman at his side. "Mr. Richter, I believe you've met my daughter, Madeleine Blake, *formerly* of the FBI."

"Formerly?" Jack muttered. "What the hell's he talking about, Maddie?"

Maddie? What the hell? How does Jack know the senator's daughter?

"My career's over," she snapped. "Seems my investigation was an embarrassment to the Bureau and they thought I'd be better suited to a desk job. It became apparent very quickly that Richter had gotten to my bosses, too, so I told them to take their dirty money and shove it up their collective asses."

"Listen," Richter interjected, the pitch of his voice higher now that he was backed into a corner. "This is all a big misunderstanding."

Maddie strode forward, her chin jutted, ready for a fight. Richter stumbled back to get away from her advance, but Jack blocked his retreat, grabbing Richter by the back of the jacket and forcing him to face her.

"You pathetic piece of shit," Maddie hissed. "You handed over technology that the government had been developing for decades, plans for defensive weaponry that could've saved millions of lives. Men *died* protecting that information and you just went and pissed on their graves. How *dare* you stand there and tell me it was all a misunderstanding? Fuck you!"

Luke jerked back a little when Maddie punched Richter's face.

Damn.

"Your father asked for justice, Maddie," Jack said, pushing Richter toward her. "And we will provide it. It's your call as to how."

"Listen," Richter blubbered, "I'll tell you whatever you want to know! Just don't—" Richter suddenly jerked, blood spraying both Maddie and the senator.

A startled curse tore from Luke as he instinctively lunged forward to grab the senator and shove him behind one of the skeletal boats for cover. "What the fuck is going on, Jack?" Luke demanded into his com. "Who else knew we were here?"

"Hell if I know," Jack grunted as more shots rang out, splintering the wood near Luke's head. "We need to get Maddie and Hal outta here."

"Copy that," Luke barked. "Head for the car, and I'll cover you." He popped up over the edge of the boat and fired off three rounds in the area where he'd seen the bullets coming from. Out of the corner of his eye, he saw Jack and Maddie making for the car and fired two more shots, making sure they got inside before dropping back down behind the boat.

Rapid gunfire tore into the boathouse, sending chunks of wood flying. *Time to go.* Luke turned toward the senator, ready to grab his arm and pull him to safety, but stopped short when he saw a pool of red spreading across the senator's chest. "Ah, Christ," he hissed. Then into his com:

"The senator's been hit. Repeat—Blake's been hit. I need an evac, Jack."

"Elijah," the senator gasped, his chest heaving in panicked breaths. "They'll come for him."

Luke shook his head, not understanding the man's ramblings, and pressed the heel of his hand against the wound in the senator's left shoulder. "Hang in there, Senator."

"That bullet wasn't for Richter." The senator covered Luke's hand with his own, grasping it so hard Luke's bones ached. "Please—they know. They'll come for Eli."

Luke frowned and was opening his mouth to ask who the hell Eli was when he heard the limo's tires squeal just outside the boathouse. "That's our ride," he mumbled instead, grabbing the senator up and pulling his arm over his shoulders. He half-carried the guy out of the broken-down door, keeping low, not surprised as bullets rained down on them, pinging off of the limo. Maddie returned fire, offering what cover she could as Luke shoved the senator into the back and dove in after him.

"They're in!" Maddie yelled, banging on the divider.

The limo instantly lurched forward, the tires squealing and throwing gravel into the air as it sped away.

Maddie dropped to her knees at her father's side and lifted his suit jacket to examine the wound. "We've got to get him to a hospital."

Luke grabbed his duffel bag and tore open the zipper, grabbing the first shirt he saw and wadding it up. Blake cried out when Luke pressed the shirt to his wound. "Hold this," Luke ordered Maddie. When she took over, he rummaged through his bag, quickly locating the field first aid kit.

"What the hell have you gotten yourself into, Blake?" he muttered, waving Maddie back from her father. He tore open the senator's shirt and quickly assessed the damage, checking for an exit wound. The bullet must still be inside him. Luke tore open a packet of quick-clotting powder and poured it onto the wound to slow the bleeding, ignoring the senator's pained cry when the chemicals made contact.

Luke placed a thick gauze pad on top of the hole in the senator's chest near his shoulder and pressed down hard with a glance at his watch to mark the time. "Who else knew you were meeting us here, Hal?"

"Jesus Christ," Maddie hissed at Luke. "Do you really think now is the best time to question him?"

Luke met her gaze, not bothering to sugarcoat it. "Might be the only chance we get. Unless *you* want to start talkin' for him."

The divider window came down at Luke's angry outburst. "Lay off, Rogan."

"Bullshit!" Luke shot back. "I don't know what kind of grab-ass side action you've got going on with the senator's daughter, Jack—"

"Hey, screw you!" Maddie snapped, talking over his tirade. "My relationship to Jack is none of your goddamned business!"

"—but somebody just took out the guy we were sent to get a confession from," Luke continued, ignoring her. "And then the senator tells me the bullet was meant for him and not Richter. So somebody want to tell me what *the fuck* is going on?"

Jack glanced over his shoulder at Maddie, who immediately looked away and turned her attention to her father. "Dad, who do you think shot you?"

The senator's face was growing dangerously pale and his eyes were losing focus, but Luke could see him trying to hang on. "They've been hounding me for months," he panted. "Threatening violence if I didn't give them the locations."

"Locations of what?" Luke asked.

The senator's gaze shifted to meet his. "The treasures."

Ah, fuck.

Senator Hal Blake wasn't just a friend to the Alliance; he was one of them, one of their most loyal operatives embedded in the government to help guard the freedoms and liberties that the Templars were sworn to protect. He was also one of the Guardians of the various treasure caches that funded the Templars' operations. If he was getting threats of any kind, why the hell hadn't he said something about it?

Luke shook his head, his mind racing as he tried to make sense of it all. Maybe Blake *had* said something about it—that kind of shit was way above Luke's pay grade. Somehow one of the most loyal Templars in the Alliance had been compromised. And they needed to find out how. Stat.

Luke lifted his eyes and briefly met Jack's in the rear-view mirror. "End of conversation, Jack," he warned with a significant glance toward Maddie. Then he added the code phrase they used when there were civilians in the room. "*Silence is golden.*"

Maddie met his gaze. "Speech is silver."

Luke's eyes narrowed. She'd given the answering response, a quote from Thomas Carlyle's poem. She knew. She knew all about them—or at least about her father's involvement with them, which made him wonder exactly what the hell else she knew. It wasn't uncommon for the offspring of a Templar to be brought into the fold at some point. But considering the knowing glances between Jack and Maddie, Luke was beginning to wonder who exactly had been her source.

"Who's Elijah?" he demanded.

"My nephew," Maddie gasped. "How do you know about him?"

"I don't," Luke assured her. "Your dad said they'd be coming for Elijah."

"Why would they want Eli?" Maddie breathed, clearly confused. "He's just a kid."

"I thought he'd be safe," Blake murmured. "I didn't think they'd ever find out where I'd hidden it. . . ."

"Hidden what?" Maddie pressed. "Dad, what did you hide?" When the senator didn't respond, her gaze darted between Jack and Luke. "What does he mean?"

Jack shook his head. "No idea, love. There are only a handful of people in the Alliance who know anything about where the treasures are hidden—the highest-ranking commanders and a few trusted *confreres*. None of the rest of us know anything about where or how they're hidden."

Luke ran a hand through his thick black hair and muttered a curse. "Well, apparently our pal Hal thought he could trust a fucking *kid* with the information."

"Hey!" Maddie snapped. "How *dare* you—"

"He's right, Maddie," Jack interjected mildly, cutting across her anger. "I don't know what your father was thinking, love. He completely disregarded protocol and has jeopardized us all. Hal isn't privy just to the treasures but to our covers, current ops—perhaps even private residences. We know a Guardian will transfer his knowledge of the treasures, but he could've shared the other information as well."

"A lot of guys could die if we don't get a lid on this and fast," Luke added.

"Dad would never put anyone at risk unnecessarily," Maddie insisted.

"Then we need to get to your nephew before anyone else does," Luke told her. "Where is he?"

Maddie sent a guarded glance in her father's direction, her eyes brimming with tears as he slipped into unconsciousness. "They're in a little town in Oregon about seven hours from here."

Luke nodded. "I'll call it in," he announced, fishing his cell phone out of his jacket pocket.

"Let me," Jack insisted. "I'll report in after we get Hal to the hospital, let Will know what's going on."

Luke met Jack's gaze again in the rearview mirror, noticing his brother-in-arms' guilty expression, wondering why the hell he wasn't willing to immediately call in their redefined objective to their commander. There was only one reason he could think of. "Commander Asher doesn't know what we're up to, does he?"

"It's my fault," Maddie defended. "I asked my dad to procure Jack's help under the radar. I'm sorry—I had no idea it would go down like this."

Luke chuckled bitterly as he pulled a hand over his face, working to keep his anger in check. This was fucking awesome. He'd just gotten his ass shot at as a personal favor to Jack's . . . *whatever*.

"We'll need guards on the senator," Jack informed him. "And Maddie isn't safe either. We'll need to get them both back to headquarters in Chicago. I'll handle things here until we can move them."

"And the kid and his parents?" Luke prompted, already guessing at the answer.

Jack shifted a little in the front seat. "I'm going to need you to bring them into protective custody."

"It's only Sarah and Eli," Maddie added. "Sarah's husband was killed in a car accident three years ago."

Luke clenched his jaw, not liking this plan one damned bit. "This is more Ian's thing, brother," he pointed out to Jack, referring to Ian Cooper, another of his brethren who was a former U.S. Marshal and had a personality far better suited to babysitting duty.

"Ian's on his way back from the Sudan, and you bloody well know it," Jack replied evenly. "Take the jet that's on standby and get your ass to Oregon to retrieve the woman and her son. Is that clear?"

Luke bit back his retort, not wanting to tangle with his friend. Jack was the one who'd recruited him, and he'd been the first—and pretty much the only one—in the Alliance to attempt to befriend him when he'd come on board. But regardless of their personal relationship, Luke had only been with the organization for five years compared to Jack's fifteen and wasn't gonna win this one. He bit back the snarl of rebellion that came to mind and said instead, "I'll need an address."

Chapter Two

Sarah Scoffield stood at the door of her classroom, ushering her students out with a smile and the occasional hug. Their happy chatter and constant enthusiasm for everything at this age never ceased to amaze her. She wished she had even a modicum of their untainted optimism.

"Bye, Mrs. Scoffield," they chirped one after another, their sweet little voices music to her ears.

She loved her job teaching first grade in Bakersville, welcomed the opportunity to shape young minds and help them grow, to foster that sense of wonder and belief in the magic of possibilities. The world would leave them jaded and cynical soon enough. A lot of these kids were the sons and daughters of farmers and ranchers, so they'd already experienced the mysteries of life and death, understood that all life eventually came to an end. But at the tender age of six or seven, they still saw the beauty in the world around them and could give the darkness just a passing glance.

Sarah felt a tug at her long denim skirt and looked down at the little girl with blond curls and wide blue eyes grinning up at her. "Yes, Mary Rose?"

Little Mary Rose pointed to a tiny gap in her mouth. "I just lost a tooth!"

Sarah gasped dramatically. "No way! Just now?"

Mary Rose nodded enthusiastically and held out her palm, where the little tooth lay. "Well, let's make sure you take it home for the tooth fairy," Sarah laughed, going to her supply cabinet and taking out a box of thimble-sized plastic treasure chests that she kept on hand for just this sort of occasion. "You don't want to miss the chance to put it under your pillow."

Mary Rose selected a pink chest and helped Sarah secure the tooth. "Do you think the tooth fairy will remember to come to my house tonight?" she asked. "Or will she be at the Fall Festival, too?"

Sarah grinned and guided Mary Rose toward the door. "I'm sure that even if she drops by the festival for a while, she'll still find time to stop at your house and leave you a little something. Just be sure to tell your mom and dad so they can make sure your tooth is under your pillow."

Mary Rose nodded solemnly. "Good idea."

"I do have them now and then," Sarah chuckled, gently scooting the girl out the door so she wouldn't miss her bus. "Now, have a great weekend. I'll see you Monday!"

Sarah was still grinning when her son, Eli, entered the room, the strong resemblance he bore to his father already at the age of eleven breaking her heart a little. It'd been three years since Greg's death and the pain had finally started to lessen a little with each day, but every time she looked at Eli, it came rushing back in a quick stab right in the center of her chest. The boy had her dark eyes, but everything else about him was his father, from the unruly dark hair to the arch of his brows to the hint of a dimple in his chin.

"Hey there, pumpkin," she greeted him, gathering him into her arms for a hug and ruffling his hair when she released him. "Did you have a good day?"

"Mom!" he admonished with a huff, smoothing his hair back down. "I told you not to do that. I'm not five anymore."

Sarah repressed a grin and held up her hands. "Sorry. Can't help myself. It's a mom thing."

"So, we're still going to the festival tonight, right?" Eli asked as Sarah went about the room, tidying up.

"Yep," Sarah said with a grin, looking forward to it as much as he was. "I promised to work at the school's booth for a while, but then we can walk around together."

Eli's face fell. "But I told Hunter I'd meet him at the haunted house."

Sarah grabbed an eraser and started clearing the white board of the day's lesson. "Well, I guess you'll have to tell him you were mistaken. I'm not comfortable with you wandering around on your own, Eli. I'm going with you. End of discussion."

He rolled his eyes. "Are you *serious?* Mom, all the other guys get to go around by themselves. How come I can't? I'm eleven years old—I'm not a baby!"

"I know you're not, Eli." Sarah glanced at her phone as she was tossing it into her purse. Noticing she'd missed a couple of calls from her sister, she made a mental note to return her sister's call in the morning, then grabbed her bag and gestured toward the door.

"Then why can't I go to the festival with my friends?" he demanded.

Sarah took a moment to lock her classroom door before answering. The truth was, she knew Eli was one of the most responsible kids around, that he'd never given her any reason not to trust him. And he was scary smart—another trait he'd inherited from his history professor father, who could've made even IRS tax guidelines fascinating—and was wise well beyond his years.

The rational side of her knew she'd have to let go sooner or later and trust that Eli would make the right decisions when he wasn't with her. But after losing her husband, the thought of losing Eli too . . .

"Look, kiddo," she said on a sigh. "I know you're old enough to hang out with your friends, but I'd feel better if you hung out with me instead, okay? Don't roll your eyes at me, Elijah Scoffield—I'm serious."

"Mom," Eli said, giving her a sardonic look, "we live in Bakersville. Nothing *ever* happens here."

Luke pulled up to the quaint yellow Queen Anne, complete with white picket fence. The place was so freaking cute he was afraid he'd go into sugar shock if he stuck around too long. Good thing he was gonna tell them to get their shit and get the hell in the car. Of course, he'd say please. No need to be an asshole about it.

He climbed the porch steps, the aging wood groaning under his weight. Lamps shone through the window, but when he knocked on the door there was no sound of movement inside. He glanced up and down the street, grunting at how freaking picturesque it was. Old-fashioned streetlamps lined the street, their pale light illuminating the growing darkness on the crisp night. The whole street was deserted. Since it was an unseasonably mild fall night, he'd expected kids to still be playing outside, cars coming and going. *Something.*

"Where the hell is everybody?" he mumbled, turning back to the door and knocking again, louder this time. He was going to be seriously pissed if he'd traveled all this way for nothing.

"No one's home."

Luke whipped around toward the sound of the voice, his hand instinctively slipping under his jacket to grasp his gun. A man with white hair and a loud cardigan sweater was standing on the sidewalk with his dog—some kind of collie from the looks of it. Luke withdrew his hand and patted his pockets to cover for his reaction. "Can't find my key," he said, forcing a friendly smile. He jabbed his thumb toward the house. "Know when they'll be back?"

The man shrugged. "No telling. Just about everyone's at the festival downtown. Goes to midnight. You a friend of Mrs. Scoffield?"

Luke nodded. "Yeah."

The man eyed him suspiciously. "She hasn't had many visitors since her husband died a few years back. Funny she's suddenly had so many people stopping by tonight. And you're supposed to have a key? Did you try calling her?"

A hot shot of adrenaline spiked through Luke's blood. "Who else has been here?" Luke demanded, ignoring the old man's questions. "Did he give you a name?"

The man shook his head. "Didn't tell me his name."

"What'd he look like?"

The man tilted his head to one side, considering the question. "Oh . . . young fella. Nice looking, I guess. I thought maybe Mrs. Scoffield had finally started dating again. Been a few years since her husband passed, after all."

Luke bounded down the steps. "Did you tell him Sarah was at the festival?"

The man nodded. "Sure. Didn't see the harm in it. Seemed to know a lot about her and little Eli already. Everything okay?"

Luke jogged to his rented Ford Expedition. "What's the quickest way to the festival?"

The man gestured toward the north. "Just follow the main road that way. Can't miss it."

Luke peeled out of the driveway and sped off down the street, hoping like hell that he got to them in time. He dialed the number Madeleine Blake had given him for her sister, but the call went straight to voicemail just as it had when Maddie had attempted to call earlier in the day. Knowing her sister kept her ringer off when she was at work, Maddie hadn't seemed worried about Sarah's lack of response and had texted Luke a few recent pictures of her sister and nephew. But he was betting whoever else was looking for the woman and her kid had more than that to go on.

Luckily, the old man was right—Luke had no problem recognizing the downtown area. He parked the Expedition in a lot and handed five bucks to the attendant before hurrying toward the center of activity. Hundreds of people milled around, talking and laughing as they celebrated the season.

Strands of yellow lights were draped on all the trees and store fronts, illuminating the dozen or so food booths and carnival games that lined the streets. In an adjacent field, carnival rides had been set up and were bustling with activity, the bright flashing lights and upbeat music blaring out of the speakers at various rides conflicting with one another and creating a disorienting cacophony of sound that put Luke's teeth on edge. But the aroma of artery-clogging goodness in the form of corn dogs, funnel cake, and pretty much every kind of meat on a stick made Luke's mouth water, reminding him he hadn't eaten since breakfast that morning. And the sweet tang of hot spiced cider about did him in. But as soon as he felt the pang of hunger, it vanished. His focus was on getting to the Scoffields before whoever the hell else had been looking for them.

Luke shoved his hands into his jeans pockets and hunched his shoulders a little, trying to blend in but drawing curious stares from several people he passed. Unfortunately, none of those faces belonged to Sarah Scoffield or her son.

How the hell was he supposed to find them among all these people? They could be anywhere. And for all he knew, they'd already left and headed home.

He groaned inwardly, liking this mission less and less. He needed backup. If he'd had one more set of eyes on the crowd, that would've at least been something. But his partner was in Seattle, pulling strings to protect the senator and his daughter and somehow keep the news of the incident from leaking to the press. And there hadn't been time to try to grab somebody from the Alliance commandery in Seattle or Portland. That's what he'd had to tell his commander a couple of hours ago when Asher had called with the express intent of chewing his ass out for going along with Jack's cluster-fuck of a plan.

That was a fun conversation. Nothing like getting your balls busted for going along with what you thought were orders and then getting an encore ball-busting for taking on *new* orders without backup. He'd be sure to thank Jack when they all got back to Chicago.

"You look like you could use something warm to drink."

Luke's head snapped up toward the sound of the voice. Behind the counter of a homemade wooden booth that sported cartoonishly large red apples painted on the front, was a woman so striking Luke actually felt his chest grow tight. Her lips curved into a smile, bringing dimples to her cheeks. Long dark auburn hair spilled over her shoulders, framing the curves of the full breasts beneath the crimson turtleneck she wore. He was so taken aback by her loveliness, it took him a full twenty seconds to realize that he was staring at Sarah Scoffield. Holy hell . . . was it really gonna be that easy?

"Yes, I'm talking to you," she teased with a laugh, motioning him over. "I guarantee this will be the best apple cider you've ever tasted, and all proceeds go to Bakersville schools. I promise you won't regret it!"

Luke sauntered over, unable to repress a grin. Sarah Scoffield was even more breathtaking the closer he got. And the picture her sister had sent didn't even begin to do her justice. Looking at her standing there smiling at him with those adorable little dimples, her wide dark eyes sparkling, Luke began to think this job might not be so bad after all.

* * *

What the hell was wrong with her?

Sarah wasn't the kind of woman to hit on a complete stranger, and yet here she was flirting mercilessly with the man on the other side of the booth. She'd seen him skulking through the crowd, his height and powerful build making him hard to miss. And that profile—she couldn't remember the last time she'd seen a man so heart-stoppingly handsome. And when he'd turned toward her and pegged her with that dark stare of his . . . well, it'd been a long time since she'd felt her heart skip a beat, let alone since she'd felt the other areas of her anatomy sit up and take notice.

As he came toward her, Sarah busied herself filling a paper cup with cider to hide her sudden onset of nerves. By the time she lifted her eyes again, she was able to steady her hands as she handed the cup over.

He took the cup from her, his fingers brushing over hers briefly during the exchange. As he lifted it to his lips, he peered over the edge and took a careful sip. "You're right," he drawled. "I don't regret it one bit."

Dear Lord . . . that *voice*! It was deeper than she'd expected and velvety smooth. She felt the heat rising to her cheeks and offered him a nervous smile. "I'm Sarah," she said, extending her hand. He took it in his massive paw and gave it a quick shake, but he didn't immediately release her, continuing to hold her hand gently in his grasp.

"Luke," he replied. "Can someone fill in for you here, Sarah?"

"I . . . uh . . . I'm supposed to be working here for the full hour. Sorry." She drew back slightly, but his grip tightened on her fingers, keeping her where she was.

He leaned across the counter until his lips were close to her ear. "Sarah, I need you to come with me."

Sarah's blood suddenly ran cold with fear. "Listen," she stammered. "You've got the wrong idea. I didn't mean—"

"Your father sent me, Sarah," he interrupted. "You're in danger."

"My father?" she scoffed. "Not very likely."

Luke glanced around as if expecting danger to close in on them at any moment. "There was an incident earlier today. Your father was injured, and your sister—"

"Look," Sarah interrupted, finally pulling her hand from his grasp. "I don't know who you are, but this isn't funny. And, by the way—it's a *lousy* pickup line. Now, if you'll excuse me, I have a job to do."

Luke downed the cider and grabbed his wallet from his back pocket, fishing out a couple of hundred-dollar bills and handing them to her. "For the cider."

She cautiously reached for the money. "It only costs a dollar."

"I'm guessing it'll cover what you would've sold for the rest of the hour," he said. "Now, I need you to come with me so I can get you and Eli to safety. I'd rather not have to throw you over my shoulder and drag you outta here kicking and screaming to do it, but I will. I'll do whatever I have to do to keep you safe. Where's your son?"

Sarah's fear was replaced by anger. "What the hell do you know about Eli?" she demanded. "You touch one hair on his head, and I swear—"

Luke cursed and strode around to the back of the booth, gently but firmly taking hold of her elbow. "Lady, I'm not the one you need to worry about."

Sarah's breath caught in her chest. At least a foot taller than she was, Luke towered over her, his powerful body crowding her as he pressed close. She put a hand against his muscled chest to stop him from getting any closer and was surprised to find his heart beating as fast as hers.

Dear God. He was looking at her with such intensity, she

almost expected him to kiss her. And something told her it wouldn't have been a tentative, uncertain kiss.

"Everything okay, Mrs. Scoffield?"

Sarah started and tore her gaze away from Luke's— which was far more difficult than she would've thought— to give the man in the booth next to hers a smile. "Yes, Mr. Thomas. Everything's fine." She turned back to Luke, narrowing her eyes at him. "Just who the hell should I be worried about? What was this *incident* you seem to know all about?"

"There was an attempt on your father's life," Luke told her in a low rumble. "I'm sorry."

"What?" She pegged Luke with a pointed stare, her anger and disbelief making her tremble. "Prove it. Prove to me that my father sent you. Prove that *any* of what you're telling me is true."

Luke heaved an exasperated sigh and took out his phone and turned it toward her. "Here."

She read the text message from the phone number she recognized as her sister Maddie's: Pic of Sarah and Eli. Please bring them home safely. Dad in surgery.

Sarah immediately called out, "Mr. Thomas! I need to take a break. Could you watch the booth for me until Mrs. Smith gets here?"

Luke didn't wait for Mr. Thomas to answer before grabbing Sarah's hand and pulling her along behind him. "Where's the boy?"

"The haunted house." Sarah gestured toward a sprawling historic home down the street that was converted into a house of horrors every year to the delight of people all over the county. She'd held firm about Eli not going, planning to have him sit with her at the booth until she was free to go with him, but then Hunter's mom had informed her that, contrary to what Hunter had hoped, she and her husband *would* be joining the boys at the festival and keeping watch over them.

Luke picked up the pace, his powerful strides forcing Sarah to take three steps to his every one. She struggled to keep up with him, her long denim skirt and brown knee boots not really suited for jogging. But as her fear and panic ramped up, she surged forward, now dragging Luke behind *her*.

"Betsy," Sarah panted when they reached the wrought-iron gates, recognizing the girl taking tickets as one of the high school girls who'd babysat for her during staff meetings. "Have you seen Eli?"

The girl blinked at Sarah—well, at Luke, really—but finally seemed to snap out of it and nodded. "Uh, yeah. He went in, like, a few minutes ago, I think. Haven't seen him come out yet. But, you know, I'm not like watching for him or anything."

Sarah bolted up the steps, ignoring Betsy's protestations about tickets, and heard Luke's heavy footfalls right behind her. "Eli!" she called when she burst inside. "Elijah!"

Luke grabbed her arm and pulled her to a stop. "Sarah—"

"Let me go, damn it," she yelled over the spooky music and artificial sound effects of creaking doors and demonic cackles. "You told me my son's in danger. Well, I'm going to go find him."

Luke pulled her a few steps toward the wall and deeper into the thick curls of artificial fog to let another group of people pass, then grasped the back of her neck and bent to speak directly into her ear, "We're not the only ones looking for him, remember?"

Sarah shuddered at the warmth of his breath on her ear and forced herself to focus on what he was saying.

"We don't want to lead them to Eli." He drew back just enough to peer down into her face, and his hand drifted from the back of her neck to cup her cheek. "Now, follow me—quickly, but calmly."

Sarah nodded and let him take her hand as they hurried through the darkness, lit only by disorienting strobe lights. They searched the faces of those they passed, looking for Eli in the crowd. Whenever she saw one of the children she recognized, she tried to ask if they'd seen her son. Those to whom she could make herself heard could do little more than nod and point, their voices lost to the noise.

More than once, costumed performers dressed as gruesome zombies, mangled murder victims, or ghosts with hollowed-out eyes leapt out at them, startling a cry from her. But Luke barely flinched. It seemed the man was completely immune to fear. Which made Sarah wonder just how the hell her father knew him.

The aura of danger that surrounded Luke was unlike any she'd seen before—and did nothing to assuage her fear for Eli's safety. If her father had sent someone like the man beside her to protect them, then the people he feared were coming for them had to be pretty damned frightening.

Her panic increasing with each passing moment that Eli wasn't with her, Sarah tightened her grip on Luke's hand. Finally, as they made their way through the crowded third-story hallway, she thought she had suddenly caught a glimpse of Eli. Without thinking, she bolted forward, squeezing her way through the crowds, frantic to keep him in sight as he and the Smith family made their way toward the back stairs.

She was just about to dart down the darkened stairwell after them when a group of giggling girls emerged from the room to her right, clogging the passageway. Sarah elbowed her way through them, drawing angry protests that were thankfully drowned out. She raced down the stairs, which were dimly lit by a dull yellow bare bulb at the top landing and another, blinking, fizzling bulb further down below like something out of those creepy slasher films from the eighties.

Her heart pounding, she took the stairs as fast as she could. As she made the first landing, she came to an abrupt halt with a loud scream, not having expected to encounter a performer sprawled on the floor as if he'd been shot in the head. A shockingly realistic splatter was painted on the wall a couple of feet above him and smeared down as if he'd hit the wall when the bullet struck him and slowly slumped to the ground.

After the initial shock, Sarah moved to go around when something about the man's face suddenly struck her as familiar. It was in the next instant that terror gripped her, making her knees momentarily weak. The man wasn't a performer. It was Mike Smith—the father of Eli's friend Hunter and the man who was supposed to be watching out for her son.

Sarah forced her feet to move, tripping over the body and nearly tumbling down the stairs. Her heart was racing, her pulse pounding so loudly in her ears she no longer could hear the haunted house sound effects bleeding through the walls into the stairwell.

Dear God.

Mike Smith was dead. Shot in the head. And the person who'd committed such a horrific murder was there in the darkness somewhere. With her son.

Sarah didn't care anymore about being quiet. All she wanted was to get to her child before it was too late. She bolted down the stairs, screaming for Eli at the top of her lungs. When she reached the bottom of the stairs, there was a heap lying in the shadows. Heedless of her own safety, she rushed forward, dropping to her knees. She reached out a trembling hand and rolled the body over.

Sarah gasped, choking back a horrified sob when she saw the wide, unblinking eyes of Patricia Smith. And beneath her lay the huddled form of a little boy with dark hair. Sarah placed a hand on his shoulder, expecting to find him dead as well, but he screamed and pulled away, cowering with his arms over his head.

"Hunter!" Sarah cried. "Hunter, honey! Where's Eli? Where'd he go?"

Hunter couldn't stop screaming, the poor boy too traumatized to respond. Fighting back the scream of frantic need to find her own son, Sarah managed to scoop up Hunter and was attempting to stand with him in her arms to take him with her when strong hands wrested the boy from her grasp.

Her protective instinct on overdrive, Sarah lashed out, kicking and clawing at the man.

"Sarah!"

The deep voice broke through her rage, bringing her assault to an abrupt halt. Her relief at seeing Luke was so intense that she had to choke back a sob, but the desperate need to get to her son kept her on her feet. "He's gone," she told Luke, her voice quavering. "And Patti and Mike . . ."

Without a word, Luke rushed through the back door and into the night, the traumatized little boy still in his arms, his piercing gaze searching the darkness, his expression deadly. Sarah's own eyes darted around, desperately trying to spot Eli.

"Oh my God! What's happened?"

Sarah's head snapped toward the voice and recognized the woman rushing toward them as a fellow teacher at the elementary school. "Helen, have you seen Eli?"

The older woman shook her grey head in confusion. "Yes, dear, I believe I saw him run out of here a moment ago. He was headed toward the midway. He must've been darned scared from the haunted house tonight. He was running like the dickens."

* * *

Luke gently handed Hunter over to Helen, pushing away the rush of emotions and horrifying images that came flooding in on him from his own childhood trauma. "There's been a murder. Call the police."

He didn't wait for the woman to respond before taking off after Sarah. Damn, the woman was fast! But he had to believe if it'd been *his* kid in danger, it would've taken an act of God to keep him from getting to his child, so he could understand her desperation. But that same love and protective instinct was going to get her killed if he didn't reach her.

Fortunately, his long strides made up for her head start. By then, they were almost to the midway, and he heard Sarah's strangled cry as she poured on a fresh burst of speed, racing past the curious festival attendees who sent confused glances her way. Luke caught sight of the little boy at almost the same moment as Sarah. But he also saw the wiry guy in a gray hoodie moving in from the boy's flank.

Sarah reached her son just before the other man, scooping him into her embrace and pivoting to shield him with her body. Luke kept running, throwing himself into the would-be kidnapper and taking him down to the ground before the guy even realized what'd hit him. But it didn't take the attacker long to recover his wits.

Luke saw the gun just as he reared back to drive his fist into the guy's face. He grabbed the man's wrist, slamming it against the ground with one hand and connecting with the guy's jaw with the other. As the gun finally slipped from the attacker's hand, Luke felt the man squirm beneath him and heard Sarah's cry of warning just in time to roll away and avoid the sharp blade of the hunting knife that the guy had apparently hidden away in a sheath at his calf.

"Who the hell are you working for?" Luke demanded as the guy squared off against him, hunched over, teeth bared.

The attacker swung his arm, slicing through the air as he

advanced on Luke, damned near catching him with the tip. Luke jumped back at the last second, catching the guy's arm as he swung past him and twisting him around into a choke hold, pressing the knife to his throat.

"I said, 'Who the hell are you working for?'" Luke growled.

The guy chuckled darkly, leaning into Luke to avoid the blade at his throat. "I serve the One True Master. And if you kill me, more will come. We will know your secrets, Templar."

Luke was about to ask how the hell the bastard knew who he was when the guy started convulsing. Sarah hastily stumbled backward with Eli, shielding his eyes.

Luke cursed under his breath and released the man, letting him fall to the ground, where he continued to convulse and spew white foam, which was soon tinged dark with blood. Luke's stream of ripe curses grew louder and more colorful when he realized the motherfucker had poisoned himself, taking the coward's way out instead of allowing himself to be questioned. When Luke regained his composure, he glanced up to encounter the horrified stares of the crowd of people who'd dared to approach them now that the assailant was on the ground. More than a few of them were on their phones, no doubt already calling 911.

Luke lunged forward and took hold of Sarah's arm, quickly leading her and Eli from the scene before the police could show up.

"Where are we going?" Sarah demanded after a few yards, digging in her heels and pulling him to a stop. "We need to stay here and tell the police what happened! You heard what that nut-job said—more will be coming."

Luke relaxed his grip and glanced down at her and then into the wide dark eyes of her son. The boy was mute with terror, but tears hovered on the edges of his long black lashes as if he was holding them back with sheer willpower. The last thing the kid needed was to hear his life was in danger, but something about the way Eli looked at him—a mixture of fear, disbelief, and awe—told him the boy could take it.

"It's because more'll be coming that I need to get you two outta here," Luke told them. "Eli, you think you can hang in there for me, buddy? You're safe right now, but I want to keep it that way. Will you trust me for a little while, help me get your mom somewhere safe?"

Eli nodded. "Yeah." He blinked a few times, swallowed, and glanced at his mom before squaring his shoulders and nodding again. "Yeah. I'm good. Let's go."

"Good man." Luke clapped him lightly on the back before meeting Sarah's gaze. "How about you?"

"I don't even know who you *are*," she breathed. "Not really. You say my father sent you, but how can I know that for sure? How do I know I can trust you any more than *that* guy?"

Luke sighed. Hell if *he* knew how to convince her to trust him. If she'd met him five years earlier, he would've told her she couldn't. He hadn't been worth trusting back then, and he probably had no right to ask a young mother to put her life and the life of her son in his hands even now. But as he stood there looking into Sarah's gaze, so fierce, so indomitable, and yet frightened and vulnerable, he somehow knew he'd give his very last breath to protect her and the boy.

"You *don't* know you can trust me," he finally answered. "But if you want to survive, Sarah, you're gonna have to."

Chapter Three

Fucking amateurs.

Jacob Stone tore off his headset and slammed it onto his desk. He knew he should've just taken care of grabbing the kid his damned self. But keeping his distance was imperative if he didn't want to blow his cover. He needed those layers of plausible deniability in case things went to shit. And, apparently, if he kept relying upon the more fanatical members of his following to take care of business for him, they were going to.

Those willing to serve him without question had their place, certainly, but they lacked finesse. They were better for broad-stroke missions, not those operations that required secrecy and stealth. He never would've thought a simple kidnapping was beyond their capabilities, but he also hadn't counted on one of the Templars managing to get there before the mission was completed. A miscalculation he wouldn't be repeating.

At least the mission wasn't a total wash. Although the senator hadn't been killed in the assassination attempt, he *was* lying in a coma from which he was unlikely to awaken. As such, everything still would be transferred to the senator's chosen heir as a precaution, just as Stone had intended.

Unfortunately, he had no fucking clue how Blake had actually transferred his knowledge of the treasures to the boy, but protocols dictated that the senator would've had some mechanism in place to ensure that the information was passed on should he become incapacitated, so that his knowledge would not be lost. If there was anything the Alliance had learned from the purge of their leaders during the Middle Ages, it was that they needed to have some redundancies in place.

Fortunately for Stone, his old friend Senator Blake had a guilty conscience about the rift between him and his younger daughter and had been all too eager to accept the advice of his long-time confidant on how to make amends. It had been Stone's idea for Blake to name the boy his heir, insisting that none of the Alliance's enemies would ever suspect Blake would pass on such crucial knowledge to a mere child.

Luckily, with Blake being required to file his succession plan with the Grand Council and leave a record of it at Central Headquarters, there would be at least a dozen suspects for the failed attempt to snatch the boy—not to mention what he imagined would be a panicked investigation when they discovered that their supposedly impenetrable files had been hacked. A nice touch, Stone had to admit, useful to some degree, and just the red herring he needed to keep them scurrying and distracted while he carried out his plan.

Stone smirked, wishing he could share his triumph with someone but contenting himself with a mental pat on the back at his own devious brilliance. He had known Hal Blake his entire life. Blake and his father had grown up together, gone through training together, entered into service together. And when Allister Stone had been killed in Russia during the Cold War, Blake had become like a second father to the young Jacob. Hell, he was one of the few *confreres* who even knew the truth of Blake's identity and mission. And yet despite being one of the most seasoned and respected Templars embedded in the government, Blake was surprisingly trusting when in the company of his ward.

It was almost sad, really. He actually felt a twinge of regret that things had taken such a turn. But he had his own agenda, and sacrifices—while unfortunate—were required.

Now he just had to make sure the gears continued to turn in spite of the little setback in Bakersville. The boy and his mother had gone underground, but it was only a matter of time before they resurfaced. He'd lay odds that they were headed to the home base in Chicago, but the commander there would tell them to stay away for a little while and let the rest of them look into who could be behind the attempted assassination and kidnapping. He wouldn't want them drawing the enemy straight to headquarters.

Will Asher, the leader of the Chicago commandery, was far too smart and savvy for that. So, fine, let the Templar take the woman and her son to some hole-in-the-wall for a while, get all snug and cozy thinking they were safe from his reach. He was a patient man. He could wait things out a while longer, wait for the perfect moment to strike again. He'd been waiting twenty years to make his move, to rectify the wrongs committed against his family. What were a few more days?

He still had a few of his most reliable followers attempting to pick up their trail and had no doubt they would. But it had become clear to him from this little snafu that he needed someone more dependable to actually extract the boy, someone he could trust to finish the job, who wouldn't let fervor for the cause interfere.

He paced the floor of his office, mulling over his options. Hiring mercs was out of the question. They had *no* loyalty. Whoever paid them the most was their boss for the day, and as vast as his own personal wealth was, it was nothing compared to what the Alliance could provide. No, if he was going to hire out, he needed someone as jaded and bitter about the Alliance as he, someone who wouldn't think twice about taking them on but who could match their level of training and experience.

What he needed was one of the very people from the Alliance he was trying to take down. But their loyalty was renowned. Infiltrating their current ranks, ferreting out a Templar who was carrying a grudge significant enough to make him want to turn against those he'd been indoctrinated to fight alongside, could take years of sowing seeds of bitterness and dissent.

He continued to walk the floor, finally pausing at the window that looked out over the city. *His* city. At least, it *should've* been. He was the right man to run this town, the only one with the vision to see it rise out of mediocrity and take its rightful place in the world order. And yet the obstacles to his rise to power remained. His hands balled into fists at his sides, his need for power rushing upon him as it did sometimes in the middle of the night when his long-awaited glory still seemed so out of reach.

But not for long.

Soon, the simpering, indolent morons of this country would know his name, would curse him for his strong hand and righteous mission, but in the end, they would understand that they owed all they had to the One True Master. History would sing his praises for centuries to come and look upon him as the great savior of the nation, the man who had delivered them.

In his mind, he pictured the throngs of people who would eventually attend his funeral decades from now, the thousands upon thousands who would wait in line for hours for a glimpse of their savior.

He grinned and closed his eyes, soaking it in, reveling in the adoration that would one day be his. He took a deep, cleansing breath and blew it out slowly, letting his hands uncurl. He wiggled his fingers, allowing the blood flow to return.

Soon.

All he needed was the right man to retrieve the boy and set the final stages of his plan in motion. He had heard of such a person, a Templar by the name of Eric Evans who'd been drummed out of the Alliance a few years before for conduct unbecoming. By all accounts, the confrontation between Evans and Will Asher had left Evans near to death, but Will had shown mercy—a mistake Will would no doubt soon regret.

Last he heard, the former Templar was in Cuba. Perhaps, for the right price, he could be persuaded to return to the United States. And if their partnership worked out well, then maybe he would consider offering a more long-term association. One never knew when one might need a highly trained killer at one's disposal.

Oh, yes. He was beginning to like this plan more and more. . . .

He turned to his desk and pressed the SPEAKER button on his cell before dialing his assistant.

"Yes, Mr. Stone?"

"Allison, my dear, I'm sorry to bother you on a Saturday, but I'm going to need you to make some flight arrangements for me."

"Of course, Mr. Stone. Just give me a moment to get to my laptop." A few seconds later, he could hear Allison typing swiftly. "Where will you be traveling, sir?"

Stone grinned. "Havana."

There was a slight pause. He could hear the lovely Allison Holt inhale as if about to ask him why in the world he would want to visit that particular country, but she had been with him long enough not to question his activities. "Of course, sir. When will you be leaving?"

"Tomorrow, if possible."

He heard her typing again and pictured her long, slender fingers, which were always manicured with such precision. Everything she did was calculated for maximum effectiveness and efficiency. He was quite lucky to have her at his beck and call, eager and willing to please. And with her luxurious blond hair, perky ass, and ample tits, she was damn fine to look at, too. He should've boned her long ago.

It wasn't like she would've said no. Hell, she was throwing out signals like a bitch in heat. He'd seen the way she looked at him, noticed how her blouse was always unbuttoned just a little too much for propriety when they held their weekly meetings. And why wouldn't she be throwing herself at him? At forty, he was in the best shape of his life and had the prowess of a man half his age. And he was never naïve enough to underestimate the allure of his bank account. He would've been shocked if she *hadn't* wanted him.

On more than one occasion, he'd fantasized about throwing her down on his desk and fucking her blind. Perhaps with his goals within reach, it was finally time to seal the deal and add a tasty bit of arm candy to his suntanned, cornfed all-American boy image.

He felt his dick growing hard at the thought of it.

In an uncharacteristically impulsive move, he drawled, "On second thought, Allison, go ahead and make that flight for two. I will be requiring your presence on this trip."

He heard her quick little intake of breath and could tell she was smiling when she replied, "Of course, Mr. Stone. Is there anything else you'll be requiring today?"

He shifted his weight, not sure how it was possible that his dick was growing even harder as he began to picture what he was going to do to her on the private jet during the long flight to Havana, how he was going to make her take it every way humanly possible and leave her begging for more. "No, not today. I think we'll have plenty of time to discuss my needs on the flight tomorrow."

He disconnected the line and hastily unzipped his slacks, freeing his cock and taking it roughly into his hand. As he pumped it furiously and felt an explosive release building, he squeezed his eyes shut. But it wasn't just images of the lovely Allison sucking him off that raced through his mind. He saw her with her head in his lap while he sat in the coveted chair in the Oval Office, as the world's most powerful leader and savior of humanity. Soon it wouldn't be just his assistant who was on her knees before him.

Will Asher strode through the underground tunnels that connected the buildings of the Alliance's compound. To the casual observer, the complex looked like any other exclusive gated community in the quiet Chicago suburb where the Alliance had set up its regional command center.

The custom homes were veritable fortresses of security, each one a private residence for the highest-ranking Templars in the region, appropriately extravagant to maintain their front as businessmen who ran one of the most lucrative investment firms in the world. Those who were still initiates, or who were still proving themselves, lived in the building that appeared to be a town hall at the center of the self-contained community.

But the vast majority of their operations took place in the underground high-tech ops center that made the fallout shelters built by NORAD look like a kid's dollhouse. The facility was a stronghold that could withstand any physical attack and would continue to operate even in the event of an electromagnetic pulse or other terrorist activity that would disable the most advanced operations elsewhere.

But not even the most impenetrable fortress could protect Will now.

He squared his shoulders and lifted his chin a notch higher as he stormed into the situation room, catching the startled faces of the rest of his team. They sat around the table at the center of the room, awaiting their briefing on the emergency that had called them in from the field at such short notice, but Will continued past them and toward his office. The briefing would have to wait. He was due on a call in less than a minute, and he was not going to risk pissing off the Grand Council any more than they already were.

His ass was already in a sling for not having better control of his men. And Jack Grayson, of all people, was the one who was behind this colossal cluster-fuck. Jack Grayson—his most dependable lieutenant and most trusted friend—had gone rogue, putting himself and his partner at risk for personal reasons that had absolutely nothing to do with Alliance business and everything to do with assuaging his own guilt.

Of course, it wasn't like Will was going to tell the Grand Council that their golden boy had shit on protocol because he was thinking with his dick. They'd see it as just making excuses. Ultimately, as commander of the Chicago commandery and thereby of the North American province, all ops were Will's responsibility. So if they went to shit, it was on his shoulders. Period.

Will slammed the door to his office and snatched up the remote that operated the flat-screen monitor hanging on his wall. He had seconds to spare when he joined the teleconference.

"Good evening, Commanders," he said, bowing slightly at the waist. "I'm sorry to keep you waiting. Thank you for joining me on this call."

Each of the members inclined his head, but it was the high commander who spoke. "Commander Asher," he said, his voice taut with disapproval. "We are curious to hear what has necessitated this emergency meeting."

Will steeled himself to deliver the news. "Senator Hal

Blake has been shot in what appears to be an assassination attempt."

"When did this occur?" asked one of the council members. "I've seen nothing in the news feeds."

"We're controlling the spin," Will assured him. "The shooting wasn't public, so we've created a cover story to release. Tomorrow's news will state the senator has had emergency surgery due to a non-life-threatening medical issue and is recovering well at an undisclosed location."

"And who is caring for Senator Blake?" the high commander asked. "Are we on top of this?"

Will inclined his head. "He was taken to a Seattle hospital where we have *confreres,* who saw to his care. We're in the process of transferring him to Chicago to our local medical facility, where our doctors will oversee his recovery and I can monitor the situation personally."

"*Will* he recover?" another council member demanded. "Should we make preparations?"

Will hesitated for a moment. "His situation is grave. We're doing everything we can."

"He has named his successor," the high commander reminded the council. "We must assume that Hal put the necessary precautions into place in that regard."

Will shifted slightly, a movement that didn't go unnoticed by the high commander.

"You have something to add, Commander Asher?"

Will kept his tone even as he said, "Late last night, one of my best field operatives was sent to take into custody Hal's successor and the boy's mother. The child was successfully extracted, but not before someone attempted to abduct the boy, killing at least two civilians in the process."

His words were met with a heavy silence as each of the Grand Council considered the implications. It was clear from their stony expressions that they were thinking the same thing Will was—that the attempt to assassinate Hal and abduct his successor meant either that one of them was a traitor or that someone outside the trusted circle of leadership within the Alliance knew their most guarded and potentially damning secrets.

It was the high commander who finally spoke, breaking the silence. "I am instituting emergency protocol Alpha Delta Zed. Commander Asher, as this has occurred under your watch, you will be coordinating asset-relocation efforts. And I expect a full investigation into the matter. Do you have any sense of how deep the breach goes?"

Will shook his head. "Not yet, sir. But my team is assessing the damage as we speak to determine what information, if any, has been compromised."

"Thank you, gentlemen," the high commander said, dismissing his fellow council members. "We will keep you apprised of the situation. That will be all."

All of the council members signed off except for the high commander. He waited thirty seconds to ensure that all lines had been cleared before fixing Will with his fiery glare. "Exactly how the hell did this happen? Where was Hal's security detail when he was shot? Who the hell dropped the ball on this, William?"

Will refused to waver under the old man's fierce gaze. "I am looking into the matter of his security detail, sir. However, it's my understanding that he dismissed them from duty and ordered them to leave him."

"He was alone then?"

At this, Will couldn't help but squirm. There was no way he was going to throw Jack and Luke under the bus. He'd deal with them himself. But he knew if he didn't tell the truth, the high commander would sense it in a heartbeat. "No, sir. He was not. His daughter Madeleine was with him. They were settling a personal matter, from what I'm told. Two of my field operatives were also there—as a favor to the Blake family."

The man made a noise of disgust. "Personal matters. There is no room for personal matters in the Alliance."

Will was well aware of the high commander's stance on anything personal, that was for damned sure. Any personal life Will had hoped to have, any semblance of a normal existence, had been unceremoniously ripped away from him years ago by the very man on his screen. One would think that Templar Priest forefathers had had it bad, but perhaps having no affiliations would be better than having only the fleeting ones they were permitted under the high commander's watch. Never mind the fact that both the high commander and his son had married and fathered children, as had several other members of the Alliance.

Fucking hypocrite.

But Will also knew from experience that it was a special person who could marry into the Alliance and all the bullshit that came with it. His grandmother and mother had been saints to put up with the shit they had over the years. . . .

All that said, he let the comment go and focused on the crisis they were facing. "Do you have any reason to doubt the members of the council, sir? Should I have my people look into their communications?"

The high commander peered down his hawkish nose, pegging Will with a chastising look. "Of course you should. You are far too trusting, William. It will be your undoing. You have already given your team far too much freedom to run their own ops. Clearly, they have little respect for your authority if they are running rogue ops and endangering the very essence of who we are. I expect you will adjust your management style accordingly."

Will bit back his furious retort. "Of course, sir."

"How long will it take to move the Alliance's assets?"

Will had no fucking clue. The last time they'd had to scramble to relocate assets after a potential breach of this magnitude had been over a hundred years before. And before then? Hell, the last major relocation had been in the early 1300s, when the leaders of the Templars had been tried for heresy and their Order officially dissolved.

At this point, there were only a handful of Templars within the Alliance who even knew where all of the treasure caches were located, all the others with that knowledge having died off. Only the members of the Grand Council and their chosen Guardian—and, apparently, the Guardian's successor—knew all of the locations. Even Will didn't know of the locations outside his regional control. He knew only that they were out there, scattered across the globe so that no one could take possession of the entire treasure should they happen upon a single cache.

"Two weeks at most," Will finally answered, pulling the number out of his ass. "I've already implemented our North American protocol. The international caches will be a challenge, but as soon as you send me the coordinates of the caches, I'll move people into place."

The man gave him a sharp nod. "I expect a full report filed by morning documenting this incident, William, as well as a complete risk assessment with the corrective measures you intend to take to control the damage."

Will's jaw clenched, and he felt the muscle in his cheek twitch. "Sir, I would prefer—"

"I don't give a damn what you'd *prefer*, Commander Asher," the high commander hissed. "I only care that you do your duty and clean up the mess you've allowed to happen."

Will took a deep breath and expelled it on a harsh sigh. "Of course, sir. Understood." Before the high commander could hang up, Will quickly added, "There's one other thing that I wanted to discuss with you, sir. I didn't want to bring it up in front of the council, but I think you should know.

The man who attempted to abduct Eli Scoffield claimed to be a follower of the One True Master."

The high commander's already fair complexion blanched at the phrase. "You will keep this information to yourself, William. Is that clear?"

"I think my men should know who we're potentially dealing with," Will argued. "They need to understand the implications—and the danger."

"You are not to mention the Illuminati in any of your conversations," the high commander snapped. "If I discover that you have disobeyed my orders in this, I will strip you of your command and have you burned from the Order."

Will clenched his hands into fists. "They killed my father. And now we have evidence that they are re-forming, making a move against the entire Alliance. And you would have me do *nothing?*"

The high commander's hard expression softened almost imperceptibly as sorrow briefly passed over his features. But the lapse was momentary. "Do you think I don't mourn my son to this day? You should hope to be half the man your father was, William."

"You can't bury your head in the sand and hope that the Illuminati are not plotting to rise against us again, Grandfather!" Will snapped. "We've already lost enough due to your unwillingness to act!"

The man's face grew red with fury. "That will be all, Commander. I look forward to your report."

The line disconnected and Will's screen went black. He sank down into his chair and ran a hand over his sable hair. His grandfather had been high commander for decades and had managed to keep the Alliance thriving during difficult times, especially during the Cold War era when it was all they could do to keep the world superpowers from annihilating one another.

But his determination to deny the facts before him was a
danger to them all. And his stubborn belief—that the men
who had murdered his son and left Will an orphan had
merely been rogue operatives invoking a defeated enemy
to instill fear and unease—might be exactly the kind of
arrogance that could bring the Alliance to its knees. . . .

Chapter Four

"You should get some sleep."

Luke glanced over to where Sarah was curled in the passenger seat. She hadn't really slept either during their long night of driving, finally dozing off for a little while as the sun rose, but in spite of the harrowing night and hours in the car, she was as beautiful as when he'd first seen her at the festival.

"I'm good," he assured her.

"Interesting choice of music," she said, with a glance toward the stereo. "Do you always listen to stuff this hard early in the morning?"

He followed her glance. Five Finger Death Punch. Good choice actually. But he honestly hadn't even noticed what was playing until now. "Sorry. I always listen to hard rock or metal when I'm driving. Helps me think. And keeps me awake."

"I can imagine." She smiled sleepily, teasing him. His stomach filled with heat. God, he'd love to see that smile on the pillow next to him. . . .

He leaned forward to adjust the volume, but she intercepted his hand, sending a shot of sensation up his arm. "It's fine," she assured him. "Trust me, I'd like you to do what you need to do to stay awake."

He gave her a terse nod and settled back into his seat. "Don't worry. I've got about three more hours in me before I need to rest."

"I could drive," she offered, emerging from beneath his biker jacket, which he'd insisted she use as a makeshift blanket.

"Probably better if I stay behind the wheel." They'd been followed for a little while a few miles outside of Bakersville, but he'd managed to shake the tail. Still, not knowing exactly who they were dealing with, he didn't want to take any chances. He'd already been in the same vehicle for too long, making their trail far too easy to pick up as it was. He was going to need to ditch the SUV ASAP, but until then, he was staying behind the wheel.

Sarah didn't argue. She stretched with a stifled yawn, then pivoted around to peer at her son, who was out cold in the back seat, his mouth hanging open just a little as he slept. "I don't know what I'm supposed to tell him," she murmured on a sigh. "I mean, *I* don't even know what's going on. How am I supposed to explain it to *him?*"

"He's a strong kid," Luke told her. "When you figure out what you want to say, don't sugarcoat it. Trust me, being straightforward is the best approach."

"Done this a few times, have you?" she joked with an attempt at a saucy grin.

He couldn't help but return it. "Well, not *this* exactly."

They sat in silence for so long after that exchange, Luke thought Sarah had nodded off again until she said, "Thank you, Luke. For everything. If you hadn't shown up . . ."

He glanced her way, surprised to see her studying him, her head tilted to one side as if she was trying to puzzle him out. The warmth in her expression made him quickly look away. "No problem."

"So what now?" she asked. "Where are we going?"

Luke shook his head. "Not sure yet. I should be hearing from my commander soon with instructions."

"What about everything that happened?" she asked. "Shouldn't we be making a report to the police or something now? And poor Hunter . . . what about him?"

"We'll do everything we possibly can," he told her. "We have resources that—"

"Who exactly is this *we* you keep talking about?" she interrupted. "And don't even think about giving me some kind of 'the less you know, the better' bullshit. I'm sick of being kept in the dark. My father always had his secrets, keeping us all ignorant of his business dealings and then his political career until my mom finally couldn't take it anymore and left us all. And now it seems those same secrets have brought danger to *my* door. So please don't sit there and presume to know what's best for me."

Luke chanced a glance at her. She looked so goddamned adorable, her cheeks red with righteous indignation, that if they hadn't been driving he would've been tempted to drag her into his arms and kiss the hell out of her. As it was, he felt his defenses weakening.

And she was right. After what they'd been through the previous night, she was entitled to know what she was part of and why she was in danger—especially since her sister seemed to be in the know. It seriously chapped his ass that the senator would tell one of his daughters all about them and not the other. What the hell was the guy's problem? From everything he'd seen, Sarah seemed like an intelligent, level-headed woman. She deserved to finally know the truth. And, hell, what was one more ass-chewing from his commander at this point? Luke heaved a long sigh, then said, "I work for an organization called Temple Knight & Associates."

"Temple Knight?" Sarah said with a laugh. "You've got

to be kidding me! My dad sent his *financial advisors* to look after us?"

Luke shifted in his seat, his back beginning to ache. "It's a little more complicated than that, Sarah."

She motioned for him to continue. "So enlighten me."

"The firm is a front," Luke explained, his tone taut as if what he was telling her was normally only pried out of him with a crowbar.

Sarah shook her head. "A front for what? The mob? Drug cartel? CIA?"

"The Knights Templar."

"You're a *Mason?*" she asked, grimacing as soon as she'd spoken, her voice sounding even more patronizing than she'd intended.

Luke sent an exasperated look her way. "No, I'm not a Mason. We're the actual Templars. After the Order was dismantled, some of the remaining knights scattered and were absorbed into other orders. Others simply changed their name—like the Order of Christ in Portugal. And some of them banded together and went underground to continue their mission of guarding the innocent, renaming the organization the Dark Alliance centuries later. They moved the caches of treasure to secure locations to keep them from being confiscated and to help fund their operations. Since then, our numbers have grown to include hundreds of Templars and hundreds more *confreres* and *consoeurs*—civilian allies who work closely with us to help us embed operatives within key business and government positions."

Okay. Wow. Maybe driving off with this guy wasn't the best idea. . . . He was either a delusional conspiracy nut or a bald-faced liar.

"Uh-huh," Sarah said, scooting closer to the door just a

little. "You know, you could've just said you didn't want to tell me. You didn't have to make something up."

"I'm not making it up," Luke insisted. "We've been operating secretly for centuries, recruiting members from the most elite soldiers and intelligence officers around the globe, insinuating our own into the highest echelons of society, working outside the law when necessary to try to right some of the wrongs in the world."

"Sure. Okay." Sarah shrugged. "If you say so."

"You gotta be shitting me," Luke mumbled. "Listen, do I seem like the kind of guy who'd waste his time just feeding you a line of bullshit? I honestly shouldn't be telling you any of this. And if you were anybody else, I wouldn't be. But seeing as how it's *your* family involved, I'm making an exception."

Sarah studied him for a long moment, watching the muscle twitch in his chiseled jaw, his irritation at being questioned clear. For the first time, she noticed the black metal band bearing a stylized silver Templar cross on his right ring finger. The ring was simple, inconspicuous—she wouldn't have found anything remarkable about it if not for the context of their conversation. Could it be that he was telling her the truth? Was there still some remnant of the Templars operating independently, guiding the fate of humanity?

Part of her wanted to believe him. *He* certainly seemed to believe it. But at this point, she wasn't sure *what* to believe. If anyone had told her a couple of days ago that some nut job would murder two people and try to abduct her son, she certainly wouldn't have believed that either. And yet here she was, riding in the car of a man she barely knew but who had already risked his life once for them.

"Why was that man after Eli?" she asked. "And how did my father know he'd be coming?"

"Because your father's one of us." Luke turned to look at her, gauging her reaction.

Even as he said it, a foggy, distant image intruded on her thoughts—a memory of her as a little girl, sitting on her father's lap as he rocked her to sleep, holding his hand and drowsily twisting the black band he wore on his finger.

"He has been for a long time. He used to work in the field for the Alliance until he decided to marry and have a family and so was embedded in the government. For security reasons, there are only a handful of people who know the secret locations where our treasures are hidden—your father is among them. Apparently, he has named your son as his successor, which means he somehow has passed on his knowledge of the treasure caches to Eli."

"Why Eli?" Sarah said, shaking her head. "He's never even met my son."

Luke shrugged. "Got me. He said something about making amends. Now you know as much as I do."

"Maddie's text said Dad was in surgery. Where's he now?" Sarah asked, her stomach twisting with fear and regret for the tension that had lingered between her and her father all these years. "Is he okay? Can I talk to him? What about my sister?"

"I'm sure we'll hear something soon." Luke glanced over at her, offering what she was sure was supposed to be a comforting smile, but it looked more like a grimace.

Sarah covered her face with her hands, trying to process everything being thrown at her. How was any of this possible? She was a schoolteacher, for crying out loud. She led an ordinary life. Eli had been right—*nothing* ever happened in the quiet little town where they lived. That's precisely why they'd stayed there. For three long years, she'd been struggling to get her life back to normal after Greg's death, and now her whole world had been turned upside down again.

"Pull over," she blurted, her stomach suddenly churning ominously. "I think I'm gonna be sick."

Luke immediately swerved to the side of the road. Sarah was throwing off her seat belt and opening the car door before he'd even come to a complete stop. A moment later, she was out of the SUV and stumbling several feet away. She doubled over, bracing her hands against her knees, waiting for her stomach to heave, but nothing happened. Instead, sobs shook her shoulders, bringing her to her knees. She sat back on her heels, wrapping her arms around herself as the tears came.

"You gonna be okay?"

Her head snapped up at the sound of Luke's deep voice, and she wiped her cheeks, swiping away the tears of fear, frustration, sorrow. "I don't know," she told him honestly, surprised to see him crouched beside her. "Two of my dear friends were murdered by some wacko trying to get to my son. And he's still in danger. I'm scared, Luke. I don't know what to do."

Her heart hitched a little as he reached out and took hold of her arm, his touch surprisingly calming. He helped her to her feet, but kept his hand where it was. "I won't let anything happen to you, Sarah," he said after a long silence, his thumb smoothing lazily over the material of her sweater. "We're gonna figure this out. You and Eli will be fine."

"You can promise that?" she asked, trembling as she felt her barely maintained hold on her fear rapidly slipping. "You know for certain that this is all going to end well? That no harm will come to either one of us?"

He pulled her into his arms, holding her close, his embrace comforting. "You have to trust me."

She pressed her cheek to his chest, closing her eyes, accepting the strength he was offering her. After a moment, the heat of his body permeated her skin, the masculine, woodsy scent of him swamping her senses, having a calming effect she hadn't anticipated. She found herself taking a step closer, her arms encircling his waist, feeling the rock-hard muscles of his back even through his T-shirt.

As her mind began to whirl with crazy, inappropriate thoughts of what it might be like to have those strong arms around her in a different setting, that harsh mouth against hers, she lifted her face and found herself wishing she could see his eyes behind his sunglasses, get a glimpse of what might be going on inside his head at that moment.

She swallowed hard, her breath growing shallower as his hold on her tightened ever so slightly, pulling her just a little closer. "I want to trust you," she said, her voice little more than a whisper.

Luke's phone buzzed, thankfully breaking through whatever it was that'd been going on between him and Sarah. What the hell was he thinking? There was no denying that Sarah was a beautiful woman, but he was letting his libido get the better of him. He had to keep it together and quit letting her get to him. As soon as this job was over, he'd never see her again. And, even on his worst day, he wasn't a big enough bastard to hook up with a woman when she was vulnerable and afraid.

Shit.

He was just tired. That was it. As soon as he got some sleep, he'd be back on his game, no problem. He took a couple of hasty steps in the opposite direction and grabbed his phone.

"Yeah."

"How you holding up?" It was his commander. Fortunately, he sounded one helluva lot less pissed off than he'd been the night before.

"I'm gonna need to stop soon, and catch some shut-eye," Luke admitted, sending a quick glance Sarah's way. "It's gonna be tomorrow before we can get to Chicago."

"Chicago?" Sarah cried, hurrying over to him and tugging on his arm. "We can't go to Chicago!"

He waved away her protest, motioning for her to be quiet. "Am I coming in to HQ or one of the safe houses?"

"Neither," Will informed him. "Whatever the hell is going on is seriously fucked up. We've had a security breach of our master files. I'm not sure how the hell someone was able get by all the shit Finn has in place, but they did. Until we lock everything down and mobilize our resources, I'm gonna need you to keep the woman and her son off the grid."

Luke nodded, understanding the implications of a security breach of that magnitude. "Copy that. How long are we talking here?"

"Couple of days," Will assured him. "Few weeks, max."

"A few—" Luke pulled his phone away from his ear and forced himself to take a deep breath and bite back the curses that came to his lips. He had a death grip on his phone when he put it back to his ear. "I'm supposed to be in Moscow next week. You tellin' me I'm off that mission?"

"I'll send one of the other guys instead," his commander replied. "No need for you to worry about it."

Luke ground his back teeth. He'd busted his ass for five years to earn the trust and admiration of his commander— a man he respected the hell out of and one of the few people whose good opinion he actually gave a damn about. The fact that he'd been selected for the Moscow mission was a vote of confidence that spoke volumes. Besides that, the less time he spent with Sarah Scoffield, the better it'd be for both of them.

"Rogan? You still there?"

Luke blew out a harsh breath. "Yes, sir, Commander. I'm here."

"This is priority one for you. You get me?"

Luke glanced over into the SUV at Eli, who was still out cold in the back seat, his young face unlined with worry or concern now—unlike last night when he'd been running for his life. And then there was Sarah, the woman who even now was looking at him with those wide dark eyes filled with tentative, fragile trust.

Shit.

Even if he wanted to bail, he realized there was no way he could. They needed him. Hell, aside from those he'd fought alongside, they were probably the only people who ever had. And he wasn't about to let them down.

"So if we're not coming in," Luke continued, "where am I supposed to take them?"

"Your call," Will told him. "Just make sure it's somewhere we don't have on record in case this bastard has dug deep enough to unearth our property holdings."

There was only one place Luke could think of that would be secure enough to keep Sarah and Eli safe and wasn't in the Alliance's records. "I got a place in mind. But I'll need a care package for the Scoffields if this is going to take that long. Anyone out in this area?"

"I'll have Finn put something together and get it to you ASAP," Will assured him.

"Copy that. Rogan out."

"Where are we going?" Sarah asked when he hung up.

"Home." He opened the passenger door to the SUV and extended a hand to her to help her climb back in.

She took his hand, her fingers cool in his grasp, and turned those soulful eyes up to his. "So, we're going back to Bakersville after all?"

"Not *your* home," Luke corrected her with a shake of his head, hoping he was making the right call. "I'm taking you to mine."

Chapter Five

Jacob Stone glanced over his shoulder where he'd left the lovely Ms. Holt panting and sighing in her seat, her black pencil skirt still up around her waist where he'd shoved it in his haste to get between her thighs. She'd seemed a little shocked when as soon as the private jet was at cruising altitude, he'd very bluntly admitted he wanted to fuck her. But then she'd come at him like a lioness on the prowl. And *damn* but the woman was just as accommodating when it came to sex as she was in the office, letting him do to her whatever the hell he wanted.

Oh, yeah, this is going to work out famously. . . .

If his cell phone hadn't rung a moment before, he would still be balls deep inside her, but that would have to wait. This was one call he'd been expecting.

"Good morning, Will," he said, forcing his tone to be congenial.

He couldn't stand the commander of the Chicago commandery. The little bastard wouldn't even be in the position if his grandfather hadn't been high commander of the Alliance. The man had dragged his grandson in from his duties with the CIA to put him in charge of the region when Will's father had been killed during a mission several years earlier. The appointment hadn't sat well with anyone in the Alliance—Templar or *confrere*.

But now it was like no one remembered how they'd been screwed over for advancement as a result of blatant nepotism. And the son of a bitch was regarded as one of the best commanders in the Western Hemisphere—possibly the world—and considered to be heir apparent to the high commander if he could be convinced to take the position. Will Asher's modesty and constant deprecation of his glory and accolades made Stone's gut twist with disgust. He'd been handed power on a silver platter and refused to embrace it while other, more deserving brothers would've been more than happy to take what they were due. Will Asher was weak, pathetic.

But not Stone. Such injustices merely galvanized his determination to take what should've been his all along.

"Good morning, Jacob," Will replied, his tone grave. "I'm sorry to call so early."

"You know my line is open to you any time, Will," Stone said, reminding himself that he'd only be kissing Will's ass for a little while longer. "To what do I owe the pleasure, my friend?"

"I'm sorry to have to do this over the phone," Will began, "but you need to know Senator Hal Blake has been shot in an assassination attempt."

"My God," Stone breathed, feigning shock and concern. "When? How? Do you have any leads?"

"Not yet," Will said. "I know Hal's like a father to you, Jacob. I promise we're going to do everything we can to figure out who's behind this."

Stone had to suppress a grin and cleared his throat as if emotion was choking him. "Thank you. I appreciate that."

"We're trying to keep it quiet, spin Hal's condition with the press," Will continued. "But I didn't want you to find out from some other source if it leaks out. I thought you should hear it from us."

"What about Maddie and Sarah? Do they know?" Stone asked, holding his breath as he waited for Will's response, hoping he'd give away a clue as to Sarah's whereabouts.

"Yeah," Will replied.

Stone waited for a moment, but when it became clear that Will wasn't going to say another word about the senator's daughters, Stone suppressed a sigh and continued, "Well, please let them know I'm thinking of them. And that if they need anything, I'm here."

When Will disconnected, Stone had to resist the urge to lob his phone across the cabin. *Cagey bastard.* The man wasn't nearly as willing to confide in Stone as some of his colleagues. And of all the commanders, Will Asher was the one he most needed in his pocket—not just because he commanded all of North America but also because of his family connections. Unfortunately, he was the commander who was proving the most difficult to win over.

Still, Stone had no concern that Will suspected his true motives or plans for the Alliance. He'd known Will long enough now to understand that his reserve wasn't personal—the guy didn't get close to *anyone*. Jack Grayson, whose family was almost as legendary and well-connected as Will Asher's, might be the one exception. Perhaps *that* was the angle Stone needed to work. . . .

"Mr. Stone?"

Stone turned at the sultry sound of Ms. Holt's voice, and all thoughts of the Alliance vanished. She was completely naked now except for her red pumps and a paisley scarf around her neck—which he'd be sure to make use of in ways she'd probably never imagined—her golden hair falling around her shoulders. "Why, Ms. Holt, I think I have underestimated just how useful you are going to be. . . ."

* * *

Jacob Stone was a fucking weasel. Will never had liked the guy, hadn't trusted his too-charming smile, his easy manners and perfect answers to any question. But the guy had gotten a shitty deal from the Alliance. If any other brother had made the same mistakes that Stone had, he would've been sanctioned, maybe stripped of any rank or at least bumped down. But Will knew when his grandfather had handed down the verdict on Stone's hearing that he'd been acting on an old vendetta against Stone's grandfather, Angus Stone. So much for not getting personal.

But Will hadn't been in a position to argue. Not back then. But if any of his men were to go up against the Grand Council now, he sure as hell wouldn't let them go down in flames like his father had done to Stone. He would defend his men, no matter the risk.

He just had to assume that his father had had reasons for burning Stone that went beyond the family rivalry. He had to believe that his father had been a good man, an excellent commander, who'd kept his oath to put the Alliance before all else. And that his grandfather had made the right call.

That was certainly easier than admitting that his family was comprised of power-tripping assholes just like the Stone family had been. Regardless, he was working damned hard to distance himself from that perception since taking command. Maybe Jacob was as well. So far, he'd proven to be an adept politician under Hal Blake's tutelage, and his meteoric rise to the spotlight had as much to do with his own talents as Hal's influence. Hell, maybe he should give the guy a chance to prove himself. Wasn't that what Will was asking from his fellow Templars?

Will rolled his head, trying to work out the tension in his neck, but it didn't do a damned bit of good. With a resigned sigh, he turned his attention back to his laptop screen, checking the most recent updates about the movement of the assets. He shook his head at the estimated time for completing relocation. It overshot his promise to his grandfather by at least two days, maybe more. "Too long."

"I get that all the time."

Will's gaze snapped up to see the wide grin of his tech specialist, Elliot "Finn" Finnegan. Normally, he appreciated Finnegan's levity and unwavering optimism. Those personality traits were certainly in short supply in the Alliance. But today he couldn't even bring himself to crack a smile in response.

"What do you have, Finn?"

"Put together the tech for Luke," Finn told him. "Should be enough to get them by until we can bring them in. I can be on the plane as soon as you say the word. But I'm hosed when it comes to picking out ladies' things. . . . Gonna have to hit up Maddie Blake to figure out what to get her sister and nephew, if that's cool with you."

Will gave him a terse nod. "I'm expecting Luke to give me a call soon to let me know the rendezvous point. Might not be able to give you much notice, so be ready."

"Copy that." Finn jerked his head toward the screen on Will's wall. "Just sent you the latest assessment."

Will tapped a sequence of keys on his laptop, and several documents popped open on the wall display. "What am I looking at?"

"A whole lotta fucked up," Finn said.

He gave him a sardonic look. "Not what I was hoping to hear, Finn."

Finn nodded. "Ah, sorry, *brah*. It's sunshine, rainbows, and pretty pink ponies."

At this, Will actually chuckled. "That's more like it," he said with a grin. "Walk me through it."

* * *

Luke's eyes were burning by the time he finally pulled into the parking lot of a roadside motel that looked like it would fit his needs—a place that wouldn't be crawling with bugs and God knew what else but where no one would bat an eye at people just needing to hole up for a few hours. Even better that it had a greasy-spoon diner a parking lot over and a gas station down the road, where he could fuel up before they continued on the next leg of the trip to his personal residence.

"Are you sure you don't just want me to drive?" Sarah asked.

He offered her a grin, knowing damn well that what she was asking was more along the lines of *Are you sure we won't catch something if we sit on a chair here?*

"We'll be fine here for a little while," he assured her. "I wouldn't take you somewhere I thought would put you and your son at risk. As soon as I check us in, we'll grab something at the diner, and you and Eli can hang out while I catch a couple hours of sleep."

She cast a hesitant glance toward the rows of cheap motel rooms with bright red doors, but nodded. "Okay."

Ten minutes later, he was leading them into the diner and sliding into a booth at the back of the room so he could keep his eye on the front door as well as the kitchen, where he assumed there was a second exit.

"How you folks doin' this morning?"

Luke lifted his eyes to the middle-aged waitress standing beside him. "I'd like coffee and your country breakfast."

The woman blinked at him. "Well, alrighty then. Guess that answers my *next* question."

"I'm sorry," Sarah said gently, reaching across the table and placing a hand over Luke's. "He's not usually so surly. We've been in the car a long time. He's just tired. Isn't that right, honey?"

When he caught her gaze, her eyes widened slightly,

giving him what he assumed was her "teacher look," silently chastising him. "Sorry, ma'am," he muttered to the waitress, suddenly feeling like he was back in school and getting in trouble for not turning in his homework again.

"Where you folks headed?" the waitress asked.

Eli sent an expectant look Luke's way, waiting for an answer, but before Luke could get a word out, Sarah stepped in.

"Michigan," she said with a friendly grin that brought her dimples to her cheeks. "Visiting family there during my son's fall break from school. It should be a *lovely* drive this time of year, don't you think? Hopefully we won't hit any snow. . . ."

Luke watched in amazement as Sarah chatted easily with the waitress, feeding her a cover story he couldn't have invented any better had he tried. Soon, the waitress was plying Eli with chocolate milk and fresh donuts and bringing Luke and Sarah freshly baked blueberry muffins that were mouth-wateringly good.

"What was that all about?" Luke asked after downing half his coffee and his second muffin.

Sarah glanced toward the lunch counter, where their waitress was bustling about helping other customers. "Well, I assumed we needed a cover story."

"The less you say, the better," he told her, realizing just how shitty that sounded the minute the words left his mouth.

"Is that right?" she snapped. She leaned toward the table, hissing, "Well, an ill-tempered man and a rather rumpled woman traveling with a school-aged boy at this time of year deserves some explanation, don't you think? The way she was looking at us, it seemed to me that she was curious. Places like this probably don't get a lot of kids as customers."

He had to admit she was right, and had his brain not been half-numb with sleep deprivation, he probably would've drawn the same conclusion and come up with something similar. As it was, it impressed the hell out of him that Sarah had so seamlessly intervened.

"Thank you," he said simply before he turned his attention back to his breakfast.

Half an hour later, they were waving good-bye to their new pal Lorraine, who'd sent them on their way with a box full of muffins for the road and to-go cups of coffee.

"How long are we staying here?" Eli asked as Luke unlocked the door to their motel room. "It doesn't look like they have decent cable."

"Just for a few hours," Sarah answered, smoothing the boy's hair from his wide, dark eyes. "Mr. Rogan needs to sleep for a little while. You and I will find something quiet to do in the meantime."

"Don't worry about being quiet," Luke assured her as he pulled back the dingy curtains just enough to check the parking lot for any cars that looked out of place. But it didn't appear that they'd been followed. "I'll be fine. Just stay in the room and don't open the door for anyone."

Eli dropped down on the end of the bed and grabbed the remote control, flipping on the TV and finding a documentary on the African Serengeti. While the boy was preoccupied, Luke strode to the bathroom and glanced inside, noting a small window over the toilet. It was for ventilation but was big enough that someone small could squeeze through.

He checked the latch to make sure it was secure and turned to head back to the bedroom, but stopped short when he saw Sarah blocking his path.

"I thought we were safe here," she said, her arms crossed over her chest.

"We're as safe here as anywhere until we get to my place," he assured her.

"Yet you're acting like you expect someone to come barging in and attack us at any moment," she accused.

He took a step closer and immediately realized his mistake when his heart started pounding at the nearness of her. *Shit.* He shoved his hands into his pockets to keep from touching her. "If being paranoid is what's going to keep you and your son alive," he said, "then guilty as charged."

"Please don't take this the wrong way, Luke," she began, edging closer, damn it all, "but why does it matter so much to you if Eli and I are safe? You don't know us. I get that you've been given an order, but I also heard you talking to your commander and know you'd rather be somewhere else. If you'd insisted that someone else watch over us, I would've understood. I can just go to the police, tell them what happened. I'm sure it'll be fine."

Luke stared at her for a long moment, trying to figure out the answer to her question. Hell if he knew why it mattered so much to him that he keep them safe. In the technical sense, he protected people every day and had for going on fifteen years when he added up his time in the military and then working for the government and now with the Alliance. But she was right—this assignment was hitting him on a level he hadn't anticipated.

"I guess because, when I wasn't much older than Eli, someone took my mother and me in, watched over *us* when we needed it," he finally said, not sure where the explanation was even coming from. "And someone else did the same thing for me again a few years ago when I was in a really dark place—except this time the enemy I was up against was myself. If it wasn't for that person stepping in, I don't know where I'd be. But dead is a damned good bet."

Sarah straightened. "Oh. God. I'm sorry."

"Don't be," Luke told her. He shook his head as his vision went a little blurry. Suddenly too tired to stand, he leaned against the edge of the sink. "I made a promise to keep you and Eli safe, Sarah. I'll keep it. There's no way I'd abandon you, so don't worry about it."

The next thing he knew, Sarah's arms were around his neck, hugging him tightly. He resisted the urge to wrap his arms around her and hold her close, to bury his face in her hair and let the warmth of her wash over him. But when she pressed a kiss to his cheek and whispered, "Thank you," in his ear, he almost gave in.

Fortunately, before he could move, she stepped away and hurried back into the room with Eli, leaving Luke gaping at the empty doorway and wondering exactly what the hell he'd gotten himself into.

Sarah had to force herself to concentrate on the documentary on TV and not to keep glancing over at the other bed, where Luke slept, breathing softly.

She'd been offering him an out when she'd told him she would understand if he wanted someone else to watch over them. But when he'd shared his reasons for wanting to make sure they were okay and promised not to abandon them, she had been secretly relieved.

And she'd impulsively thrown her arms around him, wanting to feel those protective arms around her if only for a brief moment. But he'd gone rigid with a sharp intake of breath when she'd hugged him, keeping his arms at his sides. Her initial reaction had been disappointment until she'd felt his heart pounding in his chest and her own kicked up a notch to match the frantic pace.

And when she'd brushed her lips against his cheek, she felt the almost imperceptible shudder that shook him. And for one crazy second she had the urge to kiss him again, this time on those fierce lips that he kept in a grim line, except on the rare occasions that he smiled. And *that smile* . . . it completely transformed his already handsome face. But luckily she'd come to her senses and put some distance between them before she did something colossally stupid. It was the situation, she told herself. Stress and adrenaline and some misplaced knight-in-shining-armor fascination—although come to think of it, that wasn't far off the mark with the whole Templar Knight shebang—had her waxing poetic and experiencing crazy thoughts and feelings toward this man.

Sarah sent another glance his way.

God, he was a gorgeous man. And she'd noticed that, in spite of his tall, muscular frame, he moved quietly, making almost no sound at all when he walked. Like a man who was used to being a predator. And yet, for all the deadliness she sensed in him, he treated her and Eli with such gentleness—not exactly something she would've expected from a man who radiated raw masculine power.

But there was a darkness to him as well—something he'd referenced when he'd vaguely spoken of his past when she'd cornered him in the bathroom a couple of hours ago. His piercing dark eyes had gone even darker in the remembrance of whatever it was that haunted him.

She studied him more intently, frowning a little as she tried to solve the puzzle that was Luke Rogan. What secrets was he keeping? If he knew her father, then he definitely had secrets—likely ones that were deeper and darker than she could possibly imagine.

"How long was I out?"

Sarah started so violently at the sudden sound of Luke's deep voice that she earned a worried look from Eli.

"It's okay, Mom," he said, patting her arm. "It's just Mr. Rogan."

She forced a little laugh and gave Eli a hug. "Thanks, pumpkin. I guess I'm just a little jumpy."

When she turned her attention back to Luke, he was sitting on the edge of the bed, studying her with narrowed eyes. But his gaze wasn't menacing. It was . . . curious.

Busted.

She held his gaze for a moment, but when she felt heat rising in her cheeks, she glanced toward the bedside clock. "Um . . . uh . . . a couple of hours."

Luke glanced down at his wristwatch, confirming the time, and gave her a terse nod, then grabbed his phone from the same table. "Time to check in with my commander."

He was on his feet and out the door before she realized he was even moving. A moment later, she could hear his booming voice outside the door and went to it, pressing close to try to hear what he was saying.

"—that this is a seriously bad idea."

She leaned closer as his voice got quieter, her heart sinking when she heard her name. He was trying to off-load them after all. That had to be what he meant by "bad idea."

She heard him wrapping up the conversation with an exasperated "Copy that" and hurried away from the door, pretending to inspect the air-conditioning unit under the window.

"Time to move out," he said as he shut the door behind him. "Eli, time to go, buddy."

"Where are we going now?" Sarah asked, her tone clipped.

Luke's brows twitched together in the hint of a frown. "East for about two hours. I'm meeting a colleague there to pick up some things for you and Eli. Then we'll continue to my house in Wyoming."

She shook her head slightly. "But I thought—" She bit off her words to keep from letting on that she'd been listening to his conversation. "Okay. But we'll need to get lunch somewhere along the way. Will there be someplace we can stop?"

"It's okay, Mom," Eli chimed in. "I can wait. I'm not that hungry."

She turned in time to catch her son sending Luke a wide grin and a starry-eyed look of admiration. She'd have to discourage him from getting attached to Luke, especially when the man clearly saw them as a burden, regardless of what he said to her face.

"Listen to your mom, Eli," Luke said mildly. "She's the boss."

Eli gave Luke a nod that was a very good imitation of Luke's own. "Copy that."

Luke's mouth twitched with the hint of a grin. "We'll grab some lunch at the first place we see," Luke assured them. "Eli, can you be my eyes and watch for some place? I'm used to traveling alone and not eating very often."

Eli nodded emphatically. "Sure!"

"All right then, let's move out."

Sarah started for the door, but Luke put out a restraining arm, catching her around the waist. Her cheeks flooded with heat at his touch and she lifted her eyes to his. For a moment, their gazes locked and the air between them grew thick with tension as he looked down at her, his brows drawn together in a slight frown as if he'd forgotten what he'd intended to say.

When he finally spoke, his voice was rough. "I go first. To make sure it's safe."

Her voice seemed to have deserted her, so she merely nodded and watched him as he opened the door part of the way and peered outside before stepping out and going to the SUV. He glanced around casually, as anyone else might, but Sarah could tell by the way his eyes narrowed that he was taking in every detail of their surroundings, searching for any sign of a threat.

"I like Mr. Rogan," Eli said, slipping his hand into hers. "Do you think we'll stay at his house for very long?"

Luke waved them out at that moment, so Sarah left her son's question hanging. But considering the way her stomach fluttered and her heart pounded when Luke gently placed a hand on the small of her back to guide her to the SUV, she realized the sooner they were away from Luke Rogan, the better.

Chapter Six

Luke leaned against the hood of the SUV, waiting for Finn to arrive and trying not to think about how heavy the weight of Sarah's gaze had been while he was sleeping. Even when he had been out cold, he could feel her looking at him. It made him uncomfortable—mostly because he hated what she must've been thinking of him.

He hadn't intended to make reference to his past when they were talking. It was better for everyone if that stayed buried. But it was almost like she could see right into his soul. And that made him want to yak up all the muffins he'd wolfed down at breakfast. If she'd had any idea what he'd done in his lifetime, could see even a *fraction* of the shit that gave him nightmares, she wouldn't look at him in that particular way she had that made him want to drag her into his arms and not let go.

He glanced over to where Sarah and Eli were sitting in the grassy field next to the truck stop where he'd been told to rendezvous with his fellow Templar, both of them needing to stretch their legs and be out of the SUV for a few minutes. As he watched, Sarah closed her eyes and turned her face up to the sun, her hair lifting slightly in the autumn breeze.

She was so beautiful in that unguarded moment that his

chest constricted with emotion. He'd been to more countries than he'd bothered to count, had seen some of the most beautiful places on earth. And yet it all paled in comparison to the sight before him now.

Oh, yeah. This is a seriously *bad idea. . . .*

He'd tried to get that across to Commander Asher when they'd chatted outside the motel room. Luke hadn't had the balls to come right out and tell his commander that he was attracted to the woman he'd been asked to protect, that he worried about where things might go if they spent too much time together.

There'd been no point. He knew exactly what Will would've said—*keep your dick in your pants, Rogan, and do your fucking job.* It'd been made very clear to Luke that this was a nonnegotiable condition of his employment when he'd been recruited.

There was a reason the Templars were discouraged from getting involved in romantic relationships. They were distracting. And that directive had never been an issue for Luke. Hell, he'd had a hard and fast rule about not getting serious with anybody well before he'd been recruited into the Alliance. And since then, he'd been all about the job, determined to prove to himself and his brethren that he deserved to be there. And that hadn't been a problem. Until now.

He was just going to have to keep his shit together and keep his distance. Period. Which was a great fucking plan until he felt Sarah's pulse racing every time he touched her and realized she was into him too.

Quiet footfalls on the gravel sent a spike of adrenaline through Luke's veins. He spun around, weapon drawn.

"Whoa, whoa, whoa, *brah,* It's just me." Elliot "Finn" Finnegan sauntered his way, the guy's shaggy blond hair sun-bleached and his tan surprisingly golden brown for someone who spent the vast majority of his time behind a shit ton of computers in their ops center.

Luke lowered his gun. "You were supposed to call when you got here. I damned near shot your ass." Jerking his chin toward Finn's gaudy flower-print shirt, ripped-out jeans, and flip-flops, Luke asked, "Just get back from the island?"

Finn flashed the wide, easy grin Luke knew had a way of procuring some of the best ass around in spite of the guy's being a total geek. "Fuckin' A. The waves off Waikiki were totally bitchin'. You should come with me next time, check it out."

Luke chuckled. "I'm more comfortable riding horses than riding waves, but thanks. So whatcha got for me?"

Finn handed over the black duffel bag he was carrying. "Standard field tech. Plus new, secure phones for Sarah and her son. We're still assessing just what was affected by the breach, so I've switched everyone over to a backup system I'd installed on the sly—you know, just in case."

Luke gave him a wary look. "And who exactly is kindly hosting this backup system if we've been compromised?"

Finn chuckled. "Let's just say there are certain branches of the United States government that have been most accommodating."

Luke lifted a brow. "I'm guessing they have no idea just *how* accommodating."

Finn shrugged. "Wouldn't be the first time I've taken full advantage of their generosity. Anyway, Sarah and Eli's numbers are already programmed into your contacts, and yours into theirs. Aside from calling you, each other, or my direct line at the ops center, they can't make outgoing calls. They can receive incoming calls, but we're going to be the only ones that have the numbers."

"What about email?" Luke asked.

"Their accounts have already been taken care of," Finn assured him. "I'm keeping an eye on things and monitoring incoming messages. Outgoing will be evaluated. And we're already working on making arrangements for Sarah's personal affairs. Commander Asher will fill you in on the details. Also got a new laptop for you and newly secured mi-fi for all the devices so you can check in with HQ. You'll also find new IDs and passports for all three of you, courtesy of my masterful forgery skills—just in case. I've set up a bank account and credit cards for you and Sarah under the new names, too. You're now Mr. and Mrs. Randall."

"People know my name where I'm going," Luke told him. "I've lived there for a while."

"So say she's your girlfriend then," Finn said with a shrug. "And just use the cash when you're in town so no one gets their dick twisted. Is your house in your name? Is it traceable?"

Luke shook his head, explaining as he made his way to the back of the SUV, "It's listed under a phony trust set up by one of my aliases from an op I ran before the Alliance. Someone would have to know about that to figure out it's mine."

"Still, better give me the address in case of an emergency," Finn suggested. When Luke hesitated, Finn held his arms out to his sides. "C'mon, Rogan. You've known me *how* long?"

"I don't want my address on record," Luke reminded him, opening the SUV's rear door and grabbing his own duffel. "That was the deal when I signed on."

"It won't be on record," Finn assured him. He tapped his temple. "It'll be right up here. Nowhere else. And when this is over—poof! It's gone."

Luke gave him a wary look. "Yeah right. I've never known you to forget a damned thing. But you'll just purge my address from your memory?"

Finn gave him a tolerant look and gestured at himself. "Dude. There's only so much awesome this body can take. I have to purge the shit now and then."

"Fine. But if my address gets out, it's your ass." Luke rattled off his address, earning raised eyebrows from Finn.

Finn's brows shot up. "No shit? Wyoming? So the whole thing about riding horses . . ."

"Wasn't bullshit."

Finn nodded. "Sweet."

"Now give me yours," Luke demanded, crossing his arms over his chest. "Quid pro quo."

"Don't have one," Finn said with a shrug. "Gotta keep movin'. I just go where the waves take me."

Luke shook his head. The Chicago commandery's golden boy was a piece of work, but he couldn't help but like the guy—even if he did always look more like a beach bum than a genius with three PhDs who had a price on his head in at least four countries for hacking government secrets.

"Have anything else for me?" Luke asked. "Sarah and Eli had to leave without grabbing anything."

"I've got a couple changes of clothes for each of them," Finn replied. "Maddie Blake helped me on sizes. But they'll probably want to grab some other things. There's a mall about twenty miles from here." He jabbed his thumb over his shoulder at the red SUV he'd driven up in. "You can take this fleet vehicle. I'll take care of ditching this one. You know the drill."

Luke gave him a terse nod. This was hardly his first time evading an enemy—foreign or domestic. But like most of his other colleagues, Finn only had a vague knowledge of Luke's background. Jack and Commander Asher were the only ones who knew the full story—Jack because he'd recruited him; Will because his ass was on the line if Luke fucked up.

"The commander's calling an emergency meeting of the team," Finn told him. "Bringing in anyone from ops who can be spared. You'll need to check in tonight at twenty-two hundred. Your laptop is set up and ready to go for you to conference in."

Luke slammed the rear door of the Expedition and tossed Finn the keys. "Thanks, I'll—"

"*Daaaaamn*," Finn drawled under his breath. Luke turned to follow Finn's line of sight and saw Sarah and Eli walking toward them. "Sure you want this detail? I'd be happy to take her—I mean *it*—off your hands."

Luke sent a look of warning Finn's way that made the man chuckle. Not exactly the reaction he was going for. But Finn wiped the grin from his face when Luke stepped in beside Sarah and guided her forward with his hand at the small of her back.

Luke cleared his throat and vaguely gestured in Finn's direction. "Sarah, Eli, this is Finn."

Finn's smile returned as he glanced between Luke and Sarah. "No way . . ."

Luke sent a dark look Finn's way. "Don't even go there, man."

Finn smothered his shit-eating grin, but amusement still seemed to tug at the corner of the little bastard's mouth as he reached out and shook Sarah's hand. "Don't mind him. Dude's just jealous of my good looks and is worried I'll sweep you off your feet with my irresistible charm."

Sarah laughed, clearly amused by Finn's flirting. "Well, I can see why he's concerned, Mr. Finn."

Finn slid his hands in the back pockets of his jeans, striking an Adonis-like pose that came naturally to him. "Just Finn," he said with a wink.

"Don't you have somewhere to be, 'just Finn'?" Luke snapped.

Finn shook his head, his gaze fixed on Sarah. "Nah, I'm good."

Luke strode to the other SUV and jerked open the passenger door. "Well, we do. Thanks for the care package."

Sarah sent a bemused look Luke's way, but then extended her hand to Finn. "It was nice to meet you, Finn."

Finn took her hand, holding on to it longer than Luke would've liked. But it was actually Eli who interceded. He stepped between them with a huff and grabbed his mom's hand. "Mr. Rogan says we have to go, Mom."

"Eli!" Sarah scolded softly, ushering him into the back seat. Then she sent an apologetic look Finn's way. "I'm sorry. He's normally not so rude."

Finn shrugged good-naturedly. "No worries."

Luke helped Sarah into the SUV, then turned back to Finn, whose wide grin had returned. "What?"

Finn shook his head. "Be careful, *brah*. You're headed for trouble."

Luke frowned at him. "What the hell is that supposed to mean?"

Finn chuckled. "Nothin', man," he called over his shoulder as he sauntered away. "Nothin' at all."

Luke was still frowning when he put the duffel bags into the rear of the red SUV and got behind the wheel, earning raised brows from Sarah.

"I didn't like that guy," Eli grumbled, crossing his arms. "And his shirt was stupid-ugly."

Luke chuckled as he started up the SUV and got them back on the road. "His shirts are always ugly. Don't hold it against him."

"Eli," Sarah interjected, "there was nothing wrong with Mr. Finn's shirt."

"Fine," Eli huffed. "But I didn't like the way he looked at you."

Luke grunted. He didn't like it either, but he sure as shit wasn't about to admit it.

"What are you talking about?" Sarah asked with a slight chuckle, sending a glance Luke's way.

Eli shrugged. "Nothing. I just didn't like it. He had that

look like in the movies when the guy puts his tongue in the girl's mouth."

"What?" Sarah cried. "*What* movies are you talking about? Were you watching cable at Dylan's again?"

Luke glanced in the rearview mirror in time to catch Eli rolling his eyes. "There's kissing in *all* the movies, Mom. Sheesh. But it's okay when Mr. Rogan looks at you like that. I don't mind *him* wanting to kiss you."

Luke damned near steered the SUV off the road. But his surprise was apparently nothing compared to Sarah's; she twisted around in her seat so fast it was a miracle she didn't get whiplash.

"Elijah Gregory Scoffield!" she hissed. "I suggest you hush this instant, young man. You have no idea what you're talking about."

"Sure, I do," Eli argued. He leaned forward enough to tap Luke on the shoulder. "You think my mom's pretty, right?"

Luke suddenly found himself wishing for a well-placed sinkhole to swallow up the SUV. He shifted a little in his seat and sent a glance Sarah's way. "Yeah. Sure."

"And don't guys always want to kiss pretty girls?" Eli pressed.

Luke cleared his throat, the air in the vehicle feeling too thick to draw into his lungs. "Uh . . . it's a little more complicated than that, buddy. You can't just kiss every pretty girl you see." He sent a guarded glance Sarah's way. "She has to *want* you to kiss her."

Eli sent an expectant look his mom's way. "You *want* him to kiss you, right, Mom?"

Sarah looked like she wanted to dive out of the moving vehicle, her cheeks nearly as bright as her sweater. "End of discussion, Eli."

"But—"

The look she sent the boy's way cut him off in an instant. Eli huffed again and settled back against his seat.

"So where are we going next?" he piped up after a few long moments of charged silence.

"My house," Luke told him. "You'll be safe there. But I don't want you saying anything to anyone about what happened at the festival, okay, Eli?"

Eli shrugged. "Sure. Okay."

"In fact," Luke continued, "if anyone asks, I need you to tell them you guys are Sarah and Eli Randall. Sarah's my girlfriend—"

"I knew it!" Eli cut in.

"It's just a cover story, Eli," Sarah stressed, her tone clipped. "We're only staying until Mr. Rogan is allowed to take us back home."

"When will that be?" Eli asked. "Who *was* that guy at the festival? Why did he want to hurt us?"

Luke glanced Sarah's way, willing to let her take the lead on how much she wanted to tell her son.

"We're still trying to figure that out, pumpkin," she said. "But Mr. Rogan is going to make sure we're safe until then."

Eli pressed his lips together and squared his shoulders in the way Luke had seen Sarah do earlier. The boy was more like his mother than he probably realized. "So are we going straight to your house?" he asked. "Are we almost there? How much farther do we need to go?"

Luke glanced up in the mirror again and caught the kid's dark gaze, his eyes wide with anticipation. "We're still a few hours away. And we're going shopping first."

Eli pulled a face. "Shopping? Oh, *man* . . . I *hate* shopping."

"I totally feel ya, buddy," Luke agreed. "But you're going to need a few things before we get where we're headed."

"Like what?" Eli pressed.

"Well," Luke said, "at this time of year, odds are good you're going to need some snow boots. . . ."

Chapter Seven

Jacob Stone took his seat in the café where he was supposed to meet his contact. He was early. He always made sure he arrived well in advance of any meeting so he could scope out the area first and assess any potential threats—old habits and all that.

He was enjoying his *café cubano*, appreciating the extra caffeine after his rather rigorous dalliance with Ms. Holt, when a man in light linen slacks and pale blue cotton shirt sauntered toward him. The guy sported the kind of tan one would get spending a life of leisure on a private yacht and the swagger of someone who knew he was the one in control, regardless of the situation.

Stone smiled and raised his coffee cup in salute, but stayed seated. He knew how to play this game, too.

"You need to get out in the sun more, Stone," the guy said as he took the seat across from him. "You're pale."

Stone downed his coffee and signaled to the server. "I like to spend my time in the boardroom—or the bedroom—these days, Evans. I don't miss sweating my ass off to further someone else's agenda."

"But you clearly have no qualms about asking someone else to further *yours*," Evans drawled with a smirk. He didn't even glance toward the pretty senorita who appeared at his elbow, merely held up two fingers.

As she scurried away to get their drinks, Stone mirrored his companion's nonchalance. "Favorite spot of yours?"

Evans lifted a shoulder. "I like the service."

Stone could imagine. If he didn't have Ms. Holt waiting in their hotel room for him, he would've brought back one of these tasty pieces of ass to enjoy during his stay. Hell, he still might. "Care to make a trip home?"

"I'm open to a visit," Evans replied. "For the right reason. There are people there who'd prefer I stayed gone."

A tall glass filled with rum and Tropi-Cola appeared in front of Evans with hardly a sound, and another was placed before Stone along with his coffee before the server slipped away. Apparently, Evans's friend knew how to be discreet during his meetings. "Well, I have about five million reasons that I'd be willing to share with you. Would that be sufficient?"

Evans inclined his head in a slight nod. "I suppose. When?"

"Things are a little . . . delicate at the moment," Stone said. "Everyone is on guard. Give it a few days to settle down."

"And is there a particular window of opportunity for this visit?" Evans asked.

Stone toyed with his drink. That was, indeed, the question. Will was already moving assets. All cash and investments would've been shifted within hours. The Alliance was nothing if not prepared. But the non-liquid assets would take longer, the logistics in place but requiring careful execution for the purposes of concealment. If his timing was off, if he waited too long before making another move, whatever information Eli Scoffield possessed would no longer be useful.

Blake would've most likely passed along only the shell of a contingency plan. Only the Grand Council and the commander placed in charge of relocating assets would know the final destinations. And there was no way in hell he was making a move on Will. Not yet.

"Three weeks," Stone finally answered. "Maybe less."

"Where will I be visiting?" Evans asked.

This made Stone squirm a bit. "That's the other problem. I'm not entirely sure."

Evans's smirk grew. "You want me to make a visit, but you don't know to *where?*"

Stone forced a smile, wishing he didn't need the smug son of a bitch for the job when he would've preferred to throat-punch him for being such a condescending prick. "I'll supply the information to you when you arrive in the United States."

"And who will be eagerly awaiting my arrival?" Evans asked.

Now it was Stone's turn to be smug. "The grandson of your old friend Hal Blake."

Evans paled behind his tan before his face flushed with barely restrained fury. "You should've led with that."

Stone's lips curved into a grin. "I was saving the best for last. I need the boy brought to me. He has certain information that I would like to retrieve."

Evans's jaw tightened. "Who's he with?"

Stone shrugged. "His mother. And a newer member of the Alliance—no one you know, so no chance of your being recognized if your paths cross before the extraction. He was recruited after you left."

"To fill my place, you mean," Evans spat, his cool demeanor slipping.

"Sure," Stone told him. "If that's the way you want to see it."

"What's his name?" Evans pressed. "Apparently, I'm going to need to do my homework to track them down."

Stone took another sip of his drink before answering. "Name's Luke Rogan."

Evans laughed in a harsh burst. "Are you shitting me?"

Stone eyed him askance. "So you *do* know him?"

"Only by reputation," Evans told him. "But that's enough."

"Do what you need to do," Stone said, growing tired of Evans's games. "Rogan's of no concern to me."

"Well, he's a concern to me," Evans shot back. "Rogan was Special Forces, so he's already not someone you want to dick around with. But I heard about him from some of my less . . . *savory* acquaintances. Rogan was one of the guys the government used on the kind of ops they don't like to admit to in polite company. I imagine that's how he came to the attention of our fine friends in the Alliance."

Stone eyed him evenly. "Are you telling me you're afraid to take on this Rogan?"

Evans didn't flinch. "I'm saying I'm not eager to get myself killed. And Rogan won't think twice. I'm going to have to get the drop on him first."

Stone sighed. "Fine. I'll add an additional five million reasons for you to take the job. But the boy is to be unharmed."

Evans gave him a terse nod. "Understood." He raised his glass to Stone and offered him a tight smile. "Who says you can't go home again?"

Will Asher strode down the deserted hallway of the private floor of the hospital, flanked by two of his men, Chase Nielsen and Ian Cooper. He'd been told that Hal's security guards had insisted on accompanying their charge when he was transported to Chicago, but there was no way in hell he was trusting them to guard Hal until he'd had a very long, unpleasant conversation with each of them to determine what role they'd played—if any—in the assassination attempt. He'd pulled both Chase and Ian in from other ops, their backgrounds as a Secret Service agent and as a U.S. Marshal, respectively, making them two of the best choices for the security detail.

The two Templars currently stationed outside of Hal's room looked up when they saw him approaching and dropped their gazes, knowing they were in the shit.

"You're relieved of duty," he said, his tone clipped. "But don't plan on going anywhere. Your commander has offered his full cooperation in this investigation. In fact, Rich and I are old friends, so he's more than willing to join me if you don't feel moved to open up to me."

Both of them cursed under their breath. Will's men might think he was a hard-ass with a heart of stone, but Rich's men *knew* he was. The guy had a reputation for shooting first and asking questions later, which often put him on the Grand Council's shit list. But he was effective. And his men knew better than to fuck up without a damned good reason. Will was seriously considering whether he should take a page from his fellow commander's playbook. Maybe if he'd been more of an asshole, they wouldn't be in the fucking mess they were in now. . . .

On that cheery thought, Will pushed open the hospital door and went in, trying to hide his shock when he saw Hal lying in the bed. He felt his chest go tight with emotion at seeing his old friend so helpless.

To cover his reaction, he turned to Jack and the woman he assumed was Maddie Blake. He hadn't seen Maddie since she was in pigtails. He'd heard a lot about her and her sister over the years from conversations with Hal—and, later, with Jack. In fact, he knew a hell of a lot more about Maddie Blake than she'd probably be comfortable with him knowing. Like how she'd stolen the heart of his friend and how Jack had once planned to propose to her before everything had gone to shit . . .

Jack came toward him, offering his hand. "Commander."

"Commander?" Will scoffed as he shook his hand. "*Now* you suddenly give a shit about protocol, Jack? You might've given that some thought before you conned your partner into going along with your bullshit. You could both be de-cloaked if I can't clean up this mess."

"Luke or Jack aren't to blame," Maddie insisted from where she sat near her father's bedside. "This is on me, Commander Asher. My father was only trying to help me with a situation—"

"And you thought you'd call on the Alliance?" Will inter-rupted. "We're not in the business of settling scores, Ms. Blake. I know your father brought you into his confidence a few years ago, so you know how we work. We guide. We advise. We protect. We try to mitigate the damage done by all the assholes in this world who are doing their damnedest to fuck things up. From what I understand, this man who was killed—Jonas Richter—was one of these assholes by virtue of selling secrets to hostile nations. That fact might end up being the only thing that saves Jack's neck."

"Back off, Will," Jack growled. "I could've said no. I could've refused to help Hal or Maddie when I got the call."

"Really?" Will fired back. "You could've, Jack? Do we want to go there right now?"

Maddie stepped forward, to put herself between Will and Jack, lifting her chin defiantly and pegging Will with a look that was a damned good imitation of one Will had seen her father use against adversaries back in the day when he was a field operative.

"I will accept whatever consequences there are for what's happened," she told him. "But my father was only doing what he thought was best for me. So was Jack."

Will bent slightly, not about to back down until he was damned good and ready. "You have no idea what you've set in motion, Ms. Blake. Your actions might be the catalyst that destroys the Alliance. What exactly are you prepared to do to make amends for *that?*"

"Whatever it takes," she said without hesitation. "Put me in play. You have no women among your ranks. Bring me in and I'll prove I'm not the selfish bitch I know you think I am—I can see it in your eyes when you look at me, so don't try to deny it. But I could be a tremendous asset to the Order, Commander. Just give me a chance."

"Maddie, love," Jack said softly. "You have no idea what we give up when—"

She cut him off with a pointed look. "Yes, Jack, I do," she snapped. "I know *exactly* what you give up when you join the Alliance." She then turned her attention back to Will. "Give me an opportunity to continue my father's legacy of service to the Alliance—as you continue your father's."

Will drew back at this. "You don't know a damned thing about my father."

Her expression softened with sympathy. "I know enough." When Will sent a furious look Jack's way, she quickly added, "My father told me about it once after he'd had a call from the high commander. I know that your father believed the Illuminati had formed again, that they were maneuvering for a power play, that they were intent on controlling the world instead of trying to help it. And I know he died trying to prove it."

Will regarded her for a long moment, considering her proposal. She was correct that they didn't have any female operatives. He'd long suggested that it was to the Alliance's detriment that they didn't. But the old guard in the Grand Council was so entrenched in tradition that they were always looking back instead of forward—except when it suited them.

"It's not my call," Will told her. "I can take you on as an initiate, but the Grand Council has the final say."

"That's a start," Maddie said. "I want to get started as soon as my father recovers."

Will traded a glance with Jack, silently asking just how likely that was, but Jack dropped his gaze, either unable to answer or unwilling to face the truth.

"I've stationed two of my own outside," Will told her, changing the subject. "I'm taking your father's detail back to headquarters to find out if they were involved at all in the attempt on his life."

"They weren't," Maddie insisted. "I know they weren't. They're good men."

"You're welcome to return with us," Will said. "It'd be more comfortable for you at the compound. I promise your father is in safe hands."

She shook her head. "I'm not leaving him. He needs to know I'm here. I'll just wait until my sister arrives."

"There's been a change of plans," Will told her. "Luke's taking your sister and nephew to his haven."

Her brows came together in confusion. "What? Why?"

"What's happened?" Jack demanded. "You know the safest place for the boy is here, where we can guard him."

Will's gaze shifted between Jack and Maddie. "Someone attempted to abduct your nephew."

"Oh my God!" Maddie gasped. "Is he all right? Is Sarah? When can I talk to her?"

"They're safe at the moment," Will assured her, "but we need to keep them that way. If someone was threatening Hal leading up to the attempt on his life, they know us. They know how we operate. They'd be expecting us to bring him here."

Jack cursed under his breath. "Hal was right, then. We do have a leak."

"Yeah," Will confirmed. "And if I'm right about who's behind it, my father won't have died in vain."

Chapter Eight

Sarah didn't realize she'd dozed off until her head bumped the window. She moaned, rubbing the point of impact. "Damn it."

"Sorry."

She turned to Luke and laughed a little. "There are nicer ways to wake me up, you know."

His dark eyes seemed to go darker. "I'll keep that in mind."

The intensity of his gaze made her look away, the innuendo in his words impossible to mistake. "So where are we?" she asked, glad to divert her attention to the surrounding area. The landscape had changed considerably since the last time she'd noticed. Gone was the interstate and the heavy traffic. They were now driving along wooded roads with only the occasional passing car or truck.

"We're about half an hour from my house," he told her. "I called ahead and asked my caretaker to go shopping for groceries and stock the pantry, but if we need to get anything else, we should still be able to make a quick trip to town and back before they roll up the sidewalks."

Sarah turned her attention back to him. "How remote is this place?"

He grinned. "Remote enough."

"Did you grow up in this area?" she asked.

The question seemed to make him squirm a little. "No. Not really. When my mom left my dad, we went back to the rez for a while, but she was a horse trainer, so we traveled wherever the job was—and my dad wasn't. He showed up every now and then, drunk, looking for us and determined to persuade Mom to come back to him. Which usually cost her whatever job she had at the time, so off we'd go again."

Sarah shook her head a little, trying to put together all the pieces of information he'd just imparted. Clearly, his upbringing had been far different from her own. "The rez?" she repeated. "You're Native American then?"

He gave a terse nod. "Cheyenne. Well, my mom was. My dad was white—and a drunken, abusive asshole. Mom met him when she was in college. He was from a wealthy family, trust fund kid. Mom had grown up with next to nothing. The way she told it, he was charming when he wanted to be, and she was swept off her feet. But they'd only been married a couple of years before things went to shit."

"I'm sorry," she told him. "My parents went through a nasty divorce as well. My mom left and never looked back. Did you spend much time with your mom's family?"

He shook his head. "Nah, I never saw my family. My grandparents were already dead, and my mom wasn't close to her siblings. They were traditional and saw her as a sellout, like she left because she thought she was too good for them. I wasn't really raised in my culture, never had any roots."

"So how did you settle here?" she prompted, curious to hear the rest of his story.

His expression grew dark, filled with sorrow, and his voice was heavy with emotion as he continued, "My mom got a job with a rancher named Jim Hadley. He was a widower with a young daughter. After a while, he and my mom fell for each other and got married. I was a smart-mouthed, asshole teenager—always getting in trouble, skipping school, barely passing. I seemed hell-bent on following in my useless father's footsteps. But Jim was a good guy and forced me to pull my head out of my ass and see I was breaking my mom's heart. He turned my life around. It was a good couple of years."

After a long pause, Sarah prompted, "But?"

"But my mom got cancer," he said. "She died right after my high school graduation. Jim tried to convince me to stay on and help him with the ranch, learn the business so that I could eventually take things over with his daughter, but I couldn't handle it. Had to get away. So I joined the army, eventually moving into Special Forces for a while."

Sarah waited, studying his profile as he drove. His jaw was clenched, his gaze intent, but she had a feeling he was focused more on the past than the present, reliving that time in his life. "So you were in Special Forces when you were recruited to the Alliance?" she supplied.

He seemed to snap back to that moment and sent a guarded glance her way. "No. I was working on a special assignment for the government when I was recruited."

She shook her head a little, confused. "With whom? The CIA?"

"No." Clearly, he wasn't comfortable sharing any more about that time.

"And your home here . . . ?" she pressed, switching gears.

God, it's like pulling teeth trying to get answers from the man!

"I received a signing bonus when I joined the Alliance," he told her. "I was told to create a 'safe haven,' a place where I could go to decompress—because I'd need it."

Sarah's eyes went wide. "Well that sounds ominous."

He acknowledged her comments with a brief glance and shrugged. "I was used to ominous. Anyway, I used the money to purchase a couple hundred acres of Jim's land—"

Holy shit! How much was his signing bonus?

"—and built my own ranch, purchased my own horses and cattle to help Jim supplement his income. This was the only place I'd ever really been happy, the only place that'd ever felt like home. It seemed like the best place to settle."

At that moment, Luke turned off the main road, such as it was, and onto a dirt and gravel path that Sarah assumed was supposed to be a road, based on the two well-worn tire tracks.

After maybe a half mile on the road, they came to a split-rail fence with two tall posts and a rail across the top with a carved sign bearing the name HAVEN RANCH. They traveled for maybe a couple of miles more along the road, which was now lined with the split-rail fence, before a log cabin came into view.

But it was a log cabin only in the sense that it was made from stone and logs. The two-story structure had three stone chimneys, one of which already had a fire going in it, as evidenced by the curl of smoke that tickled the sky. A porch stretched the entire length of the house and had at least half a dozen bentwood rocking chairs arranged in three groupings perfect for intimate conversations.

In the distance, Sarah spotted a barn nearly as large as the house itself and another outbuilding of some sort. Beyond that was a corral where two horses meandered. And as they drew closer, Sarah saw the last of the early evening sunlight dancing upon a river that curved behind a copse of trees and disappeared into the low hills. And all the beauty of the property was framed by snowcapped mountains.

"My God," Sarah breathed. "Luke, I've never seen anything so beautiful."

He offered her a smile that made her heart trip over itself. "I'm glad you like it."

"Like it?" Sarah said with a laugh as he parked the SUV in the gravel driveway. "How could I not? It's breathtaking. It's—"

Sarah's words died on her lips as the front door opened and a statuesque woman with a long, thick blond braid draped over her shoulder stepped out onto the porch, waving enthusiastically. The woman jogged toward them, her smile pure sunshine in her lovely face.

Luke chuckled low and got out of the SUV, meeting the woman halfway and sweeping her into a hug that lifted her from her feet.

"Who's that?"

Sarah glanced back at Eli, who'd finally removed his earbuds and turned off the e-reader Luke had bought him at the mall. "I have no idea."

"Whoa. Is this Mr. Rogan's *house?*" Eli asked, losing interest in the woman chatting animatedly with their host. Sarah wished she could do the same. But it was difficult to plaster a smile on her face as she got out of the Expedition and followed Eli toward the house.

"Hi!" the woman said, her eyes dancing. She was gorgeous, Sarah had to admit. "Welcome to Haven!"

"Sarah," Luke said, "this is my caretaker, Melanie."

Melanie grasped Sarah's hand and shook it with a laugh. "Caretaker? That's putting it mildly. This guy might look big and tough, but he'd be totally lost without me looking after this place while he's away on whatever new secret mission the army has him on."

Sarah sent a glance Luke's way and received an almost imperceptible shake of the head. Obviously, Melanie thought he was still in the military.

"This is Eli," Sarah said, bringing her son close.

Melanie then turned the full glory of her smile on Eli

and had a new admirer in an instant. "Hey there, big guy! Welcome to Haven. Do you want a tour while Luke and your mom get everything settled?"

Eli sent a pleading glance up at Sarah, who in turn sent a silent question Luke's way. He nodded, indicating it was safe to let Eli go.

"All right," she agreed. "But listen to Ms. Melanie and do what she says."

As soon as Eli and Melanie were on their way to the horse corral and safely out of earshot, Sarah said, "She's very pretty."

Luke sent a frown Sarah's way as he started pulling out the bags of clothes and other supplies from the back of the SUV. "Mel? Yeah, I guess."

Sarah cleared her throat and grabbed her fair share of the bags. "You two seem pretty close."

Luke nodded as they headed toward the porch steps. "I wouldn't trust anyone else to help me run this place when I'm away."

Sarah hadn't thought her heart could sink any further, but it did. "Have you been together long?"

Luke came to such an abrupt stop on the porch that Sarah nearly collided with him. "Together?" He turned and peered down at Sarah for a long moment, his eyes narrowed, a slight grimace curling his lips. "We're not together. Mel's Jim's daughter. She's my stepsister."

Sarah closed her eyes, her face going warm in an instant. If Luke had had any doubts about the fact that she was attracted to him, she'd pretty much shown her hand with her idiotic assumptions.

"C'mon," Luke said, giving her a slight nudge with his elbow. "Let me show you around the house."

Sarah opened her eyes in time to see him no longer attempting to smother a grin as he strode into the cabin.

Fortunately, her humiliation was replaced by awe when she entered the house.

The front door opened into a great room with vaulted ceilings supported by exposed beams. A fire blazed in a stone fireplace along one wall. On the other side of the great room was the entrance to what Sarah could see was a kitchen, but she wasn't prepared for how large and modern the kitchen was. She'd expected something far simpler—but aside from the décor, the only thing remotely rustic was a brick oven.

He gestured to a wooden door tucked into one side of the kitchen. "That leads down to the basement. My gym's down there—you're welcome to use it, if you'd like. And I'll give you the code to the storage room in case of an emergency."

Her brows lifted. "What exactly do you store there?"

"Weapons." He jerked his head. "C'mon. The dining room's this way."

The dining room could've seated twelve easily—and maybe then some—but it didn't look like it had ever been used. The library was a different story. The furniture had the look of having been sat in often, and the books weren't just showpieces.

There was another room at the end of the house, but Luke skipped over that one, instead leading Sarah upstairs to the loft overlooking the great room. Inside the loft was a huge TV mounted on the wall and several different gaming consoles.

"Bit of a gamer?" Sarah said, brows raised.

Luke shrugged. "Helps me unwind. Plus, I have to keep my skills up or the other guys'll kick my ass."

Along the hall were four doors. They passed the first one—presumably Luke's bedroom, based on the glimpse Sarah got of a huge carved bed and simple, masculine comforter. The next room was just as simple, but the bed was covered in a patchwork quilt of red, blue, white, and green, and lovely landscape paintings hung on the walls. The room had its own en suite as well as a separate sitting and dressing area.

"You can sleep in here," Luke said, ushering her inside, then setting down all but two of the bags just inside the doorway. "My office and a room for Eli are down the hall. I'll let you get settled."

Sarah turned to thank him again for harboring her and her son, but he'd already gone without a sound. She shook her head with a laugh. "I've got to find out how he does that. . . ."

She didn't waste any time putting away the clothes and other items they'd purchased to get them by for a few days. Then she took a few moments to explore the room a little. On the bedside table, in a silver frame, was a photo of a beautiful Native American woman with a radiant smile and wide dark eyes that even in the photograph seemed to dance with light. Her arms were lovingly wrapped around a dark-haired boy of maybe Eli's age. He was laughing so hard his eyes were squeezed shut, but there was no mistaking the boy's identity.

Sarah picked up the photo to study it a little closer, grinning at the obvious love between mother and son. "So Luke *did* know how to laugh at some point. . . ."

She was still grinning when she set the photo aside and strolled around the room, studying the paintings. They were skillfully done, but not museum quality—more a labor of love. She squinted at the signature. LYLA YOUNGBEAR.

Luke's mother?

Pounding footsteps in the hallway brought her out of her thoughts, and a moment later, Eli raced into the room, his cheeks flushed with excitement. "Mom! Have you seen this house? It's so cool! It's like four *times* the size of ours! And Mr. Rogan has a huge TV and all kinds of games like *Halo* and *Fallout* and *Mass Effect* and *Call of Duty*. . . . And the horses are *so* awesome! Ms. Melanie said that she'd teach me how to ride, too. Is that okay, Mom? Is it?"

Sarah felt a twinge of guilt at having to tamp down his excitement. "Oh, honey . . . I don't know how long we'll be here. I don't want you to get too attached to this place, okay? We're just visiting for a few days."

Eli's face fell and his shoulders sagged. "You never let me do *anything*."

Sarah smoothed his hair away from his forehead. "I'm not saying you can't. But I just don't want you to get too comfortable here."

Eli sighed. "*Fine*. But can I at least have a *little* fun while we're here?"

Sarah laughed and shook her head. "Nope. No way. Absolutely *no* fun allowed. You know that's *completely* off limits, pal. You will do nothing but peel rotten, smelly potatoes and practice ridiculously difficult long division problems all day, every day."

Eli gave her *the look*—the one perfected by tweens everywhere to clearly indicate that they were *way* too sophisticated and mature to let on that they found their parental figure even remotely humorous, no matter how hard they wanted to laugh.

"Very funny, Mom," he said, suppressing a grin.

She tossed him one of the bags. "Yeah, well, you should hear my whole routine. Trust me, you'll be R-O-T-F-L-M-A-O. Or would that be Y-O? *My? Your?* Not sure . . ."

"No," he said, shaking his head, giggling. "Don't do that."

"What?" Sarah asked, feigning ignorance.

"Don't try to be cool," he called over his shoulder as he headed out of the room. "Please."

"What?" Sarah said, hurrying to the doorway to poke her head into the hallway. "What are you talking about? I'm the coolest mom around! Here, check me out, Eli—I can totally bust a move."

Eli whirled around, his eyes wide in pretend horror, but he couldn't suppress his laughter. "No! Just . . . no. Don't do the Mom Dance!"

"What *Mom Dance?*" Sarah called as he disappeared into the bedroom at the end of the hall. She started doing the cabbage patch, calling out, "Come on back, Eli! Check me out, yo! You have *the* coolest mom ev-ah!"

She heard him grumble something and, laughing, turned back to her bedroom—and leaped back with a startled yelp.

Luke's lips twitched with amusement. He ducked his head, then looked up through those long, dark lashes, giving her a grin that would've been devastating if she hadn't been so damned embarrassed.

"Sorry to interrupt," he drawled, his mouth hitching up at one corner. "Just realized I forgot to tell you to help yourself to the towels if you needed to shower or anything."

Sarah pressed her lips together, then gave him a curt nod. "Uh-huh. Okay. Thanks."

"So . . . I'll just leave you to it."

Sarah watched him retreat down the hall and thought for sure she saw his broad shoulders shake with laughter. . . .

Chapter Nine

Luke didn't miss the shy glances Sarah sent his way throughout dinner, the way her cheeks flushed when their eyes met and she quickly looked away, pretending to be completely engaged in the animated chatter between Eli and Melanie. He also didn't miss the way his heart began to pound and his stomach clenched in those moments. He'd be an idiot to deny the sexual tension simmering between them—or how badly he wanted to give in to it.

Sarah was a remarkable woman. Beautiful, intelligent, strong . . . Aside from her initial reaction to the situation that had her bent over at the side of the road on the verge of yaking, she'd taken it all in stride; her determination to remain strong for her son was clear to Luke without her saying a word. She was the kind of woman a guy could fall in love with before he even knew what was happening. Hell, if he was the kind of guy to be into that kind of thing, he'd be halfway gone already. But he was the *last* guy Sarah Scoffield needed to get mixed up with.

And yet, as the thought crossed his mind, those soulful dark eyes found his across the table and heat spread through his chest, warming him in a way he'd never felt before.

"I have a call to make," he announced abruptly,

launching to his feet, bringing an equally abrupt halt to the conversation.

"Right now?" Melanie asked. "You haven't finished your spaghetti."

"Duty calls," he told her. "Gotta check in."

Sarah pushed back from the table and started toward him. "I'll come with you."

"No," he said. His need to be apart from Sarah and the way his arms wanted to reach for her every time she was near made the word come out harsher than he'd intended.

Melanie glanced between them, frowning. She had assumed that Sarah was Luke's girlfriend, and he hadn't contradicted her, sticking to their cover story. But she still seemed to be watching every move he made around Sarah, no doubt curious about the woman who'd finally lasted for more than a quick fuck-and-run—and who had a kid, no less. Melanie had seen him at his worst when they were teenagers and, after meeting his father on one unfortunate occasion, completely understood Luke's aversion to relationships. Fortunately for him, that meant Mel also knew he pretty much sucked at this kind of thing.

So the look of silent rebuke she sent his way made him mumble more politely, "I don't want to interrupt your dinner."

Sarah gave him a pointed look. "I have some things of my own to look into, remember?"

He could feel Mel's gaze heavy upon them at that moment, gauging his reaction, so he forced a grin. "Don't worry. I won't be long. Then I'll turn the office over to you."

She huffed. "Luke—"

Before he even realized what he was doing, he dropped a quick, perfunctory kiss to the corner of her mouth, cutting her off. "Be back in a few minutes."

Sarah blinked up at him in startled silence, too surprised by the kiss to respond—exactly as he'd intended. But as soon as he was in his office, he dropped down into his chair and closed his eyes for a moment, reliving the all-too-brief warmth of her lips. Then he raked his hands through his hair with a groan.

"Get your shit together, Rogan," he grumbled, booting up the laptop Finn had provided and making the call to headquarters. But he was still imagining what it would be like to fully claim Sarah's soft lips, feel her naked in his arms, when his commander's face suddenly appeared on his screen, jarring him from his thoughts.

"It's still two hours until our call," Will said by way of greeting.

"Yes, sir, I'm aware of that," Luke said.

"Then what's the problem?" his commander prompted. "Have you been made?"

Luke shook his head. "No, nothing like that."

Will waited for a long moment, but when Luke didn't continue, he said, "Luke, I have the high commander breathing down my neck demanding to know how the flying fuck someone found out about Hal's plan for succession, and a man I admire and consider a friend lying in a hospital bed on life support with no way of telling us what the hell is going on. So if you've got something to share, I suggest you get on with it."

Luke felt like an ass. His commander was right—there were far greater problems to deal with than Luke's misgivings about his current assignment. So he stowed that shit and instead decided on a different tack. "Sarah wants to make contact with her family. Can we trust Maddie Blake?"

His commander gave a terse nod. "Your partner, Jack, seems to think so. He trusts her. That's enough for me. But monitor the call. Make sure nothing is said to give away your location."

"Sarah's not going to compromise the safety of her son," Luke assured him.

Will crossed his arms over his chest. "I'm sure she wouldn't—intentionally."

"And the info Hal shared with the boy?" Luke asked. "How do you want me to get at that?"

Luke hoped to God Will wasn't going to suggest anything like their normal methods of interrogation. He wasn't one to disobey orders—at least, not these days—but he and his commander would have words if he even went there.

"Get Sarah talking," Will suggested. "We need to know what information the boy has and how it can be contained."

Luke gave his commander a wry look. "I'm not exactly known for my conversation skills."

Will's mouth twitched in amusement. "I'm aware of that, Luke, believe me. Just get her to trust you, be a friend. God knows she probably could use one right now. Maybe she'll say something that will give us what we need to know. She might not even be aware it's important."

"Why not just send her sister here to talk to her?" Luke suggested, feeling uncomfortable at the thought of manipulating Sarah into confiding in him. Hell, he'd done worse to people over the years, so why the hell did it matter now?

"Madeleine Blake refuses to leave her father's side for the moment. Doesn't trust us to keep him safe while he's in the hospital." Will grunted. "Considering the colossal cluster-fuck of an op that you and Jack ran, can't say that I blame her."

Luke clenched his jaw. Jack had already copped to running a rogue op without Luke's knowledge; Will had told him as much. But it still didn't mean that Luke was clear of responsibility. They were partners, brothers. What affected one affected all.

"Sarah should at least get the chance to talk to her sister," Luke insisted. "Maybe something Ms. Blake could tell her about the situation would trigger a memory for Sarah, give us a lead."

Will paused, then nodded. "All right. I'll get in touch with Jack and have him set up a call on this line. It's the only one we know for sure is secure at the moment. And I'm going to send you some files to look over, give you some additional context. It might give you some insight into Sarah Scoffield and her family that you can use in your conversations."

Luke shook his head. "I don't want to pry into her personal life, Commander. Keep your files."

Will sighed. "I'm going against protocol even offering these files up. They're confidential. But Sarah has the right to know the truth, don't you think? And if you're going to help her, you need to know it as well."

Luke mulled over what his commander was saying. He had to admit, the man had a point. And hadn't he been pissed all along that the truth had been withheld from Sarah? This might be the kind of information she deserved to know. "All right. Send it."

Will gave him a terse nod. "Now, fill me in on the Russia op."

For the next hour, Luke went on to brief his commander on the op he was *supposed* to be running but instead was handing off. When he'd finished sharing all the intel he'd been accumulating in preparation for the mission, he disconnected the teleconference and leaned back in his office chair, pulling a hand down his face. Then he got to work dealing with the other details of his current assignment, which had him lost in his thoughts again in no time.

A tentative knock on the door brought his head around. "Come in."

The door opened slowly and Sarah peeked her head in. "Sorry to bother you. Melanie headed home."

"You okay?" Luke asked. "How's Eli?"

Sarah offered him a tired smile. "I'm still trying to process everything. But I'll be okay. Eli's passed out on the couch at the moment. I think he's handling things much better than I am."

Luke got to his feet. "Poor kid. The only sleep he's had lately has been in the car."

He followed Sarah to the living room and had to smother a smile. She wasn't kidding that the kid was passed out. He was face down on the sofa, his arm hanging off the side of the couch, his mouth open wide.

Sarah bent to rouse her son, but Luke put a hand on her shoulder. "I got him."

He scooped up the kid and hefted him onto his shoulder. Eli was heavier than he looked—especially when he was conked out, his head lolling against Luke's shoulder. As Luke headed for the stairs, Eli whimpered in his sleep, and his arms, which had been draped over Luke's shoulders, now tightened around his neck, clinging to him.

Poor kid.

Eli might seem unaffected by the attempted kidnapping, but clearly it was just a brave front.

"I can take him," Sarah whispered at Luke's elbow.

"It's all right," he assured her, making his way up the stairs. When they reached the second floor, he headed down the long hallway to the last bedroom and gently laid Eli down on the twin bed.

The boy opened his eyes briefly and offered Luke a sleepy smile before his face went slack again. Luke felt a tug in the center of his chest and took a step back. It was one thing to work his way into Sarah's confidence, but he wasn't about to let himself get attached to the kid.

"I can take it from here," Sarah told him, resting her hand lightly on Luke's arm.

Luke flinched at her touch before he could check it. But she didn't seem to notice as she stepped past him and removed her son's shoes, so he left the room, waiting outside the door until she finished tucking in her son.

A few minutes later, Sarah came out and eased the door closed behind her before offering Luke a smile. "Thank you for taking us in."

He gave her a terse nod. "Seemed like the best option."

"I hope it's not too much of an imposition," she said. "This is a beautiful home, but I can tell you don't have many visitors."

He pushed off the wall. "I've never had *any* visitors here, not overnight anyway. Not even sure why I built so many bedrooms. I'm only home every couple of months."

"You built the cabin yourself?" Sarah asked, her eyes going wide.

"Most of it," he said with a shrug. "I suck at electrical wiring. And I had to call in contractors to help with the security I put in."

"Security?" Sarah repeated. "All the way out here? I thought you said we'd be safe."

"You will be," he assured her. "I have to take a call soon, but c'mon. I'll take you around and brief you on the security I have in place."

She followed him down the stairs and through the kitchen to the basement door. "Do you have the phone Finn gave you?" She nodded and produced it from her pocket. "I'll download the app that allows you to control the alarm system. That way, you can set it, disarm it, or send an emergency beacon wherever you are."

The basement stairs opened up into his game room, which contained a pool table and a full-service bar. He jerked his head toward the door on one side of the basement. "That's the gym." He led her to the other door, which he'd secured with a keypad and retinal scanner. "Here's the weapons storage." He bent and let the device scan his eye, then punched in the ten-digit access code. "Now you."

Sarah sent a confused look his way, but then he gestured toward the scanner. She bent slightly and kept her eye wide as the scanner swept over it. When it finished, Luke punched in the code again. "There, now you have access." Then he punched the actual access code for the room into a text message on her phone and hit SEND. "There's the code. Keep this phone with you at all times."

She nodded and tucked it into her pocket. Motion-activated lights came on the moment he stepped across the threshold. He turned back to the doorway, ushering her inside.

"Good God," she breathed, slowly surveying the wide range of weapons mounted on the wall and locked in various storage cases. "What kind of invasion are you expecting?"

"I'm not," he told her. "These are for missions."

Sarah wrapped her arms around her torso, suppressing a shudder. "I'm going to try not to think about the kinds of missions you go on."

The wariness that came into her eyes made his stomach sink. "They're not all dangerous. But you never know when one's going to go south. I have to be prepared for pretty much anything."

"I'm not a fan of guns," she told him, shrinking into herself and edging toward the doorway.

"You need to know how to defend yourself, Sarah," he reminded her. "What happens after you leave here? What happens when I'm no longer with you? If someone comes for Eli again, you need to be able to handle a weapon."

The thought of someone harming her son made her straighten with indignation. "I said I didn't like guns," she snapped. "I didn't say I don't know how to use one. My father insisted on Maddie and me being trained in marksmanship with several different weapons." She scoffed and added, "Now I guess I know why."

Luke sighed and went to her, taking hold of her arms. "Sarah, I'm really sorry for whatever lies you've been told, whatever rift there is between you and your father. But I'm here to help you and Eli. That's all. I need you to trust me."

He felt like a total asshole even asking that of her, the order he'd been given making him uneasy. The thought of deceiving her into getting close to him, knowing that as soon as this mission was over he'd never see her again, reminded him he was a lying piece of shit.

Sarah heaved a sigh. "I do trust you, Luke. I'm just scared."

"Well," he said, taking her hand in his and leading her from the basement, "if it makes you feel any better, I have perimeter sensors all around the property that alert me to vehicles approaching. There are also cameras recording twenty-four-seven, and all the windows are ballistic glass."

"Wow. So," she said, linking her fingers with his, "you weren't kidding about security. But couldn't someone on foot or horseback get by your sensors if they're just for vehicles? What if someone sneaks onto the property that way?"

He sent her a grin. "The only people getting close to you and Eli on this property will have to be invited in. And you're not going anywhere off this property without me, so any son of a bitch that wants to hurt you is going to have to come through me first."

Her grip on his hand tightened, and her other hand came up to grasp his forearm as they made their way up the stairs to the second floor and down the hallway to his office. But when he started for the doorway, she stepped in front of him, putting a hand on his chest. "Luke . . . I . . ." She paused, dropping her gaze.

He waited, giving her the time she needed and frowning to keep from dwelling on the pressure of her hand against his chest and imagining what her soft palm would feel like against his bare skin.

Just when he felt like he was going to need to covertly shift things around a bit, she took a deep breath and continued, "I just want to say thank you again. I don't think I can say it enough. I honestly don't know what would've happened to Eli and me if you hadn't shown up when you did. I can't help picturing my friends. . . ."

Unable to stand the way her voice hitched with unshed tears, he gently grasped her chin and lifted her face to his. Which was a mistake. Tears clung to her long dark lashes as she looked up at him, her eyes filled with sorrow. His thumb smoothed lightly across her skin. "I'm sorry I didn't get there in time to help them, Sarah."

She blinked and a single tear slid down her cheek. "I know."

God, she was killing him.

He brushed away the tear with the back of his fingers and slid his hand around to the nape of her neck. His gaze dropped down to her lips, which parted ever so slightly, and she stepped into him, her hand drifting down to his waist.

Shit, shit, shit . . .

He was going to kiss her. For real this time. And she wasn't going to stop him. He could feel it in the pressure of her fingertips at his waist, the way her breath quickened as his head dipped lower.

The sudden buzzing of his cell phone brought Luke's head up in an instant, and they started apart as he snatched the phone from his pocket. "Rogan."

"It's Jack."

Luke sent a glance Sarah's way, but she was avoiding his gaze, her cheeks flushed. "Impeccable timing as always, Grayson."

Sarah's gaze snapped to him, her brows drawn together in a frown. "Grayson? Jack Grayson?"

Luke returned her frown. "Yeah."

Sarah crossed her arms over her chest with a bitter laugh. "I want to talk to that son of a bitch. Right. Now."

Luke's frown deepened. *Oh, I'm definitely gonna need to get the rest of* that *story. . . .* "Hey, Jack. I think you'd better get a teleconference going. Sarah has a few things she'd like to say."

A few minutes later, they were back in Luke's office, Jack's face on Luke's laptop, his expression contrite.

"Where's my sister, you bastard?" Sarah hissed.

"She's here with me, Sarah," Jack assured her. "I'm so sorry about your father. Had I any idea—"

"You know what?" Sarah interrupted. "On second thought, I *don't* want to talk to you. Put Maddie on."

Jack sent a glance up at Luke where he stood behind Sarah, but then stepped out of view and Maddie Blake slid into the chair he'd vacated. "Hey, honey. How are you holding up?"

"Well, thanks to Luke, Eli and I are both alive," she snapped, her gaze following Luke as he silently left the room. As soon as he was gone she turned her attention back to her sister and gave her a stern look. "But I think you'd better bring me up to speed. *Now.*"

Sarah raked her hands through her hair and sat back in Luke's chair, trying to process everything her sister had just shared. "You knew about the Alliance? About Dad's involvement?"

"Only after joining the FBI," Maddie told her. "I found out when Jack was sent to assist on one of my cases. He had to come clean on things and explain why . . . why things happened the way they did, why he had to leave so suddenly before, so that I could trust him."

"And *do* you trust him?" Sarah pressed. "All the lies, all

the deception, Maddie . . . Our entire lives! How can we trust *anything* we're told at this point?"

Maddie took a deep breath and let it out slowly. "Honey, you're going to have to try. I've told you everything I know. And I'm sure Luke can fill you in even more. There's more at risk here than you can possibly imagine."

"I don't give a shit about whatever it is that someone's after," Sarah snapped. "I just want to make sure my son is safe. If anything happens to him, I will never forgive Dad for what he's done. He had no right to put Eli at risk this way."

"I'm sure he had his reasons, Sarah," Maddie said.

Sarah clenched her fists. "Stop defending him! Damn it, Maddie—you've been making excuses for that man our entire lives."

Maddie's face fell. "And you've never given him a chance. Ever since Mom left, you've been determined to cast Dad as the bad guy. Well, Mom wasn't a saint, Sarah. She knew about Dad, knew what he did and why. And she couldn't take it. She walked away and never looked back—not even to see her daughters."

Sarah pressed her fingertips to her temples, feeling a raging headache coming on. "I'm not having this fight with you again, Maddie."

"Fine," Maddie replied. "But just try to understand, okay? That's all I'm asking."

Sarah heaved a harsh sigh. "I'm not making any promises."

There was a long pause before Maddie cleared her throat. "So, are you okay where you are? Is Luke treating you okay? He seems a little . . . abrupt."

Sarah lifted her brows. *Luke? Abrupt?* Thoughts of how tender he'd been in the hallway, how gently he'd touched her, came rushing back to her. She felt the heat rising in her cheeks at the remembrance of that moment, wondering what might have happened had Jack not called when he did.

She cleared her throat and gave herself a mental shake, reminding herself that her sister was still waiting for a response. "He's great," she said in a rush. "He's taking very good care of us."

Maddie gave her a knowing look. "Be careful, Sarah. You're vulnerable right now."

Sarah flinched. "What are you talking about?"

"I'm just saying I don't want you to do anything you'll regret."

Sarah shook her head in disbelief. "Wow. Really? You're giving me a lecture now? I'm a grown woman, Maddie. And here's a news flash for you—I'm not the delicate flower you and Dad have always thought I was. If I want to go screw my brains out with some guy I've only known a couple days—who is *seriously* hot by the way and is actually the first man I've been even *remotely* attracted to since Greg's death—then that's *my* business."

"Sarah, honey, that's not what I meant—"

"I'll talk to you soon, Maddie," Sarah said, cutting her off. "Keep me posted on Dad."

She disconnected the line and swiveled around, pushing out of the chair to bolt from the room but stopping short when she saw Luke leaning against the door frame, his arms crossed.

Oh God. How much did he hear?

"You okay?" he asked, coming toward her.

She nodded, her face on fire with the heat of embarrassment. "Yeah," she croaked. If he'd heard her tirade with her sister, he wasn't letting on. "Well, I will be anyway."

Luke took hold of her shoulders. "Will you tell me if that changes?"

She drew in a deep breath and let it out slowly. "I'll try.

But I'm not used to having anyone to talk to when I'm not okay."

His expression darkened. "Me either."

She impulsively stepped closer and wrapped her arms around his waist. "Maybe we can learn together."

He straightened at the contact, and she was on the verge of backing off with an embarrassed apology when his strong arms came around her, pulling her in closer—loosely at first and then holding her tighter.

"Yeah," he muttered. "Maybe."

She wasn't sure how long they stood there, holding one another, but when he released her and took a step back, it seemed all too soon. But then his hand slid lightly down her arm until he reached her hand, which he held in his firm grasp to lead her from the office and back to her bedroom.

"I have to go get on a call with headquarters," he murmured, his gaze searching hers. "You should probably grab some sleep."

She nodded. "Probably."

The tension in the air between them grew until Sarah could hardly breathe. Then he cradled her face in his hands. His head dipped lower, slowly closing the distance between them. . . .

He dropped a kiss on her forehead, the tender pressure of his lips upon her skin making all the nerves in her body come alive, and she shuddered, unable to repress it.

"Good night, Sarah," he whispered against her skin. Then he pressed his forehead to hers for an all too brief moment before abruptly releasing her and striding down the hall, his boots heavy on the hardwood floors in his haste to put distance between them.

Her breath left her on a gasp, and she grasped the doorjamb to keep her knees from giving out on her. "Good night, Luke."

Chapter Ten

Luke dragged his sorry, tired ass out of bed and glared at his alarm clock, daring the bastard to go off again. He'd been getting up every morning at four-thirty for almost twenty years. And there were days that he'd had even less sleep than he'd had last night. But adding in the temptation of the sexy-as-hell woman lying in the bedroom next to his had not only kept him lying awake most of the night, tossing and turning, but had also tortured him in his dreams. So not only was he sleep-deprived, he was also fucking exhausted and had a serious case of blue balls.

He scrubbed a hand down his face, over the stubble on his jaw, as he began his morning routine. His shower hadn't helped clear the fog away at all. In fact, he'd been so distracted, he didn't even notice until he was already pulling on his gray T-shirt that he hadn't bothered shaving. Whatever. Like his horses were going to give a shit.

He grabbed a black button-down and the beat-up pair of boots that were still sitting at the bottom of the closet where he'd left them the last time he'd been home, then sent a glance out the window. A light but steady snow was falling. Not enough to accumulate yet, but enough to be a pain in the ass. He snatched his cattleman hat from the top shelf and his Carhartt, his work gloves still shoved into the pockets.

When he slipped out into the hallway, he sent a glance toward Sarah's closed door. He took a step in that direction but brought himself up short. What the hell was he thinking? Clearly, he wasn't. Or maybe he was just thinking with his dick—which even now was coming to attention as he imagined Sarah on the other side of the door.

He was going to have to get a handle on this shit or sleep deprivation would be the least of his problems. And it looked like he was going to be tortured for more than just a few days. The conversation he'd had with the team last night had put a damper on any plans to return Sarah and her son to their normal lives.

The Alliance was scrambling all its resources to shift around assets and bury them again. And Finn's tech team was working around the clock to lock down the network and switch over to the backup network while they worked to determine what data had been compromised. The big question that remained, of course, was who the hell was behind the breach.

Luke had shared what the asshole at the festival had said about the One True Master. Everyone on the teleconference had seemed puzzled and confused by the reference. Except their commander. Luke hadn't missed how Will's jaw had tightened. He wasn't about to call him on it in front of the others. But he sure as hell was going to demand to know what the fuck was going on when he and Will had their next debrief.

Luke was so up in his own head that he didn't notice the footfalls behind him until he was at the bottom of the stairs. Frowning, he turned to see Eli tromping down the stairs, already dressed and bundled up for the cold in the new coat and boots they'd bought on the drive there.

"What are you doing awake already?" Luke grumbled, sounding surly, even for him.

Eli flashed him a wide grin. "Melanie told me that you have to get up early to take care of the horses. So I set the alarm on the phone Finn gave me."

Luke's brows lifted. "Yeah? Well, I guess since you're already awake, I might as well take you up on your offer to help."

Eli jogged alongside Luke as they made their way to the barn, having to take several steps for each of Luke's long strides.

"So how did you learn about horses?" Eli asked. "Was it from your mom? Melanie said she was a horse trainer."

Luke peered down at the boy beside him. "You always talk this much in the morning?"

Eli smiled up at him. "Yeah. Mostly. Mom says I've always been a morning person. Even when I was a baby."

Luke nodded. "Thought so." He pulled his gloves out of his pockets, his fingers already starting to feel the sting of the cold morning. "Yeah, it was my mom who taught me about horses. She had a way with them—could work with even the most difficult ones. I think it was her voice. She had a way of talking to people and animals both that made them feel like they were the most beautiful thing alive, like they mattered—even when everyone else said they didn't."

Eli nodded. "My mom does that. One time Jordan Jakes told me I was a loser because I don't have a dad. And he said I was a nerd because I read all the time, but that I only get good grades because I can't play sports since I don't have a dad to show me how. But that was stupid—my mom could teach me. I just don't like sports. And Mom told me there's nothing wrong with being smart." He sent a sly smile Luke's way. "She said someday I'll be Jordan's boss and then he'll wish he had studied more."

"She's probably right," Luke told him, a grin tugging at

his lips. But he sobered again when he added, "Hey, I'm sorry about your dad. From what I've heard about him, he sounds like a good guy. And you're not a loser because he died. You know that, right?"

Eli shrugged. "Yeah. Mom said my dad loved me more than anything. And that some kids don't ever get that—not even for a little while."

Luke scoffed. "No shit. I can relate to that."

"Did your dad die, too?" Eli asked as they reached the barn.

"No," Luke told him. "He just wasn't around much. And when he was around, he was an asshole and we couldn't wait for him to leave again."

"That sucks."

That's an understatement.

"So, have you ever been around horses?" Luke said, changing the subject.

Eli shook his head. "No. Just at the fair and stuff."

"Well, between Mel and me, we'll teach you everything there is to know," Luke promised.

Eli's grin returned. "Sweet! But . . . do we have to get up this early every morning?"

Luke smothered a grin. "You can sleep in a little longer. How about you set your alarm for seven o'clock instead? That way, you'll get enough sleep but will still have plenty of time to help Mel and me out in the barn. Deal?"

Eli was beaming. "Deal. But don't you need to sleep too?"

"I'm a grown-up, so I don't need to get as much sleep as you do. And, besides, now it's habit. I got up this early even before I worked for my current employer. One of the requirements we have as part of our morning routine is to 'tend to our horses.' It's a holdover from the old Templar days. For me, it's a very literal requirement when I'm home. But, most of the time, it's making sure all my weapons and tech are in working order so that I'm ready to go at any moment." He sent Eli a guarded look. "You know anything about the Dark Alliance or the Templars, Eli?"

With Eli knowing information from Hal Blake and being named his successor, the boy would never have an Alliance-free life again. He was too much of a liability. Not that Eli or his mom needed to deal with that right now, but they were going to have to face the reality of the situation. And if he was going to help Eli through this, the boy needed to have at least some understanding of the legacy that had put him in danger.

Eli nodded as he hefted a bucket of feed. "Some. I read about the Templars in school. I like history—it's my favorite subject. And I heard you and Mom talking in the car. I wasn't sleeping as much as you thought I was. It's kinda crazy. I didn't realize I was even important."

Luke chuckled again and ruffled the kid's hair. "You're very important, buddy. Don't ever let anyone tell you otherwise. But I meant, did your grandfather ever tell you anything about what he shared with you, what kind of information he'd passed along and why?"

Eli shook his head, huffing and puffing with the weight of the bucket as he carried it to the stalls, but Luke had to give the kid credit—he wasn't about to ask for help. "Never met my grandfather. Mom told me he's a senator."

"He's never come to see you?" Luke pressed. "Not at school or somewhere and asked you not to tell your mom?"

Eli shook his head and plunked down the bucket. "Nope. Now what?"

Luke went about the process of feeding the half-dozen horses in his stables, explaining everything to Eli as he went, teaching him to give them just the right amount of food, the best mixture of grains to use. The kid was a quick study and hung on Luke's every word, listening intently to his instruction.

And when Luke handed him a set of brushes to help him groom the horses, Eli was a natural. He cooed and whispered to the horses, using a gentle hand as he dragged the brush over their glossy coats.

"You're pretty good at that," Luke told him, bringing to Eli's face a broad smile that lit his eyes. The kid had Sarah's smile.

"Thanks," Eli said. "I like doing this."

"I always did, too," Luke confided. "Therapeutic, I guess."

Eli groaned. "I wish I could've done this instead of going to all the stupid therapy sessions with Dr. Locke."

Luke straightened. "You had to go to therapy? For what?"

Eli heaved a sigh. "It was after my dad died. Mom thought I needed to talk to somebody. Then I had to start going again a few months ago because I started getting into fights at school."

"With little dicks like Jordan Jakes?" When Eli laughed, Luke added, "Sorry. I'm not used to having kids around. I probably should've said 'jerks' instead of 'dicks.'"

Eli giggled again. "No, he was a dick. It's cool."

Luke found himself grinning. He liked this kid.

"But yeah," Eli said. "I was getting bullied. Mom handled it at school—"

I'll bet she did. . . .

"—but she was worried that it was going to make me start feeling bad about my dad again or some crap like that."

Luke chuckled. "I take it you disagree."

Eli shrugged. "Mostly I was just tired after the sessions. But I guess they helped some." He sighed, then lifted his gaze to Luke. "I just . . . I don't remember much about my dad anymore, Mr. Rogan."

Luke crossed his arms over his chest and pegged Eli with a pointed look. "It's Luke."

"Yeah, I know. But Mom gets all freaked out if I call

grown-ups by their first names," he said, rolling his eyes. "I think it's a teacher thing."

"Odds are it's a *respect* thing," Luke corrected. "But since you're a guest at my house, I give you permission to call me Luke. How 'bout that?"

Eli beamed. "Cool. Thanks, Luke." The boy cringed comically and glanced around with a feigned fearful glance as if expecting his mother to pop out of the next stall and put the smack-down on him for bad manners.

When Luke chuckled at his joke, Eli's grin widened, but then he heaved a sigh and seemed to mentally push away the happiness he was feeling at that moment.

Luke frowned at him. "You okay, buddy?"

Eli nodded. "It's just . . . I really like it here."

Luke's brows lifted. "And that's a bad thing?"

Eli shrugged with one shoulder, returning his attention to grooming Luke's favorite mare, Molly. "Mom said we're only going to be here for a few days and that I shouldn't get too comfortable."

Luke could totally relate. He couldn't even remember how many places he and his mother had lived in during his childhood, moving from job to job. He'd learned damned quick not to get attached to anyone or anything.

Except Luke had a feeling he was breaking his own rules. Because something about the way the kid's shoulders sagged made Luke's chest go tight. "When I was about your age, we moved around so much I learned that I had to be happy wherever I was and not worry about when that happiness might end."

Eli stopped brushing midstroke and kept his eyes on the mare's coat as he said, "Like what happened at the fair. We were having so much fun at the haunted house. And now Hunter's mom and dad are dead, aren't they?"

Luke nodded. "Yeah."

Eli took a deep, shaky breath and let it out slowly. Then

he made a quick swipe at his eyes with the sleeve of his coat before turning his gaze on Luke. "I'm not sure Hunter will be happy again."

"It'll take a while," Luke agreed, patting Eli on the shoulder. "But eventually he'll be okay."

Eli's chin began to tremble. "How long does it take? Before someone's okay?"

Luke shook his head. "I don't know, kid. I guess everybody's gotta figure it out for himself."

Eli gave him a terse nod and pressed his lips together in a determined line, then returned to grooming Molly's coat. Luke studied him for a long moment. The kid was stronger than he probably realized. And smart. And really kinda funny. Hal Blake was an asshole for putting him in danger.

"Will you show me some of the stuff you did when you fought that guy at the festival?" Eli said, breaking into Luke's musings almost as if he'd been listening in.

"Sure," Luke said with a shrug. "But first tell me why you want to know how to take somebody down."

Eli lifted his gaze. "Because I need to be able to protect my mom. I'm not letting *her* get killed."

Fiery rage and icy fear warred for dominance within Luke at the thought of anything happening to Sarah. "We'll start today."

Chapter Eleven

Sarah ran her hands through her hair and checked her appearance in the mirror, then sent one last glance toward the bedside clock. Nine A.M.

She couldn't even remember the last time she'd slept past six. Normally, Eli was up at the crack of dawn—the quintessential morning person, eager to begin the day and greet whatever adventure awaited. But not today. She'd not heard a peep since she'd awakened half an hour earlier. It was like she'd walked into some kind of alternate reality.

Feeling well-rested for the first time since Greg's death, she left her room with a smile and headed down the hall to peek in on Eli. But when she got to the bedroom door, her heart leapt into her throat, choking her breath.

"Eli!" she called, pivoting and racing toward the stairs. "Eli!"

"Down here, Mom!" came a muffled reply.

Sarah nearly collapsed with relief as she raced down the stairs. "Where are you?" she called out again as she reached the bottom, her gaze taking in the great room in a glance.

"Kitchen."

It was Luke's voice—which had an entirely different effect on her heart and knees. . . .

Not wanting to let on as to just how panicked she'd been, Sarah took a deep breath and let it out slowly before forcing herself to stroll casually into the kitchen. She wasn't sure what she expected to encounter, but it wasn't the scene before her. Eli was standing on a step stool at the stove, spatula in hand, flour on his shirt and pancake batter on his cheek.

"Hey, Mom! Luke and I are making pancakes," Eli called out merrily. Then his eyes went wide and he added quickly, "Luke said it was okay for me to call him by his name."

Sarah glanced toward where Luke was leaning nonchalantly against the counter across from Eli, mug of coffee in hand. His dark gaze took her in from head to toe in one quick, heated sweep, but his tone betrayed nothing when he said, "Eli wanted to surprise you."

"Well, you succeeded," she said, coming forward as Luke poured a second mug of coffee and held it out. "I don't usually let Eli use the stove."

"I've learned lots of new stuff already today," Eli told her, wrinkling his forehead in concentration as he carefully slid the spatula beneath one of the pancakes on the griddle. "Luke taught me how to groom horses and gather the eggs from his chickens and how to make pancakes and sausage and how to get out of a choke hold—"

Sarah nearly spit her coffee across the room. "What? A *choke hold?*"

Eli nodded, grinning from ear to ear. "And he says he'll teach me how to rip someone's nuts off."

Sarah turned wide eyes on Luke.

"I was being metaphorical," he told her with a shrug, a hint of unrepentant mischief in his eyes.

"Could we chat for a minute?" she said, jerking her head toward the other room.

"That's what Mom says when she's about to rip someone a new one but doesn't want everyone to hear," Eli warned.

"*Elijah Gregory,*" Sarah hissed.

He held up his hands. "What? It's true."

Luke pushed off the counter and offered Eli a conspiratorial wink before nodding toward the stove. "Don't forget—just until they're golden brown."

The moment they were out of earshot, Sarah whirled on him. "What the hell are you *thinking?*"

Luke pulled back in response to her harsh words, which Sarah would've found amusing—big, tough guy that he was recoiling from the elementary schoolteacher who was at least a foot shorter—had she not been so angry.

"I don't see why you're pissed," Luke told her.

"Well, for starters you have my eleven-year-old *cooking,*" Sarah said, sending a nervous glance into the kitchen to check on Eli.

"He wanted to help," Luke told her. "You've never let him help you make anything?"

Sarah's anxiety continued to rise the longer she was away from the kitchen. "Sure. He's helped me make cookies. But I don't let him use the stove. It's too dangerous."

Instead of laughing at her or rolling his eyes as Sarah was used to when people criticized her overprotectiveness with her son, Luke wrinkled his brow in concern. "So is riding a bike. Or walking down the street. Or going to school every day. Hell, how many school shootings have there been in recent years? You have to let him grow up—"

"Like *you* grew up?" Sarah shot back, instantly regretting her words when she saw how Luke's expression tightened.

"I wouldn't want any kid to have the childhood I did," he assured her. "But isn't part of being a parent about guiding a kid and giving him the tools to be a responsible adult?"

Sarah studied him for a moment, trying to ascertain

whether he'd asked because he was genuinely wanting to know or because he was yet another person who couldn't possibly understand. . . . "And you think part of the guidance I've failed to provide is teaching him how to *fight?*"

"I'm not teaching him to fight," Luke corrected evenly. "I'm teaching him how to defend himself. Big difference."

"Well, he's not your son," Sarah snapped. "You don't get to make that call."

Luke's jaw tightened. Clearly, Sarah had hit a raw nerve with her comment. "I wish someone had taught me how to fight on those nights my old man was wailing on my mom. I would've been happy to rip off that fucker's nuts. Eli wanted me to show him how to protect you, Sarah. I'm not saying no to that."

Sarah's anger at Luke dissipated in an instant. "*Protect* me? No offense, Luke, but my situation isn't exactly like your mother's. Why would Eli need to protect *me?* If anything, it should be the other way around."

Luke took a sip of his coffee, his gaze boring into her over the rim. "Eli loves you and doesn't want anything to happen to you. But I don't think it's entirely about you. After what happened at the festival, he needs to feel like he has some control, like he could protect you or himself if anything happened again."

God, she could so relate to that. . . . After all, wasn't that exactly why she'd been such a hover-mother since Greg's death? Trying to protect Eli from any possible danger gave her some measure of control, of security that she wouldn't have Eli taken from her, too.

She glanced toward Eli again to see him loading up a plate with the finished pancakes. "But . . . he seems to be handling everything pretty well, all things considered. I'd planned to get him into therapy again after we get home."

"With Dr. Locke?" Luke asked.

Sarah's attention snapped back to him. "How do you know about Dr. Locke?"

"Eli told me," Luke admitted. "Did you ever get to sit in on the therapy sessions?"

Sarah shook her head. "No. Dr. Locke thought Eli would probably be more open with him if I wasn't sitting in there. But I was right outside the room the entire time. Are you insinuating something . . ." *God, she couldn't even say the words.* ". . . something *questionable* was happening in the sessions?"

Luke's thick brows came together. "No, nothing like that. Who recommended this guy to you?"

Sarah narrowed her eyes at him, wondering why he was so interested. "My father, oddly enough. My sister keeps him updated on things with us. I guess when he found out about Eli's struggles, he suggested a guy he knew in Portland who specializes in children who've lost a parent."

Luke's expression morphed into a hard mask of fury. But his voice was calm when he said, "We'd better get back."

Sarah watched in confusion as Luke stormed back into the kitchen, wondering what in the world had made him so angry about Eli's therapist. She was determined to press him on the issue, but when she entered the kitchen, Eli was busy scurrying around, setting the table.

"Wait!" Eli said, waving her back. "Close your eyes. I have to put the finishing touch on the table."

Sarah glanced at Luke, who just lifted a shoulder, pretending he had no idea what Eli was talking about; then she closed her eyes. "Okay, tell me when I can look."

She heard a shuffle of feet and then a quiet thud as Eli set something on the table. "Okay," he said. "You can open them."

In addition to having set the table, Eli had added an old watering can containing several branches boasting crimson maple leaves.

"I couldn't find any flowers," Eli told her.

Sarah pulled him close for a hug and dropped a kiss to the top of his head. "This is beautiful! Thank you so much, sweetheart. What possessed you to do all this for me?"

Eli hugged her back, holding on just a little longer than usual. "I just thought it'd be nice." He let her go then and hurried to his seat to dig into the pancakes, adding, "But the leaves were Luke's idea."

Sarah sent Luke a questioning look, the heat rising in her cheeks as he leaned in to pull out her chair. "Thank you."

He turned his head slightly, holding her gaze. "You're welcome."

"*Good morning, gang!*"

"Hi, Melanie!" Eli called out at the sound of Melanie's cheerful voice from the other room. "I made pancakes!"

Sarah dragged her gaze away from Luke's as Melanie swept into the kitchen with a wiggling armload of grey fur.

"Awesome!" Mel said to Eli, giving the puppy she carried a good scratch before setting it down on the floor. "You'd better eat up. I'm going to need your help with this guy." When Eli squatted down to play with the puppy, Mel turned her attention to Sarah and Luke, suppressing a knowing grin. "You two are *way* too cute with the flushed cheeks and guilty looks. Should I come back later when you're not gazing adoringly into one another's eyes?"

The heat in Sarah's cheeks grew, and she sent a glance Luke's way, too taken aback by Mel's sudden appearance— and the woman's astute assessment of the moment between her and Luke—to respond.

Luke merely gave his stepsister a bland look before diverting the subject. "What's with the dog?"

She washed her hands at the sink, then joined them at the table. "He's one Davis brought home. His mother was shot—probably while raiding a henhouse. Davis saw her and her two pups along the side of the road and took them to his clinic."

"Was he able to save her?" Luke asked.

Mel shook her head. "No. He tried, but she was near dead by the time he found her."

Luke eyed the dog warily. "That's a wolf-dog, Mel."

Mel nodded. "Probably. But Davis wasn't about to turn them back out. They're too young."

Luke leaned back and crossed his arms over his powerful chest. "And . . . ?"

She grinned at him. "And we're keeping one of the pups and thought you might like the other."

"*Can* we keep him, Mom?" Eli pleaded. He'd gathered the puppy into his arms and it was now licking his laughing face.

"There's no 'we,'" Sarah told him before she could catch herself. She shared a glance with Luke before adding, "We're just visiting with Luke, Eli. We don't have a place for a dog like this at our house."

"Oh," Mel stammered, looking back and forth between Sarah and Luke. "I thought . . . well, I just assumed . . ." She cleared her throat. "I'm sorry. Luke's never brought anyone here. I thought it meant . . ."

"Who's ready for pancakes?" Sarah asked, changing the subject. "Eli, put the puppy down and go wash your hands."

They enjoyed their breakfast in silence until Sarah couldn't take it any longer and asked, "So, who's Davis?"

"Davis Bell," Luke supplied. "Guy I knew in the army. He and I were at boot camp together. He got out and went to veterinary school right around the time I went into Special Forces. He has a vet clinic in town."

Melanie chuckled. "What my stepbrother *isn't* saying is that he brought Davis home with him on leave and Davis and I have been together ever since."

"I didn't *bring* him home," Luke corrected. "Dude invited himself."

"Well, I'm glad he did," Mel teased. "Are you guys going to be here long enough for the wedding?"

"You're getting married?" Eli asked, his tone betraying the disappointment of a childhood crush.

Mel rifled his hair. "Yep. Right after Thanksgiving."

"Unfortunately, we won't be staying that long," Sarah said. "I have to get back to my teaching job and Eli has to get back to school. But thank you. And congratulations."

Mel was clearly disappointed, but she smiled anyway. "Well, at least you'll get the chance to meet Davis. He's going to stop by today and check out that mare of yours that's ready to foal, Luke. And I think Dad might come with him. It's been a while since he's gotten out of the house. He wanted to come see you and meet your 'lady friend.'"

Luke gave his stepsister an irritated look. "Melanie—"

"He's coming," Mel interrupted. "Get over it."

With that, she shoved back from the table. "Thank you for the breakfast, Eli. It was delicious. You want to come help me out in the barn for a while?"

Eli sent a questioning look to Sarah, who nodded. "Go ahead. But listen to Ms. Melanie."

He jumped up and cleared his plate before racing out of the kitchen to grab his coat, the puppy at his heels with every step.

As soon as they'd gone, Luke sighed and began to clear the rest of the plates. "I'm going to end up with a dog, aren't I?"

"I'm sorry," Sarah said, grabbing the plate of remaining pancakes. "I didn't realize that Mel was going to think things between us were permanent. We'll come up with a good break-up story when it's time. Besides, I really do need to get back to my job and get Eli back to school, so—"

"That's all been taken care of," Luke assured her.

Sarah went still. "What are you talking about?"

"My commander sent an email from you to your principal last night," he told her.

Sarah gaped at him. "He did *what?*"

"Starting next week, Eli will have private tutors online to help him keep up. And you're taking a medical leave due to the trauma of the attack at the festival," he explained. "Your job is protected for up to twelve weeks by FMLA. The paperwork has already been sent over."

"Twelve weeks? Are you *kidding* me?" Sarah raged, her hands balled into fists. "What the *hell* gives you—*any* of you—the right to hack into my email and send a message on my behalf? Do you realize I don't get paid during that time? I'll have to use what little sick time I have and then use my savings to cover my bills."

"That's been taken care of as well," Luke said with a shrug as if it were the most natural thing in the freaking world.

"What has?" Sarah demanded.

He finally turned to face her. "Everything. A payment was most likely sent to your mortgage company this morning to pay off what you still owe on your house. Your utilities have been set up on automatic payments through one of the Alliance's accounts—I took care of that myself. And any remaining debt will be paid in full by the end of the week. Honestly, it wasn't much, so it's not a big deal."

Sarah was utterly dumbfounded, not sure if she should break down in tears at the Alliance's generosity or be even more pissed off at their cavalier way of handling her situation. "Why?" she asked. "Why do all this? Why not just talk with me about it all first and then let me take care of it?"

"We needed to act before whoever came after Eli could do anything to sabotage you financially. What would've taken you hours, days, to take care of, our guys were able to handle within a few minutes. All your bank, savings, and investment accounts have been closed and moved into secure accounts we manage for safekeeping. We essentially locked you down for your protection. As soon as we catch the bastard behind this, your investments and bank accounts will be turned back over to you. Until then, you can use the ones Finn has set up. The funds are at your disposal. You don't need to worry about the balance. We have people to handle that."

Sarah pressed her palm to her forehead, trying to keep at bay the monstrous headache she felt coming on. "Are you always this arrogant? Do you guys always just do as you please without any consideration for the people you're supposedly helping?"

Luke's mouth turned down briefly in what seemed to equate to a shrug. "When it comes to one of our own, we don't fuck around, Sarah."

Sarah took a deep breath and let it out slowly, trying to keep her temper in check. "Luke, I appreciate all you're doing. I really do. And I understand why the Alliance is concerned. But I *don't* appreciate being kept in the dark. From now on, I want to know the truth. And I want to be consulted about anything relating to me or my son. If you can't live with that, Eli and I will walk right out that door. Is that clear?"

Luke nodded. "Fair enough. But, remember—you *wanted* to know the truth."

Chapter Twelve

"Who the hell is responsible for this?" Stone demanded.

"I don't know, Jacob," Jack Grayson confided, his voice betraying his weariness. Stone could only imagine the kind of chaos going on within the Alliance. The high commander would've had to call an emergency meeting of the Grand Council—no easy feat with the members spread all over the world. The provincial and regional commanders would all be flying to Switzerland or teleconferencing in if their duties kept them from being there in person. Will Asher would be among the latter group, of course, since it was his men involved in the security breach.

Stone had to stifle a chuckle. He could just imagine the conversation between Will and the high commander over that one. Being the imperious bastard's grandson would only cover Will's ass to a point.

"How's Hal?" Stone asked, surprising himself with just how sincere his concern sounded. "When can I see him?"

"He's still in a coma," Jack told him. "We've transported him back to Chicago, though, so our team could oversee his care personally."

"I can be on a plane to Chicago in an hour and stay at one

of my properties there for as long as necessary," Stone said. "Just say the word, brother. Tell me how I can help."

Stone heard Jack heave a sigh. "Thanks, Jacob. I know that would mean a lot to Hal. I'll talk to Will. I'm sure an exception can be made for you. You're family."

"Have Maddie and Sarah seen him?" Stone asked. "How are they?"

"Maddie's here with him," Jack told him. "She won't leave his side. I've only been able to persuade her to leave to take a shower and to talk to Sarah."

"And Sarah?" Stone had to work to keep his voice from sounding too eager.

There was a slight hesitation on the other end before Jack said, "She's with one of our brothers. He's keeping her apprised of her father's condition."

Stone cursed silently, wondering how he should play his next move. "I know there's been some bad blood between her and Hal, but I can't believe she'd be so selfish. Hal's her father, for chrissake!"

"It's not like that." Jack was quick to defend her. "Keeping her away was our call." There was a slight pause, and then Jack cursed under his breath before adding, "Someone tried to abduct Sarah's son the same day Hal was shot."

"Are you shitting me?" Stone cried. "What the hell, Jack?"

Another pause. Jack was clearly struggling with how much he should share with his former brother in arms. "The guy was some kind of fanatic, raving about 'One True Master.' It appears Hal made Eli his successor and the man who tried to abduct him knew as much."

Stone muttered a curse. "You know as well as I do that this may not be just about the treasures. Hal was keeper to a lot of other valuable information. Then the boy will never be safe. Not until we find out who's behind this. Where is Sarah now? She can come stay at one of my homes. I have the same security measures in place that I had when I was in the field. She and Eli would be safe here."

"Thanks, I'll keep that in mind," Jack promised. "Right now, she's with Luke Rogan. He's one of our best. They're at his haven, but if anything changes, I'll let you know."

"I'm sure this Rogan is capable, but maybe I should go be with her since I'm someone she knows," Stone suggested.

"Couldn't tell you where they are, even if I wanted to," Jack said. "No one but Finn knows where Luke's haven is located."

"Damn it, Jack," Stone raged. "I need to feel like I'm being useful somehow. Did someone already make a tech drop? I'd be happy to take care of it."

"Finn already handled it," Jack assured him. "Just keep your ear to the ground, Jacob. Let us know if you hear anything on this nut job who tried to kidnap Eli or on who might be behind shooting Hal."

As soon as Stone hung up, he called another number, waiting impatiently for the son of a bitch to pick up. Finally, the ringing stopped and there was a slight pause before someone said in a bored drawl, "Go."

"Rogan's taking them to his haven. The only one who knows the location is a member of the Alliance named Elliot Finnegan," Stone told him. "He's the Chicago commandery's tech specialist. I suspect you might want to send someone to have a persuasive conversation with him."

"Won't be necessary . . . at the moment," Evans assured him. "Knowing they're at Rogan's haven is enough. If he's as good as you say, it'll take a little digging to track him down, but it can be done. I'll be in touch in a few days."

The call was disconnected before Stone could respond. He glanced at the screen. Yep, the arrogant asshole had hung up on him. No. He had *dismissed* him. Well, soon Evans would be kissing *his* ass.

"Mr. Stone?"

Stone turned to where Allison Holt was hovering in the doorway to his home office, not quite sure how to interact with him since their flight to Cuba. And the return flight.

He offered her his most charming smile and extended a hand. "Allison, really. You're going to have to stop calling me Mr. Stone. Well, privately anyway. I'll still need you to act as my assistant in the office until I can find your replacement."

Allison's lovely eyes went wide. "Mr. Stone . . . Jacob . . . are you firing me? Sir, had I known that I would lose my job, I never would've . . ."

He laughed and pulled her into his arms, pressing a kiss to her hair. "Of course not, Ally. I'm not firing you. But I can't exactly date my assistant, now can I?"

She pulled back, her face aglow. "Do you mean you actually want to have a *relationship?* With *me?* This isn't just sex to you?"

He laughed teasingly at her modesty. Oh, yes. She would make him the perfect, demure little mouse of a wife. Willing to do his every bidding as long as he pretended to worship and adore her. "You know you've been in love with me for years, Ally," he insisted, silently congratulating himself on how masterfully he could play the lovely woman in his arms. "And I honestly can't hide my feelings for you any longer. They've tormented me every day for far too long."

As expected, she threw her arms around his neck with a squeal of excitement, making him grimace. It was a good thing he actually did *like* the woman and value her usefulness. Otherwise, that high-pitched squeal would've been enough for him to slice open her pretty little throat. . . .

Will heaved a sigh, wishing he hadn't bothered to check his email. Or maybe that his grandfather had stuck to the traditional method of sending *written* missives to scold his grandson and remind him of his fuck-up instead of relying on technology to deliver his threats and insults. He'd already had three messages from the high commander since the initial briefing, each one demanding an update—in spite of Will's regular updates to the council—and a none-too-subtle reminder that Will's position as commander firmly depended on the expeditious resolution of their current crisis.

He was in the process of responding with the latest status update on the asset relocation efforts when a firm knock sounded on his door.

"Enter."

Will's brows lifted slightly at seeing Jack sauntering in, his smooth gait at odds with the concerned expression he wore. "Jack. I thought you were at the hospital."

Jack took a seat across from his desk. "I wanted to speak with you regarding Maddie's request."

Will leaned back in his chair, leveling his gaze at his friend. "I don't think there's anything to discuss, Jack. I already agreed to take Maddie on as an initiate. The rest is up to her."

Jack pressed his lips together for a moment before continuing, "I don't believe you've fully considered—"

"I don't believe it's your call," Will interrupted. Softening the edge to his tone, he leaned forward, resting his arms on the desk. "Jack, I know you care for her."

"It's far more complicated than that," Jack snapped.

Will spread his hands. "Well, then let me make things simple. This is Maddie's decision. If you don't think you can handle the emotional aspect of working together, I'll make sure you're not assigned to any ops together."

Jack shook his head. "It's not about how I feel about Maddie, Will. I love her. I always will. Being near her every day would hardly be a problem. But because I love her, I don't want her to have to give up everything for the Alliance.

I know your history as well as you know mine, my friend. We've both sacrificed too much. I would spare Maddie that heartache."

"Sacrifice has been a tenant of the Templars since the Order was conceived," Will reminded him. "You and I are hardly unique. We had a choice and we made it. Regret doesn't do anyone any good."

Jack blinked at him. "Careful, Will. There for a moment, I thought you were the high commander."

Chapter Thirteen

"Have a seat," Luke said, gesturing to his desk chair. If Sarah wanted the truth, he'd give it to her. He bent over her shoulder to open up a series of files, finally reaching the one he sought.

He'd spent the previous night going through the files his commander had sent for him to review—files on Hal Blake, his ex-wife, his daughters, his grandson . . . No surprise that the Alliance had extensive information on all of them. But the one that Luke had found most fascinating had actually belonged to Hal's son-in-law, Gregory Scoffield.

"What is this?" Sarah asked, glancing up at him in her confusion. "Why do you have a file on Greg?"

Luke straightened and went to the other side of the desk, taking the seat across from Sarah, the better to read her expressions as she read the file on her deceased husband and gauge just how well she'd known the man she'd married.

"*Gregory David Scoffield*," she read aloud, skimming through the pages of information, "*born in Halifax, Nova Scotia, on May fifth to Helen and David Scoffield. Only child. Parents killed in plane crash in 1990. Attended Columbia University . . . BA in history . . . PhD in history from Oxford University . . .*"

Sarah lifted her eyes to Luke's. "I know all this. The question is, why do *you* know it?"

"Keep reading," Luke prompted. "There's more."

She shook her head and heaved an irritated sigh. "*Received official censure for affair with Sarah Evelyn Blake, having acted against orders . . .*" At this, she slowly leaned away from the laptop and lifted her eyes once more to Luke, but this time the confusion and hurt in her gaze sent a stab of regret right through the center of Luke's chest. "'Against orders'? What the hell does that mean? *Whose* orders?"

"How did you meet Greg Scoffield?" Luke asked instead of answering her directly. She needed to make the connection herself.

"He was taking some post-doctoral classes when I was a junior," she said, with a sad smile. "We met at a campus lecture—just happened to be sitting beside each other and struck up a conversation. He asked me out for coffee afterward."

"He took quite an interest in your welfare?" Luke continued. "Asked a lot about you and your family? Just happened to bump into you often on campus after that?"

She blinked at him in dismay. "It was a small campus. Even students in other majors interacted with each other quite a bit. We fell in love before we even realized what was happening."

Luke nodded. "I don't doubt that. Especially when his job was to keep an eye on you, to protect you. But this particular assignment came with strict orders for Scoffield not to get personally involved."

"That's ridiculous," Sarah huffed.

"As ridiculous as some wack-job showing up to kidnap your son?" Luke nodded toward the laptop, prompting Sarah to continue reading.

Her lips moved slightly as she murmured to herself, devouring every word of the file. Then her reading came to an abrupt halt and she shook her head slowly in denial. She cleared her throat, but her voice still quavered with emotion when she continued reading aloud, *"Upon learning that Sarah Blake is with child, Scoffield has tendered his resignation with the Alliance. A formal complaint of dereliction of duty has been filed by* confrere *brother Senator Harold Allen Blake."*

Luke sat in silence, waiting for Sarah to absorb the facts laid out before her. After several moments, she swiped at the tears on her cheeks and took a deep, shaky breath. "He was one of you. Greg was a Templar working for the Alliance. And he'd been assigned to me by my father. Is that why Dad was so mad when Greg and I got married? Because one of you had actually fallen in love with me and acted against *orders?* Is *that* it? Or was my entire marriage a lie as well? Did Greg even really love me? Or was his marrying me just some stupid Templar obligation because he'd knocked me up?"

"I'm sure he loved you," Luke told her even though he was talking out of his ass. It was a guess. A gut feeling. How the hell would he know what Greg Scoffield's motivations were? But what man *wouldn't* love her? If Greg Scoffield hadn't loved his wife, he'd been a fucking moron.

The look of gratitude in Sarah's eyes at his words just confirmed what his gut told him. But then her expression returned to one of disbelief and sorrow as she shook her head again. "I don't know how you can be sure. I certainly can't be."

Luke leaned forward, bracing his forearms on his knees. "You have to understand, Sarah, leaving the Alliance isn't something someone does on a whim. This is more than a job for us. I don't even really know how to explain it except to say that this is a life you don't just walk away from. Not without a damned good reason. For your dad—it was his family and his duty to play a key role among our political allies. For Greg Scoffield—it was his love for you. It would take one hell of a woman to persuade one of us to leave. I guess that's what I'm saying."

They sat in silence for several moments before Sarah finally spoke again. "Could I please have some time alone?" she requested. "I just . . ."

He was on his feet in an instant. "Yeah. Sure."

"Luke?" she said, just as he reached the door.

He halted and turned back. "Yeah?"

"Thank you," she said, her eyes still on the laptop screen. "For what you said."

Luke hesitated in the doorway, not sure what to say or do. He hadn't been exaggerating when he'd told Commander Asher that he sucked at getting close to people. But something about the sorrow that weighed on Sarah, the way her shoulders sagged, brought him back into the room.

And he was really kinda shocked when he gently took her hand and pulled her to her feet and into his arms. But he liked the way her arms slipped around his waist, returning his embrace. And he welcomed the slight pressure of her cheek against his chest. And when she turned her eyes up to his, he only vaguely realized that his head was dipping toward hers. But every single inch of him was aware when his lips brushed against hers—some inches more keenly aware than others.

Her lips were soft, warm, yielding. Exactly how he'd spent the previous sleepless night imagining that they'd be. And he wanted to sink into that kiss, explore the mystery of her lips until he discovered the secret bliss that he figured only a few had ever known.

But his conscience made him end the kiss after only a brief taste. He was an asshole for even going as far as he had. Sarah was vulnerable. And it was a dick move to take advantage of that. Pissed with himself for not being the gentleman his mother had raised him to be, Luke released Sarah and, without a word, strode from the room.

Sarah watched Luke practically run down the hall to get away from her, confusion at his abrupt retreat making her head spin. Or maybe it was the aftereffect of coming down so quickly from the jolt of white-hot heat that had lanced through her when Luke had kissed her.

It had been just a brief brush of his lips against hers, almost a chaste kiss, really. But it had been enough to make Sarah's entire body buzz with awareness. She wondered where it might've led if he hadn't suddenly turned and run.

And what was with that disappearing act, by the way? How in the heck could he be so tender and compassionate only to cut and run? The man was a walking, talking riddle. And one she'd very much like to solve.

But there was another riddle begging for her attention at the moment.

Sarah returned to the laptop and began paging through the documents again, this time reading closer, discovering the secret life her husband had led, wondering which "truths" she'd always believed about the man she loved were actually *true*.

When she'd finished with his file, she turned to hers and her sister's. Maddie's had been an interesting read, that was for damned sure. It seemed Jack Grayson had been called to the carpet as well, for crossing the line with Maddie when he was assigned to be her detail. But that line of inquiry abruptly ended. Looking at the dates, it must've been when Jack had suddenly been reassigned and Maddie had gone to Quantico for training. Apparently, there'd been another operative assigned to her there—but this time without her knowledge.

And then there was Eli's file. They seemed to know a

great deal about her son, considering her father hadn't been in contact with them. Obviously, that hadn't deterred him from keeping tabs on them, in addition to what Maddie was sharing. But there was nothing at all about her father passing any information on to Eli. Not in the general file on her son. Eli's being named a successor had been a secret even from Hal Blake's fellow members of the Alliance— *brothers*, as they called each other.

The only official mention of Eli's being named a successor was in an email message from a man named Phillip Asher, high commander, to Will Asher, regional commander, North America, confirming that Hal Blake had, indeed, approached the Grand Council—which was apparently the body of senior officials in the Alliance—to apprise them of his chosen successor. But in the message, which contained a none-too-gentle reprimand to Will Asher for not managing his people better, the high commander mentioned that if he wanted additional information, Will would have to contact his seneschal for the meeting minutes. And that the elder Asher expected that Will would "handle the situation immediately" and without "further breaches" that would jeopardize his command as there were "certainly others willing to fill it."

"Wow, they're about as warm and fuzzy a family as mine," Sarah mused.

So there were no other hints as to who outside of the Alliance might've known about Eli. So far, everything Sarah had heard indicated that they suspected a breach from outside the organization. Were they looking in the wrong direction? Was it possible one of these guys in the Grand Council was jockeying for a more important seat and was using the breach to make Will Asher look bad? Was this whole thing just a bullshit *power play*?

Sarah pressed her palm to her forehead and squeezed

her eyes shut. God, it felt like her *headache* was getting a headache.

She glanced down at the clock at the bottom right corner of the laptop and her eyes went wide. It was almost noon. She'd been going through the files for hours. Frowning, she pushed back, needing to get away from the computer for a while.

She then became aware of the sounds of synthetic gunfire and explosions coming from somewhere in the house and followed them down the hall to the loft to find Eli parked in front of the huge TV, playing a video game.

"Hey, Mom," he called happily when he noticed her standing there. "Luke said I could play whichever game I wanted while he made lunch."

Sarah lifted an eyebrow at him. "I imagine Luke didn't realize there are certain games I don't allow you to play?"

Eli gave her a guilty grin, looking far too old with the gaming headset on. "Well, he didn't really have any of the ones I usually play, so I picked *Halo*. Is that okay?"

"*This* time," Sarah told him. "But we're going to have to look into some other form of entertainment for you while we're here."

A barrage of gunfire brought Eli's attention back to the screen. "Ah, man! It's so on. . . ."

"Who are you talking to?" Sarah asked, frowning at the battle waging.

"Finn," Eli told her, his forehead wrinkled in concentration.

"So you forgive him his tacky shirt?" Sarah said.

Eli shrugged. "He's okay—as long as he's not trying to date my mom. Besides he thought I was Luke at first." He giggled. "He cusses a lot when he gets his butt handed to him."

Sarah closed her eyes on a sigh. *Lovely.* This trip was

turning out to be way more educational for Eli than she'd anticipated. . . .

"Tell him I said to watch his language or he'll find out what it's *really* like to get his butt handed to him," she drawled.

Eli sent a grin her way. "Can I actually say that?"

"Sure can," Sarah told him, not bothering to correct his grammar this time. "You can *quote* me."

She heard Eli repeat what she'd said as she headed toward the stairs and couldn't help smiling to herself when she heard him add, "Dude. She *totally* means it."

She was grateful beyond words for Eli, her little ray of sunshine. No matter what darkness came into her life, just hearing his laughter lifted her spirits. She was hurt, pissed, about the secrets Greg had withheld from her. But she could never regret their relationship or the beautiful son he'd given her. And no matter the initial reason he'd come into her life, what they'd shared had been real. He'd loved her. She might have doubted it when Luke had first shown her the files. But in her heart, she knew the truth. All of it. And that assured her of Greg's love—and finally gave her the peace she'd needed.

But her grin began to fade as she made her way down the stairs and heard Luke's voice, the sound of his deep bass making her stomach flutter. She was tempted to turn around and go back upstairs, putting off having to face him after their kiss. But she couldn't exactly avoid him in his own house. And she didn't want to. She wanted to feel those strong arms around her, wanted to feel safe and protected and *desired*. God, she wanted far more than that. . . .

Sarah swallowed hard and tried to keep her heart from pounding as she approached the kitchen. But a snatch of conversation brought her up short outside the doorway.

"If you needed money, Mel, you should've told me."

"Why?" Melanie shot back. "So you can continue to

throw money at a ranch that offers you nothing in return? You give every cent of profit to Dad."

"It offers me more than you know," he assured her.

"Look, Luke," Melanie said on a sigh, "I appreciate all you do for us. I know you paid far more for this land than it was worth just so Dad would have some security. It's not about the money. You're not *here* all the time. Stuff comes up, things need to be repaired. You have a mare getting ready to foal any day. But you know Dad can't handle things anymore, not since his stroke. I'm managing both ranches, and I can't do it on my own."

"How many more hands do you need to hire?" Luke asked. Sarah could hear in his voice that he wasn't a fan of that option.

"Three," Melanie said. "I've already posted the jobs, and I'll start interviews in a few days. But, more importantly, I need to hire another ranch manager who can help me out with your place when you're not around."

Luke cursed under his breath. "How are you vetting these people?"

"Same way as always. No one is hired without a complete background check through whatever organization it is that you use."

At that moment, Luke turned his gaze toward where Sarah stood, and she got the impression that he'd known she was standing there all along. His eyes narrowed a little as if he was studying her, silently trying to determine whether she was going to be okay after the bombshell he'd dropped on her.

She offered him a tentative smile. "Sorry to interrupt. Should I come back?"

"No," Melanie said, sending Luke a pointed look. "I need to get back to work. Davis and Dad will be here for dinner, by the way. I'll bring dessert."

Luke's mouth compressed into a grim line. "Melanie—"

But before he could finish his sentence, his stepsister had slipped out the kitchen door. Sarah immediately missed the other woman's presence as an awkward silence fell between them.

Finally, needing to break the tension, she said, "So, I've been thinking about what you said . . . about Eli needing to feel empowered."

His gaze snapped toward her. "Yeah?"

"And I've decided I'm okay with you teaching Eli how to defend himself," she told him. "I just want you to discuss it with me first, okay?" When he gave her a terse nod, she cleared her throat and took a couple of steps further into the kitchen. "And I'd like you to teach me as well."

He studied her for another moment then slowly nodded. "Okay. But why the change of heart?"

She crossed her arms over her chest and lifted her chin. "Because I'm tired of everyone else treating me like I'm too precious and delicate to handle the truth. It seems you're the first person who's had the . . . the *balls* to actually be honest with me, Luke."

He grimaced a little at her statement and dropped his gaze. "Sarah . . ."

She closed the space between them and took his hand in both of hers, not willing to let him back out. "I want you to teach me everything you know."

His gaze came up at this, oddly tortured. "You don't want to know everything I do. Trust me."

The sorrow and regret she saw in his eyes was heart-breaking. "Okay," she said. "Then just teach me what you can in the time we have."

"We'll start tomorrow," he said.

She frowned at him. "Why not today?"

He heaved a sigh. "Because it looks like we're going to have to go into town today. Apparently, we're having guests tonight."

Chapter Fourteen

Luke could feel his muscles growing tenser with each mile as they drew closer to town. He'd been able to avoid making many trips in since building his haven, depending on Mel to get what he needed as the caretaker for the ranch and ordering all the rest online, then having it shipped to another property the Alliance owned a few miles away.

"You okay?" Sarah asked, startling him out of his thoughts as they drove down Main Street.

He shifted in his seat and shrugged. "Yeah, I'm good. I just don't come here often anymore."

"Why not?" Eli asked.

The back of Luke's neck began to ache. "I got into a lot of trouble when I was a teenager. Let's leave it at that."

"A lot of trouble" was an understatement. It was damned lucky for Luke that his stepfather was so well-respected or Luke's ass probably would've ended up rotting in prison with a record that would've doomed his future before it'd even gotten started.

"But that was years ago," Sarah pointed out. "I'm sure they've forgotten about that by now."

Luke grunted. "You'd think so. But local police in a small town aren't about to forget about a kid who was picked up for trespassing, underage drinking, destruction of property . . . take your pick. And that was before my mom died. It got worse after."

To his surprise, Sarah reached across the space between them and briefly squeezed his hand. "But not now. You're a different man."

He pulled into one of the few parking spots that lined the street in front of the town's only grocery store. It was little more than a convenience store really. Most folks drove an hour or more to one of the larger towns in the area and stocked up, and as soon as Luke got out of the SUV, he immediately regretted not doing the same.

"Well, I'll be damned! Luke Rogan."

Luke clenched his jaw as he helped Sarah out of the vehicle and tried to keep his expression neutral when he gave the sheriff a terse nod in greeting. "Ellis."

The man had gone completely gray since Luke's last visit to town and had added probably twenty pounds. "Been a while."

Luke took Sarah's hand in his and started toward the store. "Yep."

"Aren't you going to introduce your lady friend?" Sheriff Ellis called. "Don't recall the last time I saw you with a woman who wasn't—"

"This is Sarah and her son Eli," Luke interrupted, giving the man a warning look.

Sarah left his side and immediately stepped toward Sheriff Ellis, extending her hand and offering him a bright smile. "It's so lovely to meet you," she said. "Luke was just telling me about how much of an impact you had on his life. It sounds like your concern and guidance were invaluable in helping him get on the right path."

Sheriff Ellis blinked at her for a moment, then narrowed his eyes a little, studying her as if trying to determine whether she was being sincere. "We do what we can to help the youth of our town," he said, his tone cautious. "But I gotta say, I never expected Rogan to turn into a family man."

Sarah turned back to Luke, reclaiming his hand and urging him back to her side. "He's one of the best men I've ever known."

Luke's conscience nut-punched him at her praise. "It was good to see you, Ellis," he said, urging Sarah back toward the store's entrance and jerking his head at Eli to follow.

"You see Jim yet?" Ellis called after them. "When you do, give him my best."

Luke ground his teeth together to keep from telling the sheriff to mind his own fucking business. The last thing he needed was to get into it with the guy when he was trying to keep a low profile. Instead, he called back, "You bet."

"What was that about?" Sarah asked sotto voce as they made their way into the store.

Luke shook his head with a covert glance toward Eli. "I'll fill you in later."

Sarah let the subject drop and helped him come up with ingredients for a decent meal that evening; within half an hour, he was stowing the groceries in the back of the SUV. "We've got one more stop to make," Luke told Sarah. "I need to pick something up."

"Hey, Luke, could we go take a look at that store?" Eli asked, pointing across the street. "I want to get something for Master Chief."

Luke grimaced when he saw where Eli was pointing. It was a gourmet bakery for pets—one of the town's few concessions to the trendy. "You named the dog after a character in *Halo?*"

"Not just *any* character," Eli pointed out. "It's Master Chief. He's totally bada—I mean, he's totally cool."

Luke sighed. *Yeah, he was definitely getting a dog.*

"You go ahead and pick up what you need," Sarah told him. "Eli and I can check out the bakery."

"Mine can wait," Luke insisted. And it probably should. Picking up condoms from the local drug store—just in case—was probably asking for trouble. At least if he didn't have any protection on hand, he'd have a reason not to allow himself to give in to temptation with Sarah. Plus, it was damned presumptuous of him to think she'd even be willing. Still waging an internal debate, he added, "I'm not letting you go alone."

Sarah cocked her head to one side and gave him a chastising look. "Luke, seriously. What is going to happen? No one knows where we are. It'll be fine."

He surveyed the street, searching for anything suspicious, anyone who didn't look like they fit in, any cars that seemed out of place. But before he could respond, Sarah added, "Luke, I need a few minutes of normalcy. Please."

He exhaled a sharp breath, not wanting to deny her that, all things considered. "Fine. Ten minutes. I'll meet you back here. Don't go anywhere but the bakery."

He watched them cross the street and waited until they were in the bakery before he turned up his collar against the cold and snow that was falling again and made his way down the street.

"Come on, sweetie, make a decision," Sarah prompted, offering an apologetic smile to the woman behind the counter.

"I want to make sure it's something Chief will like," Eli reminded her.

Sarah strolled around the little bakery, browsing the shelves to fill the time. As she passed the window, she happened to catch a glimpse of their SUV. A man in a denim jacket was checking it out, trying to look nonchalant. In fact, had she not been looking for danger ever since the Fall Festival, she probably wouldn't have even noticed.

"I'm going to get these, okay, Mom?" Eli called.

Sarah fished her phone out of her pocket and dialed the first number programmed into it. Luke answered almost instantly. "Sarah? What's wrong?"

"There's a man in a denim jacket checking out the Expedition," she told him. "Where are you?"

"On my way back," he said in a rush, his voice sounding like he was already in motion. "Stay where you are."

Sarah pocketed her phone just as Luke came into view, his broad shoulders rolling as he stalked forward. In the next moment, he tackled the guy against the hood of the SUV and had him in a headlock. Out of the corner of her eye, Sarah saw a woman who was heading to a nearby car take a few stumbling steps backward and frantically fish her phone out of her purse.

Sarah cursed under her breath, calling over her shoulder as she threw open the bakery's door. "Eli, stay here!"

She raced across the street toward where Luke was wrenching the guy's arm behind him. As she approached, the woman with the cell phone was yelling hysterically at whoever was on the other end of the line.

"Who's the 'One True Master'?" Luke growled at the man as she reached his side.

"Hell if I know, man!" the guy yelled.

Luke wrenched his arm higher. "*Who is it?*"

"Shit, man, I don't know!" the guy whimpered. "*You* are?"

"Luke, stop!" Sarah cried. "It's a mistake! I made a mistake!"

Luke released the man and took a step back, his expression deadly, his body still at the ready to take the guy out should he make even the slightest move toward Sarah.

"What the fuck?" the guy spat.

"It's my fault," Sarah told him, turning to the terrified woman, who came rushing to check out the man. "I'm so sorry. It's all my fault. I thought you were breaking into our vehicle. I'm sorry. He was just protecting us."

Luke raked a hand through his hair and let fly a juicy stream of curses, then raised his hands and laced his fingers behind his head before getting down on his knees. Confused, Sarah turned to see two sheriff's cars arriving.

"On the right path, huh?" Sheriff Ellis drawled a few moments later as his deputy cuffed Luke and dragged him to his feet so he could pat him down.

"Got a gun," the deputy remarked, removing a handgun from the small of Luke's back.

Oh, God . . .

"Permit's in my wallet," Luke assured him.

"This is all my fault," Sarah pleaded. "I saw this man looking in our car—"

"Jesus, lady!" the guy cried, holding the woman close. "We're having a baby and are thinking about getting an SUV. I was just checking it out."

Sarah covered her face with her hands for a moment, feeling like a paranoid idiot. "I'm terribly sorry. *Please,* don't arrest Luke, Sheriff Ellis. I'm begging you."

The sheriff looked at the man Luke had assaulted, his brows lifted in silent question. The guy muttered under his breath, then said, "Fine. Whatever. But, shit, dial it down a notch, dude."

The sheriff jerked his chin at his deputy. "Go ahead and take their statement so we can file our reports."

As soon as they were out of earshot, the sheriff pegged Luke with a pointed look. "I've known you a long time, Rogan. Seen you through some serious shit—especially after your mom died. But what the *hell* is going on? You could've broken that guy's arm."

"Just a misunderstanding," Luke said, shrugging off the sheriff's concern. "Won't happen again."

"That's a bit more than a misunderstanding, son," Ellis told him.

Sarah stepped closer to Luke, taking his arm. "Thank you for understanding, Sheriff," she said, offering him her sweetest smile but feeling it waver under his scrutiny. "If it's all right with you, I'd just like to get my son and go home."

Not waiting for his reply, Sarah hurried back to the bakery to find Eli standing at the window watching the entire incident, wide-eyed. "How much do we owe you for the dog cookies?" she asked the woman behind the counter.

But the woman waved her off, giving her a sympathetic look. "It's okay, honey. They're on the house." Then she subtly nodded toward the window. "You have any more trouble, you know you can come to anyone in town for help. Or ask for me. My name's Nancy."

Sarah gaped at the woman's implication. Did the woman seriously think Luke would harm her? "I'm fine," Sarah assured her, offended on Luke's behalf. "There's no need to be concerned. But thank you for the treats."

Sarah grabbed Eli's hand and pulled him from the store, her heart hammering. She'd screwed up. It was that simple. Luke had wanted them to keep a low profile, to not draw too much attention to themselves. And what had she done? Overreacted like some freaking drama queen, and he was the one whose reputation was paying the price.

But, to his credit, when she got back in the SUV, Luke didn't make a single rebuke. In fact, he didn't say a word during the entire ride back to the ranch. It was only after they'd finished unloading and putting away the groceries that Luke finally spoke.

"Hey, Eli, why don't you take Chief outside to play for a few minutes," he suggested. "I need to talk to your mom."

Eli bolted toward the front door, the gangly-legged puppy bounding after him. As soon as she heard the front door slam, Sarah said in a rush as he strode toward her,

"Luke, I don't even know what to say. I'm so sorry about what happened today—"

But her words were abruptly cut off when Luke took her face in his hands and claimed her mouth in a harsh kiss—the kind of kiss she'd imagined the first time she'd seen him stalking through the crowd at the festival. She was too stunned to respond at first, but then she was kissing him back, her lips clinging to his in the all too brief moment before he lifted his head.

He cursed softly, letting his gaze drop. "Jesus, Sarah. When you called and I thought another one of those assholes had found you and Eli . . . I kinda lost my shit. But I'm sorry—I shouldn't have kissed you earlier today or just now. It's a dick move. I just . . . I'm sorry."

"I'm not," she said, the words coming out before she could stop them. She added in a rush to explain, "I mean, it's been a long time since anyone has kissed me. Not since my husband . . . and it was . . . nice."

He lifted his eyes at this, and her breath caught in her lungs as she forgot to breathe. He wanted her. She could see it in his eyes as he gazed down at her, could feel it in the heat between them, in the tension building in the air in the small space that separated them. But she could also feel his restraint, his determination not to give in to the desire they clearly both felt. And based on the conversation with Eli they'd had the other day on the way to the ranch, she realized Luke wasn't going to give in to that desire—not without her permission. And somehow that made her want him even more.

"So," she murmured, stepping closer, "I guess what I'm saying is that I *want* you to kiss me."

"No you don't, Sarah," he said on a harshly exhaled breath. "You really don't."

She could feel the tension in his entire body—his muscles taut beneath her fingertips when she placed her hand on his chest. "Yes, I do. I've wanted it since the moment I saw you coming toward me at the festival."

He hissed a curse and took a deep, ragged breath.

Sarah's heart cracked a little bit at his response, wondering if maybe she'd misread him, but then his arm went around her waist and he jerked her against him, his mouth claiming hers, his lips hard, hungry, demanding.

God, for the first time in years she felt alive, desirable and *desired*. And she wanted more.

She slipped her arms around his neck, going up on her toes so that she could press closer to him, and nipped at his bottom lip, then swept her tongue across the seam of his mouth. He groaned as he sank into the kiss, his tongue caressing hers. His arm around her tightened and his other hand tangled in the length of her hair.

Sarah shuddered as lightning hot desire filled her veins, thrilling her and terrifying her at the same time. And she abruptly pulled back, leaving them both panting. "Oh, God," she rasped. "I'm sorry."

He took a half step back, giving her some space, raising his hands as if she was aiming a gun at him. His head dipped down as his chest rose and fell with each ragged breath. "It's okay," he managed. "It's fine."

But it wasn't. Not for her. She'd thought she was ready, thought she could want another man without feeling that tug of guilt at the center of her chest. But even as much as she was drawn to Luke and in spite of the way her heart ached now at leaving his arms, she couldn't help feeling that she was betraying Greg somehow—even after all she'd learned.

"I'm just confused," she told him.

"Sarah, you don't have to explain anything to me," Luke assured her. "I get it."

But she wasn't sure he did. She wanted him. Dear God, she wanted him with an urgency that was shocking. But the way she felt, the intensity of it all, made her feel out of control—and control was something she was a little light on at the moment.

"Luke—" Her words died abruptly at the sound of the front door opening and Eli's hurried footsteps as he jogged into the kitchen.

"Hey, Luke! Mom!" Eli called. "You gotta come see this!"

They followed him back outside to see the snow coming down at a rapidly accumulating rate. Chief alternated between pouncing on the snowflakes as they hit the ground and barking at those still falling.

"Isn't he hilarious?" Eli laughed.

Luke rifled Eli's hair. "Yeah, he's an entertaining little guy, I'll give you that." At that moment, his cell phone beeped with an alert. He grabbed it off the clip at his belt and frowned.

"Everything okay?" Sarah asked.

He sighed. "Yeah. Vehicle coming in."

"Dinner guests?" she guessed. When he nodded, she slipped her hand into his, giving it a squeeze. "It'll be okay."

He turned his eyes down to her, studying her intently, no doubt wondering if she was talking about what had happened just a moment before in the kitchen or about his family's visit. His thumb smoothed over the back of her hand. "You sure?"

She didn't respond right away, not sure what to say. But then she took a deep breath and let it out slowly. "I want it to be. I really do."

At that moment, an aged Bronco pulled up in front of the house and Mel hopped out with her normal boundless energy and easy smile. A tall, handsome African-American man got out of the driver's side and sent an adoring glance Mel's way. The man was clearly and adorably head over heels for Mel.

Sarah couldn't help but smile. *So this must be Davis. . . .*

As Mel moved around to the back seat to help the third passenger, Davis came toward the porch, his hand extended.

"Good to see you, man," he said, shaking Luke's hand and pulling him in for a brief man-hug. "Been way too long."

Luke was actually grinning and appeared to be genuinely happy to see his old friend. "Good to see you, too, Davis. And congratulations. I'm happy for you and Mel."

"Thanks. She's one hell of a woman," Davis said, glancing over his shoulder at Mel.

"She'd have to be a saint to put up with your shit," Luke said with a chuckle.

"Look who's talking," Davis said, jerking his chin at Luke. Then he extended his hand to Sarah. "I hear you're the one who's managed to get this loser in line."

She shook his offered hand. "I'm Sarah. And this is my son, Eli."

Davis shook Eli's hand as well. "Mel tells me you have quite a way with horses, Eli. You want to come take a look at them with me after dinner?"

Eli's eyes lit up. "Sure!"

Sarah felt Luke stiffen next to her and followed his line of sight to see Mel escorting a frail-looking man toward the porch. Davis turned and hurried down the steps to offer his arm to the man as well. As the man made his way up the stairs, his eyes began to glimmer and a smile lifted the left side of his mouth, the right remaining turned down.

When he reached Luke, he stepped away from Mel and Davis and took Luke's face in his hands, pulling him down to press a kiss to the top of his head. "It's good to have you home, boy," he said, his words a little slurred.

Luke's voice was strained when he replied, "How are you holding up, Jim?"

The man chuckled. "Freezing my balls off at the moment. How about some coffee?"

Chapter Fifteen

Luke leaned back in his chair, listening to Jim tell Eli the same tales he'd heard during his own youth, marveling at the man's storied life. But it was tough to see the man who'd been so strong and rugged reduced to a shell of his former self. Jim's stroke had left him limited, but it hadn't dampened his sense of humor or his ability to hold his audience rapt with a story.

When Sarah got up to clear the table, Luke leaped to his feet, grabbing some of the dishes and following her to the sink.

"Jim is an incredible man," Sarah told him softly. "And Eli adores him."

Luke nodded. "I wish you could've known him before."

"We're heading out to the barn," Mel called to them.

Luke grabbed the coffee and a few cups and carried them back to the table. "Jim, you need a refill?"

The man nodded. "So, you doin' okay, Luke?"

Luke refilled his cup, then poured a cup for him and Sarah before responding, "Yeah, I'm good."

"We're enjoying our visit," Sarah said. "The property is absolutely gorgeous, Jim."

Jim offered her a smile. "Thank you. Wish I could get around it like I used to. But Mel drives me around the land at least once a week so I can take a look. When Luke's mother was alive, we'd ride out to the lake and spend the entire day there, just lying in the grass, watching the clouds."

Luke's heart ached at the remembrance of those too few happy days. As if sensing his shift in mood, Sarah reached over and took his hand.

"I'm sure it was beautiful," she said.

Luke met her gaze and impulsively brought her hand to his lips, pressing a lingering kiss to her fingertips. "I'll show it to you sometime."

"Glad to see you happy," Jim said, dragging Luke's eyes away from Sarah. "I worried about you."

Luke's conscience twisted his gut. "Jim, I owe you an apology for all the shit I put you through. I know I was a pain in the ass."

Jim chuckled and winked at Sarah. "Oh, you got that right. But a father loves his son no matter what. And I know I didn't raise you, boy, but you'll always be my son."

The twisting in Luke's gut made the meal of steak and roasted potatoes churn ominously. "I'm sorry I can't be home more."

Jim lifted his good shoulder and let it drop in a slight shrug. "Army keeps you busy."

Luke sighed, suddenly feeling the need to unburden his soul and come clean. "Jim, there's something you should know about the work I do. . . ."

Jim lifted a hand. "I don't need to know anything except that you're keepin' yourself safe."

Luke narrowed his eyes a little, studying his stepfather. The man knew more than he was letting on. There was no way he'd know about the Alliance—their existence was too buried in secrecy. But it wouldn't have been too tough to figure out Luke was no longer in the army. And yet Melanie still seemed to buy it, so Jim apparently hadn't shared the truth with her.

"I do the best I can," Luke told him. "But sometimes danger can't be avoided. It's part of the job."

Jim nodded. "Well, now you have someone to come home to. Just keep that in mind."

Luke smoothed his thumb over the back of Sarah's hand. As much as he hated to admit it, Jim was right. The way Luke was starting to feel about Sarah and Eli was a game-changer. He'd been ready to rip off the arms of that fucker in town if it meant protecting his family.

What the fuck? His family?

What the hell was he thinking? He had no right to think of them that way. They were a job—his mission was to protect them, nothing else. He needed to check that shit right fucking now. He'd been wandering his entire life, never fitting in, never feeling like he belonged until joining the Alliance. He wasn't about to screw that up by getting attached to something he had no right to.

He released Sarah's hand and massaged the back of his neck. "I should probably go see what Davis has to say about the horses," he said, abruptly standing, needing to put some distance between himself and Sarah.

But he was cut off from his escape as Mel, Davis, and Eli came inside, stamping off the snow on the rug inside the front door.

"It's really coming down, Dad," Mel called out. "We should probably head home."

A few minutes later, after a brief report from Davis, Luke helped Jim back into Mel's Bronco with a promise that he'd bring Sarah and Eli over to the main house once the weather cleared up.

As they made their way back into the house, Sarah said,

"I'm not sure how you can say you have no family, Luke. Those people love you."

Luke grunted. "That's exactly why I stay away. You've seen the kind of enemies the Alliance has, Sarah. I don't want to bring any of that shit down on them. I brought them enough grief when I was younger."

"But Luke—"

"I need to go check in with my commander," he said, cutting her off. "See how much longer you and Eli will need to be here."

He hadn't meant to hurt her with his comment—or, hell, maybe he had. It was better for both of them if things between them came to an end before they could really get started. He didn't need any emotional tangles—and the last thing Sarah needed was to get involved with him.

Still, as he went to his office and closed the door, the sound of her chatting and laughing with Eli about Chief's antics filled him with the kind of peacefulness of spirit that his mother had always spoken of to him, a harmony that she'd wanted for him.

So, half an hour later, when his commander finished reporting to his men that the relocation of Alliance assets should be completed within the next two weeks at the latest and that any security risks should be fully evaluated and addressed in the same time frame, Luke's heart began to pound.

"So, what does that mean for Sarah and Eli?" he asked, trying to keep his tone neutral.

"You should be able to deliver them to Chicago as soon as we have confirmation that the relocation is complete," Will assured him. "Then we'll evaluate what else Hal might've shared with Eli and go from there."

Two weeks max. Shit.

"I know it's an inconvenience, Luke," Will continued. "We're doing the best we can."

Luke gave him a terse nod. "Understood."

"You can tell Sarah that her father's improving," Jack chimed in. "He actually opened his eyes today."

"Is he talking yet?" Luke asked. "Did he say who he thought might be after Eli?"

Jack shook his head. "No, he wasn't coherent. Jacob Stone is coming in tomorrow to see him. We're hoping he might be able to talk with him, get some answers."

"Jacob Stone?" Luke repeated. "As in billionaire tycoon and political golden boy Jacob Stone? Word is he will be tapped for secretary of state by the presidential front-runner."

"He's one of us," Jack explained. "Or was. He was born into the Alliance—his grandfather was in line to become high commander but got involved in some shady dealings and was ousted. And Jacob's father was killed in an op in Russia. Jacob was a brother until he totally fucked up a mission."

"It was decided that his talents and skills could be better utilized as an embedded *confrere*," Will interjected. "Hal was his mentor and has guided his career, making sure Jacob reached a level of success that was most useful to us."

"And you think Stone can jog something in Blake's memory that you guys couldn't?" Luke asked.

"Stone's the son Hal never had," Jack told him, something in his voice making Luke frown. Was it possible that Jack had hoped to fill that role for the senator?

"Keep me posted," Luke said. "I'm sure Sarah will want to talk to Blake when he wakes up."

"Any progress on your end?" Will asked.

"Check into a therapist in Portland named Dr. Locke," Luke suggested. "Sarah told me that Eli was in therapy with the guy for a while. Apparently, Hal had suggested the guy—would've been right around the time he filed his plan of succession."

"You're thinking embedded memories?" Jack asked, brows raised. "Are we still doing that? I thought the practice was frowned upon."

"We only use it when necessary," Will said, his tone clipped. "It's probably still the safest way to hide classified data—for both the subject and the information he's carrying. If it's done right, he won't even know the information's there, so you can't get to it even with torture or Sodium Pentothal. The intel is buried too deep in the subconscious to be accessed without careful backtracking."

Luke ran a hand over his hair, his concern for Eli making him practically growl, "Yeah, but if it's *not* done right . . ."

Will hesitated, but then finished Luke's thought with a solemn confirmation. "Digging it out the wrong way will seriously fuck with someone's head."

Luke hissed a curse. "And Blake thought this would be safe to use on a kid? His own grandson? What the fuck? I'm beginning to think Sarah's right about her dad."

"I'm sure he wasn't anticipating this scenario," Jack interjected, his sympathetic tone only serving to piss Luke off even more.

"I don't give a rat's ass what he *anticipated*," Luke ground out. "There's no way in hell I'm letting some sadistic motherfucker dig through Eli's brain."

Will's brows lifted almost imperceptibly before he said, "Jack, that'll be all." Jack immediately disconnected, his commander's tone leaving no room for argument. As soon as they were alone on the secure line, Will gave Luke an expectant look. "Wanna tell me what that was all about?"

Luke shook his head with a shrug. "I'm just doing my job. I was assigned to protect Sarah and Eli. That's what I intend to do."

"You know how this works, Luke," Will reminded him. "We make sacrifices for a greater good, put our own personal wants and desires aside for the Alliance. I'm not saying this to be a dick. . . . . I'm telling you from experience."

Luke crossed his arms over his chest. "Does that experience have anything to do with the One True Master bullshit?" When his commander's expression hardened, Luke knew he'd hit on a nerve. "You know what that son of a bitch in Oregon was talking about, don't you?"

Will didn't immediately respond, his face impossible to read. Then he nodded. "Yeah. I've heard it before. It was mentioned in my father's notes on the op he was running when he was killed."

"And how's not getting personal working out for you?" Luke pressed.

"When this mission's over, it's over," Will barked. Luke had obviously hit on a raw nerve. "Just make sure when it's time to move on that, your shit's squared away."

Luke clenched his jaw. "Copy that."

Will rested his forehead on his clasped hands, his thumbs pressing against the bridge of his nose to try to reduce the pressure building in his head.

Luke was right. This shit was getting personal. And not just because of the possible connection between the security breach and the Illuminati. He'd long suspected those power-grabbing assholes were behind his father's death—unlike his grandfather, who preferred to keep his head up his own ass and refused to face facts. But the look he saw on Luke's face when he'd spoken of Sarah Scoffield and her son was one Will had seen before. And Luke's frustration and helplessness to protect the people he cared about were far too familiar.

Will hated himself for spouting the exact same bullshit rationalization to Luke that his grandfather had spewed to him almost a decade before. But the fiery resolve in Luke's eyes told Will that Luke wasn't about to just puss out and walk away. Not without a fight.

Will's hands slid around to grasp the nape of his neck. He wished he'd had the same resolve when he'd had to walk away from his one chance at happiness. He should've fought harder. But, God, he'd still been a kid—just twenty-six—with only a few years in the CIA when his world had been turned upside down.

But he'd made his choice. He'd left that world behind. He'd left *her* behind. And he'd regretted his decision ever since. He didn't regret his oath to the Alliance, following in his father's footsteps and taking on the role of regional commander as well as provincial commander from the word go, fulfilling his family's legacy. He'd always known on some level which direction his path would take him. But he regretted bowing to his grandfather's will and leaving behind the one person who'd mattered most. She'd trusted him with everything—with her life—and yet he couldn't bring her into his world in return.

He'd watched Jack Grayson and others under his command do the same goddamned thing. And now he was practically ordering Luke to cut and run. Jack was right. Will was becoming more and more like his grandfather— a total fucking hypocrite.

With an angry groan, Will pushed away from his desk and strode from his office, not sure which he was more pissed off with—his grandfather for being such an overbearing prick who insisted that the Templars have no life outside the Alliance unless it fit with his very narrow, grim definition or with himself for not having the balls to stand up to him. . . .

If Phillip Asher, high commander of the Alliance, wanted his grandson to demonstrate that he was worthy to ascend to the highest position of authority within the Alliance someday, then Will was sure as hell going to show him he was. And odds were the self-righteous, condescending asshole wasn't going to like it.

Chapter Sixteen

Sarah lay in bed listening to Luke's deep voice through the bedroom wall, trying to hear what he was talking about but not having any luck. She heard her name and Eli's more than once, but didn't know what he was saying. The call had been going on for three hours. Chances were, the parts she'd wanted to hear had been before she'd even gone to bed anyway.

She tossed and turned, trying to get comfortable but not having any luck. Finally, she heard Luke leave the office, his boots pounding the floor in furious strides. Before she could second-guess herself, she threw off her covers and padded softly to the doorway and into the hall, hoping to catch him. But his bedroom was empty.

Frowning, she made her way down the stairs and searched each of the rooms, but still nothing. Finally, she headed toward the one room Luke hadn't shown her during the tour of the house. The door was ajar, lamplight spilling out into the dark hallway.

She put a hand on the door to push it open, but hesitated when she heard the first few notes of music. They were soft, quiet at first, gentle. Someone was playing the piano—and beautifully. She listened intently but didn't recognize the piece.

She eased the door open just a little further. Luke sat at the baby grand piano with his profile to the door, his head down, his eyes closed as he played. Sarah watched in utter fascination, wondering if she would ever have the chance to truly know the man before her, wondering if *anyone* had ever had the chance to truly know him. The way he'd fought the man who'd attempted to abduct Eli had told her he was fierce, deadly. And his reaction to the man in town had been swift.

And in spite of the few moments he'd shared more than she imagined he had intended about his past, he'd been stoic, closed off. But then there were the moments of gentleness that spoke of a soul far more intricate and beautiful than what he seemed willing to admit.

And then there were the kisses they'd shared . . . passionate and demanding, and yet tender.

As he played, her lids grew heavy and she slid down the wall to sit in front of the doorway, determined to hear more but suddenly too tired to stand. She leaned her head back against the wall and closed her eyes, letting the music wash over her. . . .

"Hey."

Sarah started awake, disoriented for a moment, wondering why in the world she was sitting on the floor in a T-shirt and pajama pants. But then she saw Luke crouched down in front of her and she realized she must've dozed off while listening to him play.

"Sorry," she whispered, not sure why she felt the need to keep her voice low. "I couldn't sleep."

A smile tugged at the corner of his mouth. "Clearly."

She laughed sleepily. "Okay, I couldn't sleep *before* now. I heard you come downstairs and didn't want to disturb you while you were playing. It was too beautiful. So I just thought I'd sit here and listen for a moment and must've dozed off."

"So, you're saying my playing is a cure for insomnia?" he teased.

She liked this teasing, playful side of Luke. And she had a feeling people didn't get to see it very often. "Yes, that's exactly what I'm saying," she said with a grin. "So where did you study?"

He laughed—deep, smooth. Like velvet, the sultry sound of his laughter slid across her skin. "I didn't study anywhere. My mom played a little and taught me what she knew. The rest I just . . . learned."

This brought Sarah fully awake. "You taught yourself how to play like that? Luke, I studied for years growing up and can't play that well. That's incredible."

He stood and extended his hand. "Nah, it was just something to do. And then, when I joined the Alliance, we were encouraged to do something to relax and 'improve the mind,' keep balanced. Finn meditates or surfs, depending on where he is at the time. Jack fences. The commander—hell, I'm honestly not sure what Will does. Some of the guys do martial arts, woodwork, whatever. I play the piano. It was something I knew I enjoyed. I used to spend a lot of hours doing nothing on some missions, so I played music in my head sometimes, running through the notes. You know."

Sarah shook her head as she took his hand and rose to her feet. "No, I don't. Will you show me?"

His brows lifted. "What, right now? It's late."

"Just a short piece," Sarah prompted.

He took a deep breath and let it out slowly. "All right. But only if you play as well. I'm sure you're better than you think."

She shrugged. "Okay, if you want to put yourself through that torture . . ."

They took a seat next to one another on the piano bench,

but Luke's broad shoulders made it difficult for them both to comfortably get situated. "Here," Luke said, sliding his arm around her back to reach around to the keys to her right. "How's that?"

Sarah slid a little closer until she was pressed against his side. Every nerve came alive with awareness. She cleared her throat, trying to focus on the sheet music in front of her. Then her eyes went wide with surprise as she realized why she hadn't recognized the piece he'd been playing. "*You* composed this."

She felt him shrug. "It's not great. I've had a tune in my head the last couple of days and needed to get it down on paper."

She reached out to let her fingers skim over the notes on the page. It was a fairly straightforward composition, but it was beautiful in its simplicity. "What's it called?"

He hesitated, but then said, "It doesn't have a title."

She gave it one last perusal, getting a feel for the notes, and then began to play. But the heat of Luke's body seeped through the thin material of her T-shirt, making her stumble over the keys, striking notes as clumsily as she had when she'd been forced to perform in her recitals as a child.

A low chuckle rumbled in his chest, vibrating into her. "Here," he said, his fingers sliding over hers. "Like this. Gently, softly . . . like a lover's caress."

Sarah let her lids drift shut for a brief moment as his fingers stroked over hers, guiding her gently through the piece. When they played the final note of the first movement, she turned her head to offer him a smile and found his face just a breath away.

It would've taken just the slightest movement by either of them to complete the kiss that hovered in that moment between them. But then Luke pulled back and shifted on the bench so that he was straddling it.

"That wasn't so bad, was it?" he asked softly.

Sarah smiled. "No. Not bad at all." She cocked her head to one side, studying him, trying to figure out the man who was turning out to be far more complicated than he'd at first seemed. "You have a gentle soul, Luke."

His dark brows twitched together in a frown. "No. I don't. I wish I did." He brought his hand up, caressing her cheek with the back of his hand. "If for no other reason than I hate the thought of disappointing you. I like the way you see me—even if it's untrue."

Sarah shook her head. "How could you possibly—"

"I was a mercenary, Sarah," he blurted, letting his hand fall away. "You asked what I was doing when I was re-cruited into the Alliance. That was it. I'd left Special Forces to work for a special black-ops team run by the government. The shit I did during those two years . . . if you knew the half of it, you wouldn't look at me like I'm some kind of fucking hero."

Sarah recoiled, unable to believe what he was saying. "That's not true. I'm sure there's more to it than that."

"I like to think I never took out anyone who didn't de-serve it," he admitted. "But most of the time, I didn't really question my orders. Not until one particular job. That's when Jack's path crossed mine. Thank God he kicked my ass and knocked some sense into me. But there's still some-thing cold inside me, Sarah."

"Why are you telling me this?" she asked. "Are you trying to make me dislike you?"

"I just don't want you thinking I'm something I'm not," he told her.

She turned and straddled the bench as well so that she was facing him. "And what *are* you, Luke Rogan? Because you seem like a pretty damned remarkable man to me. And if not for you, my son and I might not be alive. So you can tell me whatever you want, keep me at arm's length if that's your intent. But I know what I've witnessed. I know what

I've felt. And I believe there's more to you than you care to admit."

Luke stared at her for a long moment, then allowed a smile to curve his lips. "You're one stubborn woman, you know that?"

"So I've been told." She stifled a yawn and stretched, belatedly realizing that she was braless and that her nipples were hard and growing harder by the second.

But instead of being embarrassed, her breath grew shallow when she noticed Luke's gaze snap up from her chest. "I should get you to bed," he said, his voice rough as he rose and extended a hand. He closed his eyes briefly and shook his head a little as if realizing what he'd said. "Shit. That sounded like a really lousy come-on."

She laughed and let him pull her to her feet. "Oh, it's not so bad as come-ons go," she teased.

"I'll need to step up my game," he said leading her toward the stairs. "No one's going to keep buying that you're my girlfriend if I act like an idiot every time I open my mouth around you."

"It's been quite a while since I've dated anyone," she said around another yawn, "but as I recall, acting like an idiot around the object of your desire is pretty much standard operating procedure."

His thumb smoothed over her skin. "Well, then maybe I'm doing better than I thought." He glanced her way, looking suddenly sheepish as they reached her bedroom door. His gaze locked with hers and she could feel the tension in the air. He bent forward as if he was going to kiss her again, but then cursed under his breath and straightened.

But Sarah grabbed his hand before he could pull away. "It's not okay."

* * *

Luke frowned, too distracted by the hard peaks of her breasts beneath her shirt to understand exactly what she was talking about. "Sorry?"

"When we were in the kitchen," she explained. "You said that putting the brakes on like I did was okay. But it's not." She edged a little closer, cautiously. "It wasn't fair for me to come on to you and then push you away. I'm just . . . confused. I haven't wanted to be with anyone since Greg died. But things are different with you, Luke. Because I do. Want to be with you."

Luke wasn't sure what to do or say. He peered down at her for a long moment, wanting desperately to kiss her again, to touch her, to hold her close and smooth her hair— if for no other reason than to soothe away the frown of confusion she wore. But he kept his arms at his sides, refusing to give in to his urges.

"If you just want a warm body, Sarah," he finally said, "I'll give you whatever you need. Hell, a man would have to be a total dumb-ass to walk away from an offer like that. But not until you're ready."

"And you don't think I'm ready?" she asked.

"I know you're not," he said. "Not at this very moment. You admitted you're confused. But even if you hadn't said a word, I could've seen it in your face."

She drew back a little at this, looking slightly offended. "And you know me so well after just a couple of days to-gether?"

God, had it only been a few days? It seemed as if she'd been in his life longer than that.

"Yeah, I think I do," he told her. "And I know that you're not the kind of woman to just fuck and run, Sarah." When her brows lifted in surprise, he quickly amended, "But *I've* never been with any woman more than one night. I don't get attached. I can't afford to."

"I'm not asking you to change that," Sarah assured him. "I don't *expect* anything from you. I just don't want you thinking that I'm a tease or that I'm toying with you or that I'm using you. It's not like that."

He felt like a total asshole for making her think he'd ever feel that way about her. "Jesus, Sarah, are you shitting me? I'd be even more of a bastard if I could blame you for being confused right now." Against his better judgment, he smoothed along the curve of her lovely face with the back of his fingers, his balls going tight when her eyes fluttered closed and her lips parted slightly on a gasp at his touch.

When she opened her eyes again, her gaze holding his in a heated stare, he almost forgot that he was trying to be a gentleman. And when she pulled him down to press a kiss to the corner of his mouth, his self-control completely deserted him.

His arms went around her, and he returned her kiss with a languid sweep of his mouth against hers. But he forced himself to end the kiss far sooner than he would've liked and released her with a sigh, wondering where in the hell all this fucking chivalry was coming from anyway. . . .

"Good night, Sarah," he said softly, backing away toward his own bedroom. He paused in his doorway and sent a glance her way, holding her gaze a long moment before entering his room and shutting the door.

Sarah let her head fall back against the wall and closed her eyes, focusing on the lingering warmth of Luke's lips upon hers, the feel of his arms around her. Finally, with a disappointed sigh, she slipped into her own room.

But sleep evaded her. She lay awake, waiting, hoping that any moment now he'd return and knock on her door. But no knock came. She could hear him tossing and turning in the room next to hers. And then she heard him pacing. But he never took the extra steps that would lead him to her bed.

And he wouldn't, would he? He'd left it to her to make the first move, to determine if she was ready to finally make peace with the past and try to find a little happiness, a little comfort in the arms of someone else.

The information Luke had shared with her about Greg had finally given her the closure she needed to move on. But she covered her eyes, wondering at the wisdom of giving in to the sexual tension between her and Luke.

He'd said he'd be a warm body if that's what she wanted—and, oh, yeah, she *definitely* wanted. But there was no mention of emotion or commitment of any kind. In fact, he was telling her flat out that he couldn't offer any of that. Was she willing to open herself up with no promise of anything more? Kissing him was one thing, but was she ready to cross the line he'd drawn in the sand?

The part of her that was aching to feel alive again, to feel desirable again, didn't give a damn if she was ready or not. But she'd never been able to divorce sex from emotion. Luke had been dead-on with his assessment on that one. She'd never been the kind of person who could just hook up and move on.

But the way Luke made her feel when he held her was something she'd never expected to feel again. In fact, if she was completely honest with herself, she was falling in love with the man already, even with the very pointed warning that he'd never be able to return her feelings.

Sarah rolled onto her side, trying to ignore the ache in the center of her chest. She was so screwed. For, no matter what she decided to do, Luke Rogan was going to break her heart. . . .

Chapter Seventeen

Luke's muscles burned with exhaustion, but he continued to pound the punching bag, preferring to focus on raging muscles instead of the kiss he and Sarah had shared the evening before. If he hadn't put a halt to things, he had a feeling he would've ended up in her bed, making love to her all night long as he longed to do.

And he had a feeling she would've regretted every moment of it the next morning.

There had been no mistaking the desire when she'd kissed him in the kitchen and then again when he'd walked her to her bedroom. Holy shit—he wasn't sure he'd ever been so knocked on his ass by a kiss. He'd been with his fair share of women, had even been with a few who'd taught *him* a thing or two. But Sarah damn near brought him to his knees.

And she wanted him too. She'd straight up told him so.

He punched the bag one last time with a roar of frustration.

It was official. He was the biggest dumbfuck in the world for walking away from what she was offering. He'd spent the rest of a sleepless night trying to convince himself of all the reasons why he shouldn't go marching to her room and drag her back into his arms. Because if the heat wracking his body had had any say in the matter, that's exactly what he would've done. Having her just a room away was like a persistent itch just beneath his skin that he couldn't scratch.

And that scared the shit out of him.

No other woman had ever affected him like this. So what the hell was it about Sarah that made things different this time around?

He snatched a towel from the bench and swiped at the beads of sweat on his chest and at the back of his neck, muttering a long string of juicy curses as he strode to the door. But he came to an abrupt halt as the door swung open and Sarah entered the room, dressed in curve-hugging black yoga pants and white T-shirt, her hair in a ponytail that hung down to her shoulders.

"Hey," he said, glad he could blame his breathlessness on his workout and not her sudden appearance. He went over to the shelf where his phone was hooked into the speakers and turned down the volume on the rough, gravelly music of From Ashes to New and turned back to her with a frown. "What are you doing up this early?"

"I couldn't sleep," she answered.

He studied her for a long moment before admitting, "Me either."

She cleared her throat, then said, "I thought maybe we could get started."

He did a mental double take. Oh, he wanted to get started all right, but thank Christ he had the presence of mind to clarify before dragging her into his arms and seeing if he could set a record for getting her naked. "Sorry . . . Get started?"

"You promised to teach me some of the self-defense moves you know," she reminded him.

"Oh, right. Shit. Sorry." He ran a hand over his hair and realized the last thing he needed to be doing at that moment was getting up close and personal with anyone. "Give me five minutes to grab a shower."

He snatched a clean towel from the shelf on the gym wall and headed for the small shower stall he'd installed in the tiny room adjacent to the gym area. It was little more than a four-by-four square of tile with a drain in the center of it and a shower curtain to keep the water from spraying all over the damned place. Not much of a barrier between him and Sarah as he stripped out of his clothes and stepped inside. The thought of her waiting for him just a few feet away had him turning down the temperature of the water to try to get his shit under control.

He stuck his face into the cold spray, letting the water sluice over him, hoping it would chill the raging heat within him. But it didn't do a damned bit of good. He pulled his face from the water with a curse and wiped the droplets from his face with an angry swipe.

A few minutes later, he toweled off quickly and pulled on his shorts, before heading back into the gym where Sarah was waiting. Her eyes widened slightly when he came in and he saw her swallow before shifting uneasily on her feet.

"You sure you want to do this?" he asked, coming to her and smoothing a hand down her upper arm.

She took a step back, shaking out her arms, her cheeks flushing that shade of pink he found so damned adorable, then nodded. "I'm sure."

*God*damn*, she's beautiful.*

"Start with getting out of a headlock," she suggested, turning her back to him. "You mentioned that one."

He sidled up behind her and blew out a deep breath before loosely draping one arm over her shoulder and around her neck while the other arm slipped around her waist, pulling her up against him. She bent her head forward, and the curve of her throat was so tantalizing as her ponytail fell forward, he impulsively dipped his head and pressed a kiss to the juncture where neck and shoulder met, eliciting a gasp from her.

He instantly eased his hold on her and started to step back, but she covered his hand at her waist, keeping him where he was. He hesitated for a moment, wondering what her reaction indicated, but when she said nothing, his grasp around her waist tightened. And, taking a chance, he pressed another kiss to the side of her throat, his lips lingering.

The pressure of her fingers on his arm increased, and she sighed softly before tilting her head to the side, allowing him better access. Not one to ignore such an invitation, Luke let his lips skim lightly along her skin. And when she gasped as his teeth nipped gently at the skin near her shoulder, he pressed her tighter against him.

"Grab my arm and step right," he murmured against her skin. When she did as instructed, he added, "Now tuck your chin, shove my arm up, and slip out of my hold."

She performed the action as instructed, easily getting out of the headlock. When he turned to face her, her chest was heaving in short, shallow breaths. "Show me again," she said, breathless. "At full speed."

He pulled her back into his arms and turned her around, drawing her in close as he had before. But this time, his kisses weren't as tentative and her sighs grew into moans as his hand around her waist skimmed across her belly, slipping beneath her T-shirt. And when his hand moved to cover one of her breasts, she arched slightly into his palm.

He groaned, not even bothering to stifle it, and kneaded the perfect handful. And when his thumb passed over her hardened nipple, he shuddered at the mewl that escaped her.

"Sarah," he whispered against her skin between kisses. "You need to get away from me."

She shook her head, ignoring the double-meaning of his words. "No, not yet . . ."

He closed his eyes on a ragged breath. "Are you sure?"

She cried out when he pinched her nipple, rolling it between his fingertips. "Oh, God . . . *yes*."

His hand slid back down her belly and under the waistband of her yoga pants, groaning with her as his fingertip came into contact with the bud of nerves at the top of her sex. She gasped and ground her hips against his aching groin in response. "Ah, Christ, Sarah," he gasped. "Don't do that, baby. . . . Not just yet."

But as he caressed her, her hips moved again, begging for more. His hand slid lower into her slick folds. Holy shit—she was swollen, wet, pulsing with need. And she was already close to coming, which made his cock swell even harder as he stroked her toward her release.

Her hands came up to grip the forearm that was draped across her chest, clinging to him as her hips swiveled against his palm. "Oh, God, Luke . . ." she gasped. "Please don't stop. . . ."

He ground his hips against her backside, aching for some relief of his own. He wished he could bury himself in her at that moment, but he wanted this to be all about her and her pleasure. When he felt her muscles tensing, he eased off, his caresses growing slower, more deliberate. And then he slid his hand around between them, smoothing the curve of her perfect ass, teasing along the seam of her body, slipping a finger into her when she spread her legs to grant him access. God, she was drenched.

"Oh my God, Luke," she gasped. "I'm coming. . . ."

He braced her against him with the arm across her chest as her first wave of release shook her, making her cry out. Then he shifted his hand back to the front of her sex, massaging her clit with renewed vigor, sending her over the edge with increased intensity.

Then, suddenly, she was slipping out of his hold with the move he'd shown her, putting some distance between them, her chest heaving. He held his breath, hoping he hadn't pushed her too far after the conversation they'd had the night before.

But then she came toward him in two quick strides and was dragging his head down to hers, kissing him harshly, hungry for more. "Take me upstairs," she murmured against his lips. "Now."

He pulled back just enough to peer down into her face. "Are you sure, Sarah? I don't want to be something you regret."

Her brows came together in a frown. God, the look in her eyes was killing him. She *trusted* him. He wished like hell he was worthy of that trust. Then she reached up and cupped his jaw. "I could never regret you."

Something about the look in her eyes, the warmth of her palm on his face, shattered his resolve. He grasped her around the waist, pulling her roughly to him and claiming her mouth in a harsh kiss.

Sarah only vaguely noticed as they made their way up the stairs to the second floor. It was still dark outside, and with only a light left on in the kitchen to guide them, it was amazing that they managed it without stumbling. But, seconds later, Luke was kissing her savagely as he pulled her into his bedroom and shut the door, turning the lock.

He left her mouth to press kisses along the curve of her throat. And when her arms went around his neck with a moan of need, he lifted her up, wrapping her legs around his waist, pressing her back to the wall. His hands now free, he slid them beneath her T-shirt, smoothing along her sides, around to the small of her back. As he plundered her lips, he slid a hand lower, slipping beneath her waistband to grip her ass.

She shuddered with pleasure, loving the way his rough

hands smoothed over her skin, so tender, so gentle, and yet so demanding, eliciting soul-shaking orgasms that left her equally spent and eager for more.

Apparently mistaking the reason for her shudder, he withdrew his hand and helped her to unhook her legs from around his waist. She slid down the wall until she was standing, but was glad one strong arm was wrapped around her waist, supporting her on her passion-weak knees. Luke braced his forearm against the wall, his face still close to hers. "Are you sure about this?"

"Certain," she replied. But when she took his face in her hand and tried to pull him down to kiss her, he resisted.

His gaze searched hers intently. "If I kiss you again, I'm not sure where it's going to go. I know where I want it to go, but I want you to take the reins here, Sarah."

Sarah swallowed hard, her body aching for his. She slid her hands over his shoulders, across his chest, marveling at the chiseled muscle. "Do you want me, Luke?"

"God, yeah, I want you," he said, his voice gruff. "I've wanted you since the moment I saw you. But I can't make you any promises beyond right now, Sarah. You know that."

"All I need is this moment," she said. When he opened his mouth to say more, she cut him off. "I want this, Luke. I *need* this. I need *you*."

He squeezed his eyes shut. "Ah, God . . . don't say that. You're making this harder."

Desire making her bold, she slid her palm along the hard length beneath his gym shorts. "I can tell. . . ."

He cursed under his breath. "Sarah . . ."

Her hand slid up his abdomen and back to his chest. "Your heart's racing."

His eyes opened and his gaze held hers. "So's yours."

"How can you tell?"

He offered her a sultry grin. "I can see it."

Her brows came together. "You can? Where?"

He bent and pressed a kiss to the pulse pounding in her neck, eliciting a gasp of pleasure. God, she would never tire of him kissing her there. The warmth of his lips at her pulse was enough to bring her to the brink.

But now it was her turn to take the lead. Her hands explored his skin, the contoured muscles of his back, his trim waist. She slid her hand beneath the waistband of his shorts, taking him in her hand, making him jerk with a groan. He was larger than she'd anticipated—and she'd definitely speculated.

"Tell me what you want, Luke," she whispered breathlessly, caressing his shaft. "I want to hear you say it."

"I want to touch you," he ground out, "feel your skin against mine. I want to bury myself in you, make love to you until you scream my name." He swallowed hard. "I want to lose myself in you, Sarah."

She released him to ease his shorts over his hips. He kicked his shorts aside before taking a step back, standing there naked before her. When she just stood there like an idiot, he prompted, "Undress for me, Sarah."

Sarah hesitated for a moment. She'd never been comfortable being completely nude in front of any of her handful of lovers, not even Greg. But there was something in the way that Luke's gaze devoured her that sent a thrill through her.

She toed out of her running shoes, then reached up and grabbed her ponytail holder and slowly eased it down the length of her hair, loving the way his eyes seemed to blaze with desire. She ran her fingers through her hair, shaking it out. Then she grasped the hem of her shirt and took her time bringing it up over her torso, revealing her belly slowly. She hesitated when she reached her breasts, but then she drew it up over her head and dropped it at her feet. Her bra followed a moment later.

His breath left him on a gasp as if he'd been holding it. Sarah grinned, loving the power she had over him at that moment, the rapt attention with which he studied every inch of her, his gaze hungry for more.

He swallowed hard and licked his lips when she slipped her hands under her waistband and eased her yoga pants over her hips, turning slightly as she slid them down her legs, her fingers skimming over the curves of her calves and thighs as she slowly stood.

But then, suddenly self-conscious, she shielded herself and turned her gaze to the ground, tempted to grab her discarded clothes and throw them on again. Until she felt the warmth of his body near hers. She lifted her eyes to see Luke standing inches from her. He gently took her hands and moved her arms, revealing her body to him.

Sarah's cheeks grew hot under his scrutiny. "My body was never quite the same after I had Eli."

His brows lifted. "I have no idea what you were like before, Sarah, but you're even more beautiful than I'd imagined." He bent and pressed a tender kiss to her shoulder, letting his hands skim from her fingertips to her shoulder. The back of his fingers trailed along her clavicle, between her breasts, drifted lightly over her hardened nipples. His hands smoothed down her sides to rest at her hips. And then he was kissing her again—gently, unhurriedly, until her nervous tension drifted away and her arms circled his neck.

Swiftly, Luke lifted her into his arms and carried her to his bed. He stretched her arms over her head, easing his body down beside hers and ravaging her lips until they were both panting.

When he lifted his head, the look he gave Sarah was impossible to interpret, but if she'd had to guess, she might've called it *reverent*—especially as that gaze traveled over every inch of her, taking her in as he followed along with his skimming fingertips. When his fingers had completed their exploration, his lips took over, pressing kisses to her bare shoulder, the valley between her breasts.

He took one tip in his mouth, his teeth gently scraping her already aching nipple, causing her to bow off the bed with a moan. She twined her fingers in his black hair, keeping him there for a moment but moaning anew when he moved to the other breast, his tongue flicking lightly.

After several blissful minutes, his kisses trailed down the center of her belly, along the curve of her hips, the inside of her thighs. He gently eased her thighs open, his gaze flicking up to meet hers before he lowered himself to caress her with his tongue.

Sarah instantly shattered apart with an orgasm that had her arching against his mouth, gasping his name as he drove her through it. His tongue delved deep, the intimate kiss almost more than she could stand.

"Luke," she gasped. "I need you inside me. Please."

He immediately lifted his head and crawled up the length of her body, pressing kisses to her skin as he went. When he was at eye level with her again, he kissed her languidly, slowly, as the aftershocks of her orgasm tapered off. Then he withdrew to fumble in the drawer in the bedside table, grabbing a condom, but he didn't immediately put it on.

"I'll take it slow," he told her. "If you're uncomfortable at all, I'll stop."

She stilled at his words. Good God . . . she hadn't thought about that. It'd been years since she'd been with anyone, and even with all the incredible foreplay, she might need to ease back into lovemaking.

He shifted, rolling up onto his side to slide the condom over his shaft, and then he was caressing her again, his thumb gently massaging her clit, his fingers plunging deep, readying her to receive him.

For a moment, she felt a stab of apprehension, not wanting to disappoint him when they'd come this far, but as his gentle caresses continued, her body began to ache for his.

Her need for relief, her need to feel Luke inside her, swamped her senses.

Her legs fell open as if on their own accord, welcoming him. She felt the head of his cock nudge her gently, slow thrusts bringing him in a little further each time, and then he was filling her, stretching her.

Luke ground out a curse when his next thrust sheathed him completely. Sarah gasped at the way her body accepted his—far from being painful after so many years of abstinence, pleasure engulfed her.

He withdrew and thrust again, his tempo slow as he peered down at Sarah. "Is this okay?"

"God, yes," Sarah breathed, her hips rising to meet him, matching his tempo. Her hands slid down his back, grasping his ass, encouraging him.

His tempo increased, but still he held back, letting her set the pace. She wrapped her legs over the backs of his thighs, opening herself up to him, urging him to take all she had to give. Then he was kissing her again, his tongue caressing and thrusting in time with their joined bodies.

As her muscles began to grow tighter, she urged him to go faster, thrust deeper, until he was pounding into her, their sweat-slicked skin slapping together in their frenzied love-making. When her release hit, she bit back the cry of ecstasy that threatened to erupt from her, too afraid of waking Eli down the hall.

Luke's thrusts grew slower then, longer, as his own muscles began to tense, and then he slammed into her with a low groan. He paused for a moment and then continued thrusting slowly a few more times as her own muscles continued to spasm.

Then they both went still, their breath coming in gasps. Sarah could feel his heart pounding where their chests were pressed together. But it began to slow as her fingertips trailed up and down his back.

When he at last withdrew, she moaned, suddenly feeling cold and empty. She rolled up onto her side to watch him as he walked to the adjoining bathroom, fascinated by the way his muscles stretched and contracted with each stride. But as he returned and slid between the sheets, pulling her into his embrace, she caught a glimpse of the time and sighed.

"I should probably go back to my own bed soon," she murmured, pressing a kiss to his chest. "I don't want Eli to see me leaving your room."

He pressed a kiss to the top of her head, his arm around her pulling her closer. "Probably."

"Eli looks up to you," Sarah explained. "I don't want him getting too attached or thinking that you and I have a future after we leave here."

Luke rolled her onto her back, cradling her in the crook of his arm. "We still have time."

Sarah wasn't sure what exactly he meant—was he talking about that morning or their stay with him? Or something else entirely? But as soon as their lips met, it no longer mattered.

Chapter Eighteen

The sun was fully in the sky by the time Luke jolted awake. He sent a glance toward his clock and cursed when he saw what time it was. His lack of sleep the night before and then making love to Sarah had left him completely fucking exhausted.

And it was no wonder. Holy shit. He'd never imagined how incredible it would be to bury himself in Sarah and lose himself as he'd told her he wanted to. She was even sexier and more amazing than he'd fantasized about. They'd made out again after sex, kissing and caressing, exploring one another's bodies. He'd been on the verge of grabbing another condom when floorboards had creaked down the hall.

Turned out it was just the wind buffeting the house, but it was enough to put a damper on the moment. But their final kiss was a promise for more later that night. He wasn't sure he'd be able to catch any additional sleep after she slipped from his bed to return to her room, leaving him with a raging hard-on after whispering what she planned to do to him when they came together again, but he'd dozed off before she'd even shut the door behind her.

Now he dragged his ass out of bed and quickly showered,

feeling guilty for not yet dealing with the horses. But when he went back downstairs half an hour later, he came to an abrupt halt when he saw Sarah dressed in snow pants and a ski jacket, gearing up to head out into the several inches of snow that had accumulated overnight. The way the ski jacket hugged her curves was enough to make his mouth water—and make him want to slowly unzip the thing to get to the full swells of her breasts beneath it.

"Where are you off to?" he asked, glancing around for Eli as he strolled toward her and gathered her into his arms.

"I'm going to help Eli build a snowman," she said, her words a little breathless as he began to nuzzle her neck. "You're welcome to join us."

"Can't," he told her between kisses. "Have to take care of the horses."

Her arms came up around his neck on a sigh. "Mel was already here. She and Eli took care of them. She said she was surprised you were still sleeping."

He chuckled, trying to unzip her coat, but failing when she batted his hand away. "Did you tell her you kept me up all night?"

She moaned softly as he finally managed to unzip her coat and slip his hand inside to cup her breast. "Uh-uh," she replied, pulling his head down and sucking his earlobe in a move that sent a jolt of desire straight down to his cock. "She already thinks we're a couple. I'm sure she's figured it out."

"I think we need to send Eli up to the loft to play games for a while," he murmured, nipping at her lobe and giving her a taste of her own medicine. "Then I can teach you a few more moves in the gym. . . ."

She giggled and managed to slip out of his hold, playfully shoving him away. "Later," she promised. "Now, are you coming?"

His brows lifted. "Not yet, but I hope to soon."

She rolled her eyes. "I meant, are you joining us outside?"

He grinned at her, loving the way her eyes lit up when she was bantering with him. "Yeah, give me a minute."

"Don't be too long," she called over her shoulder. But she paused after opening the door. "And remember—behave yourself."

"Can't make any promises," he told her. The look of warning she gave him made him chuckle.

Still grinning, he grabbed his gloves and headed outside. As much as he'd love to help with the snowman, he needed to start up the tractor so he could plow the driveway and at least part of the road. But he'd only made it a few yards toward the barn when a snowball smashed into his back, the snow slipping beneath the collar of his coat and making him cry out when it hit his skin.

He rounded on his assailant, ready to let loose with a few choice profanities, but Eli cried out with laughter and took off running, a delighted Chief nipping at his heels as he looked for cover. And then he saw Sarah's taunting grin before she pivoted and ran in the opposite direction.

"You guys picked the wrong man to mess with," he called out, scraping up some snow and forming it into a ball. "It's *on* now."

When Eli popped up from behind his hiding spot, Luke let the snowball fly, nailing the kid squarely in the chest. Eli clutched at his chest dramatically and fell to the ground, laughing. Luke trudged over, forming another snowball as he went.

When he loomed over Eli, he narrowed his eyes menacingly. "Do you yield?"

"I'm a Templar," Eli told him, scrambling to his feet. "I fight to the death!" With that, he lobbed a snowball he'd had concealed, nailing Luke, then took off again.

Luke jogged after him, catching him easily and scooping

him up around the waist. "I have a prisoner!" he called out. "Surrender or he gets another snowball!"

To his surprise, another mass of snow smacked into his back and he whirled around to see Sarah's eyes dancing with merriment.

"You flanked me," he said in dismay. She'd actually managed to get the drop on him. No one ever got the drop on him.

"Who's the badass now?" she asked with a wink at Eli.

Luke set Eli down with a laugh and charged toward her. She tried to run, but his long strides caught up to her in no time. When his arms went around her waist, they tripped over each other, falling into a tangle in the snow with Sarah on top of him.

Keenly aware of her body stretched out over his, Luke's laughter died on his lips, and he rolled Sarah onto her back, cradling her head in the crook of his arm. Sarah's chest was heaving as her own laughter subsided.

And before he even realized what he was doing, Luke was kissing her, taking his time, savoring the taste of her, the warmth of her in his arms.

A snowball smashed into his shoulder, spraying their faces with snow.

"I said it'd be okay to kiss her," Eli said, "but I didn't say I had to *see* it. Ewww!"

Luke grinned down at Sarah, and murmured quietly, "Guess I have trouble behaving when I'm around you. Is it okay to kiss you in front of Eli? Or should we sneak around and play grab-ass on the sly?"

Sarah laughed and pulled him back down for a quick kiss. "I think I'm okay with a kiss now and then. . . ."

"Hey!" Eli protested. "Don't make me throw another snowball. . . ."

"Okay, okay! Hold your fire!" Luke laughed. Then he said to Sarah, "How about we head back inside? Plowing roads and building snowmen can wait. It's way too cold out here."

"I don't know," Sarah said with a mischievous grin. "I'm feeling pretty warm right now."

His grin widened. "Oh, baby, *warm* is not even the word. . . ."

"I know where they are."

Stone held his phone against his shoulder and turned to his companion. "Jack, I've got to take this call. I'll meet you at Hal's room."

Jack Grayson nodded. "Sure. I'll see you upstairs."

As soon as Jack had disappeared into the hospital elevator, Stone slipped into an empty exam room. "You have seriously shitty timing. I'm supposed to call *you* when I need information."

"Fine," Evans drawled. "Would it make you feel better to call me back?"

"Don't be a smart-ass," Stone snapped. "Where are they?"

"Wyoming," Evans informed him. "Apparently, Luke Rogan's haven is a ranch he purchased from his stepfather."

Stone's brows lifted. "He has family? That could be useful."

"It may be the only way to get to him," Evans said. "The guy's security setup would give the Secret Service a hard-on."

Stone pulled open the exam door a crack, checking the hallway. "So how do you plan to earn your keep, Mr. Evans?"

"His stepsister is looking for a ranch manager," Evans told him. "I just need to make sure that they hire the right person."

"Let me guess," Stone drawled. "That person would be Eric Evans?"

"Something like that," Evans said. "I just need to get eyes on the place, gain access to the ranch without suspicion, so I can figure out the best way to extract the kid."

"Will your alias hold up to the Alliance's scrutiny? What if Rogan recognizes you?"

Evans scoffed. "I'm only found when I want to be. Rogan doesn't know me, so he won't be able to connect me to my past. Hell, considering how deep I was burned, I'm guessing my name's never even come up in casual conversation, let alone been included in the instruction videos for new recruits, warning them away from the evil temptations of," Evans whispered theatrically, "the Illuminati."

Stone rolled his eyes. "How long do you need?"

"Two weeks," Evans told him. "Tops."

"I'm not sure I can stall things that long," Stone hissed. "Apparently, my friend the senator is improving every day. And the information Eli has is only useful for so long."

"These things take time," Evans said. "If I move too quickly, I'll blow my cover. And just so we're perfectly clear—if I get made, Stone, I'm taking you down with me."

Stone heaved a sigh, considering his options. He still had his faithful who weren't nearly as concerned about such inconveniences as discretion or covering their asses. Perhaps he could make use of them. But, unfortunately, the zealots had proven they couldn't keep their fucking mouths shut. The idiot in Oregon had already revealed too much.

"Fine," Stone ground out. "But if the senator wakes up and starts spilling his guts . . ."

"I'll respond appropriately."

"I'm glad we understand each other." Stone disconnected the line, making a mental note to have Evans taken out as soon as this operation was over, then took a deep breath and donned an appropriately concerned expression before slipping out of the exam room and back into the hallway.

When he reached the floor where Blake was being cared

for, he slowed his steps. The hallway was dark, lit only by the emergency lights, and devoid of medical personnel, as if this section of the hospital had been abandoned long ago. It looked like something out of one of those zombie horror flicks—it was creepy as shit.

The only signs of life at all were the two men standing guard outside a door farther down the hall. He knew them instantly as his former Alliance brothers—Chase Nielsen and Ian Cooper. Good choices. He couldn't have chosen better for a security detail.

When they saw him coming, Chase extended his hand. "Good to see you, Jacob."

Stone shook his hand and gave him a terse nod in greeting. "You, too. Wish it was under different circumstances."

He then turned and offered his hand to Ian. The former U.S. Marshal hesitated slightly, sizing him up, before finally accepting Stone's hand. There'd always been a coolness between them, and that hadn't been made any better when Stone's miscalculation on a mission had cost the lives of their friends and had led to Stone's "reassignment."

Stone nodded toward the door they guarded. "Is Jack in there already? Am I able to see Hal?"

"Sure," Chase told him, giving his partner a pointed look as he pushed open the door.

Jacob clapped him on the shoulder as he passed, entering the room with a suitably somber expression. But he wasn't quite prepared for what he encountered. His friend and mentor lay on the hospital bed, looking pale, wan, feeble—a far cry from the powerful man who had been a surrogate father to him. Numerous monitors quietly beeped in discordant rhythm, displaying his vitals. The respirator wheezed softly as it pumped air into his lungs, keeping him alive.

Jack greeted him with a jerk of his chin, but Jacob's gaze

quickly alighted on the face of the lovely woman who sat in a chair at the side of her father's bed. Her eyes teared up when she saw him, but a smile brightened her face as she got to her feet.

"Jacob," she said with a hitch in her voice.

"Hi, Freckles," Jacob replied with a sad grin. He'd always had a soft spot in his heart for Hal's eldest daughter. It was the only thing that'd kept him from making a move on her years ago. He'd even go as far as to say he'd fallen in love with her once upon a time—if he believed in such a thing. He spread his arms. "How's my girl?"

She came forward without hesitation, hugging him tightly. "I'm so glad you came. I know it would mean a lot to Dad."

His arms tightened around her. "I'm so sorry," he whispered. "You know if I could've saved you from this I would have."

She pulled back and pressed a kiss to his cheek. "Always trying to protect us," she sighed. "Same old Jacob—I don't care what anyone says."

His brows shot up, his blood instantly beginning to boil. Who the hell was talking shit about him? He'd take the fuckers out. "What are they saying?"

She waved away his comments. "I don't even listen to all the political B.S. anymore," she said with a laugh. "I learned that after Dad's first campaign."

He heaved a mental sigh. Just the usual political bullshit then. "Well, as long as you're in my corner, Freckles, I'm golden." He then turned his attention to Jack. "So what are they saying about Hal? Has he woken up again? Said anything about who might be responsible for this?"

Jack shook his head. "No, he's only opened his eyes for a few moments. He hasn't made an effort to communicate."

Stone nodded. "And where the hell is Will? I figured he'd be here since this is all on his head."

Stone wasn't surprised that his ire earned a scowl from Jack. "If anyone's to blame, it's me."

"Stop it, Jack," Maddie interjected. "I'm the one who requested your help. You couldn't have known someone was going to try to assassinate Dad."

"No," Stone agreed, "but you all should've known better than to have the senator out in the open without his security detail. Where the hell were the other Templars actually assigned to him? Have you questioned *those* inept assholes?"

"What the hell, Jacob?" Jack spat. "Did you come here just to bust my balls about what happened? Because, I gotta tell you—"

"Enough," Maddie interrupted quietly, bringing them both to heel. "The only person to blame is the one behind this. And it's not going to do anyone any good if you're at each other's throats. And, yes, for the record, Commander Asher is questioning Dad's security detail himself. I don't know the commander that well, but from what I've seen of him during this incident, I don't envy those guys one bit."

Stone had to suppress a grin. His plan was working marvelously—more perfectly than he could've predicted. Maddie and Jack didn't suspect a thing. And Will Asher was obviously pursuing the avenue that Stone had intended to divert blame away from himself. Now he just needed to make sure Evans carried out his part of the plan before years of Stone's ass-kissing and planning went down the shitter. . . .

"Any luck?" Will asked as he entered the situation room to observe the ongoing interrogations of Hal Blake's personal security detail.

Finn shook his head, his thumbs rapidly tapping on the controller in his hands as he took out the alien invasion force on the big-screen TV devoted solely to gaming. If Will hadn't known the tech genius for years, he would've thought the guy was a just a slacker with a passion for violent video games, organic foods, and "bitchin' waves." But even when Finn didn't seem like he was paying attention, he was always listening, always soaking in everything going on around him, his mind working at a million miles a minute.

"Nah," he said with a shrug. "They were clueless. And pretty pissed off about it, too."

"You sure?" Will asked, needing to be certain that they hadn't left any avenue of inquiry unexplored.

"If Adam wasn't able to get anything out of 'em, you know they're clean," he replied.

Adam Watanabe hadn't been with them long, having transferred from the Temple Knight & Associates office in Japan just a year before at the request of his provincial commander. There'd been an incident that required him to relocate and assume a new identity. Will hadn't been briefed on the incident and Adam hadn't bothered to confide in him. But as long as he performed his duties in the board-room and in the field, Will was cool with the guy keeping his secrets.

Besides, he was a master at psychological manipulation and had proven his skills on several occasions already. So Finn had a damned good point.

But that didn't get Will any closer to knowing who the hell was behind the attempt on Hal's life or the attempted kidnapping of his grandson. Will needed a name. He needed to know if the mole was someone in the Grand Council or if it was someone closer to Hal.

He cursed under his breath. "I need a name, Finn."

"Wish I could give you one," Finn assured him. "Unfortunately, we've got nothing from these guys. You could question the members of the Grand Council, see if one of those ass-hats has a side game going on."

Will grunted. "Yeah, the high commander would love it if I hauled in his cronies. He's already told me they're off-limits as far as questioning them in person goes."

"Well, we know he didn't tell Sarah," Finn pointed out. "Who else would he trust with that info?"

Will crossed his arms over his chest. "He was closer to Maddie than Sarah."

"Nah," Finn said, shaking his head. "No way is she the one. She won't leave her father's side."

"Because she cares that much," Will asked, "or because she's afraid he'll give something up before she can stop him?"

"Damn," Finn drawled. "Your cynicism is harshing my chill."

Will grunted. "I'm not a cynic. I'm a realist. And I know that even the closest relationships might have—" He cursed under his breath, pissed with himself for not seeing another option sooner. "Where's Jacob Stone? Is he still at the hospital?"

Finn's brows went up slightly. "You think Stone knows something?"

Will's eyes narrowed as he continued to watch Hal's security detail on the monitor. "Don't know. But maybe these guys could tell us the last time Stone paid Hal a visit. How are we doing on moving the assets?"

Finn glanced up to check a bank of monitors on which code scrolled in a continuous update. "Almost there. The European caches are almost good to go. Portugal hit a snag with customs, but we're good now."

Will sighed. It was what he wanted to hear. What he'd pretty much demanded of his team. But it meant he was going to have to make a call to Luke. And he had a feeling it wasn't going to be a pleasant conversation. . . .

Sarah was cleaning up the dishes from lunch when the cell phone Finn had dropped off for her began to ring. Frowning, she dried off her hands and snatched it up from the countertop, her frown growing when she didn't recognize the number.

She thought about letting it go to voicemail—or maybe letting Luke answer. But Eli, Luke, and Chief had headed back outside as soon as the temperature hit forty degrees, eager to check on the mare who was so near her time to give birth. Besides, what was she afraid of? If someone was calling her secure line, it had to be a trusted caller. Right?

Taking a deep breath, Sarah accepted the call, hesitating a second or two before finally bringing the phone to her ear. "Hello?"

"Sarah?"

She exhaled in relief, not realizing she'd been holding her breath. "Jacob! How did you get this number?"

"From your sister," he assured her, his familiar voice bringing tears to her eyes. "I'm here with your father and Maddie. But I wanted to check on you, kiddo. Are you doing okay? Are you safe?"

She nodded, sniffling now that she'd dared allow emotion to get the better of her. "Yes, yes, I'm fine. Eli and I are safe. But how did you—" She laughed at her own naiveté. She'd been about to ask him how he knew where her father was or the truth about his condition. But the answer to that question was obvious. "You're one of them."

"Not anymore," he told her, his voice tinged with a hint of sorrow. "I was once, but I left the Alliance. I'm now just a *confrere*, like your father."

"Then you've known about everything all along," she

said, not bothering to disguise her feelings of betrayal. Even Jacob —the man who'd been like a brother to her when they were growing up, a son to her father—had deceived her.

He sighed. "I'm sorry, darling. Secrecy and deception are necessary to protect the Alliance."

She laughed bitterly. "And everyone could be trusted with the truth but me? Wow. Thanks."

"That's not what I meant," he assured her. "I was born into this, Sarah. My family has been in the Alliance since it was formed. Your father could confide in me in ways that he couldn't in you and Maddie. Maddie only came to know the truth later."

"Yeah, so I've heard," Sarah said on a sigh. Deciding to leave the past behind, she changed the subject. "How's Dad?"

There was a slight hesitation before he said, "I think you need to prepare yourself."

Sarah's knees suddenly grew weak, and she pulled out one of the bar stools at the center island and collapsed onto it. "But, I thought he was improving. . . ."

"They're obviously doing everything they can," Jacob assured her. "But I feel like someone needs to be honest with you, Sarah. Clearly, you've been kept in the dark far too long."

"I need to see him, Jacob," she insisted. "The way he and I left things . . . I'll never forgive myself if I don't get the chance to see him before . . ."

"Then you should be here," he agreed. "Come to Chicago. You can stay at my apartment in the city. Or, better yet, my house in the country."

Sarah's heart began to pound at the thought of leaving the safety of Luke's ranch and possibly putting herself and her son at risk. "I'll have to check with Luke."

"Leave Eli there with your handler," Jacob suggested.

"Then you know the boy will be safe. Or send him to me. My security detail can keep him safe. And I'll have Allison tend to him personally. He'll want for nothing while he's here."

Sarah mulled over his suggestions. "Thanks, Jacob. I appreciate it. But . . . things are complicated."

Sarah could hear Jacob sigh. "All right, but the offer stands. If you need anything—place to stay, information, just someone to talk to, you know you can call me. You and Maddie are sisters to me, Sarah. There's nothing I wouldn't do for you. You have this number now. It's secure. Use it, okay?"

Sarah swiped the tears from her cheeks. "Thank you, Jacob. I will."

She'd just hung up when Eli came rushing into the house, his snow boots slipping on the hardwood floors in his haste. "Mom! Mom, hurry up!"

Sarah's heart leapt into her throat as she ran after him. Dear God . . . had something happened to Luke?

She pulled on her boots and grabbed her coat, yanking it on as she went. Her breath was sawing in and out of her lungs when she reached the barn a few steps behind Eli, but she was finally able to swallow her heart when she saw Luke kneeling in the straw inside the stall beside his mare and her new foal.

Sarah covered her mouth with her hands, marveling at the beautiful little black filly, then turned wide eyes to Luke. "You delivered her?"

Luke shrugged. "Her mama did all the work. I just helped out a little. I honestly wasn't expecting this little gal this afternoon, but I guess she had other plans." He rose to his feet, not bothering to suppress his grin. "Guess we should give Davis and Mel a call, yeah?"

After making sure the mare and her foal were safe and warm and settled in, they made their way back to the house,

Eli giving Sarah a play-by-play of the foal's birth in vivid detail.

"Oh my gosh, Mom," he gushed. "It was so gross! It was totally cool."

He relayed the story again a couple of hours later when Davis and Mel, after coming over, returned from the barn.

"Well, I think this calls for a celebration," Mel said, ruffling Eli's hair. "What do you think, kiddo?" When Eli nodded enthusiastically, Mel turned her attention to Sarah and Luke. "What do you say? Want to join us for dinner at the main house? I promise I'll keep Davis away from the stove."

Davis laughed, raising his hands in surrender. "Hey, I never claimed to be a gourmet."

Sarah sent a look Luke's way to see if he was comfortable with their leaving the safety of the haven. When he gave a terse nod, she was glad to accept the invitation, eager to get away from the house for a little while.

And the evening proved to be as lively as she'd hoped. Eli had to tell his birthing story to Jim again after dinner when they were all gathered in the great room in front of a roaring fire. When Eli had finished, Jim then shared a few stories too, from when he was a cowboy running the ranch on his own, growing his herd of cattle little by little as he could afford it. Sarah was stunned to hear how many head of cattle and horses Jim had owned at the ranch's height. Breeding horses had been an afterthought, but a profitable one, from the sound of it, and had brought Luke's mother into Jim's life.

Sarah could see the sadness in his eyes when he spoke of Lyla and that time in their lives, but she could also see how sharing his stories, speaking of his business, and how he'd built it with his blood, sweat, and tears, completely changed his demeanor, giving her a glimpse of the man he'd been. It was too bad that he'd had to downsize since his stroke.

"Maybe, when it's time to train that little filly, Luke here can show you how it's done," Jim suggested.

Eli's face instantly brightened but then fell almost as quickly. "I don't think we'll be visiting that long."

Jim nodded, sending a wink toward Sarah. "Oh, I don't know. Your mama's awfully pretty. I think Luke might be smitten."

"Smitten?" Mel chimed in, grinning at her stepbrother when he actually blushed. "I'd say he's got it pretty bad. What do you think, Davis? You ever seen Luke with the big puppy eyes like he has when he looks at Sarah?"

"Piss off," Luke grumbled, lobbing one of the couch cushions at Mel.

"Nope, never have," Davis said on a chuckle. "But I don't know what Sarah sees in the dude. Got no sense of humor whatsoever. All he does is frown."

"That's not true," Sarah said, defending him before she realized they were teasing. But when all eyes turned to her, she linked her fingers with Luke's and offered him a loving grin. "He has a beautiful smile. It's his mother's smile."

The tone in the room immediately grew somber. "That he does," Jim agreed. "I fell in love with Lyla the first time I saw that smile." Then he nodded toward Luke. "And when I saw that her boy had the same smile, I knew there'd be something special about him too. And I was right. He keeps it hidden down deep, but Luke's heart's as big as his mama's was."

Luke suddenly stood and strode from the room. Sarah sent a confused glance around the room, but no one else seemed to think there was anything out of the ordinary in his sudden departure. They merely exchanged sad looks that left Sarah feeling like she was missing some vital piece of the puzzle.

"Hey, Eli," Davis said. "How are you at checkers? I've yet to find someone in this town who could take me on."

With Eli distracted, Sarah stood to go after Luke, but as she passed by his chair, Jim caught her hand in his gnarled fingers. "He's a good man, Sarah," he told her. "Don't let him tell you otherwise."

She gave him a quick nod, then hurried out of the room, finally finding Luke standing in front of the kitchen window, staring out into the darkness.

"You okay?" she asked softly, glad when he draped an arm around her shoulders and pulled her in close.

After a moment's hesitation, he nodded. "Yeah. Just makes me uncomfortable when Jim says things like that. I made the man's life hell for years—ungrateful, rebellious little shit that I was. I think maybe his stroke affected his memory."

Sarah wrapped her arms around his waist and peered up at him. "I don't. A father doesn't give up on his son just because he makes mistakes. And Jim obviously thinks of himself as your father. He loves you. So do Mel and Davis. They want you to be happy."

He kept his gaze trained on the window, but Sarah could see his frown deepening. "I've never told them the truth about what I did after I left Special Forces—or about the Alliance. If they knew all the shit I've done . . . they might change their minds about me."

At this, Sarah reached up and cupped his jaw and turned his face toward her, forcing him to look at her. "I didn't," she said. "And they've loved you longer." When his brows twitched together at her choice of words, she said in a rush, "I mean, they'd understand that you were doing what you thought was right, that you were trying to protect the innocent. They'd understand that you are part of something larger than yourself and are trying to make a difference in the world."

He studied her in silence for a long moment, making Sarah wonder if maybe she'd said too much. Or if maybe he was wondering if she'd been implying that she loved him when she was talking about his family. Awesome. A guy who'd already made it clear that commitment was a big, fat, never-gonna-happen, and here she was throwing the L word around. She wouldn't have been surprised if he'd suddenly turned and bolted and never looked back. God, the last thing she wanted him to think was that she was the kind of woman who was planning a wedding after one unforgettable night.

But then his lips swept over hers in a tender kiss, and then another and another until her arms slipped around his neck and the kiss deepened. At some point, he lifted her up onto the countertop and stepped into the V of her thighs. When he finally drew back, he pressed another kiss to her nose, making her grin, before resting his forehead against hers.

"I think we should head home," he murmured, his voice thick with promise.

Sarah gave him a slow smile, relieved that her unfortunate choice of words hadn't sent him racing in the opposite direction. "It's still early."

He groaned. "All right. We'll stay a little longer, but then I'm taking you home and making love to you until we're both too exhausted to move."

Sarah's breath caught in her chest at his words. He'd told her he'd never been with anyone more than once, that he couldn't risk getting attached to anyone. She blinked up at him, not daring to ask what it meant that he was willing to break what had seemed like a hard and fast rule. "Are you sure?"

He held her gaze for a long moment before finally nodding. "Yeah. I'm thinking we'll stay another hour—two max. Agreed?"

The way the heat spread through her at the mere thought of being in Luke's arms again, there was really only one way to answer. "Agreed."

Chapter Nineteen

Luke was so distracted by his thoughts of getting Sarah naked that it was hard as hell to concentrate on anything else the rest of the night. So when he agreed to meet Mel in town the next morning to interview the first few ranch manager applicants, he hadn't really been paying attention to what she'd said about where or when. Luckily, Sarah had been listening and had no qualms about kicking his ass out of her bed in time for him to get up and moving.

Well, she'd woken him up on time, anyway. But getting him out of her bed took a little longer—especially when she'd rolled over onto her back and stretched her arms over her head in an effort to shake off the last vestiges of sleep and he'd taken it as an invitation for a little morning lovin'—starting off with some attention to those perfect breasts.

But as he stood there in the bathroom, staring into the mirror as the steam from his shower filled the room, it was taking all his willpower not to go back to her room and see if she would be up to another round.

He pulled a hand down his face, trying to shake off his insatiable desire for her. It would all have to end soon. Either they'd catch the bastard who was behind Eli's attempted kidnapping or they'd wait him out until all the

Alliance's assets were safely moved and Eli's information was of no use to anyone. And then Sarah and Eli would be relocated somewhere permanent where they could get back to living their normal lives. Without him.

For some reason, the thought of not knowing how they were doing, if they were safe made him antsy, angry. Who would protect them if someone else came after them for some other reason? Or maybe just because of who Sarah's father was?

And who would be there for Eli as he got older? Luke knew what it was like to grow up without a father, to never have a man in his life to depend on, to be there for him. By the time Jim had come into Luke's life, the damage had already been done. But Luke had been too damned stubborn to accept the love and guidance of a stepfather who would've taken a bullet for him or his mother without hesitation.

The idea of Eli having to go through the same thing pissed him off. And the idea that there might eventually be someone else who *would* fill that role for the kid pissed him off even more.

But what tormented him most was the thought of not seeing Sarah's bright smile every morning, not holding her in his arms all night long. He wasn't a dumb-ass. He realized what was happening to him. He could tell by the way his chest went tight when he thought about eventually having to say good-bye. And he knew the smartest thing to do was close off, not let her get any closer than she already was.

And he had a feeling she was closer than she should've been. He'd been replaying her words from the night before over and over again. *They've loved you longer.* Did that mean she was in love with him? God, how in the hell had he let things go this far? He never should've given in to temptation. He was a Templar, for fuck's sake. Their entire Order had been built on self-discipline. But when it came to Sarah, he couldn't follow his own damned rules.

He braced his hands on the vanity countertop and let his head hang down between his shoulders, the realization of what he needed to do weighing him down. He had to end things, had to bottle his shit up and bury it deep again. He never should've let Sarah get this close and now for her own good he should pull a dick move and tell her that he'd gotten what he wanted and was ready to move on. That it'd all just been part of the act, part of their cover. That he didn't care for her.

He had to lie to her.

A soft knock on the bathroom door brought his head up. He opened it to see Sarah standing there in his shirt, her hair mussed from their lovemaking, a look of concern on her face, and he knew he was completely screwed.

"Are you okay?" she whispered, keeping her voice down so as not to wake Eli, who was still asleep down the hall. "You've been in here for a long time. Have you even taken a shower yet?"

He took her hand and pulled her inside, shutting the door quietly behind her before pulling her into his arms and pressing a kiss to the side of her throat.

"I got distracted thinking about you," he murmured against her skin when she sighed and leaned against him. "And now that you're here, I'm not sure I can keep my hands to myself."

"Who said I want you to?" she asked, smoothing her hands lightly over his shoulders and back.

When he slid a hand between them and found her ready for him, he couldn't help a self-satisfied chuckle. "You know, if we get started, it's going to be harder for me to leave," he warned, even as he caressed her—unsure whether the warning was more for him or for her.

"Well," she sighed, letting her head fall back on her shoulders, "I can't have you leaving here hard. . . ."

His laughter died on a groan as he sank to his knees,

shoving his shirt up over her hips to bare her to him. She grasped his hair as he kissed and suckled, teasing her to her release. And then she was down on her knees with him, kissing him hungrily as she stroked his shaft, bringing him near the brink before he finally grabbed her wrist to stop her.

He sank back on his heels and ran a hand through his hair and cursed, squeezing his eyes shut to keep his shit together. But his eyes popped open when he felt her straddle him. Then she was taking him in her hand and rising up only to ease down slowly, sheathing him completely with a moan.

Ah, Christ.

She felt amazing without any barrier between their bodies. Too amazing. He clenched his jaw. "Sarah," he ground out as she rose up again until he was just barely inside her, then sank down, drawing a juicy curse from him. "I don't have any condoms in here."

She increased her pace slightly, grasping the back of his neck. "Look at me, Luke."

He opened his eyes, meeting and holding her gaze as she continued to move. He didn't dare thrust to meet her for fear he'd come inside her. But with each silky caress, his willpower began to crumble.

"I want to feel you like this," she told him, breathless.

"I've never been with anyone without protection," he assured her. "I wouldn't put you at risk."

She kissed him long and deep as she continued to move. "I know," she said when the kiss ended. "I trust you."

Luke returned her kiss and wrapped his arms around her waist, guiding her up and down his shaft as he felt her muscles gripping him, pulsing, her release building. And when she came, he nearly lost it. He'd never experienced anything like this.

And then she arched back, gripping his shoulders as she

rode him. The way her pleasure continued to play out over her face was fascinating, breathtaking. He held his own release back as long as he possibly could, his own pleasure secondary to observing hers. But when he finally thrust with a groan, his seed flowing into her, he shuddered, overcome with emotion at the depth of her trust in him.

And as he cradled her tenderly against him, their bodies still joined, their hearts pounding in time with one another, Luke knew peace for the first time in his life.

Sarah took her time showering, her body still humming with pleasure from making love with Luke. As usual, they'd parted and gone their separate ways before Eli woke up. And no matter how many times she adjusted the temperature of the water, it never seemed to replace the warmth of Luke's arms around her.

When she finally went downstairs, she was surprised to see Luke and Eli watching reruns of *MythBusters* on TV, their feet propped up on the coffee table. "Don't you have to meet Melanie?" she asked Luke, glancing at the clock on the fireplace mantel.

"I called to tell her I was running late and that I was bringing you and Eli with me," Luke told her. "As long as you're up to another trip to town, that is."

She gave him a teasing grin. "As long as you promise not to accost any car-shopping tourists based merely on my crappy intel."

"It's a date then," he said with a wink, making Sarah wonder exactly what he was up to.

"Eli, you'd better have some breakfast before we go," Sarah said, heading toward the kitchen.

"Already ate," Eli called out. "Luke gave me bagels and coffee."

Sarah's brows lifted. "*Coffee?*"

"Decaf," Luke clarified. "I'm not *totally* corrupting the kid."

"And we've already taken care of the horses," Eli assured her. When she expressed her surprise, he added, "Well, you took a *long* time to get ready."

She sent a smile Luke's way. "I was distracted."

Luke chuckled, and a few moments later as they were trailing behind Eli, Luke pulled Sarah into his arms for a quick kiss. "Next time, what do you say we get distracted together?"

She kissed him back, giving his bottom lip a playful nip. "Deal."

And distracted seemed to be the word of the day. All she could think of while she and Eli sat in the orange vinyl booth at the diner where Luke and Mel were interviewing ranch hands was the way her body ached for Luke. And the sorrow that filled her whenever she reminded herself that it would soon be ending.

In fact, she was so distracted that she didn't notice the man in a black overcoat slide into the booth across from theirs until she felt the weight of his stare lingering upon her. Her gaze drifted away from Luke, who was sitting at another table with his arms crossed over his chest and his attention focused on the interviewee, and her eyes locked with the stranger's.

When he didn't look away as most people would've, she offered him a tentative smile and turned her attention back to Eli, who was chatting merrily about the tricks he was training Chief to do. But the weight of the man's stare continued to press down upon her, forcing her gaze back to his.

Exasperated, she finally asked, "I'm sorry. . . . Do I know you?"

The man's grin widened in a slow smile, and then in a blur of motion, he lunged from his table and grasped Eli's arm, pulling the boy out of the booth and into a headlock before Sarah could blink. She was on her feet in an instant, ready to spring, but the man drew a knife and brandished it at her before she could move. The diner went quiet in an instant, but in her peripheral vision, she could see Luke on his feet as well, inching forward, his shoulders hunched, ready to attack.

"All of you, empty your pockets," the man informed her with a maniacal grin, his eyes vacant. He was clearly blitzed out of his mind.

"Let my son go," Sarah demanded with a calm she didn't feel. "I'm warning you."

She had no idea where the hell her bravado was coming from, but she'd tear the son of a bitch apart before she'd let anything happen to Eli.

The guy wasn't impressed, though. He laughed with a crazed titter and slowly began to back toward the kitchen. "I want everyone's money now or the kid dies."

Sarah's gaze flicked down to Eli's and saw his expression harden. Then, in one fluid motion, he stepped right and slipped out of the headlock just as Luke had taught him. And something primal seemed to awaken in Sarah. A calm settled over her, and something buried deep within her subconscious took over.

She lashed out, grabbing the man's knife hand and rolling into him, bringing her elbow up and smashing his nose. She only vaguely registered Luke vaulting over tables and chairs to get to her as she dropped down and spun, twisting the man's arm up behind him, the sound of bones snapping as she bore down on his elbow. He dropped down onto his knees with a strangled cry, the knife falling from his grip.

But even as quickly as Luke barreled forward, another patron who'd been sitting in the booth behind Sarah and Eli jumped in, shoving the assailant to the ground and pressing his knee into the guy's back.

"You okay?" the patron asked, his gaze sweeping over Sarah and Eli. "This asshole hurt either of you?"

Sarah shook her head, clearing the rush of adrenaline that had gripped her, confused by her actions. "Yeah, yeah. I'm okay." She straightened and reached for Eli and dragged him into her arms, checking him over. The boy was trembling. But then Luke's arms were going around them, drawing them to him, holding them close. "Sarah, baby? Are you hurt? Eli?"

She shook her head and heard Eli confirm the same. She then looked down at the man who'd come to her assistance. "Thank you."

The guy grunted. "Don't know that I did much of anything. Looks like you had things pretty much under control."

The police burst into the diner at that moment, one of them relieving the patron and cuffing the guy on the ground while his fellow officers worked to calm the other patrons in the diner.

At that point, Luke extended a hand to the man still standing nearby. "Thank you for jumping in."

The guy shrugged. "Like I said, I didn't even have a chance to do much."

Sarah felt the weight of Luke's curious gaze on her for a moment, but he only said, "Still, I appreciate it."

The guy shook Luke's hand. "My pleasure. Crazy shit, huh? The guy's obviously on something, probably just drifting through and looking for some quick cash for a fix."

"Do you live around here?" Luke asked, still holding Sarah and Eli close, his tone cautious.

The man shook his head. "Nah, just passing through myself. Rancher I worked for had to pack it in, so I'm headed to Montana to see if I can find some work there."

"You should stay here and work for Luke and Mel," Sarah told him. When she glanced up and saw Luke's face go dark, she immediately realized her mistake. "I . . . I mean—"

"I'm looking for some hands and a ranch manager," Luke told him. "My sister manages the ranches, so it's ultimately her call. And you'd have to go through a thorough background check. That's *my* call."

The man blinked rapidly. "Uh, okay. Yeah, sure, that'd be fine. Who do I talk to?"

"You guys okay?" Melanie gasped, finally able to make her way to them.

Sarah nodded. "We'll be fine."

"We're leaving as soon as we talk to the police," Luke told her. "But this guy might be interested in one of the positions you want to fill."

Mel nodded, her curious gaze flitting between them. "Oh. Okay. Sure. What's your name?"

The guy offered her a wide, toothy smile and extended his hand. "Eric Evans. Nice to meet you."

Luke squinted against the afternoon sun as they drove back to the ranch, wondering exactly what in the fucking hell had just happened. All three of them sat in tense silence and Sarah looked like she was about to lose the club sandwich she'd had for lunch. But it was actually Eli who finally was the first to speak, asking the question on all their minds.

"Was that one of them?" he whispered from the back seat. "Did they find us?"

Luke sent a glance Sarah's way and saw the fear in her eyes. "No," he said. "I don't think so. That guy looked like a junkie. I'm sure it's just a coincidence."

"How can you be sure?" Sarah asked, her voice tight.

"I can't," he admitted. "But he didn't seem organized or specifically after Eli. I think it was just wrong place, wrong time. We get drifters through here, now and then, on their way to somewhere else. I'll check in with the sheriff later today to see what he can tell me."

Neither of them asked about Sarah's ability to disarm the junkie. But Luke sure as hell planned to as soon as they were alone. She'd moved like someone who'd been highly trained in disarming and debilitating an enemy. And yet, when he'd been teaching her how to get out of a headlock, she'd moved like a novice. But why the hell would she con him? Pretend not to know how to defend herself? What the hell kind of game was she playing?

He'd been planning to take Sarah and Eli around town—show them where he'd gone to high school and where he'd liked to hang out when he was in town, and take them to the coffee shop that had been his haunt when he'd had an argument with his mom or Jim and needed to get the hell away from home for a while. But it was just as well that he'd scrapped those plans and was taking them back to the ranch. If Sarah was hiding something from him, pretending to be something she wasn't, he'd already trusted her with too much, had already let her get too close.

When he parked the SUV in front of the house, none of them moved to get out of the vehicle, sitting in silence for several moments before Luke finally removed his hat and ran a hand through his hair on a sigh. "We'd better see if Chief needs to go out. I'll go with you when you're outside from now on, Eli."

Sarah's gaze snapped to him. "Then you *are* concerned."

"No," Luke said, shaking his head. "I meant what I said. But this was a wake-up call. We've been too careless, too complacent. In a lot of ways."

With this Sarah threw open the door and got out, striding toward the house without looking back.

"What's the matter with Mom?" Eli asked.

Luke didn't even know how to answer that. The thought

of confessing to Eli that he was about to lie to Sarah and put an end to what was going on between them made his throat go tight. So he just deflected with, "She's just worried about you."

Luke opened his door and motioned for Eli to come out. When the kid hopped down and slammed the door, Luke gave his shoulder a squeeze. "I'm proud of you, Eli," he told him. "You handled yourself well, kid."

"I was scared," Eli murmured low enough that only Luke could hear as they approached the house. "But don't tell my mom that, okay?"

Luke nodded. "Being scared is good, Eli," he replied, just as softly. "It can keep you alive."

It was a good hour later before Eli was comfortable enough to leave Luke's side to go upstairs and read for a while, but he was careful to keep Chief with him. Sarah had gone to her room as soon as they'd returned, but she wasn't there when Luke went in search of her to talk. He walked the house, calling out to her a couple of times, checking in with Eli to see if he'd seen her, but couldn't find her.

His heart was beginning to pound with apprehension when he finally went downstairs to the basement and found Sarah sitting in the middle of the gym floor with her legs drawn up to her chest, her forehead resting on her knees.

"What the hell happened with you at the diner?" he demanded without preamble. His phone began to buzz, but when he glanced down and saw it was his commander, he sent it to voicemail. Asher could wait.

Sarah slowly lifted her head but didn't look at him. "I don't know," she whispered so softly, he barely even caught the words.

"How *the fuck* did you know how to disarm that guy?" he pressed, his voice growing louder.

She grimaced. "*I don't know.*"

He charged into the room, determined to find out what

the hell was going on, but he came to an abrupt halt when she lifted her eyes to him and he saw her gaze was unfocused, her pupils wide and dark. He immediately dropped down to his knees and grasped her chin. "Sarah, baby, look at me. C'mon."

"I can't," she muttered, her voice slurred. "My head hurts. I can't think. Can't focus."

Realization hit Luke, making him clench his jaw to keep a furious string of curses from slipping out.

She really didn't know how she'd disarmed the junkie in the diner. And she didn't know because someone had implanted that knowledge in her head the same way they'd implanted the knowledge of the Templar treasures in Eli's. And when that knowledge had spilled out in a moment of danger, it'd taken a toll on her grey matter.

Luke pressed a kiss to her forehead, then lifted her into his arms. "It's all right, beautiful. I gotcha."

Chapter Twenty

Jacob Stone sent a furious glance at his phone as it buzzed where he'd left his pants beside the pool, fully expecting it to be yet another call from Will Asher. The son of a bitch was relentless. Apparently, the pricks who'd been assigned to Hal's security detail had placed him at Hal's mansion a few days before Hal had filed his succession plan. He'd managed to deny any knowledge of the plan and sound convincing—at least, that's what he'd thought. Except the bastard had called again, wanting Stone to come in and chat with Adam Watanabe. Yeah, right, like that was going to happen. He'd heard about the latest addition to Will's team, and there was no fucking way he was going to get in a room alone with the guy. God knew what he'd have him confessing to.

So he'd ignored the last couple of calls and voicemails, instructing Allison to inform Asher that he was in business meetings and was unable to talk. But he wouldn't be able to put him off for long. Sooner or later, Will was going to show up on his doorstep.

Hearing the countdown clock pounding like a funeral drum, Stone had entered the pool house to find Allison swimming and had been persuaded to join her to "relieve his tension." And, obliging little bitch that she was, she'd been more than willing to let him strip her out of her skimpy little bathing suit.

Things had just been starting to get interesting when the damnable phone had started to ring again. He got out of the pool, muttering a curse, and snatched up the phone. He was relieved to see it wasn't Will Asher, after all. "This had better be good, Evans. I'm in the middle of something."

"I thought you'd like to know that I have a final interview for the ranch manager position as soon as my background check goes through. Which, of course, it will."

"It'd better," Stone snapped. "How'd you convince them?"

"Planted a junkie in the diner where they were interviewing candidates," Evans said, his smug grin coming through in his voice. "Promised him a thousand dollars if he took someone hostage during a robbery attempt. I was going to take him down and present myself as the hero—of course, he didn't know that. He just knew he was going to get his next fix taken care of."

"That's risky," Stone pointed out. "Aren't you worried he'll give you up?"

"Not anymore," Evans drawled. "Sadly, my associate just happened to ingest some tainted drugs shortly before the encounter. I imagine he died on the way to the sheriff's department. I doubt anyone will be surprised. But there *was* a little surprise I hadn't anticipated."

Stone winked at Allison and held up his index finger to assure her he'd only be a moment. "What? Didn't do enough 'homework,' Evans?"

"There's no way I could've found out your pretty little schoolteacher had been trained in hand-to-hand combat," Evans hissed. "There was nothing in her background indicating she'd ever taken even a basic self-defense class. I don't like surprises, Stone."

"And I don't like your tone," Stone shot back. "Did you stop to think that perhaps Rogan has shown her a few defensive moves since she's been in his company?"

"The kid knew a couple of basic moves," Evans replied. "But the mother has been *trained*, Stone. Like one of us."

Stone's pacing slowed. "Son of a bitch." Stone laughed in a loud burst that echoed through the pool house. "That wily bastard. He embedded information in Sarah's head."

"Who?" Evans asked.

Stone chuckled, ignoring Evans's question. "He wouldn't have given someone the knowledge he held without also giving them a way to defend it."

"So is it the mom or the kid that has the information you're after?" Evans hissed.

"Well, Mr. Evans," Stone said, "that is the question, isn't it? I guess we'll just have to interrogate them both to find out for certain. . . ."

Sarah groaned as she awoke in the dark room, feeling like she had the world's worst hangover. But then her synapses began to fire and she sat up with a gasp, fear spiking in her veins when she glanced around the room in a panic, not knowing where she was.

She threw off the blanket that had been draped over her and swung her legs over the side of the bed, ready to bolt . . . *somewhere* when a hulking form took shape in the darkness, coming toward her, blocking her escape.

"It's okay, Sarah," a deep, soothing voice said.

It was familiar, comforting . . . belonged to someone she loved . . .

Loved?

She closed her eyes, pressing the heel of her palm to her temple, trying to focus. Then his name came to her, filling her with warmth. "Luke."

"Hey," he said, slowly approaching. When he reached her, he took her face in his hands and peered down at her, coming into focus as her eyes adjusted to the darkness. "Good to have you back."

She covered his hands with hers, reveling in the gentle pressure against her skin, saddened by the knowledge that soon she'd lose him.

Why? Where is he going . . . ?

"We'll be leaving soon," she mumbled. "That's why."

She felt him sigh, but he didn't respond to her statement. Instead he asked, "You doing okay? How's the headache?"

"Better," she replied. But then she frowned. "I think. What the hell happened? How's Eli? Is he okay?"

Luke kissed the top of her head and wrapped her in his arms.

Strong arms. She was safe there. She never wanted him to let go . . .

"Eli's fine," he assured her. "He's in bed."

Sarah frowned up at him. "Bed? What time is it? How long was I out?"

Luke smoothed her hair. "Several hours. I gave you something for the pain. That's the only thing you can do when the memories unfold."

"*What* memories?" Sarah asked, her confusion threatening to make her headache return. "I don't understand."

"I'll explain it all, but you need to eat something," he insisted. "C'mon. I'll warm up some dinner for you."

Sarah wasn't even remotely hungry, but apparently Luke wasn't going to budge until she was sitting in front of the fire in the great room, nibbling at the roasted chicken and vegetables that Mel had brought over for them and sipping the cup of herbal tea Luke had insisted would help with the lingering headache.

After a few minutes, she actually did start to feel better. And when she finished off the last of her dinner and Luke set her plate aside, she had to admit she'd been hungrier than she'd realized. But she didn't truly feel better until she and Luke stretched out on the couch together and she was snuggled close, her cheek resting on his chest.

"Now," she prompted, "could you please explain what's going on?"

Luke's fingertips trailed lightly up and down her arm for a moment before he finally said, "I think Eli's therapist— Dr. Locke—was working for your father, that he used a certain hypnosis technique to embed information in Eli's subconscious."

Sarah's head came up at this. "That's how he passed the information on? By messing around with my son's *mind?*"

Luke nodded. "Yeah, I think so. It was only a theory until what happened today. I thought maybe you'd lied to me, pretending to not know anything about self-defense—"

Sarah's expression twisted with indignation. "Lied to you? Why would I lie to you about that?"

He shook his head. "I know. I'm an asshole for even thinking it. But then you got the headache, lost focus. . . . All of that happens when the memories unfold in an uncontrolled way. It looks like someone's been messing with your head, too. Your memories must've kicked in because Eli was in danger."

"If that was the case, why didn't they kick in at the festival?" she asked.

Luke shrugged. "Probably because I got to the guy first."

Sarah shook her head. "It still doesn't make any sense to me. Why would my father do that to us?"

Luke sighed. "I'm sure he thought he was passing along the information in the safest way possible."

"But why put anything into *my* head?" Sarah continued. "I'm not his successor. He named Eli, right?"

Luke's brows came together. "That's what he said. But, hell, Sarah—who knows when he had somebody in your head. It could've been when you were a kid. Did you ever see a therapist?"

She shook her head. "No, I wouldn't go after my mom left. I refused."

"What about when your husband died?" Luke asked.

"I saw a counselor through the school's assistance plan," she said. "My dad didn't have any say in it."

Luke leveled his gaze on her. "What about your husband? Could he have planted this knowledge?"

Sarah pulled back at the implication that Greg could've done something like this without her knowledge. But then how could she be sure? There was no telling what he'd done. He certainly hadn't been upfront with her about anything else in their marriage.

She closed her eyes on a sigh, a long-forgotten memory coming to her. "Greg went through a meditation phase," she told Luke. "He talked me into trying it with him. Eli was just a baby. . . . It was crazy. I was exhausted. He said it would help me handle the stress at work at that time."

Luke's arms tightened around her, pulling her back against him. "I'm sure he thought he was protecting you, giving you knowledge that would keep you and Eli safe if anything ever happened to him."

Sarah blinked away the tears that blurred her vision. "Maybe. I hope so. I think Greg really was a good man—especially after what you showed me, what he gave up to be with us. But, God, Luke—I feel like nothing I loved or believed in was real."

He didn't say a word, just continued to hold her. He was silent for so long, Sarah wondered if he'd drifted off to sleep. But when she shifted so that she could peer at him, his dark gaze met hers. For a long, charged moment, neither of them moved. But then Luke lifted a hand to tuck a lock of hair behind her ear before gently grasping her nape and pulling her down to him. His kiss was so tender, it was exactly the solace she needed.

Her hand smoothed over his chest, needing to feel the firm planes of his body, to reassure herself that he was there and that she wasn't still asleep. And if there'd been any lingering doubt, the way he groaned, deep in his chest, when she slid her hand down between them to stroke the hard length straining for release, removed it.

Her fingers fumbled with the fly of his jeans and slowly pulled his zipper down, allowing her the access she sought. He hissed a sharp curse when she slipped her hand inside to caress the silky length of his shaft.

His hand slid under her shirt, lightly skimming the small of her back, his fingertips brushing just inside her jeans, the teasing contact making her shiver. She broke their kiss and sat up, letting her head fall back when his hands slid under her shirt to smooth along her sides. Practiced fingers unhooked her bra with a quick flick before cupping her breasts, kneading them as his thumbs brushed over her nipples.

"Should we go upstairs?" she breathed.

But his response was to shove up her shirt so that he could take one of her breasts into his mouth, flicking and teasing until her body ached for his to the point of pain. As if sensing her need, he eased her back, shifting positions until she was beneath him. Then he slid her jeans down over her hips with her assistance, capturing her mouth in a savage kiss as his hand slid lower, swiftly bringing her the relief she sought.

She was still shuddering when he stood and scooped her up into his arms. "*Now* we're going upstairs."

Seconds later, they were in her bedroom, tearing off each other's clothes with a desperation that made her want to weep. But her sorrow soon melted away as their bodies came together, skin to skin, heart-to-heart.

And when they lay together some time later, Luke's strong arms holding her tight against him, she lifted her eyes to his, hoping not to see the same sorrow reflected there but was disappointed.

"You've had news," she surmised.

He nodded, then gently smoothed her hair, his touch achingly loving. "My commander called earlier and left me a voicemail. He's managed to move the European caches a little faster than anticipated. I'm supposed to call him ASAP—probably so he can give me a timeline for when I need to deliver you and Eli to Chicago."

Her arms reflexively tightened around him, but she pressed her lips together. She'd known this day would come, but she'd hoped it wouldn't be so soon.

They lay together in silence for some time before Luke finally cleared his throat and said, "I was ordered to get close to you, Sarah," he confessed. "To find out what you knew—if anything—about the information your father passed along to Eli and how."

Sarah slowly pulled back, sitting up so that she could see Luke's face clearly. "What?"

He sat up with her, bringing their faces within a few inches of one another, and cupped her jaw, smoothing his thumb against her skin. "This is where I'd planned to tell you that what's happened between us was just me doing my job, that it doesn't mean anything. That it's been great, but it was just sex. And that as soon as you and Eli are in Chicago, it's over."

Her heart began to pound. "But?"

His dark brows came together in a frown. "But I can't."

She swallowed hard, suddenly finding it difficult to breathe. "Why?"

His expression was impossible to read as he stared at

her, but then he pulled her to him and kissed her, his lips conveying all she needed to know.

Luke awoke the next morning with Sarah still nestled against him. For several minutes, he lay there staring at the ceiling, enjoying the way her satiny-soft skin felt beneath his fingertips as he lightly traced her spine. But finally he heaved a resigned sigh and eased out of her arms. She stirred briefly before settling back into a peaceful sleep.

He quietly pulled his jeans on and grabbed the rest of his clothes before creeping to her door and slipping into the hallway. He pulled the door closed behind him and nearly jumped out of his skin when he heard the floorboards creak behind him.

He turned with a start to see Eli standing there, Chief at his side. "Hey, buddy," he said, narrowing his eyes as he studied the kid, his guilty conscience pricking at him for breaking Sarah's rule about leaving her room before Eli was awake. "Everything okay?"

Eli studied him for a moment before finally shrugging. "Sure. Just hungry."

The tension in Luke's shoulders lessened slightly. "Oh. Okay. Well, come on downstairs and I'll fix us some breakfast."

A few minutes later, Luke was at the stove making them bacon and eggs, trying his damnedest not to read anything into the kid's unusual silence. Normally, Eli would be talking his head off. But he just sat at the table, sipping his hot chocolate without a word. Luke could feel the weight of the kid's stare on his back as he prepared their breakfast and tried not to imagine what was going through Eli's head.

And when he set a plate in front of Eli and sat down across from him, the kid continued to study Luke, nibbling on his bacon without a single word. Unable to hold Eli's gaze for very long, Luke dug into his own breakfast with a vengeance, shoveling eggs into his mouth.

"So, are you having sex with my mom?"

Luke sputtered, choking on his scrambled eggs. When he managed to dislodge his breakfast from his windpipe, he took a swig of his coffee, then gaped at the kid. "What the hell kind of question is that? And you're ten. How do you even know about sex?"

"I'm eleven," Eli corrected. "And Mom had The Talk with me last year because my friends were telling me stuff. Besides, I've seen sex on TV."

Luke frowned. "Does your mom know you're watching that shit?"

Eli shook his head. "No. We don't have cable. It's at Dylan's house. So, do women really moan and scream like that?"

"Holy shit," Luke choked again, feeling cornered like never before. He'd rather face off against the deadliest of foes than sit here getting hammered with questions about orgasms. "I can't talk to you about this, kid. You need to talk to your mom."

Eli pegged him with an irritated look. "Dude. It's my *mom.* I can't talk to her about that."

"Sure, you can," Luke countered. "And you're going to. 'Cause I'm not pissing her off just to satisfy your curiosity."

Eli rolled his eyes. "Fine. But I can't believe *you're* afraid of my mom."

Luke picked up a strip of bacon and wagged it at the kid. "You listen to me—I'm not afraid of your mom, even though I saw her go ape-shit when that guy grabbed you yesterday, so I know she can kick some ass. But there's a difference between being afraid of a woman and respecting a woman. And I respect the hell outta your mom. She's an amazing lady and you should be proud. There's nothin' she wouldn't do for you."

Eli's wise gaze met and held his for a long moment. "I think she feels the same way about you."

Luke leaned back in his chair and said cautiously. "I hope I've earned her respect."

Eli grinned, knowingly. *Damn, the kid was too smart for his own good.* "I mean, I think she loves you, too."

Luke's brows shot up. "Eli—"

"You do *love* my mom, don't you?" Eli asked. "I mean, if you're having sex, you have to love her, right?"

Fuck.

Luke ran his hand through his hair, not quite sure what to say. He knew he cared about Sarah, knew he'd never felt anything even close to what he felt for her. But was it love? Hell, would he even recognize it if it was? "It's complicated, Eli."

"It's not complicated at all," the kid shot back. "You either love her or you don't."

Luke shoved away from the table and took his plate to the counter, but as he did he caught a glimpse of Sarah's reflection in the window over the sink. His heart seized and he turned to face her where she stood in the doorway, wondering just how much of the conversation she'd heard. From the look on her face, the anxious anticipation in her expression as she waited to hear his answer, she'd apparently heard the last part.

"Hey, Mom," Eli greeted, seeing her for the first time. He polished off the last bite of his toast and hopped up to put his dishes in the sink, not sensing the tension in the room from the question that still hung, unanswered, in the air. "I'm gonna go take Chief outside for a while, if that's okay with you."

"Yeah," she said, finally looking away from Luke and offering her son a smile. "That's fine. But it's too cold to be out there for very long. And be sure to wear your hat and gloves."

As soon as Eli was out of earshot, Luke took a step forward. "Sarah—"

"It's okay," she interrupted, stepping around him to get to the refrigerator. "You don't have to answer his question. I understand, Luke. The conversation we had last night . . . I know this hasn't been just sex. It hasn't been for me either. But I knew what I was getting into with you. And it's okay. It's not like you didn't warn me about how it was going to end."

Luke closed his eyes and let out a long sigh. God, he'd made a mess of things. When he opened his eyes again, Sarah was passing by him on her way to the table. Instinctively, Luke's hand shot out and he grasped her arm.

"You didn't let me finish," he told her, pulling her close. "I was gonna say that I've never been in love with anyone before, wouldn't know what it feels like—or what it's *supposed* to feel like. But I know what you mean to me, the way you make me feel when you walk into the room, when you smile at me. It's . . . hell, it's like nothing I've ever known, Sarah. And if that's not what it's like to fall in love with somebody . . ."

Sarah's lips curved into a smile as his words trailed off. "I think I'm falling in love with you, too."

Hearing the words affected Luke more than he ever could've expected. His throat constricted, and his chest grew tight with emotion. Not knowing how else to respond, he wrapped his arms around Sarah and captured her mouth in a hard, hungry kiss. It soon became something far more tender and sensual. If not for the chance of Eli coming back in at any moment, he would've stripped her out of those goddamned adorable pajamas and taken her right there on the kitchen floor. As it was, he finally brought the kiss to a slow close, lifted his head, and wrapped her in his embrace, pressing her against him.

God, he was in serious fucking trouble. He'd never believed it was possible for someone to love him, to accept him for who he was, and love him anyway. And he loved her, too. Loved her with everything he had. Which scared the shit out of him.

Because now he had something to lose.

Chapter Twenty-One

"Hey there," Sarah said, bringing Luke a cup of coffee in his office and pressing a kiss to the top of his head. "Anyone going to work out?'"

He turned his chair enough that he could wrap an arm around her waist and pull her down into his lap for a quick kiss before answering. "Yeah, I think so. I ran them all through the Alliance's background check protocol, and these guys came up clean enough."

Sarah pointed at the one application that still rankled for some reason. "And what about the guy from the diner?"

Luke sighed. "He's clean. Not a single mark against him."

"That's good, right?" she asked. "You want someone you can trust helping Mel."

He nodded. "I don't know. . . . The guy's almost too clean," he told her, trying to explain the nagging feeling that had never failed him before. "I didn't find a single infraction. Not even a speeding ticket."

She frowned along with him, studying his laptop screen anew. "That's not out of the realm of possibility, is it?"

He shook his head. "Not really. Something just feels off."

"Then don't hire him," she said, getting up from his

lap and kissing him again all too briefly. "You have to be comfortable with your decision, babe."

He held on to her hand, keeping her from leaving. It'd been two days since their conversation in the kitchen. Two days since he'd fully realized how much she meant to him. And yet it felt like weeks, months that he'd loved her.

Luke brought her hand to his lips and kissed her fingertips. "It's not about my feeling comfortable. I have more to worry about now."

She tilted her head to one side, a sad smile on her lips, her expression telling him that she knew their time was coming to an end soon and that she had resigned herself to it. He wished he could say the same.

"Are you coming down soon?" she asked, avoiding the subject. "Melanie and Davis are bringing Jim by for lunch. And Eli is eager to show you the new trick he's taught Chief. I swear that dog has doubled in size since we got him."

Every time she said, "we," warmth spread out across his chest and tightened it at the same time. "I'll be down in just a minute. You go ahead."

She took his face in her hands and kissed him tenderly. "Don't be too long."

His gaze lingered on the doorway to his office long after she'd left. Finally, he ran a hand through his hair in frustration and turned his attention back to the applications before him. But he couldn't concentrate. All he could think about was that soon Sarah and Eli would be who-knew-where, going on with their lives, and he'd be moving on to his next assignment.

Once, the prospect of taking on his next mission would've been an adrenaline rush, would've had him antsy to wrap shit up and get going. But not this time. The thought of saying good-bye to Sarah and never seeing her again filled him with dread. And then there was Eli. He loved the boy like he was his own flesh and blood son. For the first time, he actually understood how it was that Jim could've loved the stupid, troubled kid that Luke had been. How he loved him still even though Luke sure as hell hadn't given him any reason to.

Luke heard the front door and then the cheerful chatter of his family downstairs. *His family.* He'd been on the fence about how to handle his situation, but he'd made his decision. He opened up his email and fired off a short message before he could change his mind.

Then he shoved up from his chair and headed downstairs. But he paused at the bottom of the steps for a moment, silently watching the scene before him. This was where he belonged. With them. With the people who loved him. With the people he loved.

He was just stepping off the bottom stair when his phone buzzed at his hip. He lifted a hand in greeting when Davis glanced his way as he answered the phone. "Rogan."

"What the hell is this shit?"

The tone of his commander's voice snapped Luke's attention away from Eli's excited chatter. He headed back up the stairs to take the call. "Depends," he replied. "There's been a lot of shit going on lately, so you might want to be more specific, narrow it down a little."

"Don't fuck with me, Rogan," Will hissed. "I just got your message. You want to explain what the hell you're doing?"

"Nothing to explain," Luke told him. His jaw tightened. He wasn't about to go into his relationship with Sarah with his commander. He massaged the back of his neck, working out the growing tension there. "I think I made my position pretty clear."

"I'm not accepting your resignation," Will spat. "You're one of the best field operatives I have. I'm not dropping you down to *confrere* or watching you walk away from the Alliance."

"The way I see it, those are pretty much your only options," Luke replied calmly. "I've made my decision."

"Is this about Sarah Scoffield?" Will demanded. "If so—"

"It doesn't matter what's behind my decision to leave the Alliance," Luke snapped, cutting him off.

"Luke, for fuck's sake," his commander snapped. "Would you just shut the hell up and listen to me for a goddamn minute?"

"I've made my choice," Luke insisted through clenched teeth. "The next one's yours to make."

Sarah heard Luke's angry footfalls—uncharacteristically loud—on the hardwood and ducked into her bedroom, not wanting him to know she'd overheard the conversation. She'd noticed the hard expression on his face when he'd answered the phone and had followed him upstairs, fearing that there'd been a development with her father. She'd never anticipated hearing him discussing his resignation from the Alliance.

She leaned back against the wall and closed her eyes. Part of her was thrilled that he would give up the job he'd referred to as a calling to be with her—in fact, the thought of seeing if they could build a relationship, a life together, filled her with such happiness it brought tears to her eyes. But she'd already had one man give up his dreams, his calling, to be with her. She couldn't help but wonder if Luke would regret his decision a few weeks, months, *years* from now. . . .

And then what? Where would that leave them? It wasn't just about her and her happiness. She had to consider Eli and what it would do to him if things didn't work out. He already adored Luke. It was going to be hard enough to leave as it was.

"Sarah?"

Sarah wiped her eyes and forced a smile at the sound of Melanie's voice calling to her from the hallway. "Be right there!"

But there must've been something in her voice that sounded off because Melanie's concerned face peeked around the door frame. "Everything okay?"

Sarah nodded a little too emphatically. "Yeah. Sure. Of course."

Mel gave her a disbelieving look. "Uh-huh. Tell me another one." She entered the room and sat down on Sarah's bed. "You and Luke have a fight?"

Sarah's brows lifted. "Fight? No. Nothing like that . . ."

Mel stared at her for a long moment, her penetrating gaze all too astute. "My stepbrother can be a closed-off jackass sometimes," she said. "But he's a good man. And he loves you. I can see it whenever he looks at you. I'm glad to see him finally letting someone in. We worried about him after Lyla died."

Sarah joined her on the bed with a sigh. "It's complicated, Mel. I wish love was all that mattered."

"Isn't it?" Mel shot back. "When you get down to it, after you get past all the other bullshit that distracts us on a daily basis, isn't love the *only* thing that matters?"

Sarah shook her head. "I want to believe that, but there's more going on with Luke . . . with me . . . than what you realize."

Mel put her arm around Sarah's shoulders, giving her a comforting squeeze. "Oh, honey, we knew there was something more happening than you two were letting on when you got here. Like I said, Luke's never brought anyone home before. And I'd hoped whatever it was meant that you and Eli would stay here permanently." She laughed. "Davis and Dad and I were laying odds on whether you were pregnant, running from an ex, or something else equally dramatic."

Sarah offered Mel a smile, wishing she could tell the truth of their situation, but it wasn't her place. It was for Luke to handle. She'd grown to adore the woman and would've liked to remain at the ranch and truly get to know her better. Something told her they would've been the best of friends.

"I can tell you I'm not pregnant," Sarah assured her. "And I'm a widow. My husband died a few years ago. So no crazy ex."

Mel's face sobered. "Well," she said, "whatever it is that brought you here, I'm glad for it. You've made my brother happy—even if it's just for a short time."

When Mel rose to her feet and strode toward the door, Sarah called out, "Melanie."

The woman turned back to her. "Yeah?"

"I do love him," Sarah told her. "I love him very much—more than I thought possible in such a short time. No matter what happens, I . . . I want all of you to know that."

Mel smiled. "Then I'm sure it'll all work out like it's supposed to in the end."

Sarah watched her go, then reached over to the bedside table to pick up the photo of Luke and his mother. With a sigh, she set it aside and made her way downstairs, donning a smile to hide her heartache. But her spirits lifted when Luke turned from his conversation with Jim and met her gaze, his dark eyes filling with happiness when he extended a hand to her.

She cried out in surprise when he pulled her off-balance and she landed in his lap. She was still laughing when he brushed a quick kiss over her lips. They were still grinning at each other when Eli bounced onto the couch next to them.

"Get a picture of me, too, Mel," Eli suggested.

Sarah glanced at Melanie to see her holding up her cell phone. And she didn't even hold back the happiness that washed over her as Luke gathered her and Eli close. Chief, not to be left out, jumped into their laps, licking their faces with exuberance. But the puppy wasn't content to stay still and leaped off at full speed, Eli chasing after him with a laugh.

When Mel showed them the photos and promptly sent them to their phones, Sarah felt her eyes grow misty, grateful that she would have the moment captured forever. Later, after they'd gone and she sat alone in the kitchen, she brought up the photos again. There was one of her and Luke gazing lovingly at one another. One of them with Eli. And a third where Chief had photobombed them. Luke was laughing, his eyes squeezed shut. It was the same smile he'd had in the photo with his mother. To see him that happy, and to know that that moment together was the source of it, filled Sarah with warmth. And yet . . .

"There you are."

She looked up from the screen and smiled at Luke. "You get everything squared away with Melanie?"

He nodded and joined her at the table. "Yeah. She's going to make calls tonight to offer jobs to the men I selected."

"Good." She fumbled with her phone, her fingers trying to find something to do to keep from reaching for Luke. "So, I was thinking . . . now that things are nearly wrapped up, it'd probably be a good idea for us to visit my father."

There was a long, tense pause before Luke said, "I'd have to get clearance from my commander. I'd rather not move Eli until we're certain whatever knowledge he has is no longer valuable to anyone."

"We can't stay here any longer, Luke," she said softly, tears thick in her voice. "The longer this takes, the harder it'll be on all of us."

He reached for her hand, but she shot to her feet, avoiding his touch.

"Sarah, there's something I need to tell you," he told her, coming to her.

She shook her head, refusing to look at him when he placed his hands on her hips. "Luke—"

"I want you and Eli to stay," he interrupted. "For as long as you want."

She turned her gaze up to meet his. "At what cost, Luke? I'm not letting you give up everything you've worked for just because of what we feel for each other. That isn't fair to you."

His hands fell away and he took a step back. "That's my call to make."

"Then what about asking *us* to give up everything to stay here?" she replied gently. "You want me to uproot my son for a relationship that might or might not even work out? What happens if three months from now you decide you don't want the widow and her kid tying you down?"

His expression hardened and he nodded, taking another step back, putting more distance between them.

"Luke, please try to understand," Sarah pleaded, reaching out to him, taking his hand. "This is all going so fast. I'm just . . . I'm afraid."

He finally turned his gaze to her. "You don't think this scares the shit out of me? I told you this is all new to me. I don't know what the hell I'm doing. I have no idea how I'll feel in three days, let alone three months. You got me there, Sarah. Guilty. But I'd like to see where it goes. I'd like to at least have the chance to find out."

Sarah felt her resolve crumbling. Her head and her heart were at war, and at that moment her heart was pounding so hard it was all she could hear. She closed the gap between them in two quick steps and threw her arms around his neck, hugging him tightly. And then his arms came around her and he buried his face in her hair, holding her close.

When she finally pulled back, she took his face in her hands and kissed him once, twice. "We'll figure this out," she whispered. "I promise."

Luke pressed kisses to her forehead, her cheek, before finally claiming her lips. And that moment was all that mattered.

Chapter Twenty-Two

I'm in.

Stone excused himself from dinner when he saw the text come through, offering apologetic smiles to the dignitaries and their spouses. "Please forgive me," he said, rising to his feet. "I'm afraid I have an urgent call to make."

He gestured toward Allison, who was even more stunning than usual in the designer dress and diamonds he'd insisted on buying for her for the occasion. They'd had the desired effect, charming his guests precisely as he'd intended.

"I will leave you in the care of my lovely companion." He cast an adoring look her way. "Ms. Holt is far more enchanting than I could ever hope to be." She flushed prettily, lowering her lashes to try to hide her pleasure at his praise.

As he turned away from the dinner party, he caught the knowing smiles that passed between his guests. *Excellent.* He couldn't have asked for a better result after introducing his former assistant to some of the world's most powerful leaders. The evolution of his image to prepare the way for his ascent to power couldn't be proceeding more perfectly.

And now, it seemed, there was even more good news. As

soon as he was in his study, he dialed Evans's number. The phone rang only once before the man answered.

"Sorry to interrupt your dinner," Evans drawled. "Getting the prime minister is quite a coup."

Stone wasn't taking the bait and demanding to know how the son of a bitch knew anything about the private party. He wasn't naïve enough to think Evans didn't have eyes on him at every moment, reporting back on his smallest move to ensure he could be trusted. Just as he suspected Evans was aware that Stone had done the same to him and had several of his faithful already camped out in the small Wyoming town where Evans was currently staying.

"When do you start?" Stone demanded. "We're rapidly running out of time."

"I don't need to actually *start,* Stone," Evans assured him. "I just needed them to invite the job candidates in so I can get what I need."

Stone bit back his angry retort at the bastard's condescending tone. Instead, he kept his own tone mild when he asked, "Very well then. When do you plan on *taking* your little tour?"

"Tomorrow," Evans said. "I should have eyes on the property, including the perimeter security system during the final interview process."

"When will you extract the boy and his mother?" Stone pressed.

"As soon as the opportunity presents itself," Evans replied. "And if it doesn't . . . well, then, I will *create* an opportunity."

Stone disconnected and pocketed his phone, not bothering to suppress his grin as he returned to his guests and resumed his seat. "I hope no one missed me too much."

The prime minister, seated across from him, sent a lecherous smile Allison's way. "I believe your absence was missed most by the delightful Ms. Holt."

Stone lifted Allison's fingertips to his lips. "Is that true, my darling?"

"Of course," she replied softly, her eyes worshiping him. "Every moment without you is an eternity."

Stone's smile grew. Oh, she was good . . . perfect, in fact. And he'd see to it she was rewarded quite well later that evening, as soon as all of these freeloading assholes finally left his home. . . .

Sarah finished drying off from her shower, then slipped into nothing but a bathrobe before leaving her room to go in search of Luke. It didn't take long for her to find him sitting at the piano. He was lost in his music, playing a few notes before pausing to make a notation on the sheet music.

But, as she approached, he straightened as if sensing her presence. As she came in and closed the door behind her, he turned and offered her a smile in greeting.

"I thought you were going to bed," he said, his eyes sparking with desire as she approached.

"Not without you," she said, undoing the belt of the bathrobe with sensual motions, letting the material slide between her fingers. As she walked, the robe fell open, revealing her nakedness beneath.

She saw Luke swallow hard as she wedged herself between him and the piano, straddling his hips. When she pressed a kiss to the side of his neck, his breath left him on a harsh sigh. His hands slipped inside the folds of the robe, bringing goose bumps to her flesh as he slowly explored her skin.

"This room is soundproof, right?" she murmured.

He made a sound deep in the back of his throat in response—something between a groan and a growl—before claiming her mouth in a harsh kiss. His hands drifted up to her shoulders and under the edge of the robe, sliding it from her shoulders until it pooled at her elbows.

Then he was rising to his feet, lifting her with him. A few steps later, he was pressing her back against the wall, one arm supporting her as the other hand cupped her breast, teasing, pinching, kneading until she gasped, breaking their kiss.

Then she was sliding down his body until her feet reached the floor. With a sultry grin, she put him at arm's length and let the robe slip off to pool at her feet.

She leaned her head back, arching her neck as she smoothed her hands down her throat. Then she lifted her head, meeting his gaze as she slid her hands over her breasts, pausing to knead them and pinch her nipples, moaning as she rolled them as he had done. She heard him groan and opened her eyes, grinning at him as she caressed her stomach, teasing him with anticipation.

"Jesus Christ," he muttered. "You're killin' me here."

She moaned, leaning back against the wall as his reaction increased her own pleasure. His hand slid between her legs to join hers, their fingers working separately and together. He slid a finger inside her and then another, hitting a spot she'd never encountered before. She bit her lip to stifle the scream that rose in her throat, but, remembering where they were, she allowed the scream to come as her body jerked and light exploded in her head.

In the next instant, he was dragging her back into his embrace, easing her to the ground, accepting her help to rid himself of his clothing.

"Pocket," she gasped, fingers grasping blindly at the bathrobe. He must've understood because he snatched one of the condoms she'd stashed there before heading downstairs and donned it in hurried motions, then thrust so deep she cried out.

There was no need for silence this time, no need for

discretion, which seemed to increase the pleasure for both of them as they made love with a desperation that left them breathless when at last they collapsed together in a blissful tangle.

Sarah smoothed Luke's hair from his brow and pressed kisses to his forehead and temple, murmuring her love.

When he finally rolled away, she felt chilled to the bone. It was only as he stretched out on the floor beside her and draped her robe over them as much as it would cover and propped himself up on his arm to peer down at her that she felt warm again.

"Sorry to interrupt your music," she said, bringing a grin to his full lips.

"Feel free to interrupt me anytime," he assured her. "As often as you like." His fingertips trailed along the curve of her face until he reached her chin and tipped it up so that her gaze could not avoid his. "But what brought this on? After what you said earlier . . ."

Sarah let her lids drift closed for a moment before finally answering, "I just want to savor every moment we have together—whether that's two days or two lifetimes."

Luke leaned in and brushed his lips over hers. "Then I guess we need to make the most of it. . . ."

Luke was whistling—fucking *whistling* . . . what the hell?—as he finished arranging the breakfast he'd made for Sarah.

"Is that for Mom?" Eli asked, hopping up onto the bar stool at the kitchen island. He was already dressed and ready to go. Chief sat happily at his feet, his belly full.

"Yeah, I thought it'd be nice to give her breakfast in bed," Luke replied. "What do you think?"

Eli grinned. "It looks awesome."

"Good," Luke said. "'Cause yours is on that plate right there. Dig in. I want to make sure you eat before I head out."

"Where are you going?" Eli said, his brows coming together. "You're leaving us?"

Luke shook his head. "I have to go help Mel assess the final candidates for ranch manager. I'll be back before you know it."

"Can I go?" Eli piped up.

Luke hesitated. "I'm riding for part of the time. You've only had a couple of lessons, buddy. Plus, being on a horse for a few hours can be a pain in the ass—literally."

"That's okay," Eli assured him. "I need to learn all this stuff so I can help you."

The thought of Eli growing up on the ranch, learning all that went into it, eventually taking over for him as Mel had taken over for Jim brought Luke up short. Sarah's warning about how Eli's feelings factored into their relationship hit home in a very real way.

Luke took a deep breath and let it out slowly. "Eli, you know, you and your mom staying here . . . that's temporary. I don't know how long you'll be here, regardless of how much I'd like you guys to stay."

Eli's face fell. "I know. But maybe if Mom sees how much I can help she'll *want* to stay."

"It's a little more complicated than that, buddy." When Eli's shoulders slumped, it was more than Luke could take. "But I'll ask your mom about you helping me today. Okay?"

Eli nodded enthusiastically and hopped down to grab his plate.

Luke left the kid in the kitchen and crept upstairs. When he eased open Sarah's door, she smiled sleepily and stretched, revealing her bare breasts in that way she had that had proven effective in luring him back to bed on more than one occasion.

After the night they'd had, he would've thought that he'd

be completely satiated, but his dick was already going hard again. With an appreciative shake of his head, he sat down on the edge of the bed and set the tray on her lap.

"God, you're beautiful," he murmured.

She flushed, heat creeping across her chest and up her neck until it reached her cheeks. "Careful, we tend to get in trouble when you look at me like that."

"Oh, trust me, I'd love to stay and ogle you some more and see where it goes," he said, grinning, "but I need to go meet the final candidates for ranch manager and show them around the property. Eli wants to go with me. Is that okay with you?"

Sarah hesitated for a moment. "Luke . . . I don't know if that's such a good idea."

Luke nodded. "No problem. I'll just tell him you'd rather he stay here."

She cocked her head to one side. "But you *want* him to go with you, don't you?"

"I promise I'll make sure he wears his hat and gloves, and he can ride with me," he said. "If it gets too cold, I'll just bug out and bring him home."

Finally, she nodded. "Only for a couple of hours, though, okay?"

He dipped his chin. "I'll have him back by lunch, then I'll head back out. I probably won't be back until this evening. Stay here in the house, okay? If Eli goes out with Chief later today, make sure he comes in right after. And pay attention to your phone. Do you remember everything I showed you with the alarm system? And the weapons room? If you have any trouble, call me. If you can't reach me, call Davis."

"Luke, we'll be fine." She kissed him, then motioned him away. "Thank you for the breakfast. Now go do your thing."

He hesitated at the doorway, uneasy about leaving her

alone for so long but needing to fulfil his obligations to Melanie and the ranch. He shut the door behind him and made his way downstairs before he had second thoughts.

Half an hour later, Luke and Eli arrived at the main house, surprised to find three men standing on the porch, shoulders hunched against the cold, their expressions guarded and uncomfortable.

"Where's Melanie?" Eli asked as Luke slowed the SUV to a stop.

"Good question," Luke mumbled. "Stay here for a minute, Eli. Might as well keep warm until we head out."

At that moment, Davis came out the front door and hurried down the porch steps to meet Luke as he was getting out of the SUV. "Glad you're here, man."

"What's going on?" Luke demanded, dread creeping along his spine. "Why are these guys standing out here freezing their nuts off? Where's Mel?"

"Inside," Davis said, jerking his head toward the house. "Jim's had another episode, Luke. Fell down the stairs. I've got him stabilized, but the paramedics are on their way."

Davis was still talking, but Luke didn't hear what he said. He was already racing toward the house, vaulting up the steps and charged inside. "Mel!"

"In here!"

Luke jogged over to the base of the stairs, where Jim still lay.

"Davis didn't want to move him," Melanie said, tears in her eyes as she looked up at Luke.

He squatted down next to Jim and took his wrist, checking his pulse. "How ya doin', Jim?"

Jim's mouth curved into a lopsided smile. "Oh, been better. Damned knee gave out on me coming down the stairs."

"You hear me okay?" Luke asked, pulling up Jim's eyelids to check his pupils. "See me okay? Any blurry vision?"

"I told you that Davis or I would help you," Mel chastised, wiping her cheek against her shoulder to clear away her tears.

"And I told you I'm not helpless," Jim retorted.

"No, but you've always been stubborn as hell," Luke drawled. "Any pain?"

"Well, I think I might've busted up my leg but good," Jim said in his understated way.

"Davis thinks his ankle's probably broken," Mel told him.

Luke glanced down toward Jim's feet. Considering the angle of his right foot, It looked as if Davis's assessment was dead-on. "You're lucky if that's all that's broken."

Luke heard a shuffle of footsteps behind him and saw Davis ushering Eli inside. The kid's face twisted with worry when he saw Jim lying on the floor.

"Hey, honey, you want to make Eli some hot chocolate?" Mel suggested.

"Sure, babe," Davis said, patting Eli on the shoulder. "C'mon, buddy."

"Can the guys on the porch have some too?" Eli asked.

"I told them they didn't need to wait outside," Mel explained to Luke, "but Evans wouldn't hear of it. He insisted they all give Dad some privacy while Davis assessed his injuries."

"Didn't want to embarrass the old man more than he already was," Jim said with a chuckle that ended on a wince as the color drained from his face.

"Where the hell are the paramedics?" Mel demanded. As if on cue, they heard the wail of sirens in the distance.

A few minutes later, the paramedics took over and managed to gently lift Jim onto a stretcher and get him loaded into the ambulance.

"I'm going with Dad," Mel said. "Could you and Davis show the guys around and get them up to speed?"

Luke nodded without hesitation, even though he felt like he should be there for Jim at the hospital. God knew the man had been there for him more times than he could count, particularly on those occasions when he hadn't wanted Luke's mother to know her son had been in yet another fight and needed another ride home from the sheriff's department.

"Davis, take these guys inside and get them something hot to drink, will ya?" Luke asked as soon as the ambulance pulled away. "I'm gonna give Sarah a call and let her know what's going on."

Davis gave him a tight nod and ushered everyone inside, promising them a slice of apple pie to go along with their coffee.

Luke strolled away from the house toward the pickup trucks parked in the driveway as he dialed Sarah's number. She answered on the second ring.

"Luke? What's wrong?"

"Hey," he said, peering into each of the trucks in turn, taking mental stock of their contents—fast food bags, cans of chew, boots, gloves, CDs, jackets. . . . "Jim's had an accident. He's on the way to the hospital. Mel's with him."

"Oh my God!" she gasped. "Is he going to be okay? Do you need me to come over? I can be ready in ten minutes."

He smiled to himself, moving on to the next truck, loving her concern for his stepfather. "Nah, don't worry about it. The truck I keep at the ranch is a piece of shit. I wouldn't want you trying to drive it and getting stuck somewhere. I'll keep you posted as soon as I hear anything."

He peeked into the next pickup and started to move on, but stopped short. Frowning, he peered into the cab again, taking a closer look. There were the same types of items inside—an extra pair of work gloves, a pair of cowboy boots, a duffel bag. . . . But there was something off about them.

He opened the driver's-side door and scrutinized the contents again, taking in every detail. Then it dawned on him. . . . The items looked new, the contents staged. He picked up one of the work gloves and turned it over. Not a single stain or smudge of dirt. Unheard of for a guy claiming to be a seasoned ranch hand.

The boots were new too. And the jacket. He unzipped the duffel bag, rummaging through it. Finding nothing out of the ordinary, he felt under the seat, his jaw tightening when his fingers bumped against the cold, hard steel of the barrel of a gun. He pulled on his own work gloves, then slipped his hand under the seat again, pulling the gun out.

It was a Glock, and one that looked like it'd seen some action. He ejected the clip and then the bullet in the chamber, pocketing them before slipping the gun back under the seat. Carrying a rifle or even a handgun in a car in this part of the country wasn't unheard of. Never knew when you might encounter some kind of predator—animal *or* human. And yet something about this one just wasn't sitting well with him.

He went around to the other side of the truck and opened the glove box, removing the registration. Eric Evans. The truck definitely belonged to the man in the restaurant whose background check had been so spotless that it'd raised a warning flag.

He closed up the truck and dialed one of the numbers programmed in his phone.

"'Sup, *brah?*"

"Hey, Finn," Luke said, heading back toward the house. "I need you to run a background check on a guy for me."

There was a slight hesitation. "Uh, sure. But you should be able to do that through the laptop I gave you. What's doin'?"

"I already ran a check on the guy," Luke said. "He came back clean. But I'm not convinced. I need you to go dark on this one."

There was a screech of metal and what sounded like a door opening and closing. Then Finn cleared his throat before finally speaking again. "Dude, you know I could get my ass eighty-sixed for that kind of shit. Nobody has clearance for that level except the commander and the Grand Council."

Luke grunted. "Blame it all on me. I'm on the commander's shit list anyway. Say I threatened to blast Nanna Finnegan's coconut cake recipe online or something."

Luke could only imagine the look of horror on Finn's face when confronted with the prospect of having to confess to his tough-as-nails grandmother that the famous cake recipe that had made the family a fortune had been outed.

"Dude. My nanna would *kick my ass* if that got out to anyone outside the family. Hell, she'd kick *both* our asses. You've met my nanna. You know she could."

"Finn, your grandmother makes the godfather look like a fucking saint," Luke drawled. "The last thing I want to do is piss her off. Seriously, though, I've got a bad feeling about this guy who's trying to get a job at my ranch and need you to do me a solid. I wouldn't ask if I wasn't concerned about Sarah and Eli."

There was another pause. "All right, but you owe me one. Send me what you've got."

Luke hung up and forwarded all the info he had on Evans, then headed inside. His hackles instantly rose when he saw Eli sitting next to Evans, chatting with the men around the table, grilling them about their work experience.

Evans riffled Eli's hair with a laugh, then raised a hand to Luke when he saw him standing in the doorway. "Your boy's relentless. His questions are tougher than Ms. Hadley's."

"Eli," Luke said, his tone sharper than he'd intended.

"Let these men finish their coffee. Then we need to get going. We have a lot of ground to cover before lunch."

Though Evans's grin was friendly as he turned back to the conversation with Davis and the others, Luke didn't trust the man's easy manner. He had all the outward appearance of a capable, seasoned ranch hand, a man who was used to long days and hard work.

So why did Luke feel as if he had invited the wolf to come dine among the sheep?

Chapter Twenty-Three

Sarah wasn't entirely sure what to do with herself with Luke and Eli gone for the morning. When Luke had called to tell her about Jim's accident, she'd offered to drive over to the main house to be with Mel. But when she learned that Mel was on her way to the hospital, she decided she'd rummage through the fridge and storeroom to find the ingredients for a pot roast that they could run over later to repay the family for the times they'd done the same for her and Eli.

It was the least she could do. They'd accepted her and her son with open arms—even when they'd known something was off about the reason for their presence. And the way Sarah's stomach knotted with concern when she'd learned of Jim's fall told her all she needed to know about how much she'd come to care for Luke's family.

Thirty minutes later, the roast was in the slow cooker and she was still searching for a way to pass the time. She showered and dressed and took Chief out to play in the snow, but he quickly tired of the game and wanted to go back in.

She was still stomping the snow from her boots when she heard a clatter in the kitchen. Adrenaline spiked in her veins and she sent a glance toward the clock. It was only ten o'clock—probably too soon for Luke and Eli to have returned.

She crept into the kitchen, listening for the sound again, but didn't hear anything. Still, she checked the oven to ensure her roast was still doing okay, then made the rounds, checking all the doors and windows, ensuring they were all locked, just to be on the safe side.

Deciding that all was secure, Sarah headed back upstairs to see if she could find a movie in the loft, but a persistent beeping down the hall caught her attention. She glanced at her phone. There were no alarms from the security system, so she made her way to Luke's office, where the sound seemed to be originating.

She tapped the mouse pad on Luke's laptop and saw the source of the beeping. Someone was trying to reach him via teleconference. She sat down in his chair and answered the call. Seconds later, a handsome if stern face appeared. The man's sable hair was cropped short, the style as severe as his expression. His hazel eyes narrowed in confusion.

"Where's Rogan?" he demanded.

"He's out," Sarah told him, leaning back in the chair and lacing her hands together, peering down her nose at the screen in the way she'd seen her father do numerous times. "You can speak with me. I imagine that's why you're calling anyway."

The man inclined his head slightly. "Very well, Sarah. I'm Commander Will Asher."

"I know who you are," she interrupted. "I'd say it's nice to meet you, but that would be a lie. But, hey, from what I understand you're pretty good at telling lies . . . you know, like the one you sent my employer when you hacked into my email."

He dipped his head, acknowledging her accusation. "Fair enough. I apologize. But I assure you that we were only acting in your best interests."

"How's my father?" she demanded. "Do you think I could get an honest answer about that?"

"He's improving," Will assured her. "He still isn't able to come off the respirator, but we hope that'll happen soon. We have our best doctors in charge of his care."

Sarah met his gaze, staring him down, waiting for him to say something else. When he didn't she said, "So, if my father's fine, are you calling to tell Luke it's time to off-load us?"

"No," Will said. "Unfortunately, there was a slight delay, but that should be rectified within the week. Then you can get back to your normal life."

"Except I can't, can I?" Sarah retorted. "Because you've already wiped my life clean. Did you even bother boxing up our stuff so that we'd have it when you relocate us? Or is my life with Greg classified, locked away somewhere where only you Templars can access it?"

Will sighed and actually seemed remorseful. "I'm sorry we have to relocate you, Sarah. But providing you with new identities is for your safety and security as well as ours. I have no way to know what else you and Eli might be privy to, and we need to make sure whoever is behind this current breach won't go after you again. Your belongings will be delivered to you after you're settled."

She nodded. "Will I be able to see my family again?"

"Of course," he said. "We can work out arrangements."

Sarah pressed her lips together in an angry line. "And Luke?"

Will hesitated for a moment, his expression impossible to read. Finally, he answered, "That depends on him."

"From what I heard, it sounded like that ball's in your court, Commander," Sarah pointed out.

Will's harsh mouth curved up a little at the corners. "I see why Luke likes you. Okay then, Sarah, you're right. It's my call what happens next. I'm not thrilled with the prospect of losing one of my best men because of a . . . distraction."

Sarah's brows lifted slightly. "Distraction? That's all you think I am to Luke?"

"Do you know why Luke is one of my best men?" Will asked in response.

Sarah leveled her gaze at him. "Because he's intelligent and loyal and deadly?"

Will inclined his head, acknowledging her assessment. "Yeah. But he's also single-minded. Even before he was recruited, nothing ever distracted him from his mission. That single-minded dedication was one of the things Jack Grayson saw in Luke that made him approach him to join us."

"And you think having me in his life is nothing more than a distraction?" Sarah said.

"There are some who have a calling to this life, Sarah," Will explained, avoiding answering her question. "But sometimes we're asked to make sacrifices for a greater good. That's never been a problem for Luke. Until now."

"So you would deny Luke a chance at love, at happiness, because it doesn't suit *you?*" she demanded. "Templars are forbidden to have a personal life outside of their duties to the Alliance?"

Will shook his head, his hard expression softening a little with something that looked like regret—and sorrow. "No. It's not forbidden. It's . . . not recommended. But I'm not going to insist Luke give you up, no matter what kind of heat I take from the high commander."

Sarah's brows lifted slightly at this. That was certainly not what she'd been expecting to hear. . . .

"But I need you to understand, Sarah," he continued, "the life we lead, it's not easy for partners and spouses to accept. Your parents are perfect examples of that."

"My parents have nothing to do with my relationship to Luke," Sarah told him.

He regarded her for a long moment before asking, "How are you going to feel when Luke has to disappear without a trace—maybe for weeks at a time? How are you going to deal with the fact that he might not be able to give you any notice before he has to leave? How's *Eli* going to feel when Luke promises to be at his baseball game but doesn't show because he had to fly out to Uzbekistan and couldn't tell you ahead of time because his movements always have to be kept in the strictest confidence?"

"I don't know, Will," Sarah drawled, "probably the way you felt when that happened to you when you were a kid, I'm guessing. But I'll thank you to leave Eli out of this. He's my concern. Not yours."

"I'm just trying to prevent you and Eli from getting hurt," Will said. "And you should know that I'm not about to let Luke walk away from the Alliance—he may not realize it, but he's damned important to this organization. And he's a friend. A brother."

Sarah narrowed her gaze at the man. "Well, then I guess you need to decide what to do in order to convince him to stay, Commander. But *you* should know, I would never ask him to leave the Alliance for me or my son. I've been doing just fine on my own for the last three years. I'm not after a new dad for Eli—that's not my style. And I know what the Alliance is to Luke, what making a difference and being a part of something bigger than himself *means* to him. I wouldn't ever ask him to give that up. I care far too much for him."

Will offered her a curt nod. "Thank you, Sarah. I appreciate—"

"That said," Sarah interrupted, peering down her nose at him again, "let me make a couple of things *very* clear, Commander. My relationship with Luke is none of your goddamned business. And I don't give *a shit* about what you think is best for me or for my son. I'm the one who gets to make *that* call. Understood?"

Sarah tapped the laptop's keypad, disconnecting the call before Will could respond. Still offended that the man would think her so selfish, she shoved away from the desk with a huff and stormed from the office. She'd never wanted to punch someone so much in her life. That insufferable jackass! Like she didn't know how much Luke would be giving up if he stayed with her . . . She was well aware of it. *Painfully* aware of it, in fact.

She marched into her bedroom and quickly changed into the yoga pants and T-shirt that she'd worn the other day when she'd planned to train with Luke only to end up working out with him between the sheets instead. Heat surged in her veins at the thought of their first time together—and every time since—but she gave herself a mental shake, forcing away her desire for him and focusing on her anger at Will as she made her way downstairs to the workout room in the basement.

And it was the face of Luke's commander that she pictured as she pummeled the punching bag, his condescending accusations she heard over and over again in her head as she ran on the treadmill until her muscles burned and sweat soaked her hair and clothes.

The workout helped, but her anger still burned as she climbed the basement stairs to the kitchen, wondering just how much of the conversation she should share with Luke when he returned home soon with Eli for lunch.

She was so absorbed in her thoughts that the sound of Chief's low growl didn't at first register when she entered the kitchen. But his furious barking brought her up short, her heart leaping into her throat and cutting off her breath when she came face-to-face with the intruder that blocked her way.

* * *

Luke reined his horse to a stop and swung Eli down from behind him. "I need to get Eli back home for lunch," he told Davis, checking his watch. "Sarah's probably wondering where the hell I am. You think you have it from here?"

Davis nodded. "Go on and get outta here. Mel had some sandwiches already put together, so I'll feed these guys and then head over to your place so we can take them through the paces there."

"I'm still full from that delicious pie," Evans told them with a grin. "If you want, I can head on over with you now."

Luke traded glances with Davis, who must've picked up on Luke's wariness. He slapped Evans on the back. "You know, no reason I can't grab the sandwiches and take them over to Luke's place. We'll all head out as soon as we put the horses back in the barn."

Luke handed Aesop's reins over to one of the other men and helped Eli into the SUV, suppressing a grin when the boy bit back a grimace as he eased down onto the seat. "You okay?" Luke asked as he slid in behind the wheel.

Eli nodded. "Yep. But, man, you weren't kidding about being in a saddle for too long. I think I probably need some more practice."

Luke chuckled and started up the SUV. He took the ride slowly, avoiding any ruts in the road so as not to jostle Eli more than necessary. By the time he was entering the gate to the driveway that led to his house, there were two pickup trucks coming up the road behind him. He recognized one of the trucks as belonging to Davis. The other one was Evans's.

"I want you to stick with your mom in the house when we get home, Eli," Luke said, glancing into his rearview mirror. "Stay inside unless one of us is with you."

"Um . . . okay," Eli agreed, his eyes going a little wide at Luke's concern. "But why? What's wrong?"

"You said you'd trust me, Eli," Luke reminded him. "I need you to just do what I ask, okay, buddy?"

Eli nodded and swallowed hard. His voice was little more than a rasp when he added, "Okay."

Luke was slowing to a stop in front of the house when Eli suddenly shouted, "Chief! What's he doing out here by himself?"

Luke threw the SUV into PARK, fear sending a current of electricity up his spine. "Stay in the car, Eli."

He leaped out and pulled his gun out from under the seat, then slammed the door, locking it and shoving the key in his pocket before Eli could protest. He heard the others getting out of the trucks as he crept toward the house, making a visual sweep of the area as he moved forward.

"Who the hell is this guy?" he heard one of the other men whisper.

Davis was at his side in an instant, weapon in hand. Evans showed up on his other side, his own gun out. Luke fished out the clip he'd removed earlier and tossed it to him in an arc. "You might need this."

Evans sent a surprised glance his way.

"Davis, stay here and guard Eli," Luke ordered.

Davis shook his head slightly. "When we find Sarah, you and I are gonna have a chat about what the hell is going on, Rogan. You feel me?"

Luke gave him a curt nod and motioned to Evans for them to move in. The door was slightly ajar. He placed his palm flat on the wood and slowly swung it inward; then, testing a theory, he signaled with his left hand that he'd enter first and that Evans should cover him. And, just as he'd begun to suspect from the way Evans had moved, Evans signaled back that he understood.

The guy had tactical training—either military or law

enforcement. A fact that had not come up in his background check. And as soon as Sarah was safe, he was going to demand a goddamned explanation.

Right now, Sarah was his only concern. And based on the fact that his house was completely fucking trashed, lamps shattered, tables overturned, something sure as shit had gone down. He tamped down the fear that was making his heart pound and focused on clearing the house—and using Evans without getting his own ass shot in the process. He motioned for the man to take the upstairs, then headed into the kitchen.

The mess in the great room was nothing compared to the debris field that greeted him in the kitchen. Dishes lay shattered on the tile, crunching under his boots as he made his way toward the basement door.

"Sarah?" he called in a loud whisper. Hearing no response, he crept down the stairs, his back to the wall. But the gym and the weapons room were all empty. He silently made his way up the stairs and headed down the hall to the library. He was moving toward the open door of the music room when he heard a crash upon the piano keys and a strangled cry.

Sarah.

He rushed forward, his chest so tight with fear that he had no air to even call out to her. He was two strides away from the doorway when an enormous raccoon raced from the room. Luke jumped to one side of the hallway, then glanced back toward the music room door in time to see Sarah running toward him, broom raised over her head, a war cry ripping from her lungs.

"That's right, you little bastard!" she screamed, sliding to a halt in front of Luke, panting. "You'd better run!"

Her hair, which had been up in a ponytail—or *something*— was half hanging in her face as if she'd been in one hell of a knock-down, drag-out.

Luke slumped against the wall, laughter bubbling up from his chest before he even realized it. "A raccoon," he guffawed. "It was a fucking raccoon."

Sarah huffed, brushing her hair from her face. "Yeah, it was a raccoon," she snapped. "It got in somehow—down the chimney, I think. Chief cornered it in the kitchen and they got into it. I tried to chase it out, but it tore up the whole damned house! And then—"

Luke jerked her into his arms, stopping her angry account with a harsh kiss. "Jesus, Sarah," he murmured against her lips. "I thought . . ." He kissed her again, softer this time. Then he pressed his forehead to hers for a moment, needing a few seconds to let his pulse return to normal.

"Hey," she said softly, pulling back and peering up at him, her dark eyes searching his face. "You okay?"

He nodded, then put his arm around her shoulders, leading her back down the hall. "Yeah. It just scared the shit out of me when I drove up and saw the door standing open."

Her arms went around his waist and she offered him a grin. "Too bad I didn't have any embedded memories about doing battle with wild forest animals, eh?"

He dropped a kiss to her head and chuckled as they entered the great room and headed toward the front door, but his laughter was cut short by three sharp pops. He reflexively shoved Sarah aside and brought up his weapon.

But not soon enough.

The fourth bullet struck him in the side. He reeled but recovered almost instantly and dragged Sarah behind the couch, the only cover to be had.

"Oh my God," she breathed, pressing her palm to his wound. "You're bleeding."

He shook his head quickly. "It's okay. I think it just grazed me. Stay here and stay down."

Crouching low, he slunk toward the front door and did a quick peek around the door frame, a bullet taking a chunk out of the wood and barely missing him as he ducked back. But he'd had enough time to see three bodies on the ground—one of which was Davis.

"Send Sarah out, Rogan," Evans called. "I only wounded these guys, but in another thirty seconds, I'm putting a bullet in their heads. And I'll start with Davis."

Luke cursed under his breath. "Who are you working for, Evans? Whatever you're getting paid, I can top it."

He heard Evans chuckle. "I have no doubt about that, Rogan. But this is about more than the money. It's personal."

Luke's phone buzzed at his hip. He glanced down at it. *Finn.* No doubt calling to give him the news that Evans wasn't as clean as he'd seemed.

No shit.

"Sarah and Eli are innocent in this, Evans," Luke yelled. "Whatever your issue is, it has nothing to do with them."

"Means to an end, Rogan! You know what that's like, right?"

Luke's brows came together in a frown at Evans's words. *What the hell is he talking about?*

"Yeah, I know all about you," Evans announced. "Even that op in Kabul. C'mon, you know the one I'm talking about, Rogan. . . . It's the op that brought you into the crosshairs of the Alliance."

Luke's blood turned to ice in his veins. How the hell did the guy know about that mission? The circumstances of his recruitment were classified within the Alliance. If Evans had been behind the breach in the Alliance's files, if he'd gotten into the dark files, then God knew what he had access to . . .

"Tick-tock, *brother*," Evans taunted. "These poor men are bleeding into the snow. . . ." Before Luke could respond, Evans roared, "I'm not fucking around! Send her out or I'm putting a bullet in the head of every fucking one of them, including the kid!"

There was a sound of shattering glass.

Sarah immediately lunged to her feet, her arms raised. "I'm coming out!"

Luke sent a warning look her way. "Sarah—"

She shook her head and slowly walked toward the door. "I'm coming out, Evans! Just don't hurt my son!"

"Mom!" Eli cried out, the word ending on a whimper that enraged Luke like nothing else ever had.

"Do you see Eli?" he ground out just loudly enough that only she could hear.

Sarah dipped her chin ever so slightly.

Luke couldn't risk taking another look and possibly drawing a shot with Sarah standing in the line of fire. He'd have to rely on Sarah to reveal something, give him something he could work with.

"My father lied," she insisted, inching forward slowly. "I'm the one with the information you want. Just leave my son and the others alone, and I promise I'll come with you without a fight."

"Afraid I can't do that, Sarah," Evans insisted. "Your boyfriend's one of the deadliest snipers in Alliance history. Gonna need a little assurance that he won't do anything stupid trying to be a hero."

Sarah sent a quick glance Luke's way.

"Ah . . . didn't know about the whole sniper thing, did you?" Evans chuckled. "Well, no, I guess you wouldn't—his missions were all classified, didn't get any official recognition. But I'm pretty sure he could put a bullet between my eyes without breaking a sweat unless there's a chance I could pull the trigger first and ice his old army buddy. Or maybe your little rug rat."

Sarah stood where she was, her body beginning to tremble, her cheeks flushed. But her voice was steady when she said, "You only need me, Evans. Luke won't risk hurting me."

Evans laughed again. "You forget, Sarah—I know what

you're capable of too. I need a little assurance that you'll behave yourself."

Luke saw Sarah's jaw clench, her eyes narrow. "That's the thing, Evans," she said, her voice suddenly calm. Deadly. "You have no *idea* what I'm capable of . . . but get that gun off the others, you fucking *coward*, and I'll be *happy* to show you."

The next few seconds seemed to occur in slow motion. Sarah's brows lifted slightly and she dropped flat onto the floor. Taking it as the signal he was waiting for, Luke swung out into the doorway and fired.

Evans stood stock still, a shocked look on his face. Then a thin rivulet of blood trickled down the center of his forehead and onto the bridge of his nose, before his knees buckled and he dropped to the ground.

The bastard had called it. Right between the eyes.

Luke pressed a hand to his side and rushed outside, hurrying toward where Eli was crouched behind the Expedition, his eyes wide with fear, but Sarah had already scrambled to her feet and reached her son first, dragging him into her arms with a relieved sob and peppering his face and hair with kisses.

"Is he dead?" Eli asked, his voice choked.

Luke nodded. "Yeah, buddy. He's dead."

But to be sure, Luke turned away from Sarah and Eli and went to where Evans lay and turned him over. The man's open eyes were vacant, lifeless.

Luke snatched his phone from his waist and dialed 911 to call in the shooting as he hurried to Davis and checked his wounds. It was bad, but he was still alive. As were the other two men. "Sarah! I need my medic kit. It's in my office. Eli—come over here, buddy."

Sarah immediately spun and ran back into the house. Eli crawled to him, still obviously shaken, but keeping it together. The kid was just as strong and brave as his mother.

Luke captured Eli's gaze. "I need you to put your hand right here and press hard, okay?"

Eli nodded frantically and did as Luke told him. When Davis groaned, he reflexively pulled his hand back, but Luke guided him back to Davis's wound. "It's all right, Eli. You need to put pressure on his wound to slow the blood loss. Okay? When your mom gets back I'll put some clotting powder on it, which will help. But I need you with me, buddy. Okay?"

Eli swallowed hard and nodded again. "Okay. I'm good."

Luke went over to the other men, doing what he could to help them as he returned Finn's call. He heard Sarah running down the steps and glanced over his shoulder as she dropped down beside Eli.

"Luke said to put clotting powder on it," Eli told her.

She rummaged through the kit, spilling its contents in the snow in her rush to help Davis. She quickly sprinkled the clotting powder on Davis's wound, then brought the rest of the kit to help the other two men.

"Shit, Luke," Finn said in greeting just as Sarah handed Luke the second packet. "I was about to scramble a team, *brah*."

Luke worked quickly but his hand began to shake, scattering the package's contents. His vision went blurry, and he ass-planted in the snow.

What the fuck?

The truth of what was happening hit just as the world began to spin.

Shit.

His grip on the phone tightened as he tried to force the world to stop spinning. "Better do that anyway, brother."

He heard Sarah calling his name, her voice sounding far away, as the world went dark.

Chapter Twenty-Four

Will pressed the heels of his palms to his eyes, grinding away the sleep that threatened to overtake him. He'd completely lost track of time at this point, couldn't even remember when he'd slept last.

He blinked at the screen again, trying to make sense of the most recent report from Finn and cursed roundly, the words swimming before his eyes. When his phone rang, he didn't even bother looking at the number before he answered. "Asher."

"You failed to send an update at noon."

Shit.

He heaved a sigh.

"You do realize your position hangs in the balance, do you not, William?" his grandfather continued

"Of course I do," Will ground out. "You've reminded me during every single fucking conversation—"

"Indeed?" the high commander interrupted. "Well, then, I suppose you have discovered who is behind this?"

"We know who's behind it," Will hissed. "You just won't face the truth. I can't be effective when my high commander won't admit that we have an enemy among us."

"All you have to go on is conjecture and suspicion,

William," his grandfather said. "When you have proof, then I will listen. Until then, I refuse to believe this is anything other than an isolated incident."

Will huffed, his lack of sleep affecting his ability to hide his frustration. "Grandfather—"

"I will look for your report within the hour."

Will tossed his phone onto his desk with disgust and got to his feet, needing to get the hell out of the compound for a while. There was a sexy-as-hell CEO named Delia who'd left a standing invitation for him to stop by her office anytime he needed to relieve tension. And today certainly qualified.

But before he could reach the door, Finn burst in, his normally calm expression taut with concern. "We gotta go. Rogan's down."

Stone looked down at the display on his phone and frowned. It was not the number he was expecting to see.

He pushed back from his desk and got to his feet. "Excuse me, darling," he mumbled to Allison, who was busy proofreading the speech he was to give at a museum gala later that week. "I'll only be a moment."

He waited until the office door was shut before answering. "Jack, what is it? Is it Hal?"

"No, Hal's fine," Jack assured him. "In fact, they're planning to remove his breathing tube. We're hoping to ask him a few questions soon, if he's up to it."

Stone stopped dead in his tracks, his stomach clenching painfully. Stifling his panic, he said, "That's wonderful news. But it doesn't sound like that's why you're calling. I'm afraid to ask the reason."

"There's been an incident," Jack informed him. "Sarah and Eli's location has been compromised. Luke and a few others were wounded, but the assailant was killed."

Stone bit back a furious string of curses and felt the vein in his neck begin to pulse as rage coursed through him. He pulled the phone away from his ear for a moment, pacing in the narrow hallway as he attempted to regain his composure. So much for Evans getting the drop on Rogan first.

Finally, he heaved a harsh breath, then brought the phone back to his ear. "How did this happen, Jack?"

"We've no idea," Jack admitted, sounding defeated.

"Someone must've found Rogan's address when the Alliance's records were breached," Stone mused.

"Luke's dark," Jack insisted. "No one got that far in the breach. And no one outside the Grand Council has access to the dark files."

Stone continued to play devil's advocate, hoping it would keep the Alliance's attention diverted for as long as it would take for him to implement the plan forming in his head. "Well, none of us are completely off-grid. Someone knew where to look."

There was a slight pause. "We think it was Eric Evans, according to info Luke sent to Finn to check into."

Stone paused for a beat to give the illusion of surprise. "I thought Evans was dead."

"He is now," Jack drawled.

"Have you confirmed that?" Stone asked, torn between rage and relief.

"We'll run his face through the database once the team arrives, of course, but his Social Security number and general description matched what we had on file. Unfortunately, Finn wasn't able to get the intel back to Rogan before Evans made his move. According to the sheriff's report, Luke killed him, but not before Evans wounded him."

"How badly was Rogan hit?" Stone asked, his brow furrowing, wondering why Rogan wasn't already dead. Evans had intimated that he'd take Rogan out before moving on Sarah and her brat. Maybe he'd had to act in haste. . . .

"The wound isn't fatal," Jack told him, "but the bullets Evans was using must've been treated."

Stone swallowed a snort of appreciation. Evans had been one smart son of a bitch. He'd apparently coated his bullets with a slow-acting poison—a fairly common practice in the Alliance and a rather effective means of disabling an enemy if the bullet itself hadn't done the job. Which begged the question—how had someone so fucking smart gotten himself killed? He'd told Stone that Luke wasn't someone to underestimate.

Guess he hadn't taken his own advice. . . . It was a shame. Stone would've enjoyed having another drink with him before he offed the bastard himself.

"Do you know which one he used?" Stone asked, realizing he hadn't yet responded. "Does Rogan have a chance?"

"We're mobilizing a team as we speak," Jack assured him. "Will's taking the point on this one himself. We need to move Sarah and Eli to a new location until the final assets are relocated tomorrow."

"I'll go," Stone told him. "I can be there in the same amount of time as your team—if not sooner, as I don't have anyone but myself to coordinate. I left the city after visiting Hal in the hospital and came to my estate outside of Chicago, so no one would expect to look for them here. And I have ample security to keep them safe. Besides, who better to look after them than family—especially if you have a mole inside the Alliance? Just tell me where I need to go, brother."

There was another pause—longer this time. Experience had made Jack cautious. It was the only thing that had kept him alive this long. But he was far too trusting when it came to the people he believed to be his friends, a flaw that would be his undoing. And one that Stone was counting on.

"We couldn't ask this of you, Jacob," Jack told him. "All things considered."

He was talking about Stone being kicked out of the Alliance, humiliated and degraded in front of his peers, his friends, his own *family*. His grandfather had been mortified, too ashamed to even show his goddamned face at the de-cloaking. But Stone was nothing if not magnanimous. After all, chivalry was the Templar way. . . .

"You're *not* asking," Stone replied. "I'm *offering*. And I insist."

After getting the specifics of the hospital where Luke was, Stone strode back to his office. Allison's eyes came up as he entered and widened slightly as he grabbed her and jerked her to her feet to kiss her hungrily.

"Jacob, what is it?" she asked, her lovely brow furrowed with concern when he finally released her.

"Allison, how would you feel about marrying the most powerful man in the world?" he smirked.

She gave him a cautious look. "By that I assume you mean yourself?"

He chuckled. "Soon I will be pulling the strings of kings and presidents, making the self-righteous pricks dance to my tune, bending them to my will. They'll be lining up to kiss my ass and thanking me for my generosity for granting them the chance. And I want you by my side."

Allison's eyes brightened and she took his face in her hands. "I have been waiting for this day, Jacob. Waiting for you to accept your destiny and finally ascend to the power you deserve. Where do we begin?"

Sarah paced the hospital room, chewing her thumbnail, glancing at the monitors for the millionth time. The wound in Luke's side had been a flesh wound, just as he'd said. By no means lethal. But the unknown substance on the bullet was a different story.

One of the men who'd been shot had already died. Another

was on life support. And she knew Mel was pacing the floor down the hall where Davis lay in a coma.

"Is he gonna be okay, Mom?" Eli asked softly from where he sat in the chair tucked in the corner of the room.

Sarah forced a weak smile. "I'm sure he will. He just needs some time for his body to work through whatever it's fighting."

The sound of urgent footsteps in the hallway brought Sarah's attention to the door just as it swung open. She nearly wept with relief when she saw the familiar face.

"Jacob!" she cried, going to him and hugging him tightly for a moment. "What are you doing here?"

Jacob offered her a sympathetic smile. "When I heard what had happened, I volunteered to come collect you and Eli and get you somewhere safe until this is sorted out."

Sarah shook her head. "Thanks, but I'm not leaving Luke."

Jacob placed a comforting hand on her upper arms. "Sarah, I know you don't want to leave, but your safety has been compromised. Whoever is behind this knew you were here. You can't stay."

Sarah glanced back at Luke, his strong, muscular frame at odds with his helplessness at that moment. How could she possibly leave him in such a vulnerable state?

"What if they come looking for us?" she asked. "Who will protect Luke?"

"I've already taken care of that," he assured her. "I spoke with the sheriff on my way here. They are going to post guards outside the rooms of Rogan and his family members." When she hesitated, Jacob took hold of both her arms and bent his knees a little so that he was at eye level with her. "Think of Eli. We need to make sure he's safe, Sarah. It's for one night. Then you can come back here to be with Rogan."

"But what about the toxin?" Sarah persisted. "They still

don't know what was on Evans's bullets. What if . . ." She swallowed the tears that tightened her throat, unable to even speak the words.

Jacob glanced at the clock, clearly impatient to be on their way. "Will's sending a team, Sarah. They should be here any moment. There are certain substances that the Alliance sometimes uses to subdue their enemies, some of them deadlier than others. Knowing Evans's history, I imagine it's one of the latter."

Sarah sagged, something between a gasp and a sob shaking her to her core. Dear God, if Luke was in danger . . .

Jacob shushed her. "These are typically slow-acting," he assured her, his mouth twisting into something resembling a smile. "Trust me, the Alliance has ways of drawing out one's death. Don't worry. Finn's people will be able to figure it out within the hour."

"Then what's another hour?" Sarah argued, her heart hammering. Her knees began to shake at the thought of losing Luke when they'd only just found each other. "We can just wait here until I know for certain—"

"Damn it, Sarah!" Jacob barked.

She jerked back at his harsh tone, completely unaccustomed to such a lapse in the man's calm demeanor. In all the years she'd known Jacob, she'd never seen him angry. Granted, it'd been several years since she'd seen him—not since Greg's funeral. A lot could've changed since then. But he had always been the consummate diplomat, the one who could be counted on to keep a level head in any crisis. That's why he'd been her father's protégé, his confidant. And why word was that he would soon be tapped for a leadership position at the White House.

Jacob took a deep breath and let it out slowly. "I'm sorry. You're family, Sarah. It's hard enough to see your father in his condition. You know what he means to me. I feel I owe it to Hal to keep you and Eli safe. I can't disappoint him."

Sarah could hear the genuine emotion in Jacob's voice, could see the emotional toll the situation was taking on him.

"And, besides," Jacob said gently, "don't you think Rogan would want to know that you and Eli are safe with family when he's unable to protect you? Do you think he'd want you to put yourself and your son at risk for him? I don't know Rogan, but it's not the Templar way to put ourselves before others when there is danger nearby."

Jacob had a point. Her rational self knew he spoke the truth. Luke was the least selfish person she'd ever met. But the idea of leaving him . . .

But she had to put aside her own feelings. She had Eli to consider. And she had nearly failed him once already today. She wasn't about to do it again.

She went to Luke's bedside and smoothed his dark hair, wishing she could will him awake, that she could hear his voice, feel his arms around her. But he didn't seem aware of her touch upon his brow, didn't respond at all when she bent and brushed a kiss to his lips nor when she whispered in his ear, "I love you."

"Sarah," Jacob called softly.

She nodded, her gaze lingering on Luke's beloved face for a moment longer before she finally turned away. "Okay," she said, reaching for Eli's hand and pulling him close. "Let's go."

Sarah grasped Eli's hand tightly in hers as Jacob led them through the hospital corridors. Her brow furrowed when they took a turn into an area she didn't recognize. "I think the exit is the other way."

"I'm taking you out another entrance," he informed her. "It's one that's harder to observe if someone's watching for you to come out. There's more cover."

Sarah shook off her apprehension and allowed him to lead the way. When they finally reached the exit doors, she paused, sending a glance over her shoulder as if expecting

Luke to be standing there, wearing the grin that made her heart trip over itself.

"Sarah," Jacob prompted. "We need to go."

Sarah took a deep breath and let it out on a resigned sigh and forced her feet to move. Waiting outside was a black limousine, half-hidden in shadow, with two other black cars flanking it.

"Who are they?"

Jacob opened the back door to the limo. "My security detail. Pay them no mind."

She and Eli slid inside the car while Jacob took the seat across from them, next to a lovely blond woman in a pale green pencil skirt and jacket.

The woman smiled. "Hello, Sarah, Eli. It's lovely to meet you. I'm Allison Holt."

Jacob took Allison's hand and brought it to his lips. "Allison was my assistant until recently."

She turned adoring eyes on Jacob. "I have the plane ready and waiting, my love. We can take off as soon as we arrive."

He sent a reassuring grin Sarah's way. "Excellent. We should be in Chicago in no time at all."

Luke awoke with a gasp, his entire body bowing off the bed. He took in the situation in an instant, his memory of what had happened suddenly returning. His hand shot out, grasping the neck of the man beside the hospital bed.

"You son of a bitch," he hissed as Commander Asher and another of their Alliance brothers, Adam Watanabe, rushed forward to try to pry his fingers loose from Finn's neck. "How did Evans know about me? How did he know how to find me? No one knew but you!"

Finn coughed and sputtered as he stumbled a step back

out of Luke's reach. "What the hell, *brah?* I have no fucking clue how Evans knew anything about you. I didn't tell him shit!"

"Stand down, Rogan," Will ordered, his tone calm and even but leaving no room for argument. "Finn's not to blame for this, and I'm sure you'll realize that as soon as you get over the adrenaline shot."

Luke frowned and looked down at his chest. Sure enough a huge-ass needle was sticking out of his chest. "What happened after I blacked out? Where's Sarah?"

"She's safe," Will assured him, but his expression was at odds with his words. "Jack contacted Jacob Stone. When he found out what had happened, Stone insisted on taking Sarah and Eli to his hunting lodge—more of a country estate in the woods—that sits about an hour outside of Chicago."

"Why the look?" Luke charged his commander. "And don't tell me 'nothing'—I can see it in your face. You didn't sign off on Sarah going with Stone, did you?"

Will regarded him for a moment. "No. I've been trying to contact Stone and get him to come in for a chat. He's close to Hal. It's possible he knew about Eli being Hal's successor. Jack wasn't aware of my desire to talk to Stone before he spoke to Jacob."

Fear spiked in Luke's veins at the thought of having Sarah and Eli so far away. He sat up and threw off the hospital blankets, but the world spun and three sets of hands grabbed him before he could get to his feet.

"Where are they going?" he demanded. "Do we have an eye on them?"

"I have their flight plan," Finn assured him. "They're heading to Chicago, just as he said they were. The satellite feed is locked on to them, so if they deviate, we'll know it. Then I'll have eyes on them when they leave the airport to head to Jacob's estate. If he was the one behind this, he'd be an idiot to go to Chicago or any of our other strongholds where everyone's on alert."

Luke pegged his commander with an expectant look. "And you agree? You're cool with this?"

Will hesitated for a moment. "I think we should've vetted him sooner and been more cautious about him picking up Sarah and Eli, but I trust Finn's surveillance. And as soon as you're ready to move, we'll head out to rendezvous with them in Chicago."

"Then let's move out," he barked. "I have to get to them. I promised to keep them safe."

"Jacob has a security detail at every one of his properties," Will stressed. "And I've sent some of our own to keep an eye on things as well. It'll be better guarded than your haven."

Luke sent a furious glare his commander's way, mostly because what the man said was probably true. If Luke hadn't gotten distracted by personal matters, Sarah and Eli wouldn't have been put in harm's way. He'd failed them. And now they were gone. Maybe never to cross paths with him again.

"How are Davis and the others?" Luke asked, his voice raspy, choked, as he tried to push aside his emotions at the thought of never seeing Sarah again.

The men traded glances, but it was once again his commander who spoke, "Your stepsister's fiancé is fine. We gave him the same treatment when we discovered what substance Evans had used. He's already awake. The other men . . . one of them was gone before we got here. The other has been treated, but it's touch and go. Not sure if he'll pull through."

Luke's shoulders sagged. Apparently, it wasn't just Sarah and Eli he'd failed. A good man was dead because *he*'d missed something crucial, and another might follow. He cursed under his breath and ran a hand over his hair. "I need to see Davis and Mel, talk to them about what happened. And I want to see Evans's body when you ID him."

Will nodded. "Your actual wound wasn't bad, but take it easy. You're going to feel shit-faced for a while from the drugs."

As soon as his brothers left, Luke slowly got out of bed and slipped into the black fatigues and combat boots they'd left for him. He winced when he reached for his phone on the tray beside his hospital bed, and pressed a hand to his side where his wound was bandaged.

Needing to get his conversation with his family over with, Luke sighed and headed for the door, but his phone buzzed with an incoming text message. He halted, his heart hammering, when he saw who it was from.

Please be okay. We love you. And miss you.

Attached to the text was the picture that Mel had taken of him, Sarah, Eli, and Chief. He stared at it for a long moment until his eyes began to sting. Then he cleared his throat and shook off the emotions washing over him. He started to respond, to tell her he loved her, too, that he'd see them soon, but paused before sending the message.

Maybe it was better—for all of them—if they made a clean break, if he just let them go. He pinched the bridge of his nose and squeezed his eyes shut, his heart and his head at war. In the end, he deleted the message, instead responding, **Just woke up. Checking on Davis. Will call you soon.**

It was cold, impersonal, completely devoid of emotion. Probably not at all what she expected. Feeling like a total asshole, he pocketed his phone and made his way into the hallway. Adam Watanabe jerked his head down the hall, indicating where Davis's room was.

When Luke slowly opened the door to the room, he wasn't sure what to expect, but it certainly wasn't his stepsister rushing to him to throw her arms around his neck and hug him tightly.

"Thank God," she whispered.

He returned her hug, then set her at arm's length. "How's he doing? How's Jim?"

Mel made a swipe at her cheeks. "They're both going to be okay. Dad's going to be in a cast for six weeks, but no other problems. And Davis . . ." She paused to blink away new tears. "Your friends said he'll be okay."

"I feel like shit," Davis rasped, breaking into their conversation. "And you and I still need to have that conversation, Rogan."

Luke came over to the bed and clasped his friend on the shoulder. "I'm sorry for getting you involved in my bullshit, Davis. The conversation we need to have is going to take longer than I can go into right now, but there are a few things I have to tell you. . . ."

When Luke finished going through the CliffsNotes version of the last decade, Davis and Mel stared at him in silence.

"I'm sorry I misled you," Luke told them, meaning it. "I was trying to keep you safe."

"You're right," Mel said, an angry edge to her voice, "you do owe us a longer conversation. Does Sarah know any of this?"

Luke nodded. "Yeah. She knows. She and Eli have been under my protection."

"But you didn't expect to fall in love with her, did you?" Mel asked, her tone softening. When Luke opened his mouth to deny it, to claim he wasn't in love with Sarah, Mel lifted a single brow at him. "Whatever lie you were about to tell, you can save it. We all could see what was happening between the two of you."

"It doesn't matter," Luke said, shaking his head. "It's over."

Mel got to her feet and came to him to press a kiss to his hair. "Luke, you're my brother, and I love you. But you can be a stubborn jackass. If you want to lie to us, fine. But don't lie to yourself. Not about this. Not when you have a chance at true happiness for the first time in your life."

A quiet knock on the door brought their attention around. Finn opened the door and peeked in. He jerked his head at Davis. "Glad to see you're okay, *brah*."

"Sounds like I have you to thank for that," Davis replied. "Thanks. I owe you one, man."

"Nah, we're good." Finn offered him his toothy smile, then turned his gaze on Luke. "We're heading down to the morgue. You comin' with?"

Luke nodded. "Gimme a minute." As soon as Finn closed the door, Luke stood and hugged Mel, then shook Davis's hand. "I have to go identify Evans. When I get back from Chicago, we'll have that longer conversation."

Davis nodded. "We'll have you and Sarah and Eli over for dinner again."

Luke snorted. "Just get better so you can get the hell outta here, okay?"

He nodded at his team when he exited Davis's room and followed them to the elevators, moving slowly, still struggling with the cloud of grogginess surrounding him. "How long has Sarah been gone?"

"Hospital staff said she left about half an hour before we got here," Adam informed him. "And that was a couple hours ago. Odds are good they'll be landing soon if they haven't already."

Luke nodded. "Someone going to follow them from the airport? Make sure they reach Stone's house okay?"

"We have some of our *confreres* from Chicago PD on it," Finn said.

Luke rolled his head, shrugged his shoulders, feeling uneasy. He didn't like it. It wasn't enough. Nothing was enough when it came to Sarah and Eli's safety.

The elevator finally reached the basement, the doors barely open before Luke charged through, following the signs to the morgue. He was damned near bouncing on his toes like a boxer getting ready to enter the ring when the attendant finally led them to the drawer where they'd put Evans's body. He half-expected it not to be the son of a bitch he'd taken out when they pulled the sheet off his face. But he let out his breath on a harsh exhale when he saw the same lifeless eyes he'd seen hours before.

"Yeah," he said. "That's him."

"No, it's not," Will ground out.

Luke's gaze snapped to his commander. "The hell it isn't. That's Eric Evans."

"He may have called himself that," Finn confirmed, "but that's not the guy I found in the dark files. This guy resembles Evans—hell, could be a brother. But it's not him. Different hairline, different nose, slightly different build . . . but a damned good double."

"Get me on that plane to Chicago, Will," Luke demanded, suddenly unable to draw a breath, not giving a shit if his commander kicked his ass from here to Thursday for insubordination. "Right. Fucking. Now."

As they all charged from the morgue, Will got on his phone, barking out orders to whoever was on the other end of the line. "Change of plans. I want wheels up in thirty."

Chapter Twenty-Five

"Do you like cookies, Eli?" Allison asked, holding his hand as they climbed steps to the side entrance to the mansion. She punched in an alarm code on the door before adding, "I think Chef Jean-Claude was baking some for a charity event tomorrow when we left the house. I'm sure we could sneak one or two cookies for you."

Sarah nodded when Eli sent a questioning look her way. "Thank you again for taking us in, Jacob," she said, following them down a hallway that appeared to open into the kitchen.

Jacob gave her a tight smile in reply and checked his watch. "Of course," he said. "You're family, Sarah. What's mine is yours. I hope you know I would be happy to share any of my wealth with you."

Sarah's brows drew together at the curious phrasing. "I appreciate that, Jacob."

"But, I'm afraid I do have to ask a favor," he said. "And I hope you'll understand that I would prefer not to have to ask it at all. In fact, I tried to avoid it coming to this—"

Sarah's phone began to ring, cutting off whatever it was that Jacob was about to say. She pulled the phone out of her pocket, her heart lifting when she saw Luke's name on the display. She had to fight to keep the emotion out of her voice as she answered. "Luke! Thank God!"

"Sarah, are you okay?" Luke demanded, breathless as if he was running.

"Yes, I'm fine," she assured him, her gaze flicking over to where Jacob was pacing. Why was he acting so agitated? "I was going to ask you the same thing."

"Where are you?" he asked, ignoring her concern about him.

"We're at Jacob's house near Chicago," she said. "We just arrived."

"Stay there," Luke told her. "I'm on my way. Keep your phone close. And if anything happens, call me right away. We're sending additional security over to guard the house."

Sarah's stomach dropped. "What's wrong? What's happened?"

Jacob's pacing stopped and his gaze held hers.

"Evans is alive," Luke told her. "The man I shot was just masquerading as Evans."

Sarah's mouth was suddenly dry. "A decoy."

"Decoy?" Jacob repeated, taking a few rapid steps toward her. "What do you mean? What was a decoy?"

"I'm on the plane now," Luke told her. "I'll call again as soon as we're on the ground."

"Okay," she managed to grind out, wishing like hell that he was already there, that his quiet strength was wrapped around her, making her feel safe no matter what should come their way. "Luke?"

"Yeah?"

"Did you get my text?"

There was a pause. "Yeah."

She waited, expecting him to say something. But the line was silent for several moments before he finally said, "Sarah, I . . . I'll see you soon."

She heard him mutter a curse before he disconnected the

line. Baffled by his sudden distance, she could only stare at her phone for a moment. But a comforting hand on her shoulder brought her gaze up.

Jacob's brows were furrowed with concern. "What did they say? What's this business about a decoy?"

Sarah pocketed her phone and sent a glance over her shoulder at Eli, who was chatting with Allison over a plate of cookies. When she turned back to Jacob, she said quietly, "The man that Luke shot, it wasn't Eric Evans. The real Evans is still alive."

Jacob's face visibly paled at the news. "There must be some mistake."

She shook her head. "I don't think so. Luke sounded pretty certain."

"How would he know?" Jacob snapped. "Rogan's never met Evans."

Sarah drew away, taking a step back and out of Jacob's grasp. "How do you know that?"

There was a pause. Jacob, normally so composed and polished, was clearly distracted and Sarah might even have called him panicked. But he quickly recovered. "Evans was burned by the Alliance long before Rogan joined."

The knot of misgiving in Sarah's stomach slowly unwound. "So what now?"

Jacob's brows came together and he snatched his phone from his jacket pocket and hit a number on speed dial. "Get here. Now. Your services are required." Then he pocketed the phone again and said to Sarah, "We're moving you and Eli to a more secure location within the house. Allison, bring—"

A shrill alarm cut off his words, the sound piercing Sarah's ears and making her wince. Eli was covering his ears, his face scrunched up with pain at the offending sound.

"What the hell is going on?" Sarah demanded.

Jacob's face became a mask of fury as he reached under his jacket to the small of his back and withdrew a handgun. "I believe we have a guest."

Sarah's heart sank. "We need to get out of here!" she shouted. "Get back to the cars!" When Jacob didn't move, she added, "Jacob, let's go!"

Jacob grasped her arm as she turned to go and leaned closer so that she could hear clearly. "The cars will be disabled. It's one of the first things you do before going in."

"Going in?" Sarah repeated. "I thought we were safe here."

Jacob's jaw tightened. "Follow me."

Sarah motioned frantically for Eli, who immediately ran to her and grabbed her outstretched hand, while Allison jogged behind him on her high heels. They were hurrying after Jacob into the hallway when the alarm was suddenly cut off.

"False alarm?" Allison whispered.

Jacob shook his head. "Shut off."

"Where's your security detail?" Sarah hissed, desperately wishing that Luke was at her side instead of the man who'd been her surrogate brother. She didn't doubt that Jacob would do what he could to protect them, but she would've felt far more secure with the man she loved standing there, gripping her hand as he had in the haunted house the night he'd entered her life.

"Probably dead," Jacob murmured. Then he crept down the hallway, slower than before, his entire body taut with tension.

The relief Sarah had felt earlier had completely vanished, replaced by bone-cold fear. She shoved her free hand into her jeans pocket, intending to pull out her phone and update Luke on the situation when a shadowy figure stepped into their path.

"Please refrain from any sudden movements, Sarah."

Sarah slowly removed her hand from her pocket and edged in front of Eli, shielding him from sight.

The man walked forward, his hand outstretched, a gun aimed at Sarah's chest. As he entered the ambient light, she could see a man of similar height, build, and appearance to the one who'd called himself Eric Evans. The resemblance was uncanny.

"Hello, Jacob," the man drawled, with a grin. "Good to see you."

"You traitorous son of a bitch," Jacob hissed.

Evans's grin widened. "Oh, let's not trade insults, Stone. I have a few of my own I could bring to the table. Do you really want me to share them with you in front of polite company? I will, however, take your gun."

Sarah glanced at Jacob, expecting him to put up a fight, to defend them. Luke would've given his life to protect her and Eli—and very nearly had.

But Jacob muttered something under his breath and let his gun hang from his index finger, then crouched slowly and set it on the floor before kicking it toward Evans.

"The Alliance knows the man we thought was Eric Evans was a fake," Sarah told him.

Evans made a slight bow. "I knew the late Mr. Troy would come in handy one of these days when he and I crossed paths in Havana. All it took was feeding him enough information to be able to play the part and gather intel. Plus the promise of a lot of money, of course."

"You know the Alliance will come for us," Sarah hissed.

Evans chuckled. "Sweetheart, I'm counting on it."

He motioned with his gun. For a moment Sarah thought he was indicating that they should move, but then she heard Eli cry out and turned to see another man grabbing her son up around the waist.

"Eli!" Sarah cried, launching herself at the man before she even realized she was moving, the heel of her hand connecting with his face. The guy dropped Eli to grasp his nose, and Sarah was able to get in a jab to his solar plexus before a blow to her lower back dropped her to her knees.

"Mom!" Eli cried, starting toward her.

"Run, baby!" she ordered, bringing her elbow up and nailing the assailant in the groin as he grabbed for her. She scrambled to her feet and spun around to face the attacker and saw Jacob landing a punch of his own before snatching his gun up from the floor.

"Get the kid, goddamn it!" Evans roared.

But Jacob was already racing after Eli, with Allison close behind. Sarah started after them, but a pair of arms came around her, lifting her from her feet and dragging her in the other direction. She kicked but couldn't land a blow. Desperate, she brought her head back hard against the face of her attacker, gratified to hear the crunch of bone.

"Bitch!" the man growled. He threw her to the ground and drew his gun as Sarah rolled to her feet, ready to take on the asshole again, as whatever embedded information Greg had hidden away spilled out with a vengeance. Unfortunately, the headache she'd experienced before when the memories had burst forth was already setting in, her vision began to blur and narrow as she fought to stay focused.

"Don't shoot her," Evans said, his voice even. "We need her alive for the moment." Evans jerked his chin at two of his goons. "Go after Stone and the kid. I need to find out what he knows."

"You're too late," Sarah panted. "The treasure's already been relocated."

Evans strolled toward her. "Hmm. Well, that's unfortunate. Stone will be sorely disappointed."

Sarah shook her head. "Jacob? What does he have to do with anything?"

Evans leaned closer. "I'm an enterprising son of a bitch, Sarah," he said in a stage whisper, "but I wouldn't have come after the whole fucking Alliance, not like this, unless there'd been some serious bank behind it."

"Jacob wouldn't have put you up to this," she insisted. "We're family. And he's a trusted friend to the Alliance . . ." She searched for the word she'd heard Luke use. "A *confrere.*"

"Oh, sweet, lovely, naïve Sarah," Evans sighed. "You have no idea what you're caught up in. Do you think I'm really after the *treasure?*"

Sarah went still, her head pounding but not nearly as badly as her heart. "You're not? I thought that was the knowledge my father passed along to Eli."

Evans shrugged. "Perhaps. The vast wealth of the Templars is certainly to be envied by those who wish to bring the Alliance to its knees and would no doubt be one hell of a morale killer should it fall into enemy hands. But going after the treasure was just a way to keep the Alliance scurrying around in a panic. There's something far more important at stake here, Sarah."

She swallowed hard. "What's that?"

Evans's harsh mouth curved into a grin. "Control."

Sarah frowned at him. *Control? Of what?*

"Everything," he said. "Absolutely everything."

"We have to go back for my mom!" Eli protested, digging in his heels and pulling against Stone's hold. "He'll kill her!"

Stone tried not to sound pissed when he replied, "She'll be fine, Eli. You saw how she fought back. Besides, they won't kill her. They need her right now."

"Then call Luke," Eli insisted, struggling to get loose. "He'll save her."

Stone heaved an exasperated sigh. "I'm sure he will," he

mumbled, dragging the kid to the Lincoln Navigator that idled a few feet away.

The driver, dressed in a suit to blend in with Stone's typical security detail, came rushing toward him, his anxiety far too evident. "Master, are you all right—"

"I'm fine," Stone snapped, sending a glance in Eli's direction to see if he'd picked up on the title his faithful had used. "Where are the others?"

The man opened the car door for them, handing Allison into the back seat. "En route. They should be here any moment. Should we wait?"

Stone sent a glance toward the drive that led to his home, pissed not to see reinforcement—of any variety. Fucking worthless. All of them were totally fucking worthless. Someday soon they'd realize just how worthless they were. He'd make sure of it.

"No," he said. "We need to get the child out of here. We'll go to my penthouse in the city."

"I'm not leaving!" Eli insisted. He brought his fist down on Stone's forearm and took off when Stone's grasp weakened.

Stone hissed a curse and pivoted to grab him, but his faithful was already giving chase. The man grabbed up Eli just as Evans's men burst outside.

"Get in the *fucking* car!" Stone barked. He fired off two quick shots, buying them time, dropping one of Evans's henchmen and sending the other diving for cover.

This time, Eli did as he was told, but when Stone joined them in the back seat, the boy had tears on his cheeks and gave Stone a furious glare. "You left her."

"No, I didn't *leave her*," Stone told him evenly. "I made a strategic retreat to protect *you*. Do you think your mother would want me to put you in danger to rescue her?"

Eli turned away, swiping angrily at his eyes. "We're going to get her back, though, right? You're going to call

Luke and tell him where she is so the Alliance can save her, right?"

Stone traded a glance with Allison.

She pulled Eli close and gave him a hug. "Of course, angel," she cooed, helping him buckle his seat belt. "Your Uncle Jacob will do everything he can. But there's something you can do as well."

Eli straightened, alert and ready for action. "What is it? Whatever it is, I'll do it."

Stone grinned in admiration. The boy was as tenacious as his mother and apparently as strong willed as his father had been. "You have some very important information tucked away in your mind, Eli," he told him. "If you could share that with me, we can use it to negotiate for your mother."

"That's what everybody wants," Eli said. "I heard Mom and Luke talking about it. I'm not supposed to tell anybody."

"Yes, but you can tell your Uncle Jacob," Allison assured him. "He's family. If you can't trust family, who *can* you trust?"

Eli looked back and forth between the two of them. "I don't really *know* the information, though. I mean, if I do, I don't remember it. How am I supposed to tell you something I don't know?"

Stone offered the boy a comforting smile and patted his cheek. "As it happens, I know a way that we can find out the information. But it might not be very pleasant, Eli. You'd have to be brave."

Eli swallowed hard, but then nodded. "Okay. If it'll help my mom."

Stone's grin widened. "Excellent."

"Oh my God!" Allison cried, wrapping her arms protectively around Eli.

Stone's head came up at her cry just as the impact threw

him off the seat. He slammed into the back of the driver's seat, but recovered quickly and sent a frantic look around to see what the hell had just happened. The car that had hit them had driven past and was now stopped, but as Stone looked on, it was whipping around, preparing to come back toward them.

"Are you all right?" he demanded of Allison and Eli.

When they both nodded, he glanced up at the driver, who was passed out in the front seat, blood on the window where his head had smacked against it.

"Jacob?" Allison asked.

"Get out," he ordered. "Run to the woods."

They threw open the door and raced for the woods on one side of the road. When Allison and Eli made the tree line, Stone opened fire on the car speeding toward them. One of the bullets must've struck the driver, for the car suddenly veered off in one direction before drifting to a stop.

"What now?" Allison panted when Jacob caught up to where they'd paused to wait for him.

Stone clenched his jaw, glancing around the woods, weighing his options. His nearest neighbor was a few miles away—too far to walk in the cold. And Evans wasn't going to sit around with a thumb up his ass, waiting for his thugs to return with them. If they weren't back in a few minutes, he'd send someone else for them. Where the hell were the rest of his so-called faithful? They'd sent *one fucking person*?

Unless they were already at his mansion, attempting to take out Evans and his men.

Shit.

"Uncle Jacob," Eli whispered. "We need to go."

"Yes, I realize that, Eli—"

"No," he hissed, pointing. "We have to go *now*."

Stone turned in the direction he was pointing and saw

three men circling the wrecked car. One of them opened the driver's door and fired two shots in rapid succession.

Allison started with a gasp, her hand covering her mouth.

Stone cursed under his breath. "Go, go, go!" he said, shoving them in front of him.

But they'd only run a few yards when Allison's heels caught on the underbrush, and she pitched forward, taking Eli with her as she fell, crying out in pain. Stone quickly pulled them both back to their feet, but Allison's tumble had cost them. The men were running toward them, their guns drawn.

"Don't move, Stone!" one of them growled.

Stone cursed furiously and halted, raising his hands as he turned.

"I'm so sorry," Allison said, holding her side as she hobbled closer to him.

Stone cast a look down at Eli, whose eyes were wide with fear. "Looks like we're going back for your mom after all, Elijah. . . ."

Chapter Twenty-Six

"Something's wrong," Luke ground out, pacing the plane like a caged tiger. "She's not answering her phone."

Will disconnected his phone with a hissed curse. "Neither are Miles and Davenport."

"We're ten minutes out of Chicago," Adam reminded them. "The vehicles are loaded up and waiting for us there with the rest of the response team. Jacob's estate is about fifty minutes away."

Finn frowned down at his phone for a moment, then closed his eyes, his lips moving slightly as he made some calculations. "We can do it in thirty. But it'll require some alternate routes. And probably calling in a favor from our *confreres* in Chicago PD. You cool with that?"

"Whatever gets us there," Luke told him, ready to tear the door off the goddamned plane and leap out with a parachute just to feel like he was making some progress.

When they finally touched down a few minutes later, he was standing at the door, waiting for the plane to finally stop. The second the door opened, he shoved past the landing crew, who were still trying to get the roll away ladder in place, and charged toward the waiting black H2.

"What'd you bring?" he demanded of Jack by way of

greeting, as his friend threw him a com device. He sent a glance toward Sarah's sister, almost not recognizing her in the Alliance's tactical gear. He'd have to get the story on that one later.

"Whatever you need," Jack assured him as they scrambled into the H2 with Finn and Maddie. "Your M24 is in the back, just in case."

That Jack had thought to grab Luke's sniper rifle told him they expected to find the house fully guarded and weren't planning for an easy entry.

The knot of fear in Luke's stomach twisted tighter as he pulled on the winter gear—welcome in the ball-aching cold.

"Everybody in?" Finn called from behind the wheel.

Will's voice came in over the com. "Make it happen."

Luke had to give Finn credit—dude didn't fuck around. And he wasn't shitting with them about "alternate routes," by which he'd apparently meant driving on the shoulder of the interstate, hopping medians, and cutting through neighborhoods and parking lots and all other kinds of crazy shit. Thank Christ there hadn't been any snow on the ground. As it was, they'd been lucky more than a couple of times. But, true to his word, thirty minutes later they were spreading out through the woods that surrounded Jacob Stone's estate, taking up positions around the house.

"There are two guards posted at each entrance," Luke heard Adam whisper over the com. "No sign of Stone's insignia on their jackets. They're hostiles."

"Copy that," Will said. "Do we have eyes on the hostages?"

Luke peered through his scope, scanning the windows, looking for movement anywhere in the house, as the rest of the team all replied in the negative.

Shit. Where were they?

"Finn, do you have the layout of the house?" Will asked. "Where are we going in?"

"South entrance," Finn told him.

"That's on me," Luke murmured when he had the first guard in his sights. "Target acquired. But they'll hear the report inside the house if I take the shot from this distance."

His commander cursed, knowing they could be walking into an ambush once they breached the entrance if they'd given away their presence at the house. "Adam, Jack," Will said. "I need those guards taken out. Silently."

"Copy that."

A moment later, Luke saw movement below as Adam crept up behind one of the guards and slit his throat, then dropped the body and spun, slicing open the other guard's throat before the man could even react.

He scanned the area again, checking to see if any additional guards were headed that way. He was just about to give the all clear when he caught a glimpse of movement to his left. He swung his scope back in that direction, searching for what had caught his attention.

Adrenaline shot through him like lightning.

Sarah.

"I already told you, he doesn't know anything," Sarah spat, her teeth chattering. The fully enclosed, indoor pool house was heated, but she was drenched from the repeated dunking in the water to make her or Eli talk. She'd tried to fight back, but the ropes binding her hands and feet didn't give her much to work with against the three men holding her.

"Leave my mom alone!" Eli screamed, struggling against the duct tape they'd used to bind his wrists. He managed to break free and raced to Sarah, looping his arms around her neck and clinging to her.

"I'd be happy to, Eli," Evans drawled over Sarah's furious protestations as his men pulled Eli from her. "All you have to do is share a little information. You say you don't remember any of it, and I believe you, I really do."

He draped an arm around Eli's shoulders when his men shoved the boy at him.

"You see," he said, turning Eli back around so he could see her, "What I need to know is tucked deep down in your subconscious. All we have to do is"—he shook his fist back and forth, making a gurgling noise in the back of his throat—"rattle it loose."

He gestured to his men. They immediately jerked Sarah up from the chair and dragged her toward the pool again. She struggled and kicked, screaming every obscenity she could think of, digging in her heels in a futile effort to keep them from holding her head under water again.

"Now, Eli," Evans yelled over Sarah's screams of rage and Eli's sobs, "how about that little chat?"

"Okay!" Eli yelled. "Okay! Just don't hurt my mom!"

Sarah sent a wide-eyed look Eli's way, wondering if he really remembered anything or if he was just stalling. "Eli—"

"I had to memorize a code," Eli said, meeting her gaze. "They're coordinates, I think. Like on a map."

Evans held out his cell phone for Eli to speak into. "Whenever you're ready, Elijah."

"Got 'em," Luke said. "Pool house. Ten o'clock. Adam, can you confirm number of hostiles from your position?"

"Stand by."

Luke continued to watch through his scope, taking in what he could see of the pool house. He could see Sarah where she sat shivering in a chair poolside, her arms and legs bound, her hair wet and matted to her face. His blood began to boil with rage, and it took every ounce of self-control not to abandon his positon and charge the pool house to take out the fuckers holding her.

But he forced himself to stay calm and further assess the situation, weighing his options. He didn't recognize any of the other three people in the pool house. And there was no sign of Eli.

"I have four hostiles," Adam reported back. "Only one friendly. Check that. Two friendlies. They have the boy."

As Adam spoke, Luke watched through his scope as Eli came running toward his mother, throwing his arms around her neck and trying to hold on to her, but one of the assholes dragged the boy away in spite of Sarah's furious protest.

"Fuck this," he growled. "I'm going in."

"Negative," Will barked. "Hold your position. Adam, do you have eyes on Evans or Stone?"

"Affirmative on Evans," Adam confirmed. "Negative on Stone."

"Luke, I'm coming around to you," Will said. "*Hold your position*. We'll move in on my mark. I want Evans taken alive, understood? I need to know who he's working for."

Luke ground his teeth together, not willing to acknowledge the order. If it came down to saving Sarah and Eli or putting a bullet in the *real* Eric Evans, he'd do what he had to do and deal with the fallout later.

A moment later, Will was dropping into position at Luke's side, sighting through his own sniper rifle. "Luke and I'll clear the pool house. Adam, be ready to move in. Jack, Finn, clear the house and find Stone. Maddie, watch our six. You copy?"

"Yes, sir—shit," Maddie hissed over the com. "We've got company. Car coming up the drive. Three occupants. We need to get this show on the road, boys."

At that moment, two of the bastards holding Sarah jerked her to her feet and dragged her toward the water.

Luke felt his restraint crumbling. "Fuck! We gotta go now!"

Will cursed, then muttered, "On my mark . . ."

Luke pulled in a breath, bringing his shit back under control and felt the familiar, steady calm rush over him, as years of finely honed skill had long ago become instinct. And everything else around him disappeared except what he saw through his scope.

Sarah's gaze turned his way, her eyes widening slightly as if she saw him there on the hill.

Don't move, baby, don't move. . . .

"Three . . . two . . . one . . ."

Luke exhaled slowly, his finger curled around the trigger, waiting for Will's command.

"Send it."

As Eli rattled off a series of numbers and letters into the recorder on Evans's phone, Sarah searched frantically for some way to escape, some sign of hope. Then, as she looked out through the glass wall facing the woods that surrounded Jacob's estate, the sun glinted off of something metallic. Her eyes widened when she realized what she was seeing.

Luke.

A split second later, there was a pop as something struck the glass and each of the men holding her jerked with the impact as the bullets hit them. Sarah cringed, dropping low as Evans scooped up Eli and rushed toward the door behind them that connected to the pathway leading to the house.

"Grab her!" he called over his shoulder to his remaining thug. The guy started toward Sarah, but at the same moment a man in black tactical gear burst in, taking him down. But the two seemed evenly matched. As they fought, Sarah searched the bodies of the dead men, looking for a pocket knife or key—*something*—to cut the duct tape around her ankles so she could go after her son.

She'd finally located a switchblade when the man in black slid across the wet tile, knocking into the body at her feet. The impact was enough to knock her off balance, sending her stumbling back over the edge of the pool.

The water stung as it smacked her face and then pulled her down. She tried to kick to the surface, but seemed to be going nowhere. By some miracle, she still had the knife and bent her knees, bringing her legs up high enough that she could saw the tape around her ankles.

Just as the last of the tape gave way, a huge splash disturbed the water. And the next thing she knew, she was rushing toward the surface. She sucked in a huge breath when she broke the surface and blinked rapidly, clearing the water from her eyes, nearly sobbing with relief when she realized her arms were around Luke's neck.

"I gotcha, beautiful," he assured her, swimming toward the edge of the pool.

"Evans has Eli," she gasped.

The man in black pulled her out of the water, then extended a hand to help Luke out when she had her footing. A few feet away lay the man who'd been sent for her, his head twisted at a sickening angle. Sarah dragged her gaze away and back to Luke.

"Which way?" he panted as the other man cut through the tape around her wrists.

"Here." Sarah grabbed Luke's hand, pulling him toward the door through which Evans had disappeared.

"Rogan!"

Luke turned, catching the gun belt Commander Asher tossed to him, swiftly wrapping it around his waist in practiced motions. But when Sarah turned back to the doorway, he pulled her to a stop and drew his SIG. "Adam, take Sarah back to the H2—"

"Like hell," she hissed.

Luke grasped the nape of her neck, forcing her to meet his gaze. "I need to know you're safe. Please, go with Adam. Maddie's waiting for you." When she opened her mouth to protest, he added, "I swear to you, Sarah, I will get Eli back. I would protect him with my life."

He didn't wait for her response before releasing her and entering the house. Will Asher followed close behind, gun drawn, covering Luke.

Every instinct told her to go after him, but when she started forward, the man—Adam—grabbed her arm.

"This way," he said softly. "Don't make him worry about you, too."

Sarah muttered a curse, then turned and followed Adam.

Stone's gaze followed the man left behind to guard them as he paced the bedroom—well, he followed him with his good eye, the other completely swollen shut from being the jackass's punching bag. The idiot was clearly irritated at being left out of the more important session going on with Sarah and Eli elsewhere in his house and had decided to take it out on him.

Evans had wisely separated them all initially, but he could hear Allison's angry demands in the room next to his as she pounded on the door, insisting she be released.

"I really need to have a conversation with my builder," he drawled. "These walls are entirely too thin."

The man sent an annoyed look his way.

"You realize I'm a billionaire," Stone told him. "I could pay you more than what Evans does." He chuckled. "Honestly, it's my money he's getting anyway."

The guy snorted at this. "Yeah, right. You're just one of the guys Evans has on the hook."

Stone lifted a single brow. "Oh? Who else?"

The guy gave him a dismissive look. "Like I'm telling you."

"We both know I'm a dead man as soon as Evans gets

what he wants from the boy," Stone said. "You might as well tell me who else is behind this little adventure."

The man smirked. "Couldn't tell you if I wanted to. I just know you ain't the only one sent for Evans."

Stone struggled to keep his reaction from showing in his expression. Either he had competition or someone among his acquaintances had doubted his ability to successfully complete this assignment. Turned out, they'd all underestimated that bastard Evans and his ability to play everyone involved.

"And yet something tells me that Evans had no intention of honoring his deal with either of us," Stone mused. "He planned to use the information for his own gain. Am I right?"

The guy snorted again and resumed his pacing.

"What was he after?" Jacob pressed. "It can't just be the treasure. There's something more."

"Hell if I—"

The sound of gunfire suddenly cut across the man's words, and they both looked toward the bedroom door.

"Ah," Stone said. "I believe it's time for me to go."

Before the guard could react, the door burst open. His body jerked as a hail of gunfire riddled his body. As soon as the guard dropped, two men dressed in gray hoodies and jeans rushed in.

"It's about damned time," Stone snapped as the men cut him free. "Where are Evans and the boy?"

"We haven't seen them, Master," one of the faithful told him.

Damn it.

Stone grabbed the gun from the guard's hand and stormed toward the door. He peeked around the door frame and into the hallway, making sure no one was waiting to ambush him. At this point, he had no idea how many of Evans's people were left, where they might be. And he was beginning to wonder if a last-ditch effort to grab the kid and salvage what intel they could was worth risking his own ass.

"How many of you are here?" he demanded of his faithful.

"Three," one of them responded.

Stone cursed through clenched teeth. What the fuck was going on? Why wasn't the whole goddamned place crawling with his faithful? Going up against Evans with such pitiful numbers was bad enough, but it was only a matter of time before Will and his people arrived, if they hadn't already.

"Get Ms. Holt," he ordered, gesturing toward the room where Allison was being held. "We're leaving."

"But we were told to extract only you and the boy," one of them said.

"I'm redefining our objectives," he snapped. "Now move."

Luke crept along the hallway, listening intently for any movement. He turned down an adjoining passage that led into the east wing, clearing each room as he went, stepping over the bodies of two of Evans's associates who'd been taken down.

"I want all eyes on the exits," Will whispered into his com. "Evans is not getting out of here with the boy. Jack, Finn, what's your position?"

"Second floor, west wing," Jack reported. "No sign of Stone."

"Found Miles and Davenport, though," Finn added.

Luke cursed silently and ground his back teeth together, his fury at losing two of their brothers causing the muscle in his jaw to tick.

"Commander, I have movement at the west exit," Maddie announced, her voice edged with urgency. "Shit. It's Jacob and his assistant, Allison Holt. Our late arrivals have them. I'm leaving my position to assist."

"Negative," Will hissed. "Hold your position."

"Commander—"

"Luke!"

Eli's cry cut across Maddie's words. Luke swung around toward the other end of the hallway in time to see Evans dragging Eli in front of him, a wicked knife at Eli's neck, positioned perfectly to severe his carotid with one quick slice. And unlike the man in the diner or the imposter at the ranch, Evans knew exactly how to hold on to Eli to keep him from slipping out of his grasp.

"Let him go, Evans," Luke ordered, slowly advancing, his gun aimed at Evans's chest just above Eli's head. "I took out that poser you sent to Wyoming. I'll erase you too."

Evans chuckled. "Nah, you won't. I know your commander, Rogan. He won't let you take me out. He'll want to bring me in for a chat, try to find out who hired me . . . what connections they have to the Illuminati . . ." He gasped. "Oh, I said the magic word, didn't I, Will?"

Luke felt his commander go tense, knew the guy was holding his breath. He knew Evans was right. Will's duty was to the Alliance. He needed the intel, needed to confirm his suspicions. Luke didn't know his commander all that well even after serving the Alliance for several years, but he *did* know that the guy wouldn't be able to sleep at night if he had to choose between doing his duty and doing the right thing. He wouldn't ever forgive himself if he sacrificed the life or sanity of a child to get the information he needed to ensure the Alliance's enemies didn't gain the upper hand. . . .

And that was confirmed when he heard Will curse softly, felt the man's indecision like a palpable force in the room.

"So, because you're both a couple of Alliance *pussies*, here's how this is going to go down," Evans taunted, backing up slowly and dragging Eli with him.

Luke advanced with him, assessing his options. He didn't have enough room to wing the guy as long as he held Eli in front of him. It was a kill shot or nothing. And doing nothing meant letting Evans walk out of there with Sarah's son.

"I'm going to take this little meat sack with me and find out what else he knows," Evans drawled. "And then I'll be in touch to see what sort of arrangements we can make for his return. Maybe I'll even be willing to share what *I* know—for the right price."

"Stand down, Rogan," Will said, his voice strained. "He's right, I need his intel."

Luke ignored him.

"Can't promise what kind of shape he'll be in when I'm finished with him," Evans continued, a few paces from the foyer and freedom, "but, hey, what the fuck do you care anyway, Rogan? He's not even your brat. So just be a good little Templar and do what your commander says."

"There's one little problem with your plan, Evans," Luke said, his tone deadly.

Evan's lips curled in derision. "Yeah? What's that?"

Luke's eyes narrowed. "I quit."

Will's enraged cry was drowned out by the report of Luke's weapon. The bullet ripped into Evans. He stumbled back, eyes wide.

"Goddamn it, Rogan!" Will snarled.

But Luke didn't give a shit about his commander's furious rant. He'd taken a knee the second Eli had broken free of Evans's death grip to run to Luke and throw his arms around his neck in a fierce hug. Luke hugged him back, relief washing over him. Then, fear spiked in his veins, and he pulled back to take Eli's face in his hands, his anxious gaze taking him in.

"Are you okay, buddy? Are you hurt?" he demanded.

Eli, clearly shaken but unharmed, shook his head. "No. I'm okay. Where's my mom?"

"She's safe," Luke assured him. Motion out of the corner

of his eye brought his head up. Will was walking toward Evans's body, his shoulders hunched.

"I'm sorry, Commander," Luke told him truthfully. "I had to make the call. For Eli's sake. And yours."

Will glanced over his shoulder, his brows drawn together. Then he gave Luke a terse nod before crouching down next to Evans's body. Luke got to his feet and turned to take Eli from the scene when Will's sharp intake of breath brought him up short.

"What's doing?" Luke asked.

Will took his phone out of the pocket of his tactical vest and snapped a picture of the inside of Evans's arm. He jerked his chin in greeting as Finn and Jack joined them in the foyer, a look of triumph in his eyes as he turned his phone around to show them the photo he'd taken.

Tattooed on the inside of the dead man's forearm was a pyramid surrounded by a stylized starburst. And in the center of the pyramid was the all-seeing eye.

The symbol of the Illuminati.

"Glad bag this asshole," Will ordered. "I need to make a call to my grandfather."

Sarah sat in the front seat of the H2, shivering in spite of the heat blasting through the vents and the heavy blanket Adam had wrapped around her. The man had wasted no time in getting her to safety and out of the cold in spite of her repeated protests and attempts to reason with him and persuade him to take her back inside.

He hadn't bothered to respond to her, even when she'd pulled out the tears. She'd begun to wonder if the man was just as cold and emotionless as the men who'd held her and Eli. Until they'd reached the H2 and he'd wrapped the blanket around her, giving her a look so full of sympathy and understanding that it made her wonder what exactly he'd been through himself.

But she'd only spared him a moment's thought before her worries for Eli and Luke came crashing back down on her, chilling her far worse than her wet clothes and the frigid Chicago autumn air. She gnawed on the edge of her thumb in silence, her gaze lasered in on the path from the house, her stomach knotted so tightly with fear that she could barely take a breath.

When Adam reached over and placed a hand on her shoulder, she started so violently it even startled him. He held up his hands in front of him in a calming gesture when her head whipped toward him. "My apologies, Sarah."

"What is it?" she asked in a rush. "Have you heard something? Are they okay?"

He offered her a smile and jerked his head toward the front of the H2. "See for yourself."

Sarah's gaze snapped back to the path she'd been watching, and her heart leapt into her throat and tears sprung to her eyes as Luke emerged from the woods, Eli at his side. She made a little strangled sound of relief in the back of her throat as she threw open the vehicle's door and ran to meet her son, scooping him up in her arms and hugging him so tightly the cold melted away. She squeezed her eyes shut, focusing on the fact that her sweet baby boy was in her arms again, safe and sound.

When she opened her eyes again, she had to blink away the tears to clearly see Luke's beloved face. He stood a few feet away, his forehead wrinkled in an uncertain frown until she set Eli back on his feet, keeping one arm around him and extending the other to Luke.

And he closed the distance between them in two strides and pressed a tender kiss to her forehead before wrapping his arms around her and Eli and holding them close. Her heart felt like it would burst with joy.

"We should go."

It wasn't until she heard Commander Asher's quiet words that she realized there were several others with them—including her sister.

Maddie came forward to hug her sister and nephew, then turned her eyes up to Luke. "My family owes you a great deal." Then, before he could respond, Sarah gasped as a sudden thought occurred to her.

"The code!" she said, turning to Commander Asher. "Evans recorded something Eli remembered and sent it to whoever he was working with."

"Don't worry, Mom," Eli chimed in, grinning from ear to ear. "I lied."

She frowned down at him. "You lied? What were those codes then?"

"Cheat codes from a video game," Eli said, his grin growing when Finn burst into laughter. "That's all I could think of that sounded like what he was wanting. But don't worry, Mom. I never used the cheat codes. I only memorized them—just *in case* I ever needed them."

Finn came forward, still laughing, fist extended. "Give it up, little dude."

Eli fist bumped Finn and even earned a smile from Commander Asher as the man ruffled his hair. "Good job, Eli."

As they all fell out to their vehicles, Maddie ushered Sarah and Eli back to the H2 to get them out of the cold. Luke was silent when he got in the back seat with them and put his arm around Sarah, pulling her against his side. And the silence continued for the entire drive until they arrived at the gates of a community in the suburbs of Chicago.

It was only then that Luke finally spoke. "Drop us at my place."

Adam glanced up in the rearview mirror. "Commander wants to debrief."

Maddie wasn't as subtle as she twisted around from the

front seat. "My sister needs to get into dry clothes. And then I'm sure she'd like to see our father."

Luke met her gaze evenly, his arm tightening around Sarah. "I'll see to it she's taken care of. And she'll see your father when she's ready. Not until then." Then he said to Adam, "I'll head to the situation room after I get Sarah and Eli settled."

A moment later, Adam pulled into the driveway of a gorgeous yet modest brick house. It was neither the smallest nor the largest house in the neighborhood, its façade more functional and straightforward than some of its neighbors. She recognized Luke's personality in an instant. And when she noticed the bay window to one side of the house and could see a baby grand piano, she couldn't help but grin.

She was still grinning a while later when she got out of the shower and saw Luke leaning against the edge of the vanity, arms crossed. As usual, she hadn't even heard him come in.

"Hey," he said, looking at her through lowered lashes as she finished drying and came toward him.

"Hey there," she said, extending her hand to him.

He pulled her to him, wrapping his strong arms around her and holding her for a long moment before finally claiming her lips in a long, languid kiss. When he drew the kiss to a close, he brushed another brief kiss to her brow before heaving a sigh. "I have to go meet up with Commander Asher and the others for a while. Adam brought over some dinner, so Eli has eaten. He and your sister are currently getting a grand tour of the compound. Maddie brought you some clothes before they left. They'll probably be gone for an hour or so, but then she wants to take you to visit your father. I told her I'd let you know, but you don't have to go if you'd rather wait."

Sarah shook her head. "No, it's time."

He nodded, but didn't release her, didn't move out of her arms.

Finally, she forced herself to pull away. "And then what?"

His brows lifted. "Sorry?"

"Then where are Eli and I going?" she asked. "I'm assuming your commander has some ideas about that."

His head bobbed in a nod. "I'm sure he does. But what *you* want is all that matters to me."

She swallowed hard, knowing exactly what she wanted. "Well, if your offer still stands for Eli and me to stay with you for a while . . . to try to figure things out . . . then I think that might be okay." His head came up at this, his expression so intense, Sarah wondered if she'd misspoken. "I mean, if that's still okay with you. Because I don't want to impose or push this on you if you have any doubts—"

He cut off her words with a hungry kiss. And when her towel fell away, Luke made it very clear where he stood on the issue. . . .

Chapter Twenty-Seven

Stone gripped Allison's hand tightly in his own as the guards led them down the stone steps that took them deep into the bowels of the abandoned observatory. They shoved him to his knees in the center of the torch-lit chamber. He could sense the presence of the others who lingered in the shadows, but did not see their faces. Never had. Their identities were secret to everyone except his grandfather.

"Forgive me," he pleaded, his voice echoing eerily. "I've failed you, failed my father, failed our family name."

"You don't deserve the power that has been granted you," his grandfather hissed, stepping into the light. "You are a *disgrace!*"

The man's robes of authority billowed out behind him as he stormed in agitated indignation within the secret chamber while his cloaked minions looked on in silence.

"You were given *every* opportunity to succeed, Jacob!" he continued to rage. "Had you not interfered with the faithful's plans to extract the child, we would now have in our hands the most extensive wealth in the world and the knowledge we needed to eliminate every last Templar who has pledged allegiance to the Alliance. But your ego has once again cost us all I've worked for!"

"All *you've* worked for?"

Stone's gaze snapped up to see his lovely Allison standing beside him, her hands clenched into fists at her sides, her porcelain complexion flushed an alluring shade of pink in her indignation. "Ally, darling, don't—"

"What exactly have *you* done?" she spat at his grand-father. "The agreement was that you would seat him as the head of the Illuminati—the One True Master—if he did your bidding. That was what you promised me."

Stone blinked at her, startled by her harsh words. How long had she known the truth of his mission? How long had she been secretly urging him on at every turn, seeming so eager to please, so compliant and meek? Was it *all* an act? Was there anything genuine?

"Now, you who sit in judgment of Jacob," she raged, "declare him a failure, a disgrace, when all he has ever done has been to promote your agenda? To see you rise to glory at the expense of *his* blood and tears? You are *nothing* with-out him."

"You forget yourself," his grandfather barked.

Allison threw her head back, ignoring him, and squatted down before Jacob, her ice-blue eyes drilling into his with strength he never knew she possessed. "Get up," she ordered. "Get on your feet."

"Allison," he pleaded softly, "*please*. You'll get us both killed."

She gripped his chin, her fingers squeezing to the point of pain. "You kneel before no one, Jacob," she hissed. "You've worked too hard for this—*we've* worked too hard for this—for you to give up. Get. Off. Your. Knees."

Jacob felt his chest swell with hope. Sweet Jesus. With a woman like Allison at his side, he would be unstoppable. He slowly rose to his feet, his gaze fixed on Allison for a long moment, and took her hand, linking their fingers.

A slow, seductive smile curved her lips, and she turned

to face his grandfather. "Now," she drawled. "I believe we have a few new terms to discuss."

The members of the Grand Council all looked as if they'd just sucked shit through a straw. Will stood at ease, his hands clasped behind his back, waiting in respectful silence.

Finally, one of the council members cleared his throat. "It seems we've underestimated Commander Asher's previous claims."

"Indeed," the high commander drawled. "And what do you suggest? That we run around with our hands in the air screaming in panic? We have nothing more to go on than a dead man with a tattoo and a greedy, duplicitous politician. Neither are particularly rare."

"Both Stone and Evans were burned by the Alliance," Will reminded him. "You have to admit—"

"I don't have to admit anything, Commander Asher," Will's grandfather interrupted. "Until we have more concrete information, I see no reason to assign resources to a further investigation."

"You stubborn jackass," Will spat. "You'd rather put everything we've worked for in jeopardy than admit you didn't destroy the Illuminati as our history would have us all believe?"

"That will be all, Commander Asher."

"Sir—"

"Thank you, gentlemen." The screen went dark, leaving Will standing in the center of the room, dumbfounded by his grandfather's stubborn pride, which kept him from admitting that he'd made a mistake, that he'd failed to take down the Illuminati as he'd claimed. Was he truly that afraid to see the truth? Did he think he'd be ousted from his position as high commander? Or was there a darker, more sinister reason for his resistance?

Will rubbed the back of his neck, trying to work out the tension. There was no way his grandfather could be in league with the Illuminati. It simply wasn't possible.

But even as he thought it, the years of denial and refusing to look further into Will's suspicions about his father's death made him doubt. But he knew that if he was ever going to get the Grand Council to wake the fuck up, he needed proof they couldn't explain away—regardless of where that proof led them.

He heaved a harsh breath, then placed a call, knowing there was really only one person he could trust to look into things for him and keep it quiet. "Jack, I have an op for you. This one's personal."

Chapter Twenty-Eight

"I'll be out here if you need me," Luke assured Sarah as she lingered outside her father's hospital room door. He'd insisted on coming with her to the hospital to offer his support. She'd tried to assure him that she'd be fine, but considering it had taken her until the next day to work up the nerve to finally make the trip, she was now glad that he was there.

She nodded, then took a deep breath and let it out slowly before pushing open the door. The room was quiet except for the rhythmic beeping of the monitors and she'd nearly turned to leave when she heard her father inhale sharply.

"Sarah."

She swallowed hard and came toward the hospital bed, barely recognizing the man who lay there. He had a lot more gray in his hair than the last time she'd seen him. And the stress of his ordeal had taken its toll. But the strength and will in his eyes were still there when he looked at her.

"Hi, Dad," she said softly, emotion making her voice quaver.

"My sweet girl," he murmured, his lips trembling. "Please forgive me. I was an idiot in so many ways. I never should've said the things I did when I found out about you and Greg, and—"

"I'll forgive you," Sarah interrupted. "But it's going to take some time. I won't lie. You all kept so much from me. . . . I'm going to need a while to sort through everything. But I want to move forward. I want you to know your grandson."

Her father nodded. "I understand."

"But I need to know why you put Eli at risk, Dad," she insisted. "Why make him your successor without our knowledge?"

He closed his eyes for a moment. "I wanted to leave Eli a legacy. I wanted to make amends for the mistakes I'd made. It turns out this was just one more in a very long list. I trusted the Grand Council. I trusted Jacob—"

"Jacob?" Sarah interrupted.

Hal sighed and took her hand, giving it a squeeze. "No one has made any accusations. But he was the only other person who knew I'd made Eli my successor. If the traitor isn't among the Grand Council . . ."

Sarah felt her knees turning to jelly and had to sit on the edge of her father's bed. Jacob? Could it be true? Was what Evans had told her accurate? She hadn't believed him at the time, but now she regretted not telling Luke and Will about the information Evans had relayed to her. Was he the one who'd been behind all of this? The man who'd been like a brother to her almost her entire life . . . ? It was just one more deception. Sarah's entire life was shifting like quicksand, the foundation of everything she'd ever believed crumbling.

"I've been told that all the treasure has been moved elsewhere now, so at least that part of the information is no longer valuable to anyone."

"What else did you have embedded in Eli's mind, Dad?" Sarah demanded.

He heaved a sigh. "Sarah . . . there are things I know about the Alliance, about artifacts and assets that we hold that could utterly devastate the world's balance of power if someone were to get his hands on them."

"Then he'll never be out of danger, will he?" Sarah asked, fear making her chest go tight.

"Not unless we remove the memories," her father told her. "It's a slow process when done correctly to prevent any lasting side effects. And he'll be out of danger as soon as I name a new successor."

Sarah pressed her lips together and nodded. "When can we get started?"

Luke knew he was over an hour late for that night's meeting with his commander. Finally being able to reconcile with her father and getting his assurances that soon Eli would no longer be in danger had given Sarah the peace of mind she'd needed, and the light-hearted, playful spirit he'd seen glimpses of had been too goddamned adorable to resist that night after Eli had gone to bed.

He had to force the grin from his face when he entered the situation room, knowing he was about to catch hell from a roomful of pissed off Templars, but he couldn't bring himself to give a shit. Not when the reason for his being late had everything to do with making love to Sarah.

But when he entered the room and found no one but Will sitting at the conference table, he frowned. "Where's everybody?"

Will met his gaze, betraying no emotion at all. "Dismissed about an hour ago. Have a seat, Rogan."

Luke took a chair several down from Will, steeling himself for an ass-chewing. But his commander merely regarded him for a moment before announcing, "We've confirmed the identity of Eric Evans—the real one—and have sent the preliminary report to the high commander along with the photos I took of Evans's tattoo. And Finn was able to pull info from Evans's phone that indicated he'd been in contact with Jacob Stone. We don't know the extent of Jacob's involvement, but it's not looking good."

Luke frowned. "This is gonna crush Sarah."

Will shrugged. "I'm going to have Finn and Jack do some more digging. Jack and Jacob were old friends, so he's furious. I'm holding off breaking the news to the Blakes, though, until Hal is a little stronger. This is going to hit them pretty hard."

Luke nodded, waiting for the rest of the shit to hit the fan.

Will glanced at his watch. "I know it's late, so I'll keep this short."

He slid a single sheet of paper across the table to Luke.

Luke's brows came together. "What's this?"

"The agreement for your leave of absence," he told him.

Luke shook his head. "Sorry? I thought I made it clear that I was resigning."

Will leaned back in his chair. "And I thought I made it clear that I'm not accepting your resignation. It's bullshit. So you're taking a leave of absence to figure your shit out. Spend time with Sarah and Eli. Sort out what's going on there. And then you can get your ass back to work. As it turns out, there's a pending merger between two major Canadian corporations that could benefit from the Alliance's guidance. The global market needs this one to go through. I want you on it in January. Can't guarantee Canada in January is going to be a picnic, but you'll be a short plane ride from your haven. Or your house here on the compound. Wherever you and Sarah decide you want to settle."

"Commander—"

"And in March I have a field op in Argentina that's going to require your particular talents," Will continued, "so block that month off on your schedule. I'll send the preliminary intel after the holidays so you can get up to speed."

"What are you doing, Will?" Luke asked, confused.

"I'm doing you a favor," Will told him.

Luke studied his commander for a long moment. "Why?"

Will's face clouded for a moment, his eyes taking on a hint of sorrow before his mask of stoicism fell back into place. "Because I wish someone had done the same thing for me."

"What's the Grand Council going to think about this?" Luke pressed.

Will shrugged. "Don't give a shit. I think it's time to make a few changes within the Alliance, Luke. This is just one of them."

Luke turned his gaze down to the document before him, reading over it quickly, his mind racing. He had no fucking clue how things were going to turn out with him and Sarah. But he had the chance to find out. And that scared the hell out of him.

A light scraping on the table brought his eyes up. Will had slid a pen toward him.

"You owe it to yourself and to Sarah, Luke," his commander urged. "Don't walk away from the love of a woman like her. It might not come your way again. Trust me."

Chapter Twenty-Nine

Six months later . . .

Luke rested his head in Sarah's lap, soaking in the beauty and serenity of the mountains and the soft murmur of the nearby river. For the first time in his life, he'd missed being home. And, more than anything, he'd missed being in Sarah's arms. It'd taken all his self-control not to throw her over his shoulder and carry her upstairs the moment he'd gotten home from Argentina.

But catching up with Sarah and Eli over dinner and hearing about school and the new tricks Eli had trained Chief to do and hanging out instead of trying to connect over teleconference made him realize just what it was like to have a family to come home to. And what he'd had all along with his stepfamily but had been too stubborn and afraid to accept.

For the first time in his life, Luke felt like he had the roots that he'd always lacked, the peaceful spirit that his mother had always wished for him. He had Sarah's love to thank for that. She'd seen something of value in him and had forced him to take a good, long look until he could see himself through her eyes.

So when he and Sarah were finally alone that night, he'd taken the opportunity to make up for the month they'd been apart.

Two weeks later, he still couldn't help grinning when he thought about what a homecoming he'd had. With a sigh, he closed his eyes, enjoying the warmth of the spring sun on his face as Sarah ran her fingers through his hair.

"Everything okay?" she said softly. "You're awfully quiet."

He gently grasped her hand and brought it to his lips, kissing the center of her palm before he sat up and turned to face her, his brow furrowed. "I just want to make sure you're certain, Sarah. I might really suck at this."

She brushed a kiss against his lips. "I'm positive, Luke. And you'll be amazing. How could you not be?" She grinned, bringing out her dimples. "Besides, all of our things are being delivered tomorrow. Kinda late to change my mind now."

He fidgeted, the question he wanted to ask burning like acid on his tongue, but he couldn't seem to spit it out. Christ—he'd just taken on one of the most notorious drug lords in South America in the midst of a brutal turf war. And yet he couldn't grow enough of a pair now to ask one simple question?

What the fuck?

He cleared his throat, fidgeted some more. "If you ever do change your mind—"

She pressed her fingertips against his lips, shushing him. "I won't." When he gave her a doubtful look, she added, "Luke, *I love you*. My God . . . I love you more than I ever thought I'd ever love anyone again. What I feel for you has shaken me to the core. I can't imagine being any happier than I am right now."

"But you know what it was like when I had to be gone on

and off throughout the winter," he reminded her. "I hated being away from you and Eli."

"We missed you too," she assured him. "But we had Mel and Davis and Jim to keep us company. And Abe kept an eye on us for you."

Abe Michaels had retired from the Alliance two years before and had been looking to settle out west in his golden years. Will Asher had recommended the man to Luke when he'd made his decision to come back to the ranch during his leave of absence. The guy had fit right in, becoming a good friend to Luke's family and another surrogate grandfather to Eli.

And he'd been someone Luke knew he could trust to look after the ranch and be there to protect Sarah and Eli while Luke was tending to the Alliance's business in Canada and then later during his mission in South America—especially with Jacob Stone still unaccounted for. The guy had vanished, gone underground. A man with his kind of wealth could be anywhere. Plotting anything. It was still unclear whether he'd really been the one pulling the strings or just a pawn in a much larger game.

Will Asher was convinced that the Illuminati were behind it, that they had not been destroyed as everyone believed. Luke had no idea if that was really the case or if his commander was just seeing what he wanted to see. Didn't matter. He'd have his commander's back, regardless of which assholes were making a power play. All that mattered to him was that Sarah and Eli were safe.

Eli's embedded memories had been carefully purged and a new successor named—and that information had been broadcast within the Alliance, guaranteeing that the word got out through whatever leak was still out there, ensuring he was no longer in danger.

But Luke still hadn't wanted to leave them for even a few days and had worried every single freaking minute he'd been away. There'd been some days he'd wanted to just say, "Fuck it," and order the Alliance's jet to turn around.

"It'll get easier," Sarah assured him.

He caressed her cheek. "It'll never be easy to leave you."

She kissed him again, longer this time. "Well, I hope not," she murmured against his lips before pulling back to grin up at him. "But it'll get easier to deal with being apart."

His frown deepened. "But I don't want to miss a minute of this, Sarah."

She placed her hand lightly upon his cheek, her gaze searching his. "What's really going on?"

He took a deep breath and forced it out on a controlled sigh. Then he cupped her cheek, his gaze holding hers. "I love you. I never thought I'd say that to anyone. I sure as hell never thought anyone would say that to me. But I want to spend the rest of my life telling you how much you mean to me. I want . . ."

Her voice was barely above a whisper when she prompted, "What do you want?"

His thumb smoothed over her skin. "I want to sleep with you in my arms every night and wake up next to you every morning. I want to spend every day of the rest of my life trying to make you as happy as you've made me." He pressed his forehead to hers for a moment before finally adding, "I want to marry you, Sarah."

He heard her quiet gasp and pulled back enough to see that her eyes were wide with surprise. They widened even more when he reached into his jacket pocket and pulled out the velvet box that had been delivered to his Chicago address and forwarded to the post office box he kept in town so that Sarah wouldn't discover what he was up to.

He opened the box, but then cursed under his breath. "Hang on," he said, shifting positions. "I should be on one knee, right? Hell, I'm a Templar for chrissake—you'd think

I'd have this chivalry thing down." Now on one knee before her, he blew out a bracing breath. "Sarah, will you—"

"Yes," she interrupted. "Definitely yes." She threw her arms around his neck, knocking him off-balance and sending them tumbling onto the blanket they'd spread out for their afternoon alone, their laughter ending when he claimed her lips in a tender kiss.

When the kiss finally ended, he cradled her in the crook of his arm, peering down at her, unsure what he'd done to deserve the love of such a woman. "Should we head back to the house and tell Eli?"

"Not just yet," she said, a seductive smile gracing the lips he couldn't seem to get enough of.

He'd learned early on just what that kind of smile meant. "You know," he drawled, his voice rough as a wave of desire made him shudder, "when you smile at me that way, you make it very difficult to keep my hands to myself."

Sarah slipped her arms around his neck, her smile growing as she pulled him down to her. "That's the idea. . . ."

Read on for an excerpt from the next
Dark Alliance novel
by Kate SeRine,

CONCEALED,

coming in April 2017.

Jack Grayson took a sip of his beer and covertly adjusted the earpiece he wore, trying to ignore the bead of sweat trickling down his back. A childhood spent in London had hardly prepared him for tropical climates.

He spared a glance toward the third-story window of the building across the street and saw a glint of light, reassuring himself that Luke Rogan, the Alliance's deadliest sniper and one of the few men he knew he could trust unequivocally, was still in place in case they needed cover.

"Where the hell is Ralston?" Luke murmured over the com, his deep voice gruffer than usual. "This op's been pissing me off from the start."

Jack could relate. He'd spent the last eight months gathering intel on the man who'd been hired to take out Luke and the woman who was now Luke's fiancée, in the hopes that the trail would lead them to Jacob Stone—the traitorous son of a bitch who'd been behind it all. Without Stone, the Alliance lacked the proof that the Illuminati had not been eliminated as they'd thought and were in fact growing in strength, preparing to make their next move.

The trail had taken Jack from Luke and Sarah's home in Wyoming to a rogue assassin's villa in Cuba to a drug runner's warehouse in Miami and now to this shitty hotel in

Mexico City, where someone working on Jacob's behalf had made contact with the local drug cartel, presumably setting up a deal to help fund Stone's operations now that he'd been burned by every reputable organization in the United States.

Unfortunately, Jack had no idea where the hell Stone himself had holed up when his bid to steal the Templar treasure was thwarted. But as soon as Stone's lackey returned, Jack sure as hell intended to find out.

He took another sip of his beer, surreptitiously taking in his surroundings at a glance. The slowly whirling ceiling fans attached to the vine-covered pergola did little more than stir up the oppressive, moist air that hung about the incongruously heavy European tables packed in among the potted palm trees and suffocating heat of the hotel's outdoor café.

Most of the other patrons were obviously tourists, laughing and talking too loudly as their margaritas took effect. To his experienced eye, the only one who didn't seem to fit was a lone man tucked in the corner who looked like he was heading out on safari, his khaki pants and cotton shirt a little too *turista* to be legitimate. He was also trying far too hard to blend in with the crowd, standing out more conspicuously for the effort and setting off Jack's finely tuned internal shit-storm alarm.

"Look alive, ladies and gentlemen," Jack announced, experiencing a familiar heaviness in the air that was independent of the intense tropical heat as his muscles tensed, preparing for action. "Looks like we have company. Three o'clock. Safari hat."

"Got him in my sights," Luke confirmed.

"Don't take a shot unless I give the word, even if he moves in on Ralston," Jack ordered calmly. "Let's just see how Dr. Livingstone here plays into our little drama, shall we?"

"Dr. *who?*"

At the sound of Ian Cooper's Texas drawl over the com, Jack glanced toward where the man lounged on a bench across from the café, pretending to read the local newspaper. The former U.S. Marshal was one of their own, having been recruited to the Alliance several years earlier. He'd proven to be a tremendous asset in the field and a shrewd negotiator in the boardroom when acting for their front company, Temple Knight & Associates. But there were days he seemed seriously damned young. Of course, the older Jack got, the younger and younger *all* the new recruits seemed . . .

"*Livingstone*," Jack said. "The nineteenth-century explorer who went missing in Africa? 'Dr. Livingstone, I presume?'" When he was met by only silence, Jack added, "You've seriously never heard of him?"

"Sorry, brother, not ringing any bells," Ian told him.

"So, Jack, you think this 'Livingstone' guy's cartel?" Luke interrupted.

Jack's gaze flicked toward the subject of their conversation, taking another look. "If so, he's not local. Regardless, we're clearly not the only ones who'd like to chat with Ralston. Ian, can you get a facial rec on our friend?"

Ian casually rose from the bench and strolled into the café with his cell phone to his ear. He lingered near the bar as if waiting for a seat and pulled his phone away from his ear, fiddling with it as if texting but Jack knew he was snapping a photo of the man in the safari hat to send back to their tech team at headquarters. "Sending it through now," Ian murmured. "Standby."

"Watch your back," Jack murmured, scanning the patrons in the café once again. There were some new faces among the crowd—and they didn't look like they were there to tie one on. "Two spooks three o'clock."

"Copy that," Ian affirmed.

Jack allowed his gaze to casually drift back toward the hotel. "Maddie? What's your twenty? Do you need backup?"

Maddie Blake, the only female member of the team, heaved a sigh over the com. "I'm in position. And, no, I don't need any backup, Jack."

"Is there a problem?" he asked, slightly taken aback by her obvious offense at his question.

"Yeah, there's a problem," she snapped. "I may be new to the Alliance, but I'm a big girl, Jack. I don't need you to babysit me."

Her no-nonsense attitude was one of the things that had first drawn him to her all those years ago, and he'd fallen in love with her before he'd even realized it. Unfortunately, he'd had to walk away from her without a word of explanation, thinking he'd been protecting her when really he'd been too much of a fucking coward to explain the truth. And now he was paying for that with the daily torture of having her within arms' length since she'd joined the Alliance and yet forever out of his reach.

He ran a hand through his hair and took a moment to consider his response. The last damned thing he wanted to do was hash out their issues in front of the others. There was damned little that was private in the Alliance, but what he'd once shared with Maddie was too precious to him to open it up for discussion. "I'm not babysitting, Maddie. I'm just ensuring that a member of my team is safe."

There was a long, tense pause over the com, neither of the others apparently wanting to be the first to break the silence. Finally, there was a quiet cough and Ian asked, "So, how's the uniform workin' out? Anyone give you a second glance?"

Maddie grunted. "Only because the shirt is about two sizes too small. One false move and the girls are gonna burst out. And these shorts are ridiculous."

"Sorry 'bout that," Ian admitted. "Didn't get much notice you'd be joining us on this little excursion. I had to guess at your size. But I'm happy to gather that intel first-hand next time, Maddie, if you're up for it."

"Lock that shit down, Cooper," Luke growled, "and show some fucking respect."

But Maddie just scoffed at Ian's insinuation. "Gee, I don't know, Ian . . . from what I hear from the other guys, your hand is probably otherwise engaged . . ."

Ian chuckled. "Ah, honey, don't you listen to their jaw jackin'. They're just jealous that they're all hat and no horse . . ."

"Stay on task," Jack cut in, his British accent, normally just a hint of what it had once been after so many years of living in the U.S., growing thicker in his irritation.

The thought of Maddie being with another man made him want to put his fist through a wall. But as Maddie had reminded him not too long ago, he'd given up the right to an opinion where she was concerned. He'd been the one who'd walked away all those years ago.